RETIEF'S PEACE

RETIEF'S PEACE

created by
Keith Laumer

William H. Keith

RETIEF'S PEACE

This is a work of fiction. All the characters and events portrayed in this book are fictional, and any resemblance to real people or incidents is purely coincidental.

A Baen Books Original

Baen Publishing Enterprises
P.O. Box 1403
Riverdale, NY 10471
www.baen.com

ISBN-13: 978-1-4165-0900-4
ISBN-10: 1-4165-0900-3

Cover art by Kurt Miller

First printing, September 2005

Library of Congress Cataloging-in-Publication Data

Keith, William H.
 Retief's peace / William H. Keith
    p. cm.
 "Created by Keith Laumer."
 "A Baen Books original"--T.p. verso.
 ISBN 1-4165-0900-3 (hc)
 1. Retief (Fictitious character)--Fiction. I. Laumer, Keith, 1925- II. Title.

PS3561.E37747R48 2005
813'.54--dc22

                                                               2005016176

Distributed by Simon & Schuster
1230 Avenue of the Americas
New York, NY 10020

Production & design by Windhaven Press, Auburn, NH (www.windhaven.com)
Printed in the United States of America

10   9   8   7   6   5   4   3   2   1

RETIEF'S PEACE

CHAPTER ONE

1

Second suns-set was an hour past, but the sky, ablaze with the myriad gleaming suns of the Shamballa Cluster, shone with brilliance enough to read even the five-point italic type of a footnote to a standard CDT Stern Note of Protest rendered in its most tightly spaced third-level obfuscese. Second Assistant Deputy Undersecretary Jame Retief of the *Corps Diplomatique Terrestrienne* was at that moment less interested in the radiance of B'rukley's night sky, however, than he was with the angry tenor of the gathering crowd.

The mob had been building itself to a frenzy all afternoon, beginning with a demonstration at the university campus at firstnoon, then spilling out in all directions until seemingly every street and corner of the sprawling Terry enclave of High Gnashberry was packed either with marching, chanting protesters or the silent throngs of B'ruklian natives enjoying the spectacle.

1

The focus of the march, apparently, was the Plaza of Articulate Naiveté, directly in front of the glass, faux marble, and antique plasteel elegance of the Terran Embassy. The plaza already was packed, standing room only, and more and more protesters were streaming in from every direction.

Retief had a good view, standing, as he did, head and shoulders—and a bit more—above the heads of the thronging local populace. He struck a dopestick alight and leaned against the ivy-cluttered façade of a university bookstore, typical of such establishments, filled with books, tapes, and tri-D disks on everything from theoretical economic calculus and artistic meditation to pornographic histories of galactic exploration. The store was empty at the moment. Everyone in the city, it seemed, had turned out on this star-radiant evening to watch the marching Terries.

"Whatcher doin' there, Terry?" a leather-faced local grated in harshly gargled Standard at Retief's elbow. "Why'n't youse marchin' fer a piece of yer valiant comrades an' their war?"

"I thought I'd sit this one out," he replied easily in B'rukkk, the local patois. "All that marching for either piece *or* peace can be hard on the feet."

"Unh," the local agreed in the same language, nodding his massive, knobbed and wrinkled head. The long-jawed, crocodilian head showed uneven rows of carnivore teeth. "Good point. Though, I dunno. You Terries is only got two feet to get sore. Now, when a B'ruklian gets sore feet, he's got something to gripe about! Like the Holy Mystic Fortune Cookies say, if you muffle your noofnard, you'll regret it come suns-rise."

"Wise words to live by," Retief agreed. "But then, all of our weight is distributed on two feet instead of on eight. Four times the ground pressure, you see?"

"Yeah . . . yeah." The octocentauroid native nodded as he chewed on the idea. "Never thought of it that way." He shifted back to Standard. "Geeze, how d'youse Terries manage, anyway?"

"We're tougher than we look," Retief replied, matching the local's linguistic shift. "Some of us sit through four-hour staff meetings on economic policy to build up our stamina. After a few of those, a twenty-mile hike sounds like heaven."

"Yeah? What's this . . . whatchacallum . . . 'sit'?"

Retief glanced along the length of the native's body—stocky, massive, four-armed, and with a heavy, segmented abdomen supported by eight stubby legs. "It's something we Terries do when two legs aren't enough. We kind of fold over in the middle to redistribute the ground pressure."

The local nodded sagely. "I get it. Like the Holy Mystic Fortune Cookies say, it's a poor grullard what can't hold his drollops."

"You just might have something there, friend," Retief said, exhaling a stream of hyacinth-scented smoke. "I'm not certain what, exactly, but I think you *do* have something."

A particularly boisterous knot of students tromped down the broad avenue opposite Retief's vantage point, chanting with considerable fervor.

"Peace! Peace! We want peace!
"Peace! Peace! We want peace!
"Peace! Peace! We want peace!"

"I just wonder," the local said slowly, "what it is they want a piece of."

"Ambassador Crapwell's hide, possibly," Retief said judiciously. "Or possibly they'd settle for a piece of the hide of the military attaché. But they're definitely interested in getting their message across to the Terry Embassy."

"I guess mebee they don't like th' way your war's goin' out on Odiousita."

"They don't like the fact that the war is going at all. And in that, I don't blame them one bit. Still, though . . . I wonder . . ."

"Whatcha wonder, Terry?"

"I'm just having a little trouble believing that *all* of these protesters are from USC."

A number of hand-lettered signs were in evidence, wielded overhead like blunt weapons. "Hands off Odiousita V!" one read.

"Have sex, not a kitten," another proclaimed. "The Krll are friends we just haven't met yet!" declared a third.

"Hey, you read Terry words, right?" the local said, nudging Retief's side.

"Occasionally."

"That sign there, the big one . . . does it say what I think it does? Somethin' about the Krll bein' our friends?"

"Words paraphrased directly from the Preface to the CDT Embassy Manual," Retief told him. "The 85th Edition, Revised, Annotated, and Expurgated, to be precise."

"Yeah? What's that?"

"Something like your Holy Mystic Fortune Cookies," he replied. "Only somewhat longer-winded."

"Well, each being to its own brand o' ritual suicide," the local said with a philosophical shrug of his massive shoulders. "But I gotta wonder if those Terries ever seen a Krll in the flesh . . . uh . . . Krll in the durasteel, I mean. They ain't exactly whatcha call friendly, if'n ya know what I means."

"Maybe that's just because we don't really know them," Retief said. " 'To know all is to forgive all,' right?"

The B'ruklian snorted, a sound not unlike a peculiarly productive nasal blast into a large pocket handkerchief. "That ain't what the Holy Mystic Fortune Cookies say."

"Really? What do they have to say about the Krll?"

"Nothing about *them* babies. But . . . 'Know where your gnash-berries are snickered,' that's one. An' 'A garbling groftpot natters no nookkem.' That's another. I think that's my favorite."

"I like that," Retief said, nodding. "Mind if I use it sometime?"

"Hey, be my guest, pal. The Wisdom o' the Ancients is there fer all, y'know? Ain't got my copyright on it."

"You know," Retief said after another long moment, "I really had no idea there were so many Terry students at the university here."

"Well, hey! The University of the Shamballa Cluster is *the* place o' higher learning and graduate study in th' whole Shamballa Cluster. They gotta have a student body of five, mebee six thou, somethin' like that."

"The enrollment records for this year indicate a student population of four thousand, eight hundred and seven," Retief said, thoughtful.

"Like I said. Five thou, near enough."

"Very true. But that number includes one thousand, seven hundred eighty-five students of Terry descent, most from Terry-colonized worlds here in the Cluster. The rest are Yaha, Fustian, Atlu, Gaspierran, Yill, Prutians ... quite a menagerie, in fact."

"And us B'ruk! Don't fergit us B'ruk!"

"How could I? USC started off as a B'ruk educational establishment ... what, almost a thousand years ago standard, now, isn't it?"

"Durned straight. B'ruk Middle-High Elementary and Charm School, PS-18, established in 827 AB. And now look at her! The whatchacallum premier cornerstone of higher education fer th' whole Armpit."

"I see you've been reading the university's public relations brochures."

"I'm on th' faculty, if that's whatcher mean."

"Really?"

"Yup. Doctor Dunudiddledinldink," he said, nodding. He then added, formally, in B'ruk Common, "That's Professor-Doctor Dinwiddle Dunudiddledinldink."

"Pleased to meet you, Doctor," he replied in the same language. "I'm Retief."

"Charmed, I'm sure." He switched back to thickly accented Standard. "Anyways, most us here city-zens of High Gnashberry work fer the university one way or another. S'what's yer point?"

"Only that it looks to me like we have more than seventeen hundred Terries in the street today."

"How can you tell? Ya count 'em all?"

"Nope. Just an off-the-cuff impression."

"Well, mebee you should wait until you can make an on-the-cuff impression. More accurate, don'cha know."

"Could be. You said you were on the faculty. What do you teach?"

"Irrational Numerology an' the formal mathematics of the

eight-footed gavotte. I also fill in fer th' diction an' granma department, onna 'count of they's short-footed right now."

Retief continued watching the chanting, sign-waving parade march past. There were, he noted, a number of other races represented, though most appeared to be human. Directly in front of him, a Fustian, massive, wrinkled, and ponderous despite the absence of the heavy shell of an oldster, held aloft a crudely claw-hieroglyphed sign in Old High Fustian reading "Don't Be Hasty." The more fleet-of-foot and/or -tentacled beings in the crowd around him—and that meant *all* of them—were surging past, impatient with the testudoid's stately pace.

One large and turbulent knot of protesters spilled past the Fustian and as a result jostled close to the walkway where Retief leaned against the wall. Both his height and his clothing—he was wearing his sequined powder-blue-with-magenta trim hemi-demi-informal coveralls, mid-to-late afternoon, for use during—made him more than a little conspicuous.

"Hey, mister!" a college-aged girl cried out. "Like, join us!"

The knot tumbled closer, scattering the B'ruks lining the street. The young woman, Retief saw, was quite fetching in her formal school bikini briefs, beret, and cloak, all three in the USC hot pink, Day-Glo chartreuse, and International Orange tartan colors. Her nipple rings flickered dizzyingly in red and pink flashes of LED light. Not much taller than the locals, she looked up at him with a bright and inviting grin. "So, whatcha, like, standin' there for? Like, the action is, y'know, like out here!"

"Like, I like it here, miss," Retief replied, shifting to her like-dialect. "But, like, I do like the invitation. Thank you."

"Hey, like, wait a sec," one of the other students, a pimply-faced youth in a Grateful Reincarnated T-shirt, said, crowding closer. He pointed at the small, gold CDT crest on Retief's hemi-demi-coveralls. "It's, like, wunna th' pigs!"

"Like, I think you need to brush up on your species identification, son."

"Huh?"

"Naw, Marty," the girl said. "He's, like, y'know, too sweet t'be wunna them!"

"Marty's right," another student cried. "That's, like, a CDT patch!"

"It's not *like* a CDT patch," Retief told him, shifting to Standard. "It *is* one. Do you have a problem with that?"

"You, like, makin' fun a' the way I talk?"

"Not particularly. I much prefer having stimulating conversations with people fluent in Standard."

"Yeah, pops? Stimulate *this*!" Marty threw a hard right straight at Retief's face. Retief caught the young tough's wrist in his right hand and held it, hard, the fist still twelve inches in front of his face.

"Hey! Leggo!" Marty tried to pull his hand back, but the fist remained immobile in Retief's grasp. He brought up his free hand and tried to prize Retief's one-handed grip loose, with no success. "No fair! Lemmee go!"

"Nice ring," Retief commented, observing the bright blue stone set in imitation plastic on Marty's pinky. "Sigma Omicron Beta. I didn't know they had a chapter at USC."

"Whazit to you? Geeze, fella! C'mon! That *hurts*! Let go!"

"I haven't heard the magic word."

"*Pleeeease!*"

Retief released Marty's arm, and the kid dropped to his knees, cradling his bruised wrist.

"Where are you kids from?" Retief asked, addressing the group.

"We, like, uh . . . like . . ." one explained carefully.

"It's, uh, like this, like, uh . . ." the girl suggested.

"Yeah, an', like, we gotta be, like, goin', man," another added helpfully. The group began fading back into the marching mob of protesters.

"I still think he's, like, cute," the girl said.

"Shaddap!" Marty told her, rising to his feet and hustling her back toward the street.

"Like, look me up, mister!" she called back over a shapely shoulder. "At, like, the Student Union? After the demonstration?"

"I, like, said, like, shaddap, Aquaria!" Marty snapped. "That old guy's, like, trouble!"

"Get real, Marty! He's, like, not so old!" And then the crowd of demonstrators swallowed them.

"Interesting," Retief said. "Were any of them students of yours, by chance?"

"How should I know?" Dunudiddledinldink replied with a complicated shrug of all four shoulders. "Sorry, but all youse Terries look alike to me. I mean, not meanin' to comment on racial deficiencies an' all, but youse only got the two legs an' the two arms an' you usually keep your zoobles covered up in them artificial integuments youse all wear, which it makes it hard t'read your emotions an' all. No offense, see?"

"None taken, Professor. I doubt very much you'd *want* to see the emotions displayed by our zoobles, however. Some things are best left covered."

"Yeah, ya got that right. Like the Holy Mystic Fortune Cookies say, 'It's best to leave dangling gnashberries high, cuz th' low ones'll garfle yer dillidums.' An' they *will*, too."

"And I, for one, don't care to have my dillidums garfled," Retief said.

"Well, hey! Who does? Uh-oh."

"What is it, Professor?"

The local lifted his massive head, pointing with a jutting chin across the street, which was momentarily unblocked by sign-waving marchers. The pimple-faced tough who'd confronted Retief a moment before was in the watching crowd opposite, apparently in conversation with a hulking, heavily cloaked Grothelwaith.

"Don't look now, but isn't that there th' guy you just sent packin'?"

"Sure is. I thought you said you couldn't tell one Terry from another?"

"Can't, usually," he said, shifting back to B'ruk Common. "But I recognize the pattern of lesions on that one's . . . *groz*. What's the word in Standard? The bumpy area round your oculars."

"Face," Retief supplied. "And you're right. That's our acne-prone friend Marty."

"So what's he doing with that Grothelwaith? Them folks ain't what you call gracious social mixers."

"I don't know, Professor. I've been watching those two for several minutes, now. My impression is that Marty is giving his friend a detailed rundown on our conversation."

"That ain't so good, Retief. Marty was mad, th' way you being-handled him, an' all, and Grothelwaiths can be mean-honkin' customers!"

A thin, high-pitched warble cut through the crowd noise.

"*Ow!*" Dunudiddledinldink said, clapping two of his hands over his noof-organs. "Them snarf-vibrations is shrill enough to garfle a dead limlom!"

"Sorry, Professor." Retief plucked his handphone from its hip holster and thumbed down the volume on the ringer. He held it to his ear. "Retief."

"Retief!" a reedy voice sounded, the edge to the name waver-ing somewhere between urgency and desperation. "Where in the Name of Undeclared Ambiguity are you?"

"Hello, Mr. Magnan," Retief told his boss. "I'm right here."

"Yes, but where is *here*? Ah! Never mind that now. The Ambas-sador is most upset, Retief, *most* upset! He has ordered an all-hands evolution. . . ."

"Good," Retief said. "Some of the hands could use some evolving."

"Your flippancy does you no credit, Retief. I will remind you that your semiquarterly ERs are coming up, and you are not, at the moment, well positioned in that regard, careerwise!"

"And what would a well position be, Mr. Magnan?"

"For starters, it would be here. In my office! The staff has been directed to gather in ten minutes!"

Retief cast a glance across the sea of chanting, gesticulating beings filling the Plaza of Articulate Naiveté. Beyond rose the high wall of gray stone surrounding the Terran Embassy and the chancery. The Marine guards, he noted, had withdrawn inside the iron bars of the front gate. Getting through the mob between the gate and him would take more than ten minutes, he estimated, even if the crowd wasn't against him.

"I'll see what I can do, Mr. Magnan. But go ahead and start without me if you have to."

He snapped the handphone shut, cutting off Magnan's voice in mid-squawk. There was, fortunately, another way....

2

Half a block down from where Retief had been watching the parade and around the corner onto the Avenue of Much Walking, tucked away within an unprepossessing greenstone façade, a bar and bookstore resided beneath a tastefully garish neon sign in alien script that looked for all the world like the word "Thingamaboob," rendered in sweepingly ornate cursive strokes. A ramp designed for stubby B'ruklian legs led down to a street entryway with a recessed door. Inside, artificial smoke hung in dense clouds near the pink lights on the ceiling, and the heavy silence of the latest thing in nomusic throbbed in the air. An alligator-faced local looked up from the low bar and stopped polishing the surface in mid-swipe.

"Hey, Mr. Retief!" the bartender called, showing a rubbery-lipped smile that hid the rows of carnivore teeth beyond. "Long time, no *groz*!"

"Hi, Joe. What's the problem? Not many customers this evening."

Joe surveyed the empty bar. He and Retief were the only macroscopic life-forms present. "Ah, everyone's out watching the parade. Not that that's any scales off my nose, of course. Empty or full house, I get paid, just the same." He gave Retief a broad wink. "Like the Holy Mystic Fortune Cookies say, it's a yellow burble that can't defenestrate."

"True enough. And I'm sure you'll have plenty of business after a bit. Protesting is thirsty work."

"Maybe." He began polishing a glass with two hands, while continuing to wipe down the counter with the other two. His name, Retief knew, was Jolopoppoppalnlnit, but for some reason the embassy staff called him "Joe." Joe's Bar and Bookstore—the translation of the neon sign outside—was *the* local watering hole for Terry diplomats, newsmen, and spies in High Gnashberry. The B'ruklian furnishings of the outer bar were more for show than for serious drinking.

"Y'know, though," Joe continued, still polishing the already sparkling glass, "my best customers haven't put in an appearance today."

"What?" Retief exclaimed in tones of mock alarm. "Not for elevenses? Or the traditional ritual of the three-martini lunch? The early afternoon cocktail hour? Or . . . not even *happy hour*?"

"Nope. Nary a nip."

"If I didn't know better, I'd say that they don't care for crowds."

"What crowds? This joint's been quiet as a metaphor all day!"

"I meant outside, Joe. My esteemed colleagues may feel safer behind walls and the ceremonial weapons of a platoon of Marine Embassy guards."

"Oh, yeah." Joe shrugged two sets of narrow shoulders. "Well, their loss. Like I says, I get paid either way."

"Yes, that is a sweet deal you have with the Embassy commissariat. I gather you're on a very nice retainer, and all you have to do is maintain the place for thirsty diplomats and reporters."

"And spies, Mr. Retief. Don't forget the spies! This whole thing was dreamed up by your own Mr. Smith, y'know."

"Ah, yes. John Smith, of the embassy's Covert Illegal Actions desk."

"Huh? I heard it was the department of Casually Innocent Activities."

"It all depends on your point of view, Joe. You get many spies in here?"

"Yeah, they come and they go. Lousy tippers, though."

"Well, I hope you stay in business long enough to assemble a new and more generous clientele. Especially after you lose the subsidy."

"Yeah, you got that right, Retief. Why, I wouldn't be surprised if . . . huh?" He stopped his polishing in mid-polish. "Whaddaya mean after I lose the subsidy? What subsidy?"

"The CIA black-operations money that keeps you in business. That crowd out there seems pretty determined to run the Terry Embassy out of town. If the diplomats leave, you might have to start running a *real* business. No more freebies from the government."

Joe looked startled, an effect created by having both eyes open wide, one rolling in its socket to stare at the bar's front door while the other remained fixed on Retief. "Aw, no! You CDT Johnnies ain't thinkin' of *leaving*, are you?"

"Well, listen to them out there," Retief invited.

Someone had instigated a mass chant, pulsing waves of sound thundering from the Plaza of Articulate Naiveté, just around the corner. "*Terries go home! Terries go home! Terries go home! . . .*"

"I can't be sure," Retief told the startled bartender, "but it sounds to me like we aren't welcome."

"Aw, geeze, Retief! Them's just college kids, y'know? Youthful high spirits! The indiscretions of children! Fraternity hijinks! That's all!"

"I don't know, Joe. That sounds like more than a fraternity beer-bust out there."

"No, no, you got it all wrong! Why, most of them protesters out there are Terries themselves! You know . . . the ones with only two legs and two arms? You can't miss 'em! I mean . . . why would they want to send themselves home? They can't crawl back into the nest! Like the Holy Mystic Fortune Cookies say, 'An egg twice broken makes a very poor drooze.'"

"Now I'm worried. That almost made sense. Do the fortune cookies say anything about making omelets?"

"Only that you can't make them without grobbling a chutwinkle. But, listen here, Retief. All this higher philosophy and stuff aside . . . are things really that serious? You embassy Johnnies might be leaving?"

"As to that, I'm not sure even your Holy Mystic Fortune Cookies can say for sure. The embassy's mission here on B'rukley is twofold, after all—providing diplomatic relations with the B'ruks and providing consul facilities for the large Terry student population here. Now, Terra will want to maintain diplomatic relations with your world for as long as the Krll permit, but if the students don't want our services, we will at the very least have to scale back on our presence here. And if the Krll have *their* way . . ."

"Naw, naw, Mr. Retief! You can't let a few boisterous high spirits get you shook! And, as for the Krll, well, sure they get carried away with the speech-making and rhetoric every once in a while. You know, symbolic saber-rattling, ritual drum-beating, ceremonial chest-thumping. It don't mean nothin'!"

"I take it you don't want to see the Terries leave, Joe."

"Course I don't! I know which side of my bread substitute has the ikky-wax!"

"How do you think other B'ruks feel about it?"

"We're a practical people, Mr. Retief. We live by the Sacred Pronouncements of the Holy Mystical Fortune Cookies and put a high premium on rational thought and sanity. Half the population of High Gnashberry works for the university, and the other half works for them. If the Terries leave, the university is dead . . . and if the Krll come through, the university is blown up, burned out, torn down, *and* dead *and* buried, with salt sown on the grave and a steak grilled on both its hearts!"

"Yes, but how do you *really* feel?"

"Geeze, Mr. Retief! How do we feel? Do you think we're fleaglin' *berries*?"

" 'Nuts,' Joe."

"Sure, Mr. Retief." He slid a bowl of shelled thribble nuts across the counter. "Help yourself."

Retief helped himself to a small handful. They had a delicate flavor behind the sharp crunch, somewhere between almonds and cashews.

The door to the bar opened, allowing the chanting outside to become momentarily louder. A tall and statuesque woman walked in, then stood by the door, surveying the bar. Gorgeously attired in a long, low-cut, formal evening miniskirt, with large dark glasses and a dress trench coat slung by one finger over her shoulder, she seemed to be looking for somebody.

"Evening, miss," Joe said. "Can we help you?"

"No, thanks," she replied. "I'm meeting someone. May I . . . ?"

Joe gestured with three of his arms toward the room in back. "Help yourself. Can I get you a drink?"

"No, thank you," she replied coolly. She gave Retief a searching glance, then walked through the bar and into the lounge in the back.

"Well," Retief told Joe, "looks like maybe you'll be doing all right tonight after all! And after the festivities die down outside, you may find business picking up even more. After all, *talking* is thirsty work too, and the evening is still young."

"Yeah. But you still got me worried, Mr. Retief. I don't want to see you Terries leave!"

"And in this modern galaxy, that is a most refreshing change, Joe. Thank you. I'll see what I can do."

"That's great, Mr. Retief. Good luck t'you! Hey, y'want something to wet your whazoo? Glass of Bacchian black, mebee?"

"Not this time, Joe. My whazoo has to wait. Duty calls."

"Right you are, Mr. Retief. I'll cycle you through." He reached beneath the bar and pulled down one of the dispenser handles. "And, like the Holy Mystic Fortune Cookies say, hold on to your jizzlestross, 'cause that first gnosh is a dowser."

"My jizzlestross, Mr. Jolopoppoppalnlnit," Retief said in B'rukkk, "is *always* firmly in hand."

Retief threaded his way past several dozen empty tables—all quite low to the floor and without any chairs, in deference to B'ruklian anatomy. The back room, however, a large and ornate lounge, was tastefully appointed in faux-plastic booths and tables and chairs appropriate to normal Terry articulation, with larger-than-life-sized trideos hanging from the walls of various Great Men in CDT history—Pouncetrifle, Sternwheeler, Nitworth, Straphanger, and a dozen others. The woman, Retief noted, had taken a seat in one of the back-corner booths. She glanced up as he entered, then looked away, carefully avoiding eye contact behind her dark glasses.

Recognizing the glasses for what they were, Retief gave her a cheerful nod, certain she was studying him closely. Those glasses, he thought, were Russian imitations of a Groaci theft of a Bogan copy of an ancient Japanese design popular with the CIA and other covert groups and would be fully equipped with range finder, X-ray scanning, weapons detection, radar, homing and tracking, stereoscopic telephoto, long-range audiopickup, deluxe entertainment center, and even filters for both UV and bright light.

"I like the sunglasses, darling," Retief murmured in a whisper so low it was barely audible to himself and smiled as the woman jumped, startled.

He considered striking up a conversation with her, but a glance at his fingerwatch told him he didn't have the time. Instead, he turned off to the left.

There, up a short flight of stairs and as was popular in many of the finer bars throughout the Eastern Arm, a small bookstore and reading area had been tucked away in a back corner of the lounge, so that serious drinkers had a place to relax as they imbibed.

Slipping into an aisle between the shelves in the back, Retief went straight to the section labeled "Games and Philosophy," found the copy of Machiavelli's *The Prince*, and gave the tome a tug. Immediately, with a soft *snick*, the rack of bookshelves rotated, exposing a hidden passageway. THIS WAY TO THE TOP SECRET BACK DOOR TO THE EMBASSY read a sign stenciled on the wall.

Boot steps echoing off ferrocrete walls and ceiling, Retief followed the sub-B'ruklian tunnel as it sloped gently downward, then leveled off as it passed beneath the Avenue of Much Walking.

3

"*Where* the devil have you been!" Deputy Undersecretary Ben Magnan exclaimed. "The Ambassador is beside himself!"

"If he's beside himself," Retief replied, walking into Magnan's spacious office, "he doesn't need me. Three's a crowd, and crowds make him nervous."

"Your japes, as usual, betray your inappropriately cavalier attitude toward your chosen career path, Retief. As for crowds, you would do well to note the crowd gathering in the plaza outside the Embassy front gates. Their mood is ugly, and we must prepare to run for it—that is, prepare for the worst, if necessary."

"I've seen the crowd, Mr. Magnan. It *is* pretty ugly, in spots, I'll grant you, though some of the protesters look quite nice, actually."

"You were in the crowd?" Magnan exclaimed, his normally dour features animated by a carefully rehearsed expression of Shocked Surprise (82-F) mingled with Genuine Alarm (54-B). "Surely you weren't taking part in the protest march!"

"Oh, some of them invited me to join in, Mr. Magnan, but I regretfully declined."

"I should think so! These peace marches have cast our diplomatic mission here in a decidedly reactionary and undignified light. It wouldn't do at all to give out the impression that CDT personnel were actually marching on our own Embassy and protesting our own war!"

"Perish the thought. War is so good for business, after all."

"Exactly! Uh, what?" Magnan stopped and glared at Retief, an expression of Anger, Barely Restrained (173-G) leavened with a studied Watch It, Bub (215-K). "That is, our *police action* here in the Shamballa Cluster serves a variety of social and governmental needs, not least of which is the necessity of restraining the somewhat youthfully exuberant Krll interests in acquisitions of planetary real estate beyond the Galactic Core."

"What I don't understand, Mr. Magnan," Retief said, "is . . . if this is a police action, why don't we just go in and arrest the Krll? Aggravated criminal trespass. Breaking and entering. Littering without a permit. Gross military escalation without an escalator. Warmongering out of season. We could throw the book at them."

"Save your undignified japes for someone who cares, Retief," Magnan sniffed, applying an expression of Lack of Concern for Unimportant Issues Sniffed at With Disdain (1221-Q).

"Are your allergies acting up again, Mr. Magnan?" Retief asked, assaying a 455-E, Concern for One's Superior's Health.

"Your 455 needs work, Retief. For a moment, I thought you were attempting a 961, Have Your People Talk to My People and We'll Do Lunch. About a 'K,' I would say."

"To tell the truth, Mr. Magnan, I could never really tell the difference between a 455 and a 961."

"You do grimace with a slight accent, Retief. Now, however, is not the time for practicing face-making protocol." Magnan stood, gathering his briefcase, for middle-grade embassy staff use of, and started for the door. "Ambassador Crapwell has called an emergency staff meeting to discuss the apparent threat to the embassy, and our presence is required."

"Why? Is the Ambassador looking for scapegoats already?"

"Ambassador Crapwell is among the most distinguished and accomplished of senior Great Men within the Corps, Retief. You would do well to remember that. Great Men of his caliber don't require scapegoats, unless the situation has already degenerated into abject disaster."

"Well," Retief told the back of his boss's semiformal late-afternoon CDT undress blazer as they walked out of Magnan's office and into the corridor beyond, "that is a great relief."

4

"The situation," Ambassador Chauncey Crapwell said above precisely steepled, pudgy fingers, "has already degenerated into abject disaster. We need to put on our thinking caps and find a reasonable solution to this contretemps."

"Good heavens, man!" Colonel Marwonger, the military attaché, exclaimed, bringing a beefy fist down hard on the polished iridium surface of the Conference Room table with a thump. "Do you mean to say the Krll have broken through our boys' lines on Odiousita? That's bad!"

"Or . . . or worse!" First Secretary and Cultural Attaché Bird-bush quavered. "Their warwalkers are here? On B'rukley? That's very bad!"

"I knew it!" the Political Officer, Willy Hanglow, said, rising from his chair. "The Navy's done gone and abandoned us! They've pulled out and left us to the tender mercies of the Krll, which they ain't got none! That's very, *very* bad!"

"Nonsense!" Fleet Captain Tathbub said, glaring. "The 10th Fleet would most certainly not have left without me . . . that is to say, I mean, without us . . . not unless . . . unless . . ."

"Unless what, Eustace?" Marwonger asked the naval attaché.

"Unless the damned Krlljoys managed to wipe out the Fleet!" Tathbub said in a hoarse whisper. "That would be very, very, *very* bad! My God, what a disaster, unparalleled in the history of naval—"

"You can't possibly mean," Undersecretary Dinewiner cried, "that the Embassy liquor stores have been pilfered by the locals! That would be very, very, very, *very*—"

"Gentlemen, please!" the Ambassador called over the rising tide of very bads from his place at the head of the conference table. The Great Man leaned back in his Hip-U-Matic contour chair, fingers now interlacing over his rounded abdomen as he surveyed the near-riot within his domain. Crapwell was a most distinguished-looking senior diplomat, which was to say weak of chin, myopic of vision, bald of pate, and pot of belly, the whole transformed into Authority Personified by the four thousand–GUC pinstripe suit, early evening, demiformal, ambassadorial personnel, for use by, with optional power lapels. He assumed an expression of Patient Longsuffering Held Rigidly in Check But Growing Thin (226-R) overlaid by just a hint of Knock It Off, Knuckleheads (992-A). "Your attitude of blind panic is most unseemly. I'll tell you when to panic, do you hear?"

"Goodness, Retief," Magnan said, sotto voce. "Did you see His Excellency's masterful application of a 226 playing off a 992? We are indeed privileged to witness true and masterful Greatness in Action!"

"I had no idea, Mr. Magnan," Retief murmured. "And here I thought it was just gas."

"A little more diligence in your studies of Manfried's *Ritual Expressionism: A Study in Political Facial Dynamics* would not go amiss for you, careerwise, that is."

"*Mister* Magnan!" Crapwell boomed from the table's head. "What can be so important that we must put a seven-nova nuclear-meltdown emergency Galactic Utter Top Secret embassy staff conference on hold while you discuss matters with the junior staff? Would you care to share your observations with the rest of us?"

"Ah . . . erp!" Magnan squeaked, taking in the two long rows of silent faces all turned now to regard him with an array of steely 1106s (Distasteful Examination of Something Unpleasant on the Nether Surface of a Pedal Extremity), the expressions ranging from Hy Felix's mildly reproving and disinterested level "B" on up to Colonel Marwonger's scathing "V."

"Speak up, man," the Ambassador said, his voice now carrying a cold, hard edge. "We'd all be very interested in hearing what you have to say."

"I was . . . I mean, that is to say . . . that is . . . Retief was just saying . . . or, rather, I was, that . . ."

"Come, come, man! Enough with the excuses. Spit it out!"

"I was . . . er . . . that is, I was admiring your incredibly facile application of advanced parenthetical grimacing applied to tactical advantage within conversational martial arts, a respectful aside in no way intended to disrupt the proceedings!"

"Watch then, Magnan," the Great Man said, "and learn!" The Ambassador's face rearranged itself in an almost puttylike way into a stern 623-Q (Greatness Sorely Tried), slipped down two numbers to a 621-J (Restrained Impatience), edged up a few degrees to a 621-W (*Severely* Restrained Impatience), fluttered a bit between a 602-A and a 927-S (Indignation and Viewing With Alarm, Second Degree), then writhed into a goggle-eyed 1231 (Astonishment at a Gaffe of Unprecedented Proportions) before settling with a masterful blending of rapidly escalating expressions into a cold-eyed 999-K (Don't Make Me Warn You Again) lightly seasoned with a delicately executed 1195-B (I Do Hope You've Learned Your Lesson).

"Amazing!" Magnan cried, rising and clapping his hands wildly. "A stunning, a virtuoso performance, I *must* say!"

"*Must* you, Ben?" Hy Felix said from across the table. The information service attaché was a small, baggy-looking man with trousers to match. "All this here ritual grimacing and stuff is all very well, but I'd still like someone to tell me what the heck the emergency is! I'll have you all know that I had to put a very hot date on hold tonight in order to attend tonight's . . . festivities." He nudged Willy Hanglow, who was sitting at his left, with an elbow jab to the ribs. "I don't want to keep the young lady waiting longer than necessary, if you know what I mean, eh, Willy?"

"Why, Felix!" Horace Smallbody, the Career Minister, exclaimed. "Who'd have ever thought that *you* . . . ?"

"Sit down, Mr. Magnan," Crapwell said, letting his features shift easily into the composed moue of an 881-C (You See What I Have to Put Up With) for the benefit of the others at the table. He did appear somewhat mollified by Magnan's rave review of his performance, however. "The wolf is at the door."

"Wolf?" General Services Officer Marvin Lackluster cried, whirling in his chair. "What wolf?"

"A figure of speech, Marvin. A metaphor, if you will, of the nightmare threat even now hammering at the embassy gates!"

"Which we'd have already known all about if it weren't for the grimacing," Felix pointed out.

"I speak," Crapwell said in tones of Grave Warning (411-C), edged with just a shade of Impending Doom (731-A), "of none other than the student radical revolt in the streets of High Gnashberry outside the precincts of the Embassy itself! They show every sign of adhering to those ancient high ceremonial rituals of student revolt as practiced by religious fundamentalists, fanatic demagogues, and archconservatives of every stripe, to wit, a desire to rush the gates, storm the embassy, and take the senior diplomatic staff hostage!"

"It's a *peace* march, Your Excellency," Secretary Birdbush pointed out. "Not a military assault!"

"Indeed, Thurman?" Crapwell said. "I trust you'll find that comforting when the dacoits break through the gates to lay violent hands upon your person!"

"They don't sound very peace-loving," Colonel Marwonger observed. "Listen to 'em! You can hear 'em all the way in here . . . '*Peace! Peace! Peace!*' It's enough to turn your stomach!"

"Well, peace is okay in its place," Undersecretary Dinewiner said. "I mean, just so long as one is not extremist about it."

"They'll change their tune when the Krll show up," Captain Tathbub pointed out. "From all reports, the Krll love peace. Planetary surfaces scorched lifeless by orbital bombardment can be *very* peaceful."

"Gentlemen!" Crapwell barked, mastering a difficult Determination to Get the Discussion Back on Topic (1313-G). "I will entertain suggestions as to how we should deal with the crisis."

"Entertain?" Hanglow asked, puzzled. "You mean, like, with a song and dance?"

"He means," Smallbody suggested, "that His Ex is fresh out of ideas as to how to cover his ass, and he's looking for us to help him out."

"A big job," Felix noted. He held up his hands, as though framing a headline. "Terran Ambassador's Ass Covered." As Crapwell glared at him, he shrugged. "Story at eleven," he added.

"*If* we can continue," the Ambassador continued with dogged determination, "I would like to address the problem of the peace demonstrators and their presumed intent to storm this embassy."

"Shoot 'em," Colonel Marwonger said.

"Now, now, Heracles," Crapwell chided the military attaché. "A less precipitous solution would be more in tune with the essentially diplomatic character of this mission. Further, a massacre might reflect poorly on our participation in the Interplanetary Tribunal for the Curtailment of Hostilities. We would definitely lose points at the peace table . . . assuming, of course, that ITCH is indeed able to bring the Krll to the peace table. Thus far the Krll Empire has been most intransigent."

"Of course they have, Chauncey," Marwonger replied. "They don't have a single reason to come to the peace table when all their bets are riding on the war table. Our stand on Odiousita V is the first time the Krll juggernaut has even been slowed down.

"In fact, we believe that they may be induced to negotiate if our forces deal them a severe enough drubbing on Odiousita. Of course, that presupposes that we give them the drubbing and not have them give the drubbing to us."

"Gentlemen, gentlemen, please!" Crapwell cried. "In the first place, the sacred halls of a CDT embassy are no place for a discussion of such a warlike nature! In the second, we are not here to discuss the Krll and their aspirations, but the threat to the embassy and its staff presented by the noisy rabble outside the gates!"

"Shoot 'em," Marwonger suggested.

"Are there any *other* suggestions?" the Ambassador said, disfavoring the military attaché with a Withering Glance (346-D).

"Well," the Embassy Chief of Security, Rupert Numbly, said, "not to get put down my ownself with one of your deadly 346s, Chief . . . but, like, howzabout letting the embassy Marines carry loaded weapons?"

"What?" Birdbush demanded. "Rupert, have you gone nuts? That is exactly the sort of inflammatory and ill-conceived action that could precipitate a disastrous conflagration, peacekeeperwise."

"Unthinkable!" Dinewiner added.

"Preposterous!" Mortimer Moriarity, the Personnel Officer, exclaimed.

"I wonder why the Marines even have weapons," Retief said, addressing no one in particular.

"Eh? What was that?" Crapwell demanded. "You, sir. At the far end of the table. Who are you?"

"Retief, Your Excellency. Second Assistant Deputy Undersecretary of Operations."

"Was that intended as some sort of radical remark? A criticism of established doctrine?"

"Not at all, sir. I simply note that the Embassy's Marine guard detachment is equipped with blast rifles, Mark XXX power pistols, and a number of other technological toys which do represent considerable firepower. Since standing orders require that they shoulder those weapons without power packs or magazines, it seems something of a waste to even carry them."

"Harrumph," the Ambassador harrumphed. "Obviously, you are new to the diplomatic arena. The key word, sir, you said yourself. Marine weapons *represent* firepower. With such representation, there is no need for the actual article."

"I dunno, Your Excellency," Dinewiner said. "Retief may have a point. Having the Marines carry rifles openly may be provoking the mob."

"I suggest we have the Marine guards disarm at once," Birdbush said.

"Excellent idea, Thurman." Crapwell examined the fingernails of his left hand, then rapidly poked at them with the right, entering a note on his Fingernail Pilot. "See to it, Numbly."

"Yes, sir." The Security Chief shook his head. "But why do we even *have* Marines if they can't protect us!"

"For one thing, Numbly," Crapwell pointed out reasonably, "they're *pretty*. Those blue and red full-dress uniforms ... very snazzy. And furthermore, the firepower they represent is fully sufficient to keep hostile parties at bay, just as this gentleman ... what did you say your name was?"

"Retief, Your Excellency."

"As Retief, here, pointed out." He favored Retief with a Warm Glow of Beneficent Approbation, a look unusual enough at most diplomatic functions, high-level negotiations, and staff meetings that it had no formal code designation. "Good job, Retief," the Great Man said. "A most cogent observation on your part."

"Sir, that wasn't what I meant to—"

Magnan elbowed Retief in the arm. "Shush, man!" he whispered with urgent ferocity. "You've just won at least five full career advancement points with that coup! Don't give His Ex reason to have second thoughts!"

"I'd rather hoped that he might have some first thoughts," Retief said, standing up. "Mr. Ambassador!"

"Eh? What is it, young man?"

"Disarming the Marines was not my idea, sir, cogent or otherwise. The CDT Regulations Handbook specifically calls for the Marines to provide operational security at all diplomatic installations, stations, and embassies . . . that would be as called for under Articles and Regulations; Article XXI; Section 3, Security, Embassy, Maintenance of; Subsection 12, paragraphs 5 through 9. Subsection 13 specifies the use of weapons in order to employ deadly force, as authorized by the relevant command authority, in order to safeguard Terran diplomatic, military, and civilian personnel, property, and diplomatic installations from all threats, foreign and domestic—"

"I *know* the regulations, young man!" Crapwell barked.

"I'm relieved to hear it, sir."

"Sit down, sir, and be still! You are young and inexperienced in the milieu of galactic politics and, as such, a certain amount of youthful indiscretion can be tolerated, even, I daresay, overlooked. But you overreach yourself in quoting CDT Regulations Handbook chapter and verse to *me*!"

The Great Man paused to glare at the faces of the other staff members around the polished table. No one dared meet his eyes or Retief's. Indeed, Magnan, on Retief's right, and Marvin Lackluster, on his left, edged their chairs away from his, lest they be contaminated by fallout from the detonation of Unrestrained Ambassadorial Wrath.

Crapwell made another note on his Fingernail Pilot. "I am deducting ten career advancement points for that gaffe, Retief. No! Make that twelve! See to that, Morty."

"Yes, sir," the personnel officer said, making a note of his own.

"I have heard rumor," Crapwell went on, "of some bizarre, to say the least, episodes involving flagrant disregard for Corps policy, decorum, and discipline, episodes revolving around a junior Corps officer by the name of Retief. Would that, by any chance, be you, young man?"

"It's certainly possible, sir. Especially the decorum part."

"Harrumph! Well, be advised that I will tolerate *no* deviation from established and official Corps policy at this installation and that the traditional discipline and decorum of the Corps *will* be maintained. *Do* I make myself clear?"

"Perfectly, sir."

"And for your information, sir, the key line in the regulations you so unadvisedly quoted at me a moment ago was *as authorized by the relevant command authority*. As the senior Terran diplomatic officer on B'rukley, the command authority resides with me, which means that it is I who determines the advisability of arming *my* Marines. Who is your supervisor?"

"That would be Mr. Magnan, sir."

"Magnan?"

"Ah . . . erp? That is to say, yes, Your Excellency?"

"This Retief is *your* responsibility, sir. You will keep an eye on him. I will tolerate no radicals, no rabble-rousers, no metaphorical loose cannons in my command! Do you understand?"

"Yes, sir! Absolutely, sir! No radical-rousing, no loose cannons, and no metaphors, sir!"

"Good. Now . . . where were we?"

"We were explaining why I had to tell my hot date to cool her heels while I came to get briefed on the emergency," Hy Felix said, "which you still haven't done anything about."

"Why should we do something about your date, Hy?" Dinewiner said, looking Confused (32-F).

"Let's just get this meeting over with so I can go apologize to her. She's awfully sensitive, poor thing."

"I'm afraid your love life will have to wait, Hy," Crapwell told him. "If we survive this night with the revolutionaries storming our barricades, metaphorically speaking—"

"I thought we weren't allowed to use metaphors," Dinewiner said, extending his 32-F to a 32-J.

" . . . if, indeed," Crapwell continued, ignoring the comment, "the embassy still stands in the morning, perhaps then . . ."

"In the morning!" Felix wailed.

" . . . perhaps then we all may return to the blessed normalcy of everyday life in the arms of family and loved ones . . ."

"Naw, I just want to have dinner with her . . ."

" . . . holding them close to our bosoms . . ."

"...maybe a little dancing afterward, at this little disco I know on the Street of Libidinous Expectations..."

"...indeed, when we can rest, all of us, secure in the blessed knowledge that nocturnal Jacobins shall not rouse us from our slumber, battering down the very gates of our domestic habitats, securitywise...."

"...and, well, I guess maybe a bit of snuggling later, at the Spaceport Motel, which has some really nice rooms with fake fireplaces and heart-shaped hot tubs..."

"...but, in the meantime, it remains the sacred duty of each and every one of us, as we man our stations onboard this ship of diplomatic state, rising to the occasion..."

"...well, maybe we'll do a little more than just snuggle, seeing as how she is so hot and all..."

"...indeed, our honor, our heroic caliber, the very nature of our character, as diplomats and as upright men, is now being tested to the very fullest..."

"...and I'm betting she's really good at..."

"...and indeed we must not be found limp and spent, manhoodwise, in this hour of gravest peril..."

Retief slid his chair back quietly and rose.

"Ssst!" Magnan hissed, grasping his arm. "Where do you think you're going?"

Retief nodded toward the Great Man at the head of the table, who was now warming to the rolling-thunder rhythm of his monologue.

"His Ex has just slipped into Full Grandiloquent Mode," Retief whispered back. "I figure I have at least twenty minutes."

"Retief!" Magnan said in a worried, nasal whisper. "You heard what he said! And I'm supposed to be responsible for you!"

"Don't worry, sir," Retief reassured him. "I promise not to use a single metaphor."

"But where are you going?"

"I feel the need to use a euphemism."

"Ah. The little diplomat's room? Very well. But hurry back! His Excellency is indeed in FGM, but the urgency of the situation may curtail his eloquence to a mere fifteen minutes or so. Do not tarry!"

"I'm sure you can carry on without me, Mr. Magnan. Your survival skills at enduring extreme eloquence in the course of interminable staff meetings are nothing short of legendary."

"Well, thank you, Retief. Most kind of you. I must say that . . . Retief?"

But Retief was gone.

CHAPTER TWO

1

After a brief stop at the embassy's online resource center and a few quick words with Miss Mellonocker, the resource librarian, Retief made his way down two levels to the broad, high-ceilinged splendor of the entryway.

George, the janitor, was mopping up the floor, a jet-black sheet with a mirror's polish, representing the vast, star-clotted spiral of the Galaxy. "You fixin' on goin' out there, Mr. Retief?" he asked, looking up from his scuffzapper. The crowd noise rumbled ominously just beyond the embassy doors.

"I thought I'd take in a bit of the night air, George, yes."

"That's a durned ugly crowd out there, Mr. Retief. You be careful!"

"It can't possibly be any uglier than His Excellency on an eloquence jag."

"Oh, yeah. I sees whatcha mean. Have a nice stroll, sir."

"I'll do that."

Stepping through the high, broad, double doors, he stood on the small front portico. A trio of steps led down to the front yard, where a walkway split around a rather grotesque B'ruklian statue of an eight-legged cherub, a fountain spilling from its uplifted dagger-toothed mouth.

Beyond was the wall encircling the embassy grounds, and the front gate—high and ornately imposing in black iron bars and gingerbread.

The crowd outside was pressed up against the gate so tightly that the nearest members of the mob were literally pinned against the bars, their faces, arms, and torsos squeezed into the spaces in interesting displays of forced contortion.

The two young Marines on gate duty stood inside the grounds and to either side of the gate, rigidly at parade rest, but with a nervous cast to their features as the gate creaked ominously beneath the weight of many, many bodies. They heard Retief's approach, spun to face him, and snapped to attention, presenting ceremonial arms in a snappy dual salute.

"At ease, boys," Retief told them. "I'm not the saluting kind. How's it going?"

"Oh, hi, Mr. Retief," one of the Marines said, relaxing. "Thought you might be old Garter Guts checking up on us."

" 'Garter Guts?' "

"Uh, Captain Martinet. Our CO."

"Yeah," the other guard said. "He always says he's gonna have guts for garters. Uh . . . do you know what garters are, Mr. Retief?"

"A kind of snake, native to Terra, among other things."

"Really? Poisonous?"

"Deadly."

"Wow." The Marine straightened a bit, standing a bit taller. "Cool!"

"Let's see what these folks want." Retief walked up to the gate, folded his arms, and leaned against the frame. Hundreds of people, all young, most human, swarmed in the plaza outside. Retief caught a distinctive, sweet smell, like sage, adrift in the air. A sandy-haired kid had his face and one arm trapped between the bars, pinned in place by the press of the crowd.

"Good evening," Retief said pleasantly.

"Uh . . . hi," the kid said, rolling his eyes to look up at Retief.

"That looks uncomfortable."

"Uh . . . that's, like, 'cause it is, y'know?"

"Why are you doing it?"

"Well, on accounta I can't move, see? I'm, like, stuck."

"So I see." Retief took the boy's limp hand and examined the class ring adorning one finger. "Sigma Omicron Beta," he observed. "Good fraternity?"

"Oh, it's, like, totally awesome, man!"

"Too right, dude," the student pinned next to the first kid said. "Like party-down central, y'know?"

"Lots of parties, eh?"

"Like fleaglin' right, man! It's like all the fleaglin' beer you can drink, all the fleaglin' joyweed you can smoke, all the fleaglin' nekkid chicks you can—"

"Good ol' Sig-Om-Bet, man," the first student said, nodding as well as he could with his head wedged against the bars of the gate. "It's the greatest, right, Bruce?"

"Right on, Zippie!"

"So . . . what are you doing here?"

Bruce tried to extricate his face from the gate, failed, and gave up. "We're like, exercisin' our rights t'peacefully assemble an', like, demonstrate in support of the, like, you know, like, the thingie, you know. . . ."

"I'm afraid I don't. What are you supporting?"

"Peace!" a girl caught in the press of the crowd a few feet back from the gate called out. "We support peace!"

"Uh-huh. So do I. But what are you doing demonstrating here?"

"This is the Terran Embassy!" the girl shouted. "It's, like, you know, government bureaucrats and stuff! Establishment PIGs, as in Purveyors of Ignominious Glibness! We're ordinary private citizens marching in order to exercise our Constitutional rights and to deliver our message to those in power: *We want peace!*"

"Those government bureaucrats and stuff are here to assist the peace process. . . ."

But the crowd had taken up the girl's battle cry. "*We want peace! We want peace! We want peace! We wa—*"

"I hear you!" Retief shouted, and the authoritative whip crack of his voice halted the chant in mid-want. In the startled silence, he added in a milder tone, "Just what is it you'd like us to do for you?"

"Uh . . . stop the war on Odiousita!" the girl said.

"Yeah," Bruce added. "Like, right on! Like, do the peace thingie, man!"

"As I said, I'm all for peace myself," Retief told them. "Unfortunately, some large and short-tempered folks who call themselves the Krll have decided to move into the Shamballa Cluster. They've snapped up a few dozen worlds already, and now they're trying to swallow Odiousita V. Corps Peace Enforcers were deployed there to catch the Krll's interest."

"You call using Hellbores and fractional-kiloton orbital bombardment a way to get someone's interest?" the girl yelled.

"Sometimes you need to whack the other guy upside the head with a two-by-four to get his attention, miss," Retief told her. "This is one of those times. So far, every negotiator and peace feeler we've sent to Odiousita has failed to come back. It's kind of hard to do the peace thingie one-sided." He tilted his head to the side, intrigued. "You sound like a young woman of considerable experience, however. Who are you with?"

"I am an ordinary private citizen marching in order to exercise my legal—"

"Yeah, I got that part. Where did you learn about Hellbores and fractional-kiloton bombardments?"

"Uh . . . in school? Damned military-industrial-educational complex, always looking for ways to—"

"USC? I don't think so. They're strictly liberal arts, not a military university at all. They don't even have a Star Naval Officer's Training Cadre on campus, and if they don't have a Snotsie unit, you can hardly accuse them of being pro-war, now, can you?"

"Uh . . ."

"You guys who are in Sigma Omicron Beta . . . USC doesn't have a chapter. Just where did you people come from, anyway?"

"We're ordinary private citizens marching—"

"Yes, you are, and you're doing it very well, too. But someone organized all of this. And someone paid to bring you here to B'rukley. Now I happen to know that none of you from off-planet have visas or passports. If you had, we would have processed them through the embassy here, and we haven't. You! Zippie! Where are you from?"

"Uh . . . Dead End, man."

"Where's that?"

"Newbraska."

"That's an agro world about fifty lights from here. That's a heck of a long distance to march. You go to school there?"

"Sure do. Cornfed Veterinary, Horticultural, and Miscellaneous College of Conservative Arts."

"Bruce? How about you?"

"Uh, like, Maladu II, dude. Maladu Unitarian Surfin' Technology University, man."

"MUST U?"

"Like, sometimes, dude, yeah. When you gotta, you gotta, y'know?"

"Maladu is a good eighty lights away. You guys come up with the gucks to make this trip all by yourselves?"

"Uh . . . college students? Man, like, you gotta be kiddin'!"

"All right, all right," the girl said. She was wedged into the crowd so tightly she could hardly move, but she managed to pull one arm up higher . . . higher . . .

"Ow! Hey, watch it!"

"Sorry." She finally reached her chest and plucked a card from her tightly filled sports bra. With much wiggling and shifting, she managed to extend her arm past Bruce's chin and hand the card to Retief.

"Aroused Citizenry for Halting Expansionism," he read. "Okay. That makes sense, I suppose. I've worked with ACHE before. But you're not saying that ACHE foots the bill. They're not exactly well financed."

"We have our sources," the girl said.

He glanced at the name under the ACHE logo. "Well, Miss Ann Thrope. If ACHE's not footing the bill for this little frat party, who is?"

"That's none of your business! We're ordinary private—"

"Let me explain some things, Miss Thrope. The Terran Embassy is here to serve the needs of distressed humans on B'rukley. You folks up in front look like you're turning blue, so you certainly qualify. However, if you hold visas issued by another government, you'll need to talk to them.

"Next. We here at the embassy do not make Corps policy when it comes to issues such as the current state of affairs on Odiousita. If, however, you would care to elect a small group of spokespersons, I'm sure someone in the embassy would be delighted to hear what you have to say and to deliver any message you might have to Sector Headquarters on Aldo Cerise.

"And last. If whoever is backing you is genuinely concerned about bringing peace to the Shamballa Cluster, I suggest you have them get in touch with the Interplanetary Tribunal for Curtailment of Hostilities. ITCH is sponsored in part by the Terran government but includes representatives from several interested worlds. Several members of the Embassy staff are on the ITCH panel. I can set up a meeting for your sponsors. Now . . . is there anything else I can help you kids with? Or shall we call it a night?"

"You can't brush us off that easy!" Ann screamed. "We demand action! We demand to be heard!"

"I think I've heard you."

"We're gonna come over that wall and make sure you did!" a heavyset student behind Ann yelled. He turned his head and addressed the crowd at his back. "It's like the lady says, guys! These embassy-types is just Purveyors of Ignominious Glibness! That means they talk fast and you can't trust 'em! I says we go over the wall now! Who's with me?"

"You're forgetting the Marine guards, fellows," Retief said mildly. "I'm sure they don't want to hurt anyone, but they are under orders to protect this installation."

"Haw! Them guys?" another male voice bellowed. "They don't even got loaded guns!"

"Really?" Retief asked, looking surprised. "Let's see about that!" Turning, he walked back to the two Marine guards. "Attention on deck!" Retief snapped. Both Marines came to rigid positions of attention by force of conditioned reflex.

"Inspection . . . *harms!*"

The guard in front of him went to present arms, extending his weapon in front of him. Retief took the blast rifle, made a show of snapping open the charge chamber, and flipping a power pack free.

"Huh?" The Marine started to say something, but Retief froze him with a hard glare.

"Easy, son," he said just loudly enough for the boy to hear. "Play along."

He examined the power pack carefully, holding it up and turning it under the brilliant starlight for a close look, then ostentatiously snapped it back into the charge chamber, snicked the receiver slide shut, and tossed the rifle back to the Marine. Performing a crisp about-face, he strode three paces forward to stand in front of the other guard. As before, he took the guard's blast rifle, popped a power pack out for close inspection, reinserted it, and tossed it back to its owner.

"Carry on, men!" Retief growled.

The crowd had grown strangely silent during this brief ritual; silent, that was, except for a flurry of quickly whispered warnings.

"Geeze! Didja see that?"

"Those blast rifles are charged!"

"Toby said the guards didn't have no power packs in their guns!"

"Yeah! Somebody's been lyin' to us!"

"Hey, I gotta go back to the dorm, man. Homework, y'know?"

"Hey, get outa my way!"

"Move it! C'mon! Move!"

"Getchur thumb outa my eye!"

"Ow!"

Slowly, like the changing of the tide, the mob began to pull back from the embassy gates. Bruce and Zippie were the last two remaining, trying to pry themselves free from the iron bars.

"You boys need a hand?"

"Uh, no, thanks, mister! We was just, like, goin', y'know?" Bruce pulled his head free with an audible *pop!*, rubbed the startling red indentations on either side of his face, and worked his jaw back and forth. "Man! Like, I didn't think I was ever gonna, like, get outa there!"

"Let's get back to the hotel, dude," Zippie said. "We gotta talk to the Broodie about this!"

"I'm with ya, man."

In another few moments, the plaza beyond the gates was deserted, forlornly empty save for scattered beer and soda cans, and a number of leaflets scudding about with the breeze. Retief reached down through the bars, picked up one of the leaflets, and glanced through it.

Turning, then, he nodded at the two Marines. "Good work, men. You seem to have dispersed the crowd quite nicely."

"Uh, it wasn't us, Mr. Retief!"

"No!" the other Marine said. "And how didja do that trick with the power packs? I know my power rifle had an empty charge chamber, 'cause Captain Martinet inspected it before we came out here!"

"Yeah, Mr. Retief! What gives?"

"Oh," Retief said, producing a Mark XVII MOD 5 M-29 blast rifle power pack in his hand. He tossed it, caught it, turned his hand . . . then opened his hand again—empty. He passed one hand over the other, turned his hand over—and the power pack was back. Another pass, a twist of the wrist—and the hand was empty. With his other hand, Retief reached out and pulled the wandering power pack from the startled Marine's left ear.

He tucked the pack into the guard's jacket pocket. "You should be more careful of these, son. Don't let them wander off like that." Turning to the other Marine, he pulled a second power pack from behind the man's head and dropped it into his uniform pocket.

"Just in case, fellows," Retief said.

"Hey, thanks!"

"Yeah! I don't feel quite so naked now!"

"Don't lock and load unless it's absolutely necessary," Retief told them. "And . . . it's our little secret, right?"

"Right, Mr. Retief!"

"*Semper fi*, fellows." Retief opened the gate and stepped out into the deserted plaza. "Watch the store. I'll be back in a little while."

And he walked off into the starlit night.

2

While the Plaza of Articulate Naiveté had been nicely cleared out, the web of streets and avenues leading to the plaza remained fairly crowded. While many of the marchers appeared to be wandering off to wherever it was they'd come from, a carnival atmosphere had embraced those who remained. Shops, restaurants, and bars were reopening if they weren't open already in order to take advantage of the influx of tourists.

Of those students who'd been closest to the embassy gate, however, there was no sign. "Too bad," Retief murmured to himself. "I wonder who 'Broodie' is?"

Deciding to follow up on a feeling he had, Retief strolled through the crowds toward the Avenue of Much Walking. The neon sign for Joe's Bar and Bookstore was visible up ahead when Retief decided that he'd picked up a tail.

And a fairly obvious one at that. He stopped in front of a window display filled with native crafts and pretended to look at the contents while stealing a sideways look at his follower.

The moment Retief stopped to look in the window, the other stopped as well, feigning interest in the produce of a native gopplefruit stand. He couldn't be certain, but Retief was pretty sure it was the same Grothelwaith he'd noticed earlier in the evening. Most of the members of that somewhat shy and furtive race tended to be tall and lean, some as tall as seven feet, their graceful forms all but masked by the long, black cloaks and hoods they favored. This one stood only about five feet from his cloak-hidden feet to the pointed top of his hood, and he had a tubby, somewhat stiff look about him.

Turning, suddenly, Retief walked straight toward the loitering Grothelwaith, who seemed momentarily paralyzed by indecision when he saw the Terry diplomat bearing down on him. He started to turn left, then right, then executed a wobbly dither in mid-street.

"Hello, there!" Retief called cheerily. "Haven't we met before?"

Twin yellow lights gleamed brightly within the depths of the hood, but the being gave no reply. Instead, when Retief was almost upon him, he whirled and began walking quickly away.

Retief took an extra long step, bringing his foot down on the swirling hem of the being's cloak. The Grothelwaith took another shuffling step forward, uttered a harshly sibilant cry, and fell over onto his back.

"Oh, I'm so sorry!" Retief said. "Let me help you up! ..." Reaching down, he grasped the hood of the alien's garment and gave a sharp tug.

"Littermate of drones!" the being rasped in a throaty whisper. "To unhand me, vile soft one! ..."

With the hood pulled back, a pair of penlights with round, yellow lenses mounted atop a pair of stiff wires were revealed as the alien's glowing eyes; behind and between the fake oculars, five weirdly stalked eyes protruded from the being's cloaked shoulders, weaving back and forth and even twisting around one another in agitation.

"Why ... Broodmaster Shtliff! I wasn't expecting to see you on B'rukley." He shifted into accent-free Groaci as he pulled the being to his feet. "To be a long way indeed from the pleasant hives and warm sand pits of noble Groac. To be wondering what you are doing here disguised as a soft one."

"To be none of your business, nebsnoot Terry," Shtliff hissed, angrily jerking the hood back into place. "To keep your oversized gloof organ out of the business of your betters!"

The Groaci's normally breathy whisper sounded muffled, as though he was speaking through a mask, and Retief thought he could hear the faint and rhythmic *whishh-pop* of some sort of breathing device.

"I will," Retief said, shifting back to Standard, "if you can tell my gloof organ why you were following me and why the Groaci First Assistant Minister of Sneaky Affairs on B'rukley is wearing such unfashionable attire."

"As to the second," Shtliff said with breathy disdain in the same language, "I find the long cloak keeps out the night chill of this dank and unwholesome planet. As to the first, I fear your delusional misapprehension is but further evidence of the well-known tendency of Terries to xenophobic paranoia!"

Yes, Shtliff was definitely wearing some sort of breathing unit, Retief decided. Why? Groaci breathed standard oxy-nitrogen mix, the same as humans. All Retief could see of the alien, however, were his five eyes writhing in an agitated manner at the ends of their stalks.

"Well, I'm sure you know that paranoia can lead to some pretty unpleasant misunderstandings. For example, I'm beginning to think you might be hiding something from me."

"And why ever would a Groaci First Assistant Minister of Sneaky Affairs wish to hide anything from a mere soft one?" Retief heard the muffled clack of mandibles signifying wry amusement emanating from the depths of the cloak. "To release me instanter, and I shall magnanimously overlook this unseemly breach of diplomatic protocol."

"To be wondering what the Groaci have to do with an antiwar march on B'rukley. And to be wondering why said Groaci wish to stay out of the limelight."

"To stuff lint up your nostrils, soft one."

"To spill the beans, Shtliff. To tell all in a spirit of eternal interplanetary chumship."

"To go jump in the proverbial pool of dihydrogen oxide."

"To give, Shtliff, before you see how paranoid I can be."

"To look behind you, soft one."

Retief glanced up at the display window behind the disguised Groaci, then turned to face the gathering crowd of students. Thirty or forty had begun clustering in the street at Retief's back.

"Like, Grothel-dude," one said. "Is this here suit, like, hasslin' you, man?"

"A PIG!" the Groaci cried out in Standard, his voice a soft shrill. "Halp! A Purveyor of Ignominious Glibness seeks to lay violent hands on your guru!"

"Hey, man." A student who towered a full head above Retief's six-three, and who weighed at least three hundred pounds, lumbered forward. "It ain't cool t'lay hands on our guru, see?"

"Get him, Tiny!" someone yelled.

"Yeah, Tiny! Show the PIG we mean business!"

Letting go of Shtliff, Retief reached across Tiny's out-thrust right hand, grasped it, and flipped it down and back. The big man bellowed and dropped to his knees. "Ow! Hey! No fair! Lemme go!"

Still holding Tiny's hand sharply folded at the wrist, he pretended to examine the student's fingers. "My, my, Tiny," he said. "Such dirty fingernails. Do your teachers let you come to class this way?"

Tiny reached for Retief with his free hand; Retief increased the pressure and the giant folded. "Owww! Stop, mister! Yer killin' me!"

"What school do you represent, Tiny?"

"Jockstrap-U! On Thudelphia!"

"J-U? That's one of the big top-ten conference schools for crunchball, isn't it?"

"Yeah! Ow! Yeah!"

"You took the championship last year at the Galactic Popcorn Bowl, I believe."

"Uh! Uh! Yeah! Please, mister . . . !"

"What position do you play?"

"Throwback!"

"I'm impressed, Tiny," Retief said, relaxing the pressure on the wrist just a bit. "But I'm a little surprised at a student from such a fine school turning up here at a spontaneous peace march. Who sponsored you?"

"I dunno. Some . . . whatchacallum . . ."

"A political action group," a bearded student in the crowd offered. "It's called SMERCH. Now let the poor guy up, huh?"

"Ah, yes," Retief said, nodding. "I saw some of your literature just now in the plaza. 'Students Marching to End Rapacious and Colonialist Hegemony,' is that it?"

"That's right, mister! Us students got rights! We demand to be heard!"

"How about it, Tiny?" Retief asked his captive. "Are you marching to end rapacious and colonialist hegemony?"

"Uh . . ."

"Do you know what the words 'rapacious and colonialist hegemony' mean?"

"Uh . . . 'money.' I know what that is. It's, like, what people pays you so's you can buy food and beer and stuff. Is 'hegemony' like, I dunno, money fer buyin' hegems?"

"Be careful, Tiny," Retief warned. "You don't want to go and sprain your cerebrum just before a big game."

"Gosh, no! Thanks, mister! Geeze, I didn't even know I had one of them!"

"You can't be too careful. And now, as much as I hate to end our little chat, it's time for us to go our separate ways."

"Not so fast, mister," the bearded student said. "You still gotta answer for roughin' up our guru!"

Again, Retief caught the sweet-sage scent in the air. Several in the crowd were smoking what looked like hand-rolled dopesticks.

"I couldn't have roughed him up too badly," Retief pointed out. "Not to judge by his speed at scuttling out of here. He's your guru, huh?"

"Yeah, man," another student said. "Our, like, spiritual leader in the pursuit of Cosmic Peace and Chumship, man. It's like totally cosmic, dude."

"Totally!" another agreed.

"Aw, fer cryin' out loud," still another student growled.

"Drop the cosmic yivshish and let's just take this bum apart, right?"

"Right!"

The crowd surged forward.

"Excuse me, Tiny," Retief told the crunchball player, twisting the student's arm to bring him off his knees and onto his toes. "I'd like to see an example of your blocking skill."

"Huh? Oh, yeah! Sure!"

"Thank you." Deftly, Retief spun the crunchball player around, hooking his leg around Tiny's size 14 feet and giving him a hard shove. The hulking student toppled into the advancing mob and sent them all sprawling onto the street. Dodging several out-thrust arms, Retief slipped past the mob and broke into a trot. Joe's was just ahead.

Behind him, the mob struggled to get clear of Tiny.

"Ow! Get this big lummox off'n me!"

"Where'd that guy go?"

"Hey! Watch it!"

Retief had walked perhaps ten feet at a brisk pace when he stopped. Blocking his way was the woman he'd seen in Joe's ear-lier, with the trench coat and spyglasses. She wore neither now as she held up a hand and, in an imperious voice, commanded, "Hold it right there, buster!"

A late-model hovercam floated on silent jets a few feet away. The woman turned to face the snout of its lens, patted her meticulously arranged hair, held up three fingers, and said, "On me in three . . . two . . ."

She lowered her fingers with the countdown, dropping the last silently as she shifted into full professional on-camera mode. "This is Desiree Goodeleigh, Galactic News Network, live on the streets of High Gnashberry, B'rukley, where moments ago a member of the Terran diplomatic staff to this world created a riot by assaulting several Terry students and a tourist from the Grothelwaith system. This attack, apparently launched without provocation, gives lie to CDT claims of seeking peace in this sector, already deeply torn by the so-called police action on nearby Odiousita V. You, sir!" She whirled to face Retief, the hovercam pivoting in midair to focus on his face. "Why did you start that riot just now?"

"For the same reason that I've stopped beating my wife."

"You are wearing sequined powder-blue-with-magenta trim hemi-demi-informal coveralls, mid-to-late afternoon, for use during, with a gold CDT patch on your chest. Obviously you are a member of the Terran diplomatic staff at the embassy here."

"Actually," Retief said modestly, "I'm just the gopher. They sent me out for doughnuts."

"In the course of which you callously started a major riot on the Avenue of Much Walking. Would you care to explain why you were seen using physical violence against both a human student and an innocent Grothelwaith tourist?"

"No, actually."

The mob by this time had untangled itself from Tiny. "There he is!" someone shouted. "After him!"

"Would you care to comment on the CDT's obvious foot-dragging and duplicity in the Krll affair on Odiousita V?"

"I suggest you ask them," Retief said, indicating the advancing throng, now swollen to several hundred members. As Desiree and the hovercam pivoted to face them, Retief slipped past her and down the steps into Joe's Bar and Bookstore.

"Hey, Mr. Retief!" Joe called. "Ain't seen you in, lessee . . . forty-five minutes!"

"It's been a busy night, Joe." He looked around the bar, which was this time filled to capacity—some native B'ruks, but most of the patrons human students. "I see business picked up for you, too.

"Cycle me through, Joe."

A thunder of crowd noise sounded outside the bar. Hundreds of voices had picked up a now-familiar chant. *"Terries go home! Terries go home! Terries go home!"*

"And you might want to forget you've seen me."

"You got it, Mr. Retief."

"But . . . before I go, how about a couple of dozen doughnuts to go? I have a feeling Ambassador Crapwell is going to need something to chew on while he watches the evening news."

3

"Great heavens, Retief!" Magnan cried. "Where have you been this time?"

"Don't tell me His Excellency is beside himself again."

"I won't. Not if it means more of your ill-considered attempts at humor, space-time-displacementwise. This time, I fear you've really gone too far!"

"Let's not be overdramatic, Mr. Magnan. I just went around the corner to pick up some doughnuts. See? Sourball and persimmon. His Ex's favorite."

"An admirable attempt, apple-polishingwise, but it shan't be enough to save you this time. You told me you would be back before the end of His Excellency's FGM. You were gone..." Magnan checked his fingerwatch, a genuine Japanese imitation Minnie Mouse, and scowled, "... no less than forty-two minutes! When His Excellency returned to the matter at hand, he realized at once that you were gone. I was at a complete loss to explain your absence!"

"Actually, Mr. Magnan, I was talking to the demonstrators in front of the gate. I was able to convince them to take their business elsewhere."

"Hmm," Magnan hmmed. "Hmm...I see. Between you and me, I would have to say well done. However, I wouldn't count on your success to save you from His Ex's wrath. The fact that you left a high-level staff meeting in order to actually do something about the selfsame topic of that meeting could be misconstrued in some quarters."

"You mean the fact that I did something about it, instead of talking it to death?"

Magnan gave Retief a pained expression—a 70-G, he thought.

"Retief, I know that you are seasoned enough in diplomatic work to be well aware of just how vital discussion is in the resolution of problems, diplomacy-wise. Indeed, talking a problem to death is widely viewed as the most direct—if somewhat sanguinary—means of making a problem go away. But your cavalier attitude could be misinterpreted as sarcasm if you were overheard. Please have a care!"

"I understand, Mr. Magnan. Far be it from me to suggest that the Corps would ever be so déclassé as to actually *do* something when something needed to be done."

"Very good, Retief. I knew you understood the true subtlety of the diplomatic spirit. Still, as I said, your success may not be enough to shield me . . . that is, to shield you. You are in grave trouble just now, and I, as your supervisor, may be forced to take some measure of the r-word as a result!"

"Really? Resourcefulness? That's good, isn't it?"

"Not *that* r-word, Retief!" Magnan glanced to left and right, as though fearful of being overheard. He leaned forward, motioned Retief closer, and whispered it. "*Responsibility!*"

"You're saying I got you into trouble."

"It may not be too late to salvage my career. To do so, however, I may have to jettison yours. I trust you were already wearying of the give-and-take of diplomatic exchanges. Over the past few years as we've worked together, I've noticed in you a certain lack of enthusiasm at times, as though you were less than pleased with the vision, scope, and efficiency of the *Corps Diplomatique.*"

"I'm not ready to write my note of resignation just yet, Mr. Magnan. What is it that I've allegedly done?"

"Done? Why—"

"*Magnan!*" bellowed from the intercom on Magnan's desk. "Is that criminal Retief back here, yet?"

"Um . . . that is, yes, sir. He's in my office now, sir, as we speak!"

"Well, stop speaking to him and have him get up here to the Intelligence Center here this picosecond!"

"Right away, Your Excellency!"

"You, too, Magnan! I fear you have some share of the r-word in this matter!"

"Yes, sir!" Magnan squeaked. He looked up at Retief with an expression of Doomed Hopelessness (86-Q). "It may be worse than I feared! From the sound of it, His Ex is readying the firing squad now!"

"Magnan!" Crapwell's voice thundered. "I told you to stop speaking to the scoundrel and get in here! Literally trillions of picoseconds have already trickled by, and you still have not obeyed my direct command!"

"Eep!" Magnan jerked his finger off the intercom talk switch as though he'd been burned.

"And don't count on anything so magnanimous or pleasant as a firing squad! Either of you!"

Magnan's 86-Q crinkled into an 86-Y. "Come along, Retief. His Excellency awaits."

4

The Embassy Intelligence Center was located on the third floor, a closely guarded shrine with access restricted to key personnel with Galactic Universal Top Secret clearance only.

Clearance which Magnan did not have.

"What do you mean you can't let me in!" Magnan yelled at the indifferent Marine sergeant posted in front of the vaultlike door. The words SENIOR STAFF TV ROOM above the door had been crossed out, and the words INTELLIGENCE CENTER: G-2, GUTS CLEARANCE REQUIRED, KEEP OUT, NO ADMITTANCE, THIS MEANS YOU written in underneath. "Ambassador Crapwell just ordered me to meet him here!"

"Sorry, sir," the Marine said. "Like they say, no GUTS, no glory . . . with 'glory' bein', in this case, you bein' allowed to go in there."

"But His Excellency *told* me—"

"That don't cut no mustard with me, Mac. How do I know you ain't a sneaky sticky-fingers Groaci tryin' to sneak in there? Take a hike."

"The effrontery!" Magnan exclaimed. "Do I even remotely look like a Groaci?"

"Nope. Do you think a Groaci spy would just waltz in lookin' like his own self, without some sort of disguise? Don't make me laugh!"

"Look . . . why don't you just go in and ask His Excellency? I'm sure he'll tell you to admit us."

The guard laughed, then glowered. "I *tole* ya not to make me laugh, din't I? No, way, Mac. I ain't supposed to leave my post, see? Besides . . . you think a Marine sergeant rates GUTS clearance?"

"Excuse me, Sergeant," Retief said. "I think I can clear this up."

Stepping forward, he leaned close to the lens of the retina scanner mounted on the wall next to the door. There was a deep thump of heavy tumblers falling, and the vault door swung open.

"Geeze, Mac," the Marine said. "Go on in!"

"Thanks." He jerked a thumb at Magnan. "He's with me."

"Oh, sure! Have a nice day, sir!"

Magnan followed Retief into the intelligence sanctum sanctorum. "Good heavens, Retief! When did you ever receive GUTS clearance?"

"Oh, I've had it for quite a while, Mr. Magnan. It comes in handy sometimes."

"I should think so! Admission to the Intelligence Center alone is a lofty privilege! Too bad you may be about to lose that privilege, as well as so many others!"

The Intelligence Center looked like an ordinary TV lounge, with sofas and overstuffed chairs positioned about a wall-sized tri-V television screen.

In fact, and as suggested by the sign outside, the Intelligence Center had started off as the senior staff television room. It had become the embassy's primary G-2 resource with a very important discovery some years before: whatever was going down in the outside world, GNN *always* knew about it long before the various government intelligence services did. Indeed, by now, not only ambassadors, but government heads of state and the intelligence services themselves all used GNN as a primary intelligence source.

Ambassador Crapwell was sitting in one of the sofas, watching the eight-foot-tall face of Desiree Goodeleigh as she earnestly reported the news.

"And you," the giant face was saying. "What happened to you?"

The camera view switched to one of the students Retief had encountered in the street. Fake blood had been liberally smeared on his face, and his clothing was torn. "Oh, yeah, like, it was awful, like, you know, really awful! Th' guy just went berserk! Threw poor Tiny right into us!"

"And you . . . you're Tiny? What happened?"

The camera switched to a close-up of Tiny's dull features. "Duhh . . . he wanted t'see my blockin' style. . . ."

"Clearly, some of the students here have suffered brain damage," Desiree said as the camera swung back to her. "The fact that the assailant appeared to be a member of the *Corps Diplomatique Terrestrienne* makes this monstrous assault all the more puzzling. Here is a replay of the beginning of the riot. Note the sheer brutal ferocity of the man in the blue CDT coveralls. . . ."

The scene shifted to a recognizable shot of Retief in the midst of a crowd of angry students. There was a blur of motion too quick to follow, and then Retief had grabbed and hurled Tiny into the crowd, scattering them like twenty or thirty tenpins.

"And here," Desiree's voice-over continued, "is our exclusive interview, moments ago, with the miscreant. . . ."

Retief's face appeared on-screen.

"You, sir!" Desiree's voice said off-camera. "Why did you start that riot just now?"

"For the same reason that I've stopped beating my wife."

"You are wearing sequined powder-blue-with-magenta trim hemi-demi-informal coveralls, mid-to-late afternoon, for use during, with a gold CDT patch on your chest. Obviously you are a member of the Terran diplomatic staff at the embassy here."

"Actually, I'm just the gopher. They sent me out for doughnuts."

"In the course of which you callously started a major riot on the Avenue of Much Walking. Would you care to explain why you were seen using physical violence against both a human student and an innocent Grothelwaith tourist?"

"No, actually."

"There you have it," Desiree's voice said as the close-up of Retief's face went freeze-frame, his face frozen in what might have been Ruthlessness, Masked by a Civilized Veneer, 668-A or possibly a B. "Is this the face of a CDT criminal hiding behind the shelter of diplomatic immunity? Are scores of innocent children engaged in lawful demonstration here on B'rukley against the Concordiat's unjust war of aggression on Odiousita at risk from psychopathic elements within the Terran diplomatic bureaucracy running loose on the streets of High Gnashberry? We'll get back to that story, after this . . . !"

The GNN news show broke for a commercial. Crapwell turned in the sofa, looking at Retief and Magnan with a complex four-digit expression . . . blending a masterful 1231 (Astonishment at a Gaffe of Unprecedented Proportions) with a less certain but still well-grounded 1190 (You're Gonna Burn Over A Slow Fire for This One, Charlie, and I'm Gonna Eat Popcorn While I Watch)—both of them at the mid-range of the expression spectrum . . . an L or an M.

"In all my long years as a civil servant and as a representative of sovereign Terra, I have never, never witnessed such pusillanimous, such misdirected, such . . . such *undiplomatic* behavior! You, sir, are a menace to the good name of Terra, and to the golden respect accorded as their right to diplomats of every world and race! What can you possibly have to say in your own defense?"

Retief shrugged his broad shoulders. "I was misquoted."

"I just heard you, man, admit to being a wife beater!"

"The idea!" Magnan added. "And here I didn't even know you were married!"

"I'm not."

"Then that makes it worse," Crapwell shrilled. "You are a liar, claiming to be married when you are not!"

"And here I thought lying was one of the Seven Virtues of Diplomacy."

"Well . . . it is, of course," Crapwell said, his tirade halted for the moment. "Still, the idea is to lie without the other fellow knowing you're doing it! That . . . that display I just witnessed on the GNN Early-to-Late-Mid-Evening News presented the Corps in a most unfavorable light . . . a *most* unfavorable light!"

"It's true she didn't get my good side," Retief admitted. "And you're right. The lighting wasn't very flattering. She had a bit too much purple invective in the mix, her impartiality wasn't, and the balance and fairness were both way off."

"Don't you go getting technical with me, young man! Or trying to make excuses for your behavior! I want you to—"

Crapwell's personal phone warbled. Breaking off in mid-tirade, he picked it up and flipped it open. "Yes." He listened for a strained moment. "Ambassador Nish, how nice of you to call. . . . Yes, I've been watching. . . . What? No! Of course not! Eh? . . . No, Nish, we have not begun slaughtering helpless Terran students and alien nationals in the streets. . . . No, Ambassador Nish. . . . Yes, I know GNN is a Very Reliable Source. . . . Yes, we use it for our intelligence gathering, too. . . . Nish, you really shouldn't read too much into this one news item. . . . No, Ambassador Nish. . . . Yes, of course, I am aware of the treaty provisions of the Yalcan Accords. . . . Yes. . . . Yes. . . . No. Look, Nish, I really can't talk about this now. Let me call you back. Yes . . . very well. And how is the lovely Mrs. Nish and all the grubs? Charming, charming . . . yes. Oh, and are we still on for our golf date next Wednesday? Good. Yes, I'm looking forward to it. Good-bye, Ambassador Nish."

Angrily, he snapped the handphone shut and glared at Magnan and Retief. "That, gentlemen—and I use the term very advisedly— was absolutely the last straw! For that slimy excuse for a Groaci ambassador to call me up and lecture me, *me*, on the behavior of my staff! . . . It is not to be borne!"

"It's a pity you didn't ask him what his First Assistant Minister of Sneaky Affairs was doing in that peace demonstration disguised as a Grothelwaith."

"Eh? You said what? That doesn't make sense."

"The Groaci disdain for what they consider to be inferior species is well known, Retief," Magnan said. "I can't imagine a Groaci being caught dead disguised as a member of another species."

"It has been known to happen from time to time," Retief pointed out. "There was that affair on Quopp, you'll recall, when General Hish of the Groaci Legation disguised himself as a Voion. . . ."

"But what was all that about a Grothelwaith?" Crapwell demanded.

"I noticed I was being tailed by one," Retief said. "Not very well. They kind of stand out in the crowd."

"Creepy beings," Magnan said with a slight shudder.

"I'll have no speciesist remarks within the hallowed halls of this embassy, Magnan. The fact that they look like a caricature of Death in those cloaks and hoods is no concern of ours."

"Of course, sir. I only meant to say—"

"Put a lid on it, Magnan. We're discussing Retief's future career—or, rather, the lack of it, not the sartorial preferences of creepy alien critters!"

"However," Retief went on, as though he'd not been interrupted, "it turned out not to be a Grothelwaith at all . . . but our friend Broodmaster Shtliff wearing a rather elaborate getup to make him look like one."

"Why?" Magnan wanted to know.

"He declined to say. However, I detect Groac's sticky fingers in the B'ruklian pot. We have a very large number of students, most of them human, arriving on B'rukley from all over this part of the Galactic Arm, apparently organized by ACHE and by an organization I've not heard of before, SMERCH." He dropped the flyer he'd picked up next to Crapwell, who picked it up and glanced through it.

"Students Marching to End Rapacious and Colonialist Hegemony," the Ambassador read. "Sounds harmless enough. Another means for children to feel as though they are participating in the democratic process, nothing more."

"I believe it's more, sir. Someone—either SMERCH, or some-one behind SMERCH—is paying a great deal of money to ship these students in. You'll notice that they don't have Terran visas or passports, which means they're here under the sponsorship of some other government. I'd bet Groac."

"Nonsense, man," Crapwell said. "The Groaci are notorious tightwads unless a clear material gain for them is in the offing. Why would they bring in human students? Interstellar shipping rates alone make such a proposition economically unattractive."

"Point two. The students aren't very politically savvy, most of them. They have only a vague idea of what it is they're protesting."

Magnan chuckled. "There's nothing sinister about that," he said. "Such a slender grasp of world affairs within the younger generation is, I believe, traditional."

"As is a certain amount of apathy," Retief agreed. "Why did they come here at all?"

"An exchange-student program?" Magnan suggested.

"I very much doubt it. The Groaci are offering them some-thing . . . and they're trying to keep their own participation in this affair undercover. I heard Shtliff referred to as a 'guru' by some of the students, which suggests he's put himself in the position of spiritual leader for at least some of them."

Crapwell shook his head. "That does not tally well with what I understand of Groaci religious practice. I believe they adhere to the idea that each of them can, through conniving, become a god him- or herself."

"Maybe being a guru is a first step to godhood?" Magnan suggested.

"It seems more likely it's a first step to gaining considerable influence over impressionable young minds," Retief replied. "The question is . . . why? What's in it for Groac? Publicly, they've pretty much refused to take sides in the Krll War."

"Ah! Ah!" Crapwell raised an admonitory finger. "Not war, sir. Police action!"

"Excuse me. The Krll police action. Other than taking the odd potshot at Terry warmongering, they've stayed clear of it. What do they have to gain by subsidizing peace marches and Terry college students?"

"I can't imagine."

"Neither can I, sir. But I submit that we'd better find out. This has 'big' written all over it in Groaci italic curlicues, and we'd better find out what they're up to."

Crapwell lapsed into what passed for deep thought, tugging absently at his lower lip. Suddenly, he sat up and glared at Retief. "Bah! Young man! You've sought to derail me in the course of my disciplining you! It won't do, you know. It won't do! You have disgraced the Corps on a Galaxywide news broadcast. Now . . . I am an understanding and compassionate man. I know that these news reporters can get you so tangled up with their questions that you could end up coming across as evil incarnate . . . or at least as idiot incarnate. I remember one time, on Hooligan, when I was a young undersecretary not yet marked for Greatness . . . harrumph!" He scowled and shook his head. "Never mind! Forget it."

"Already forgotten, sir."

"I don't like to say this, Retief . . . or Magnan . . . but the Corps has lost serious face in that news broadcast just now. Perhaps you had reason to manhandle that student, Retief, and perhaps you did not. The fact that you uncovered a Groaci worm in the B'ruklian apple will not serve to repair a shattered Enlightened Galactic Opinion vis-à-vis Terra or the diplomatic service!"

"We should examine the possibility that the Groaci are also behind the bad press."

"Eh? What do you mean?"

"I mean that the Groaci worm may have rendered that apple rotten to the Corps, and that they did it with malice aforethought. But there may be a way to use that to our advantage."

"Tell me," Crapwell said. "And believe me, you'd better make it good!"

5

"Retief," Magnan said, shaking his head with something akin to wonder as they entered the older man's office once more, "you have the most amazing aptitude for falling into sewage pits and coming out redolent of jasmine and *eau de sainteté*. How did you manage that bit of legerdemain in there?"

"I'm not sure I know what you mean, sir," Retief said. "It sounded to me like I'm out on my ear."

"Yes, yes, that's the *official* story, of course, for Goodeleigh and her bunch. But you were not hung, shot, nor drawn and quartered, for a start, and His Ex sounded most pleased with your devious little plan when you explained it to him."

"True, though I suspect that he likes the idea most because it offers him plausible deniability. If this idea of mine doesn't work, he can just shrug and explain that I was given the boot and am no longer affiliated with the CDT. For *real*."

"There is that," Magnan agreed. "You are taking a terrible risk, careerwise."

"Mr. Magnan, I'm sure this will come as a terrific shock . . . but it's not *always* about career."

Magnan looked startled. "It's not?"

"Nope. And if this doesn't work out, I could always sell my story to GNN."

"Retief! You wouldn't! I mean . . . that's consorting with the enemy! . . ."

"Don't worry, Mr. Magnan. I'll see to it that they spell your name right."

"Will you? I mean, no! That's not the point! Desiree Goodeleigh appears to have it in for both the CDT and for Terran intentions in the Shamballa Cluster. Her reporting is not what you would call impartial, balanced, or evenhanded!"

"True. Don't you find that interesting?"

"I find that alarming. Conducting diplomacy under circumstances in which lying or other, shall we say, irregularities violating the assumed social contract between governed and governing might at any time be ferreted out and exposed to the light of day by an ambitious newshound is bad enough. To have such charges laid at one's door without cause smacks of the worst excesses of the Spanish Inquisition!"

"Ah, but no one ever expects the Spanish Inquisition."

"I beg your pardon?"

"Never mind."

A knock sounded at the door. "Yes?" Magnan demanded.

Hy Felix stuck his head into the office. "Okay, guys. I called the press conference like you said. Nine-seventy-five AM tomorrow, out back on the parade ground."

"Tell me something, Hy."

"Yeah, Retief?"

"Did you know your hot date was Desiree Goodeleigh?"

"Nope. Or, rather, I knew that was her name, yeah. But I sure didn't know she was with GNN. I guess I have to thank you for stepping in and taking the fall for me."

"How's that?"

"Well, c'mon." Hy's long and mournful face grew, if anything, longer and more mournful. "Look at me! A gorgeous, classy dame like that, wanting an intimate tête-à-tête with an old shoe like me? I figure now she was just trying to get a line on inside information out of the embassy, maybe even trying to find someone to take a fall. She sure wasn't chatting me up because she wanted me to show her a good time." He shook his head sadly. "She really had me fooled, but when I saw her taking you apart on that news broadcast, Retief, I knew what she was up to ... I mean, I knew to what she was up."

"Now is not the time to be concerned about one's grammar, Hy," Magnan chided.

"And what was she up to?" Retief asked. "Or to what, if you like."

"Why, giving her own career a boost by finding something exciting and controversial to get all bent out of shape about! Nothing like a nice little scandal uncovered by an alert newsie to help said newsie scramble up another step or three on the old career pyramid, know what I mean? No offense, but I'm just glad it was you and not me, know what I mean?"

"None taken, Hy."

"I guess there's no fool like an old fool, huh?"

"I wouldn't worry, Hy," Retief told him. "Not every woman is after you because you can help her career. If it's romance you're looking for, I'm sure you'll find it."

"Romance, nothing. I just want to get laid once in a while. But that's neither there nor here. You sure you want to go through with this, Retief?"

"It doesn't appear that I have much choice, Hy."

"Aw, sure you got choice. You could sneak out the back and disappear! I mean, there's lots of nice little planets in this part of the Arm where a disgraced ex-diplomat could just kind of disappear, only except you're not really disgraced and you aren't going to disappear, if you know what I mean. . . ." Hy stopped and blinked confusion. "Uh, that is, I mean . . ."

"Actually, I'm about to be a disgraced ex-diplomat and I'm just about to disappear."

"Yeah, sure, but you don't have to go through with all the publicity and limelight, know what I mean? You could just, you know, disappear."

"Which would leave Mr. Magnan holding the bag," Retief replied, "and Ambassador Crapwell still in serious need of a sacrificial offering. If someone's going to be offered up, Hy, it's going to have to be me."

"For which I am eternally in your debt, Retief," Magnan said with feeling, "seeing as how His Excellency seems willing to agree that the responsibility for your unfortunate encounter with GNN lies squarely on your shoulders and not on mine."

"Don't feel too indebted, Mr. Magnan," Retief told him. "You still have to go through with your part of this, or it all will be for nothing."

"True. But I *don't* have to like it."

6

"That concludes my introductory remarks," Hy Felix was saying from his perch behind the speaker's podium set up at the edge of the parade ground. At his back, the embassy's Marine Guard was drawn up in full dress. Before him, on the grass at the edge of the parade ground, on thirty folding chairs, were thirty invited members of various news media, all watching with expressions ranging from sharklike anticipation to apathetic boredom, all sporting recorders of various makes and models, ranging from spyglasses to emotion recorders to hovering hovercams to pen and notebook. And to the right, inside a shaded observer's booth, were a few dozen members of the embassy's staff present as solemn witnesses—Birdbush, Smallbody, Hanglow, Moriarity, and others. Conspicuous by their absence were the higher-ranking CDT officers—Dinewiner, Marwonger, or Ambassador Crapwell himself.

"At this time," Hy went on, "I'd like to invite my friend Ben Magnan out here to deliver a few brief remarks regarding this regrettable situation, after which he will conduct the ceremony. Ah . . . we do have time now for a couple of questions. Are there any? Yes . . . Sid . . . in the back."

"Yeah, Hy. Sid Chatterly, of the *Galactic Herald-Times-Review-Dispatch*. How come this here Magnan fellow is doin' the honors? Why not the Ambassador himself?"

"Well, as to that, of course, Ambassador Crapwell is a very busy man. In any case, this is an intradepartmental disciplinary action and, as such, does not properly fall within the ambassadorial purview. Mr. Magnan is Mr. Retief's supervisor. Yes. In the third row."

"Marsha Neesernockin, of the *Newbraskan Agro Chicken Breeder Express*. Are you clowns really gonna toss this Retief guy out on his ear for, like, getting in a brawl or something?"

"Just watch us, Ms. Neesernockin. You'll find that we of the CDT take these matters very seriously indeed. Very well. If there are no further questions?" Several other hands were up, but he ignored them. "Ladies and gentlemen of the media," Hy said, stepping back from the speaker's podium and gestured stage left, "without further ado, I give you First Deputy Undersecretary Benjamin O. Magnan, of the Corps Diplomatique Terrestrienne."

Magnan, nattily resplendent in his full-formal mid-morning dress chartreuses, with pink stripes and sash, purple cutaway with silver epaulets, medals and orders, multiple chrome-plated lapels, top hat, gloves, *and* scabbarded two-foot gold ceremonial pen, strode onto the parade ground behind the chancery and took his place behind the podium beneath a warm morning's firstsun.

"Thank you, Hy, for those heartfelt words," Magnan said. Looking out over the audience, but connecting with none of them, Magnan sighed. "Ladies and gentlemen of the media, it is with a heavy heart that I appear before you this day. A fellow member of the Corps, a young man who might have gone far in diplomatic circles had he been constitutionally able to restrain his wilder impulses, my subordinate and my good friend, is to be publicly chastised this morning and formally expelled from the Corps Diplomatique Terrestrienne.

"By now, all of you have seen the news footage broadcast over local GNN affiliates last night, thanks to one of your number—Ms. Desiree Goodeleigh." Here, Magnan flashed the woman a dazzling and ingratiating smile—no less than a 484-R. Desiree, seated in the front row left, made no response.

"Second Assistant Deputy Undersecretary Jame Retief," Magnan went on, "a very junior officer of the CDT, committed the diplomatically unconscionable crime of laying violent hands on several civilians in the streets of High Gnashberry yesterday and doing them bodily harm. I needn't add that the Corps Diplomatique abjures and condemns any such violent act, violating, as it does, the spirit and the heart of civilized diplomatic conduct...."

There was more to the speech, quite a lot more. In fact, it was an hour past firstsunrise and secondsun was already peeking over the city skyline in a harsh blaze of white and violet when Magnan finally concluded his few brief remarks.

"And in conclusion," Magnan said—and the words were accompanied by a distinct collective sigh of relief from the audience—"permit me to extend sincere apologies to any, *any*, I say, who were offended by the lamentable events of last night, on behalf of the Corps Diplomatique Terrestrienne, on behalf of Ambassador Crapwell, his staff, and the Terran Embassy on B'rukley itself, and for myself, personally—"

"Don't overdo it, Ben," Sid called from the back. "A light class-C grovel is all that's necessary!" A smattering of laughter smattered through the crowd.

Magnan tossed him a suitable withering 346-E.

"Aw, lay off the 346, Ben!" another reporter called. "It makes you look like you got the pip!"

"Ahem. As I was saying, the Terran Embassy deeply, deeply regrets that Retief was caught . . . that is, that one of our number could be caught in such flagrant . . . what I mean to say is . . . that any diplomat worthy of the name could possibly be found conducting himself in such a churlish manner!" He stepped back from the podium. "Jame Retief! Front and center!"

To a canned drumroll, Retief marched out onto the tarmac and came to a halt facing Magnan. He was wearing formal attire identical to Magnan's, save that his epaulettes were smaller, and he only had two chrome-plated lapels, as befitted his position as a mere Second Assistant Deputy Undersecretary. Silence descended on the parade ground. The crowd leaned forward. In the sky to the south, a black, unmarked helicopter of distinctive Groaci design hovered silently just beyond the boundaries of embassy airspace.

"Jame Retief," Magnan intoned, dropping his normally high-pitched voice a full octave to demonstrate the seriousness of the moment. "You have been tried in the courts of public opinion and of the oversight of your superiors and been found guilty of reckless endangerment of the diplomatic goals and aspirations of sovereign Terra on the world of B'rukley; of gross assault on the persons of various human and nonhuman persons in a most undignified and undiplomatic fashion, of placing at least one pedal extremity within your buccal orifice in the presence of witnesses of the fourth estate, again in an egregiously undiplomatic manner; and of conduct prejudicial and detrimental to the honor, the name, and the sacred mission of the Corps Diplomatique Terrestrienne. Retief, you are a disgrace to the CDT!

"For this reason, we, your superiors in the Corps, do hereby and thereunto, according to the powers vested in us by Chapter XV, Section 12, Subsection 28, paragraphs 72 through 95, inclusive of the Handbook of the CDT, and in accordance with all relevant and binding treaties, assignations, laws, regulations, torts, tarts, and strongly worded recommendations and pertinent interoffice memos, do hereby, thereby, and therefore strip you, Jame Retief, of what little authority you may have thought you had within the most solemn ranks of the Corps, relieving you hereby of all rank, title, power, dignity, investiture, standing, association, and relationship, actual, imagined, and presumed, within the sacred and hallowed organization of the CDT."

Pausing for Dramatic Effect (87-B), Magnan leaned forward, his face inches from Retief's.

"Retief, you've been very, very naughty!" He held out his hand, palm up. "Your pen, if you please!"

As the canned drumroll started up again, Retief drew his two-foot ceremonial pen from its scabbard and handed it to Magnan.

"Extend your hands!" When Retief complied, Magnan sharply rapped him on both sets of knuckles with the pen. "*Bad* Retief! Bad, *bad* Retief!" Then, raising his leg, and wobbling only a little as he balanced precariously on one foot, Magnan snapped the pen in two over his knee, then tossed the broken halves aside.

Reaching up, Magnan snatched Retief's ceremonial black topper from his head, held it up, then drove one fist through the crown with a loud pop. Next, he grasped Retief's pink sash and ripped it from his chest, wadded it up, and cast it down.

Next came Retief's epaulettes, which had been removed ahead

of time and reattached with lightweight thread. The effect was spectacular, however, as the tiny speakers imbedded in each epaulette gave voice to a loud ripping sound as they were torn away.

Next, Magnan reached for Retief's lapels.

"No!" a woman in the second row cried. "Not *that!*"

Coldly ignoring her plea, Magnan grasped first the left chrome-plated lapel and ripped it off of Retief's dress chartreuses, and then the right. There was a loud clatter as they hit the tarmac.

Next came the medals and insignia of orders—the Legion of Meritorious Good Conduct, with fig-leaf clusters; the Grand Order of File Clerks, Second Class, with three battle stars and an "E" for Excellence; the Staff Meeting Perfect Attendance Award; the Gedunk Cross, First Class, with Peach Pit in lieu of a second award; the Good Dental Hygiene Medal; the Master of Grimacing, First Class Award; the Serene Order of Authority Delegated, Third Class, Junior Grade; the Gold Star of Political Damage Control, First Rank, with twenty-seven star clusters . . . and more. *Many* more. One by one, Magnan ceremoniously plucked them from Retief's formal diplomatic dickey and dropped them on the ground. Then he pulled Retief's cravat from his throat, jerked his shirttail out, and plucked the pink, silk, CDT-monogrammed hanky from his cutaway breast pocket.

Finally, with solemn gravity, Magnan kneeled at Retief's feet, almost as though he were proposing. One by one, with delicate deliberation, Magnan peeled off each and every one of the violet pinstripes on Retief's chartreuse trousers, wadded them up, and tossed them back over his shoulder.

By the time he was done, several women in the audience were openly weeping, and there were moist eyes among several of the men as well. Desiree Goodeleigh watched avidly and with dry eyes.

As Magnan stood up, the drumroll ceased. He reached into a pocket and extracted a Techno Marker™, with which he drew a bold, bright-red X on Retief's forehead. "Retief, I give you the scarlet 'X' for 'Expunged.' Never more will you enjoy coffee and croissants at a morning staff conference with your betters! Never

more will you be 'in the know' in matters diplomatic and poli-
tic. Never more will you gather with embassy staff members at
the ceremonial watercooler or trade bon mots with your fellows
of the Corps! And never more will you know the joy, the keen
thrill of competition, the delight of the chase as you scramble up
the career pyramid in pursuit of your next promotion! You are
broken! Finished! Out on your can! Be gone hence, and never
darken an embassy doorway again, save as a mere civilian in
search of embassy assistance while traveling abroad! I cast you
forth, and do hereby, thenceforth, and forevermore *banish* you in
the sacred name of the Corps!"

Imperiously, Magnan extended his right arm, pointing to his
right. "Go!"

Without a word, Retief executed a left-face and marched to
a position in front of the Marines. Captain Martinet barked
a command, and four Marines took up positions surrounding
Retief, ahead and behind, their blast rifles at their shoulders in
the inverted position.

"Forrard . . . *harchhh!*"

The drumroll paced out a dreary dirge. A canned Groaci nose-
flute duet piped out "The Scalawag's March." They marched him
toward the embassy's back gate.

"You're getting a damned raw deal, Mr. Retief," one of his
guards muttered, just loud enough to be heard. It was one of the
two sentries Retief had spoken to the night before. "Just wanted
you to know. . . ."

"Thanks, Marine," Retief added in the same low tones. "It's
good to know I have friends."

They reached the back gate—the tradesman's entrance. George,
the janitor, opened the gate. "I'm sorry t'see ya go, Mr. Retief."

"Thanks, George. I doubt that you're rid of me for good."

Retief walked out into the alley behind the embassy compound.
At his back, the media shouted and yelled, bombarding Magnan
with questions.

"Good luck, Ben," Retief said quietly, smiling. "You'll need
it!"

CHAPTER THREE

1

"Hey, Mr. Retief." Joe set a glass of Bacchian black on the low counter in front of him. "This'n's on the house."

"Thanks, Joe. I'm not quite flat out yet."

"Nah." The alligator jaws twisted briefly in a tight-lipped parody of a human smile. "Didn't say you were. I just don't like what they did to you. Isn't right!"

"Well, thanks for the kind thought. What do the Holy Mystic Fortune Cookies have to say about being out of work?"

"That it sucks small orange and purple gamchucks. So . . . whatcha gonna do now? You mebee headed back to Terra?"

"That takes a fair bit of money, Joe. Looks like I'm stranded for a while."

"You got a job lined up?"

"Not yet. But I'm sure something will turn up pretty soon."

"That's the spirit! Like the Holy Mystic Fortune Cookies say, a burbling momgroth urdles no yerdles."

"I can't argue with that, Joe."

"Well . . . if you find yourself hard up, I could use some help around this place. Busin' tables, cleanin' up, that kind of thing. Pay's not that good, but you got your free meals and a room in the back."

"Thanks, Joe. I'll keep that in mind if things get really tight."

He leaned closer over the counter. "I'd take you on as a server, but I'm afraid you aren't as pretty as my regular girls." He nodded toward a particularly chunky B'ruklian female in spiked heels—eight of them—and carrying a tray of drinks. "Gotta keep the payin' customers comin' back for more, right?"

"Somehow, Joe, I just don't think cocktailing is my thing. Especially if I have to wear shoes like those."

"You got a place to stay?"

"I got a room at the Starport Inn yesterday. Paid through to the end of the week."

"Well, you need anything, Mr. Retief, you just give a growl. You got a friend here if'n you need one!" He turned away to attend to a customer at the end of the bar.

The customers in Joe's Bar and Bookstore this afternoon were a varied lot—B'ruklians, humans, and a few others. The humans all looked like students; several, he noticed, kept stealing sidelong glances at him from their tables.

Retief turned back to the bar, ignoring them.

"Hey, fella. Are you, like, that CDT guy?"

"I *was* that CDT guy," Retief replied. He turned. "Is there something I can do for you?"

Three students had approached him from behind. The speaker was a skinny, geekish-looking guy. Behind him were two that Retief recognized from the march of two days before—the complexion-challenged guy with the Grateful Reincarnated T-shirt—apparently he hadn't changed in two days—and the girl with the flashing nipple rings.

"Smallwick," the first student said, holding out a hand. "Freddy Smallwick. And these are—"

"Marty and Aquaria. We've met."

"Ooh, like, he remembers!" Aquaria said in a breathy near-whisper.

"I'm Retief."

"We, like, saw you tossing Tiny Dumbrowski around on the tube the other night," Marty said. "That was, like, somethin'!"

"I'm sure it was. Like something, that is."

"You pack quite a wallop, mister."

"Thanks. How's the wrist?"

Marty rubbed his wrist as though it were still sore. "It's, like, okay. Thanks."

"Listen, Mr. Retief," Freddy said. "We're with the Student Union . . . Local 3.14159."

"Oh? So you have a union beef with me? Tiny was just showing me his crunchball blocking technique. The crowd was getting a little unruly."

"No, no!" Aquaria said. She took hold of Retief's arm. "We're not mad! We want you to, like, join us!"

"My student days are long behind me, Aquaria."

"Nah, it's like, like this," Marty said. "What we got a beef with is, like, the government waging, like, unjust war against the Krll."

"Yeah," Aquaria said. "Like, the Krll are, like, just friends we haven't met yet!"

Freddy nodded. "And the CDT is, like, representing the government out here in the Cluster, y'know?"

"I think I'm following you so far."

"So, it's like, duuuuuude," Marty told him. "You're the man! Dig?"

"Now you've lost me."

Aquaria squeezed his arm against her substantial chest. "There's like this big be-in tonight, y'know?"

"No, I didn't."

"Oooh, yeah. It's, like, the kickiest! Everyone's, like, gonna be there!"

"It's a really big deal, Mr. Retief," Freddy said. "Big concert by the Why. Lots of speeches. Lots of joyweed. A local theater group is putting on an all-nude production of *Scales*. The Guru's gonna be there, like spreading peace and benediction and everything. And it's all, like, climaxed by a big forn-in. It's like, y'know, totally mediocre!"

"Sorry, Aquaria. I'm lost again. 'Mediocre'?"

"It's, like, the tall nail gets hammered, y'know, man?" Freddy told him. "It's, like, in school, you don't want to be fleaglin' noticed, y'know? So it's, like, mediocre to the max."

"Gotcha. So where is this mediocre be-in supposed to take place?"

"At the Phark, man," Marty said.

"The Phark?"

"Yeah, dude! Like the Phark of Phenomenally Phlogistic Pheremones, man."

"Is it phree?"

"Just a love offering, man."

"Are you coming, Mr. Retief?" Aquaria wanted to know.

"Young lady, I wouldn't miss it for the planet."

2

Firstsun was setting amid a splendor of towering green and gold clouds as Retief entered the B'rukley Starport just west of the city, and secondsun blazed like a pinpoint-tiny blue arclight high in the sky. Clad in a nondescript black shipsuit, Retief looked like just another crewman or port cargo handler, though there were few enough other humans evident in the crowds.

The Shamballa Cluster was located close to the nebula-strewn border of the Hub, where the Eastern Arm first spun off from the curdled starclouds of the galactic core. Deeper into the Hub, radiation levels rose dangerously, until human-crewed ships could venture only with powerful screens raised against the sleeting storms of charged particles whipping about the galactic center, and only extremely hardy, tough-hided, and gene-stable species like the Turvah or the Krultch found worlds they considered habitable.

So the Shamballa Cluster had become a kind of cosmopolitan end-point to human colonization coreward down the Eastern Arm, a crossroads meeting place for many diverse alien cultures, including human, but one where humans were definitely in the minority.

And that was what made the large and growing human student population on B'ruk so unlikely.

Retief found an out-of-the-way vantage point on a railed balcony overlooking the main passenger concourse. He wasn't entirely sure what he was looking for, but a passenger liner, the *Theodosius*, was due in today from out-arm, with her last stop at Newbraska. It might be instructive to watch her passengers coming through the gate.

While he was waiting, his attention was caught by a pair of men in cheap striped suits leaning against the wall next to the tunnel leading to baggage claim. Both wore technofedoras, the type with high-quality Japanese commo electronics built into the brims, both wore dark spyglasses, and both were absently flipping quarter-guck pieces in perfect, gleaming unison. They appeared to be waiting for someone.

Retief reached into a pocket and brought out his own spyglasses, which Magnan had checked out of Supply for him the night before his expulsion. Using the zoom-eye feature, he magnified the view until he could clearly see the men's faces beneath their fedoras. He thought he recognized one of them—Louis the Libido, a small-time hood in the Galactic Organized Syndicate of Humanoids, Local 1066. He didn't know the other one but thought he had the look of a "made man," quite possibly one made in Japan, a Yakuza Series *ichi-man*.

As he watched, an older man approached the two, looking furtively over his shoulder every now and again. Through the zoom-eye, Retief could see the insignia of a merchant captain on the old-timer's collar and guessed he was the skipper of one of the small tramps that called periodically at B'rukley. The patch on his sleeve read *Starmaid*.

Retief recorded all three faces for identification later. Using his spyglasses' zoom-ear attachment, he tried to pick up their speech. It wasn't easy; the concourse was noisy, and the government-issue glasses weren't quite up to the job of filtering out all of the background racket. Still, he managed to pick up and record a few words. Possibly the sound could be cleaned up and enhanced later, electronically.

"It's getting' too risky, I tell ya," the old man said.

"Youz got a lifetime contrack wid us, pops, see?" the made man told him. Retief missed the next handful of words. Then, " . . . if ya knowz—*zzzzt!*—what's good fer ya. See?"

"Look, there's nothin' . . . do about it, fellas! There's . . . peace enforcer . . . orbit. It's gettin' so's . . . shot at every . . . hit atmosphere!"

"Yeah, but you gotta unnerstand our . . . an' do what we says?" Louis told him. "Or else."

"Dat's right, see? Mr. Bug wouldn't . . . any udder way, see? *Zzzzt!*"

"Yeah," Louis added. "Mr. Bug was real . . . that last shipment you lost."

"*Real* upset, see? *Zzzt!*"

"Yeah, well, you tell Mr. Bug from me that it's getting too . . ." The words were lost behind the sudden commotion of a Japanese tour group gathering nearby, talking loudly while taking pictures of one another and everything else in sight.

The three continued talking with one another. Then, after a few moments, the tramp skipper walked with studied nonchalance through to baggage claim, while the GOSH hoods waited another moment, then followed.

Interesting. According to intelligence reports he'd seen at the embassy, GOSH held a monopoly on the transport of controlled substances throughout the sector. What wasn't clear was how they were smuggling the contraband—joyweed, mostly, but also airplane glue, antique Perry Como albums, and a cheap imitation of aged Pepsi. Apparently, they'd enlisted the aid of local tramp skippers. *Very* interesting.

His musings were cut short, however, by the arrival of the

Theodosius, a titanic liner with the size and general appearance of a flying skyscraper, the pride of the Blue Star Line. He watched her approach through the transparent dome of the concourse as she gentled herself out of the sky and onto the landing field with a spooling-down whine of gravitics. Enclosed debarkation tubes connected with the mighty liner's side, and within a few minutes, the first of her passengers began off-loading into the concourse.

First came representatives of several species native to this part of the Arm—ponderously stalking Yahyas, rolling Tugalubs, bouncing Boroveers, and cloaked and hooded Grothelwaiths. In twos and threes, however, a number of young humans began gathering on the concourse just inside the gate, recognizable as students by the backpacks they carried. When about thirty of them had assembled, a human woman arrived from elsewhere in the concourse, motioned them together, and began talking to them as a group. Retief used his spyglasses to zoom in for a close look at her face.

Ann Thrope.

Retief tuned in on her speech. She had a shrill voice that carried well, and he had less trouble picking up the words than he'd had with the GOSH thugs and the tramp skipper.

" . . . you won't have to do any studying, of course," she was telling them, "though we'll register you at USC as exchange students, just to avoid any . . . irregularities with the government. You'll be staying at Camp Concentration, just outside the city."

Retief lost the next few hundred words as a group of yellow-clad Hare Krishnoids hared across the concourse, chanting loudly.

"Loudly . . . loudly . . . loudly . . . loudly . . ."

Then Thorpe's words came through once more. " . . . and the next spontaneous demonstration is planned for the day after tomorrow, at four-eighty pee-em, and you're all expected to be there. Tomorrow, there's a be-in and free concert at a local park. I encourage you especially to try to make it to a meditation class being held by Grady, the Garrulous Guru. He'll be talking about some of the special programs we've arranged here on B'rukley for you, including the PEAS Corps initiative at Weederham. It's an excellent program, and I strongly urge you to attend.

"Now, I'm sure you're all tired after your trip. I have a bus waiting outside that'll take you to your new home away from home. So . . . if you'll follow me . . ."

She led them off toward the tunnel leading to the baggage claim.

Also interesting. He would have to check that camp out. First, though, he wanted to have a look at a tramp cargo carrier called the *Starmaid*.

3

Half an hour later, Retief was outside, walking through the section of the port landing facilities reserved for cargo vessels, close by the warehouses. A handful of freighters were grounded here today, their stubby and inelegant lines all but masked by gantries and cargo cranes clustered about them. The dockyard was fenced off with a single gate; a dozen signs in as many languages told him to KEEP OUT and AUTHORIZED PERSONNEL ONLY ADMITTED BEYOND THIS POINT.

He bluffed his way past the bored B'ruklian guard at the gate by flashing his Aldo Cerise library card; the guard scarcely glanced at it before waving him in and returning to a close perusal of a lovingly worn copy of *Playbeing*, the local B'rukley edition, Retief presumed.

"Hey, you!" a voice barked from behind. "Stop where you are!"

Retief obeyed and turned slowly. A B'ruklian dockworker multi-footed it up to him.

"Can I help you?" Retief asked.

"No, but mebee I can help you," the local growled. "Where's your hard hat?"

"Sorry. Must've forgotten it."

"Here. Take mine. I got another back at the office. You humans got soft heads. You shouldn't go wandering around where things could whack you from above, know what I mean?"

"Thanks a lot. I appreciate that."

"Don't mention it. Lookin' for a ship in particular?"

"As a matter of fact, yes. The *Starmaid*. Know her?"

"Yeah, sure. That's her, right over there." He pointed at a rusty and decrepit-looking vessel resting in a blast pit a hundred yards away. "Captain Rufus. Whatcha want with the *'Maid*?"

"I was wondering if Captain Rufus was hiring."

The B'ruklian goggled at him. "He might be. But, yiminy, fella! Do you know what the *'Maid*'s route is?"

"Can't say that I do."

"Flies the Kordoban Circuit... B'rukley to Kordoban to Odiousita, then back to B'rukley!"

"Really? Odiousita, huh?"

"Durned straight! I hear the *'Maid*'s been potted at a dozen times, by Peace Enforcers and Krll deathcruisers alike! A being would have to be nuts to wanna sign on with her!"

"Why does Rufus put in at Odiousita V? What cargo would be worth the danger of flying into a war zone?"

"Ya got me, though there're rumors. What's Odiousita's biggest cash crop, anyway?"

"I didn't know they had one, aside from casualties."

"Joyweed, Terry! Joyweed! Don't know what you Terries see in the stuff, but you sure seem to like it! The five-eyes, too."

"Oh? The Groaci are interested in joyweed cultivation?"

"Yeah, but the word is that the Syndicate has the weed harvest on Odiousita all sewed up. Tramps like the *Starmaid*, and private boats, they make the run here from Odiousita every so often and smuggle in what they can. 'Course, transporting controlled substances like joyweed is against the Terry-Shamballa Accord, even if it's legal here on B'ruk, and the skippers that try it are takin' a mighty big risk."

"Well, thanks for the warning. I think I'd still like to take a look. You mind?"

"Help yourself. Long as you got a helmet!" The being waddled off.

Retief tried the helmet on. It had a self-molding inner band, so it fit him well enough, though its oblong shape was overlong for a human head. It had the look of the ceremonial headgear worn by devotees of religious racing-bicyclers. Then, suitably attired, he made his way toward the *Starmaid*, where a dozen B'ruklian and human dockworkers were hauling cargo crates off of the *'Maid*'s gantry and onto flatbed robohaulers for transport to the warehouse.

Interposing a stack of off-loaded crates between himself and the workers, Retief made his way closer. A number of smaller crates, he saw, were being stacked off to the side. He made his way to this pile, careful to keep out of sight.

Settling down behind the stack, he took a look at the cargo manifest, which was stapled to the outside of each crate. This load, apparently, consisted of textbooks and was slated for shipment to USC.

The receiver was listed as "Ms. A. Thrope," and the manifest was stamped as being precleared through customs.

Retief pulled out his penknife and carefully prized back the lid of one of the crates of books. Inside, indeed, was a stack of books—a shipment of *Elementary Economic Metacalculus as Interpreted Through Keynesian Philosophy*, the twenty-third edition. Lifting one of the tomes out of the crate, he hefted it, curious. It didn't feel like it weighed quite enough for its thickness. Opening it, he saw that the pages had been glued together and an opening carved out of the center, leaving a concealed space inside.

And tucked into that space was a plastic bag filled with what looked like dried leaves.

Swiftly, Retief unfastened the twist tie holding the bag shut and extracted one of the slender, serrated leaves. Crushing it, he held it to his nose and sniffed cautiously. The scent of joyweed, sweet and a bit like sage, was unmistakable.

Retying the bag, he put it back in the book and closed it again. Replacing the book where he'd found it, he closed the crate, then returned it to its place on the stack and began to work his way clear.

Whir-click!

Retief stopped at the sound of machinery grinding. It was coming from—

"Well, well. Whaddawe—*zzzt!*—got here? *Whir-click!*" The made man he'd seen from the observation deck earlier stepped around the corner formed by stacks of cargo crates, blocking Retief's path, a seven-foot mountain of synthflesh in a cheap striped suit. "Whadda you—*bleep!*—doin' here, which you're not supposed t' be, see?"

"Whassamatter, Seven?" another voice said. A second later, Louis the Libido rounded the corner as well. "So! We got us a snoop, looks like!"

"Hi, Louis," Retief said. "How's the libido?"

"Huh? Howdja know my name, punk?"

"Because Mr. Bug told them to me," Retief said breezily. "He sent me to check up on you two."

"Oh, he did, did he?"

"That's right. And he said to tell you that if another shipment went astray like that last one, he'd hold you two personally responsible."

That bit of news appeared to have an affect on both of the hoods.

"Geeze!" Seven said. "Dat wasn't—*zzzzt!*—our fault, see?"

"Yeah," Louis said. "It was that tramp skipper, Rufus! Mr. Bug doesn't know how hard it is t'find good help these days!"

"Funny," Retief said. "Mr. Bug was saying the same thing about you two."

"Ulp . . . he was? I mean . . . hey! You just go back and tell Mr. Bug that Louis and Seven got the whole thing unner control, okay?"

"It's all unner control, see? *Whirr-click!*"

"Yeah! Like he says."

"Don't worry. I believe you. I checked the shipment, and it all seems to be there. Sheer genius, hiding the shipment inside textbooks."

"Yeah, you like that?" Louis preened. "That was my idea. I mean, it's a natural, this bein' a college city, an' all."

"Do you two deliver the stuff? Or does Ann pick it up herself?"

"Naw, she sends somebody to get it. Seven an' me, we was just checking t'make sure the shipment arrived all right. Can't be too careful, y'know?"

"Well, you two certainly do seem to be on the ball. I'll give Mr. Bug a good report."

"Hey, that's real good of ya, fella. What's your name, anyway? I don't remember seein' youz before."

"They call me Jimmy the Juridical."

"Yeah? Well, we'll be watchin' for ya, Jimmy. Hey, that 'juridical' thing. That's somethin' good, right?"

"Absolutely. It means I'm one of the good guys."

"Oh, yeah. Right!" Louis laughed. "Good joke!"

"One question?"

"Sure, Jimmy! Shoot!"

"Later, maybe. Why does Seven always say 'see'?"

Louis looked embarrassed. "Aw, he can't help it, Jimmy. He's a really old model. I mean, *really* old. They used a really ancient programming language on him. . . ."

Retief closed his eyes. "Don't tell me. 'C'?"

"That's the one, Jimmy."

"Yeah," Seven said. "C, see?"

"*Si*," Retief told him. "I'll catch you fellows later."

"Sure thing, Jimmy. Ta!"

"Yeah, see?" *Zzzzt!* "Ta . . . see?"

4

The hour was well past secondsunset when Retief again entered Joe's Bar and Bookstore and found a corner booth in the back room, out of the way and positioned so he could keep an unobtrusive eye on whoever entered the establishment. One of Joe's waitresses brought him a passable local imitation of a wine cooler, setting it down with a flirtatious snap of her alligator jaws. He waited nearly forty minutes before a slender figure muffled in a heavy dun trench coat and dark glasses entered the bar and wended its way back to where Retief was sitting.

The figure thumped hard against the table. "Ow!"

"Maybe you shouldn't wear the dark glasses inside, Mr. Magnan," Retief told the figure. "Or else switch them to their low-light mode."

"Shh! Retief, please! No names! This is a covert operation."

"Ah. Excuse me." He pulled a hyacinth-scented dopestick out of his jumper pocket and puffed it alight. "I forgot."

"For the duration, you will address me as . . . Agent M. And you, of course, will be Agent R."

"Do you really think that's necessary?"

"Retief! I've been reading up on the topic. Why, the technological sophistication of some of the devices used by our security and espionage services is nothing less than breathtaking in their abilities! Why, there are spy satellites that can see through the roof of a building such as this and reconstruct our conversation by measuring the density variance of the air around us! There's a device that can measure the internal pressure of a wallet and deduce from its interaction with the muscles of one's gluteal region the amount of money you're carrying! There's a device—"

"If all of that's true, sir, we might as well admit it. Clandestine meetings are an impossibility. Why don't you sit down, sir, before you attract any more attention with that getup."

"Yes. Ah . . . where's the chair?"

"Move to your right. Put out your hand . . ."

"Ah. There it is." Magnan sat down, doing his best to look inconspicuous.

"I genuinely doubt, sir," Retief told his superior, "that the cloak-and-dagger is necessary. No one is going to be suspicious of two former colleagues meeting for a drink at a favorite local watering hole."

"Who said anything about a dagger?" Magnan wanted to know. "Or a cloak, for that matter. This is the latest in high-tech trench-coat wear from the boys in Intelligence. Pretty snazzy, huh?"

"Very."

Magnan rubbed the fabric of the coat's lapel almost reverently. "It is resistant to the most powerful chemical solvent known," he whispered. "And . . . it's reversible!"

"Waterproof, eh? What won't they think of next!"

"As for assumptions about the thoughts of possible hostile observers, I can only say that one can't be too careful in the world of covert operations. One mistake, one minor oversight, and our mutual identities would be exploded!"

"You mean our covers would be blown."

"That too. What do you have for me?"

Retief passed him a tiny sealed capsule. "My report's in there. Basically, though, it's what we thought. GOSH is smuggling joyweed to B'rukley in bulk. An organizer for the local chapter of ACHE is orchestrating things at this end. As it happens, she's also involved in bringing all of the off-world students for these peace rallies, through SMERCH. I don't know yet what that's all about."

"Excellent work, Retief," Magnan said, ostentatiously palming the capsule in an attempt to pick it up without having the act noticed. Somehow, he missed his pass and sent the silvery capsule clattering onto the floor. Ducking down, he tried to get it, couldn't see it because he still had his spyglasses on, then slammed the back of his head into the bottom of the table with a loud thud. "*Oww!*"

Retief picked the capsule up off the floor, carefully reached inside Magnan's trench coat, and dropped it into a jumper pocket while his superior gingerly rubbed his head.

"Names and photographs of the principal players are in that report," Retief told Magnan, "along with recordings of my conversations with some of them."

"Good . . . good work." Magnan removed the glasses, winced, and touched the back of his head again, lightly. "I expect this will nicely wrap things up all around."

"Not quite, sir," Retief told him. "We don't know where the contraband is coming from, other than that it's originating in the Odiousita system. Nor do we know how they're distributing it. And we don't know the identity of the GOSH leadership—the one they call 'Mr. Bug.'

"But what I'm most concerned about is the Groaci."

"Indeed? And what part do our sticky-fingered friends from Groac play in this drama?"

"I don't know, and that's what worries me."

"I spoke rhetorically, Retief . . . er . . .that is, Agent R. We have no reason to believe the Groaci are involved in this at all!"

"But we do. Broodmaster Shtliff was being amusingly conspicuous in his attempts to remain inconspicuous the other evening, and there is his apparent penetration of the local student scene as a religious leader. It stands to reason, though. If GOSH is involved, there's money to be made here . . . a *lot* of money. I don't think they're working with the organized crime people. That's not their style. But it could be that the Groaci are trying to cut themselves in for a piece of the action."

"That seems peculiarly opportunistic even for them," Magnan protested. "Planetary conquest, overthrowing local regimes, undermining legitimate Terran aspirations throughout the sector, that's all in a day's work for the Groaci, a part and parcel of the status quo. But stooping to crime and drug trafficking . . ."

"The illegality of the operation is still in question," Retief reminded him, taking another puff on his dopestick. "Joyweed's legal on B'rukley. The locals use it for roughage in their salad."

"True. But the fact that its transport from one system to another is illegal according to the Terran-Shamballa Accords should give one pause. There is also the matter of associating with a known and notorious criminal element, to wit, the Galactic Organized Syndicate of Humanoids."

"We'll know more after tomorrow night, Mr. Magnan, when I check out the student be-in at the park."

"It's 'Agent M,'" he corrected. "'Be-in'? What's that?"

"A happening, sir. Love, peace, enlightenment, and letting it all hang out."

"That sounds . . . dangerous. Even illegal."

"That's why we arranged this cover, Mr. Magnan."

"'Agent M,'" Magnan corrected him again. "Agreed. Still . . . you be careful. Religious enlightenment, especially, can constitute a serious risk to one's mental equilibrium."

"It's not the enlightenment that worries me, sir. It's all of that free love."

"Free . . . free love?" Magnan's eyebrows crawled higher on his thin face.

"I've found that free love very often is not." He stood up. "See you in two days . . . Agent M."

"Magnan," Magnan corrected him.

But he was already gone.

5

The be-in, Retief found, was a whirling carnival of sight and color, of sound and sensation.

The atmosphere was considerably more relaxed than it had been during the demonstration the other day. College kids—mostly human but representing several species—lazed about in various stages of dress and undress, talking, making out, wandering about, smoking hand-rolled dopesticks. There was a lot of the latter going on, and the air was thick with the sweet odor of joyweed.

The haze was thick enough, in fact, that Retief stopped and pulled out a small plastic case. Inside were a pair of high-tech BreatheSafe™ nose filters. One slipped up each nostril; he wanted to stay sharp and didn't care to get high on secondhand smoke.

On a crudely made stage, eight young humans and a couple of young Naghans, agleam in iridescent scales, danced and cavorted in the nude—an amateur production of the hit musical *Scales*.

One of the Naghans was crooning into a microphone, the words blaring from the enormous speakers rising from either side of the stage.

> "*She asks me why I'll*
> *Be just a scaly reptile.*

I'm scaly all the night
I think scales are all right. . . ."

"Hey there," a voice said from behind him. "You, like, came!"

"Hello, Aquaria. I wouldn't have missed it." For a moment, he thought his spy glasses were set to X-ray mode, but when he took them off he saw that Aquaria really was fetchingly attired in flower-print sandals and nothing else. "Are you in the show?"

"Huh?"

"Your costume."

She looked down at herself. "Oh, like, no way! I'm just, like, being, y'know? People are way too, like, uptight about their bodies. They're just, like, y'know, *bodies*. People, like, need to relax and, like, get on the beam, and, like, let it all hang out."

"Which you do very nicely indeed."

On stage, the performers were bouncing into the number's chorus.

"Gimme a bod with scales,
Green beautiful scales.
Shining, gleaming
Seeming iridescent. . . ."

"I was hoping you'd come. What's your name?"

"I'd be pleased if you would call me Jame."

"Jame. I like that."

"Why did you want me here?"

"Because you, like, seem like a cool guy."

"I'm a bit on the old side for this crowd, don't you think?"

She made a face. "That's just it. All of the guys, like, my age are such, such, like, *children*. I could go for a mature guy, y'know?"

"Ah. I see."

"Scales, scales, scales, scales, scales, scales, scales
Opalescent, luminescent
Makes me quite the adolescent . . .
My scales! . . ."

"Hey, babe, dude," a scraggly-looking teenager with a blank expression said. "Ya wanna hit? Like, good stuff."

"Like, do me." She accepted a hand-twisted joyweed joint and sucked down a double lungful. "Totally mediocre," she said breathily. "Here, Jame! Try a puff?"

"Thank you, Aquaria, no," he gently refused. "Your radiant visual charms are quite enough to get me high."

"Aw, you're sweet." She took another drag.

"Hey, hey," the boy said, gesturing for the joint. "Don't pull a bogie."

"Good stuff," she said, handing the joint back. "Totally beamie."

"Like, ya wanna?"

"Nah." She took hold of Retief's arm. "I got my date."

"Like, cool." The kid wandered off, his blank expression unmoved.

"How do you feel?" Retief asked her.

"Oh, like, stellarific, to the maxi. Beaming up the starclouds, man. Galloping the sevens to the ice, with gorgeous grow-mes in the flutterbox."

"I'll take that as a 'good.' What was that phrase our friend just used? Pulling a bogie?"

"Aw, like, Bogie was an ancient tri-vid star who, like, always had a dopestick dangling from his, like, lips, y'know? So if you pull a bogie, you're hogging the weed."

"I see." As the joyweed hit her, Aquaria was becoming increasingly vacant. Her body twitched and jerked in interesting ways to the beat of the music from the stage.

"Say, where's that guru giving his talk this afternoon?" Retief said, changing the subject.

"You wanna go, like, see him?"

"I'd like to get a little further from those speakers."

"Sure! Like, totally beamy!"

"Beamy?"

"Like . . . on the beam, in the groove, like, you know?"

"No, but I'm learning."

6

"The Grothel-dude guru, he's, like, over this way!"

Retief followed Aquaria across the red-ocher grass of the park, crossing a low rise and descending into a bowl-shaped depression that formed a natural amphitheater far enough from the stage that the thundering music was muted to a dull rumble largely masked by the intervening ridge.

A crowd of several hundred had gathered in the bowl, seated or sprawled on the grass or on blankets brought for the occasion. Some couples were enthusiastically engaged in other activities involving repetitive movements and few clothes, but most were quietly listening to the guru as he delivered his oration. The sweet-heavy smell of joyweed was thick in the air.

A stage had been built here as well, though it was low and ramped about with earth, creating a squat, truncated pyramid perhaps five feet high. The Grothelwaith—or, rather, Shtliff in his Grothelwaith disguise—sat on a colorful blanket at the center of the mound, a circle of smoking joss sticks planted in the earth around him. A banner raised behind him proclaimed: MAKE PEACE! MAKE LOVE! A pair of young, human females wearing not much of anything at all flanked him, like ceremonial handmaidens.

Or perhaps they'd just grabbed the best seats in the house.

Retief and Aquaria found a seat on the slope of the bowl affording them a good view. Retief pulled out his spyglasses and gave the guru a thorough long-range examination.

Set in X-ray mode, Shtliff's black robes faded to a hazy outline, and the Groaci's spindly-legged, dumpy-torsoed body was revealed beneath, his five stalked eyes erect behind the pair of lights mimicking glowing eyes within the hood. And, sure enough, Shtliff was wearing a mechanism suspended over his narrow chest that, from this angle, at least, looked like an air-filtration system and respirator. The unit also appeared to have a built-in voice amplifier; Shtliff's normal voice, as for all Groaci, was a sibilant, breathy whisper, but he was addressing his audience now in strong, commanding tones that echoed back from distant buildings and all but drowned out the musical next door.

" . . . and thus we know, because it is written in the Book of Ages, that service to your fellow beings is the true path to enlightenment!" Shtliff was saying, speaking Standard with only a trace of an accent. "Finding joy in honest labor, your hands deep in the good rich soil of a bountiful world, tending the Creator's green acre of growing things, ripe for the harvest!"

There was something about Shtliff's amplified voice . . . an overtone or a harmonic that Retief couldn't quite pin down, at once grating, like nails on a blackboard, and commanding. Odd. Reaching up, he touched the pressure control on the frame of the spyglasses that projected a tiny heads-up display across the inside of the left lens. Shtliff's electronics were putting out some very unusual harmonics, many of them in the infrasonic range, below the threshold of human hearing.

Conscious human hearing, that is. He set the glasses to record. The sounds could be fully analyzed later. In the meantime, Retief studied the other listeners gathered in the amphitheater. With a few exceptions that had more to do with love than peace, all seemed riveted on Shtliff's presentation. And that was odd as well, since Shtliff's material, while nicely orated, was hardly the stuff of spellbinding epics.

"It so happens that just such a venue for wholesome work and enlightenment exists here on this world of enlightenment. I refer, of course, to the PEAS Corps. My assistants will pass out the necessary information. . . ."

"PEAS Corps?" Retief said. "Do you know anything about that?"

"No, but it sounds like the *beamiest.*"

The two young women who'd been up on the stage were handing out brochures, passing stacks of them along each row of the audience. When a bundle came to Retief, he took one and passed the rest along.

The PEAS Corps, he learned, was the Politically Enlightened Alliance of Students, a group formed under the sponsorship of both ACHE and SMERCH, and dedicated to bringing thousands of students to the warm glow and fulfillment of life on an agro commune.

"Working on a farm?" Retief prompted. "Hard work, no pay, plain meals . . . that sounds beamy?"

Her eyes were closed, and she was swaying gently back and forth. "Like, awesomely beamy."

"Where are you from, Aquaria?"

"Like, Newbraska, Jame. I grew up on a farm on New-braska."

"Why did you leave? Why did you come here?"

"Aw, like, I just wanted to get off of that farm, y'know? Nothing but work, work, work, doin' the chores, feeding the livestock, mucking out the hydroponics. So I decided to go to school."

"At the Cornfed Veterinary, Horticultural, and Miscellaneous College of Conservative Arts, by any chance?"

"Yeah! Like, beamy! You know the place?"

"By reputation only."

"Well, it wasn't that great, but at least I was off the farm, y'know? Then I got the chance to sign up with a SMERCH tour to come out here to USC B'rukley. And it's ever so much beamier, with all the cool guys and the good weed and the, like . . . wow, a chance to join the PEAS Corps. . . ."

She seemed to be drifting out of the conversation. He shook her gently by the shoulder. "Stay with me, Aquaria. Let me get this straight. You couldn't wait to get off the farm where you grew up because you hated that life . . . and now you can't wait to join a commune where you'll be working on a farm again. . . ."

"Like, totally cosmic rad, like, awesome mediocrity! Isn't that the beamiest? So totally moxsome to the maxi . . ."

Retief reached over and pulled up Aquaria's left eyelid . . . then the right. Her pupils were widely dilated. She didn't appear to see him. He moved his hand up and down in front of her face without getting a reaction, though she continued to mumble a long ramble filled with "likes," "awesomes," and "totally beamies."

"The PEAS Corps needs young beings like yourselves," Shtliff was saying from his dais. "With the PEAS Corps, you will find enlightenment, bliss, understanding, *peace*...."

He looked around at the rest of Shtliff's audience. Quite a few were sprawled out on the ground now, apparently oblivious to everything around them. A few were up and dancing, which was a little strange because the sounds from *Scales* had ceased, and they were dancing to music that evidently only they could hear.

"The PEAS Corps wants you. The PEAS Corps is *home*...."

A number more were getting up off the ground and wandering off vacantly, wearing empty expressions like masks.

Aquaria started to get up.

"Where are you going?"

"I . . . need to . . . like . . . join the PEAS Corps," she said. "They need me. Enlightenment...."

"Sit down, Aquaria."

Obediently, she sat.

"Can you hear me?"

"Yes."

"Where are you staying?"

"At the . . . StarBrite Hotel . . . in town. Room 540. But the PEAS Corps is my home...."

"Aquaria, I want you to go to your room at the StarBrite Hotel. Get dressed. Then go straight to the Terran Embassy, at the Plaza of Articulate Naiveté. Ask for Ben Magnan."

"Ben Magnan."

"That's right. Tell him you claim asylum as a distressed tourist. He'll have a doctor look you over. Do you understand?"

"Yes."

"What did I just tell you?"

"I should go to my room at the StarBrite . . . get dressed . . . Terran Embassy . . . Ask for Ben Magnan . . . say I'm a distressed tourist...."

"Good girl." He took another look at the pupils of her eyes. She acted as though someone had slipped her a powerful hypnotic.

That joyweed joint? Whatever it was had made her extremely suggestible.

And it appeared to have affected quite a few other human students gathered in the amphitheater.

Vacantly, Aquaria stood up and walked off in the general direction of the center of High Gnashberry.

And Retief decided to have a little talk with the guru.

7

Shtliff apparently had not yet seen Retief. The heavy black hood of his disguise seriously restricted his vision, even for a being with five eyes, and Retief had no problem walking around to the rear of his dais, making his way to the top, and sitting down cross-legged at Shtliff's side.

"Well, well, well," Retief said. "And what would the Groaci First Assistant Minister of Sneaky Affairs on B'rukley be doing preaching sermons from a mountaintop?"

At the very first "well," Shtliff started so violently he nearly fell over.

"To be not doing that, Retief!" the being said, his whispered Groaci amplified to a commanding declaration. "To be scaring me out of ten years' growth!"

"What's the idea, Shtliff," Retief demanded in Standard. "What's the angle with the PEAS Corp? The Groaci aren't farmers and they don't go in for civil-works projects."

"Get out!" the agitated Shtliff ordered in Standard. "Go away! *Shoo!*" He shifted back to Groaci. "To not want you here to cramp my style!"

The students in the audience, Retief noticed, were getting up and wandering off in all directions, obeying Shtliff's unintentional command. The two handmaidens stood nearby, looking stunned.

"You've got those students in a highly suggestible hypnotic trance," Retief told the alien. "What'd you do? Spike the joyweed handouts?"

"To be interfering with the mission-field work of a simple laborer in the vineyards!" Shtliff scrambled backward away from Retief, his hood going astray, his five stalked eyes lashing about wildly. "To be messing things up for the Church! To be racking up serious bad karma!"

"To burn later a serious buttload of sacred joss sticks in penance," Retief said, grabbing the hem of the Groaci's robe. "You know, Broodmaster, the Peace Enforcers take a very dim view of slavery. They might be quite interested in your little scam, here—drugging Terry students, hypnotizing them into doing free labor. Just what is it your little agro community is supposed to be growing, Shtliff?"

"To be perilously close to blasphemy, vile Terry! The religious work of a simple preacher in the mission fields, to be none of the business of you or the Peace Enforcers!"

"Let our guru go," one of the young women ordered. Retief glanced up and saw that both of them were holding small but deadly Groaci power pistols and were aiming them at his head.

"Put the guns down, girls," he told them.

"Uh-uh. You let Broodie go!" Both of them, he now saw, were wearing nose filters like his. Slowly, he released Shtliff's robe and raised his hands.

"Where were you hiding those?" he asked with genuine interest. Neither girl wore enough clothes to hide a pack of dopesticks, much less a pistol.

"Shut up. Turn around."

He turned. "I take it you don't care that your guru is actually a Groaci disguised as a Grothelwaith."

Something—the butt of a pistol, he thought—cracked against the base of his skull, and Retief dropped into darkness.

CHAPTER FOUR

1

As Retief began to regain consciousness, he felt himself being half dragged, half carried by strong arms supporting him beneath the armpits. This seemed puzzling, in a muzzy-headed way; neither of the women on that stage could have dragged his six-foot-plus frame very far, and Groaci frames were frail and spindly, barely able to carry fifty pounds, much less almost five times that weight.

His hands were bound by a plastic lock-strip. He tried to shake his head to clear it, but pain exploded from the back of his skull. Better take it easy. . . .

"Okay, you wants him—*Ssst!*—in the back?" a gruff voice said from just above his head. It then added, "See?"

So Seven was in on this. Were the Groaci actually working with GOSH?

"I'll get the door," a woman's voice replied.

Retief heard the door to a vehicle hiss open. A moment later, he was unceremoniously dumped atop a dirty blanket on the floor of some sort of van or delivery vehicle. A moment later, other doors hissed and thumped shut, and he heard the vehicle's drive keening to life. He decided to feign unconsciousness; if his captives were at all chatty, he might learn something.

"Where are we taking him?" A woman's voice again.

"To the Farm." That was the breathy whisper of a Groaci; Shtliff must have removed the respirator and voice amplifier.

"We should just waste him, see?" Seven observed.

"No!" Shtliff replied sharply. "This happens to be the Terry diplomat who was kicked out of the CDT's exalted ranks the other diurnal period. He knows much. He may be useful."

"So he's going to end up on a Groaci conversation rack?" one of the women asked. "Pity."

"The ideal would be to turn him, which eventuality would be to our advantage."

"I still think we should—*zzzzt!*—waste da bum, see? *Whirr-click!*"

"Patience, patience, my dear Five. If our Terry friend back there fails to see reason, you will have your chance."

Shtliff had called the GOSH torpedo "Five." The guy sounded the same as Seven, right down to the programming glitch in his speech, but made men tended to be pretty much identical within each series. This must be another one. How many GOSH heavies were employed in this operation? And . . . was GOSH running the show, with Groaci help? Or was it the other way around?

Conversation ceased. Retief tried to make a mental note of the turnings the van was taking, but the information would do him little good, since he wasn't sure where the vehicle had been when it started. He would need to be alert to other clues if he was going to figure out where this "farm" they'd mentioned might be. Opening his eyes a slit, he was able to see the van's rear windows above and behind him. His vantage point on the floor meant he couldn't see anything but sky, but he did get a glimpse of the reddish light of firstsun. It was afternoon when they grabbed him; the van must be heading east.

Retief estimated that no more than ten minutes passed before the van finally whined to a stop. Given that such vehicles had a cruising speed of no more than 150, the Farm must be located within twenty-five miles of High Gnashberry.

He listened to the assorted bangs, hisses, and scrapings of people exiting the vehicle. A moment later, the back door sighed open.

"Please, Terry," Shtliff's voice whispered. "Cytheria couldn't have hit you *that* hard. Surely you are rejoicing to the fact that you yet possess life!"

"I don't know that rejoicing is quite the word I'd use," Retief said. He opened his eyes and sat up carefully. "You look better without the cloak, Shtliff. Black just isn't your color."

"Youz comin' outta there—*zzzzt!*—your own self?" Five demanded. "Or does I gotta drag youz, see?" *Whirr-click!*

"Patience, Five," Shtliff told the hulking GOSH thug. "Let the poor Terry get his bearings. Cytheria must have, to employ a Terry phrase, really walloped him."

"Cracked the butt of my pistol," the woman said. "He's got a thick skull."

Retief feigned weakness, moving to the edge of the van's open hatchback and taking the opportunity to study the landscape. They were, as he'd suspected, well out in the B'ruklian countryside. The characteristic gold and red canopy of a B'ruklian forest surrounded them, but several acres had evidently been logged out, creating a glade surrounded by woods. The clearing had been covered over, however, by a chameleonet, a thick webwork supporting living foliage fastened to the encircling trees. Sunlight filtered through the net, creating a dim, red-hued twilight.

And within that twilight, a number of young men and women labored with primitive tools in long, plowed furrows, tending the cultivated rows of spiky black shrubs that Retief guessed must be joyweed.

"Dis way, youz, see?" *Zzzzt!*

Five grasped Retief's elbow and pulled him from the vehicle.

Shtliff was holding a Groaci power pistol in one spatulate-fingered hand. "Come along, Terry. The name *is* Retief, is it not? I believe we met at a formal diplomatic function several months ago."

"Not to mention on the Avenue of Much Walking," Retief said.

"To be sure. All of you Terries look alike to me, but I thought your sense-organ cluster was familiar. I have been following your recent exploits with considerable interest, Retief." He gestured with the pistol. "This way, if you please."

They guided him around the edge of the joyweed field to a cluster of bubblehuts at the edge of the forest. A large, hand-lettered sign in front spelled out CAMP CONCENTRATION in friendly block letters, while smaller letters beneath read A WHOLLY OWNED SUBSIDIARY OF ENLIGHTENMENT ENTERPRISES. Through the trees, Retief could see another clearing covered by a chameleonet, this one serving as the landing pad for a small grounded spacecraft. It was tough to see from here, but he thought it might be a Groaci Class J scout.

They were leading him to a small bubble off to the side with the word STOREROOM written in Groaci curlicues above the door.

"We'll see you back at the office," one of the women said.

"To be sure. Please check the break room on your way in. If, as is usually the case, one of my elite commando troopers is present, gilding rectilinear construction materials, tell him to report to the storeroom for guard duty."

"You got it, Broodie." Turning, they sauntered off toward one of the larger domes.

"I trust you won't mind somewhat spartan living conditions for the nonce," Shtliff told Retief breezily, using a magnetic-strip card to open the storeroom door. The interior was empty, save for a few sealed crates. "This facility is still new and lacks some of the civilized amenities, such as a dedicated confinement facility and interrogation chamber."

"Not a problem, Shtliff," Retief told him. "How about untying my hands, though? We Terries talk better if we can use our hands."

"Why not? Your helplessness is complete. Five? Cut his bonds."

"So," Retief asked casually as the GOSH thug used a penknife to slice apart the plastic strip binding his wrists. "How much of this little operation of yours does Mr. Bug already know about?"

All five of Shtliff's stalked eyes came to rigid attention, quivering with shocked surprise. "To be wondering what you know of . . . *him!*" the Groaci whispered harshly, slipping back into his own language.

"What, Mr. Bug?" Retief shrugged. "Sure, he and I go way back. Met him through a friend here on B'rukley, by the name of Louis the Libido."

"Huh?" Five said. "If'n youz know Mr. Bug . . ." *Zzzzt!* His head turned with a whining of servomotors, until he was looking at Shtliff. "Dis could be bad news, boss, see?" *Whirr-click!*

"Be calm, Five," Shtliff told him. "This is no time to panic!"

Five's head whined as it swiveled back to glare at Retief. "If'n youz know Louis—*zzzzt!*—who'z da guy what works wid him, see?"

"You must mean Seven," Retief replied. "A rather distinguished-looking made man of your series—*Yakuza ichi-man* . . . the ten-thousand series."

Five looked at Shtliff. "Can we—*zzzzt!*—panic now?"

"An excellent idea, Five. Please proceed. I will join you anon." He motioned Retief inside the storage dome with his pistol.

"Five seems a bit upset that I know Mr. Bug," Retief commented. "Could it be that GOSH doesn't know what it is you're doing out here in the woods, Shtliff?"

"To maintain silence, Terry miscreant! To be thinking you may not know as much as you claim to know about Operation Weed."

"To be thinking you have ingested more than you can masticate, Broodmaster Shtliff. To be offering you my help if you make a clean breast of things."

Shtliff gave a harsh and decidedly negative clack of his mandibles, sealing the door shut behind Retief.

2

A quick inspection of his new quarters showed no immediate possibility of escape. Floor was melded to dome walls seamlessly, and the structure was cast of a tough, all-weather, all-temperature polymer that he was unlikely to tunnel through with anything less powerful than a small Hellbore. He managed to pry open one of the crates and found it stuffed with leaves . . . dried and shredded joyweed leaves. Evidently, this was the first harvest from the commune farm.

Or . . . on second thought . . . those wooden crates were familiar. They were the same design as the one he'd examined at the starport yesterday. He could even see where the shipping manifests had been stapled. He was willing to bet that these crates had been used to ship economics textbooks to B'rukley, textbooks carefully hollowed out and stuffed with joyweed. *This* joyweed. The plants he'd seen in the field outside had been small and scraggly things, nowhere close to mature.

Perhaps this was a supply brought in by GOSH to keep the PEAS Corps workers content until they brought in the first harvest.

The wood was dry and hard. Pulling up several slats from the top of a crate, he exposed the nails that had held the top in place. Inside were dry, almost powdery crumbles of joyweed, half a crate full.

It gave him an idea.

Using one exposed nail, he began digging at the edge of one of the loose, wooden slats, sawing away at the soft wood to create a V-shaped notch in the middle of one long side. It took almost twenty minutes of scraping with his makeshift file, but at last he had the notch deep enough for his purposes and cut to a sharp right angle. Taking another slat, he slid the long side back and forth along the notch. Yes . . . that would work just fine.

A scrabble at the door warned him that he had company. Swiftly, he scooped up the two slats, put them back on the opened crate, and sat on it. The door sighed open.

"To exit, Terry prisoner of noble Groac," a guard in flared hip cloak and dun-colored eyeshields demanded in a breathy whisper. "To keep your manipulatory appendages in plain view, and to come along quietly."

"To come in and get me," Retief suggested.

"To not be permitted. To emerge from vile durance on your own, or to be burned down where you sit!"

"When you're that persuasive, how can I refuse?" Retief walked out of the storeroom. One Groaci soldier kept him covered with a power pistol, while the other relocked the door. "To come with us, soft one."

They led him along a dirt path to the largest of the bubbledomes. Along the way, Retief took note of several human students working in the fields. They had a dead, empty look to them and didn't seem to notice when he passed.

He also noticed that their crop wasn't doing well at all. The plants were puny and shriveled, the long, slender leaves half-wilted.

A made man waited impassively for them inside the main dome, leaning against the door frame endlessly flipping a quarter-guck piece. "Hello, Five," Retief said. "Holding up the wall?"

"I'm not—*zzzt!*—Five," the GOSH thug said, his grammar better than that of the other *ichi-man*. "I'm Eight, see? This way." *Whirr-click!*

Eight dismissed the Groaci soldier and led Retief down a hallway to a guarded door. Inside was a nicely appointed office, complete with lush shag carpeting in an eye-crossing pattern of plaid and paisley, a nine-foot desk and a floor-to-ceiling wall screen. The screen was on, but set at the moment to show only the Groaci coat of arms—Groaci warrior *rampant* upon a *bend sinister sable*, beneath five eyes *erect*, bestriding a world *azure*, holding aloft a vaguely humanoid figure by the ankles *gules*, spilling coins *argent et or* from its pockets, and with the motto, in Groaci, "All the traffic will bear, and then some."

Shtliff stood to one side. A second Groaci, wearing jewel-studded platinum eyeshields and the rank insignia of a field general, leaned back in a Hip-U-Matic contour chair of Terran manufacture, puffing at a Groaci dopestick.

"Well, well," Retief said. "General Snish, isn't it?"

"Your lies have caught up with you, Retief," Snish told him. "I've been checking up on your story."

"Oh? I trust you found it entertaining."

"Most." He leaned back in the chair, and its servos whined in protest. "Broodmaster Shtliff, here, tells me you claim to work for Mr. Bug. However, it seems that Mr. Bug has never heard of you."

"Very interesting."

"Might you have an explanation?"

"Mr. Bug runs a rather large and complex operation, true?"

"Quite true, Terry. One interplanetary in scope!"

"Exactly. Mr. Bug can't possibly keep track of everyone on his payroll now, can he?"

"A plausible supposition, Retief. However, for a crime lord, even one of Mr. Bug's stature, to have a diplomat of the CDT on his payroll would, you must admit, be something of a coup. I would think he would remember hiring such, don't you?"

"That assumes the diplomat in question represented himself as a diplomat when he was hired."

"Ah." Two of Snish's eyestalks drooped at that, an expression meaning, roughly, *Oops. Didn't think of that.* "But . . . could it be, my dear Retief, that you are playing some sort of dangerous double game? Perhaps seeking to learn more of Mr. Bug's organization for your CDT masters?"

"I don't have CDT masters anymore, Snish. You should know. Your helicopter was watching the eviction proceedings the other day."

"Indeed, though one wonders if that might not have been a clever sham designed to perpetrate an erroneous impression for motives still unclear."

"Do you really think that GNN would have participated in a hoax? My departure was displayed on the evening news rather prominently, you'll recall."

"Very true." Snish exchanged a five-eyed glance with Shtliff, and clacked his lower mandibles thoughtfully. "And GNN *is* a class-triple-A unimpeachable prime intelligence source, trustworthinesswise."

"Besides, the CDT isn't interested in a little drug trafficking here and there. The B'ruklian embassy is here to represent Terran interests on B'rukley, not fight the Galactic Organized Syndicate of Humanoids."

"True, though I daresay there are those within the Concordiat government that would like to see GOSH put out of business, especially here in the Shamballa Cluster, and with the threat implicit in the Krll incursion."

"Enough!" a deep voice boomed in basso profundo from hidden speakers in the walls. "Snish, you five-eyed little parasite, if you keep blabbing like that, you'll give away the whole shebang!"

The Groaci coat of arms vanished from the wall screen, replaced by the immense, chitonesque visage of a monstrous insect. The face, Retief thought with interest, looked like that of a cockroach, with glittering black eyes peeking out from beneath the flat, red-brown curve of a heavy carapace. Two sets of whip-slender antennae flicked this way and that; a disturbing tangle of complex mouthparts worked this way and that behind delicately mobile palps.

"Mr. Bug, I presume," Retief said.

"You presume right, little human," the giant arthropod thundered. "But you're playing way out of your league, pally. You don't work for me, and I ain't never seen you before in my life."

"I, ah, knew that all along, Your Supreme Scuttlery," Snish said. "I was simply cleverly drawing him out to see what I could learn of his perfidious plans."

"Yeah, and while you were doing it, you were telling him everything he wanted to know." The glittering eyes seemed to shift slightly, back to Retief. "I was listening to the whole thing, with my camera off, so you didn't know I was here." He spoke slowly, almost ponderously, though Retief couldn't tell if that was his actual speech pattern, or the result of the giant being trying to speak slowly so that intellectual inferiors could keep up.

"Very clever," Retief said.

"Yeah. That's why they call me the brain bug, because I'm the brains of this whole operation." A harsh buzz sounded. "Bah!"

Mr. Bug turned away from his screen pickup, and as he did so, Retief caught a glimpse of the room behind him. It appeared to be decorated in Early Period Disaster; a large window bathed the room in a harsh, bluish light, like the glare of an arc lamp. "I told you I didn't want to be interrupted!" Mr. Bug rumbled off-camera. "What's that? No! Tell the Lord General to wait! I'm busy!"

The giant insect turned back, the roachish face once again completely filling the screen. "Excuse me. Interruptions, interruptions. Where was I?"

"You were telling me that you were the brains of this outfit."

"Yeah. And don't you forget it! Or . . . rather . . ." The being broke off, emitting a sound like a head-on collision between two Mark XVIII Bolos. "I guess you can forget it, if you want. You won't be around long enough for the memory to do you any good! Snish, you slimy, sticky-fingered little *gweech*!"

Snish's eyestalks worked furiously in a barely repressed expression of cold fury. "Yes, Your Crawliness!"

"Take this bum out and fit him for a pair of poured-stone slippers!"

"You mean . . . !"

"Yeah! Let him doze with the dishes!"

"Um, don't you mean, Your Omnivoracity, 'sleep with the fishes'?"

"Don't you tell me what I mean, five-eyes! Just do it!" And the screen blanked off.

"I hate him," Snish said after staring at the dead wall screen a moment. "I mean, I really, *really* hate him."

"Really? Do you hate him enough to pull a fast one on him?"

Two of Snish's five eyes swung around to stare unwinkingly at

Retief. "No. I don't hate him *that* much. Not enough to risk my currently and thankfully intact exoskeleton."

Casually, Retief sat down in a chair next to Snish's desk and plucked a Groaci dopestick from the built-in humidor. "I find that attitude fascinating, Snish," Retief said evenly, flicking the dopestick alight, "in view of the fact that you're already hip-cloak deep in some double-crossing intrigue with GOSH."

All five of Snish's eyes whipped around to face him, followed by the rest of the triangular head. "Ulp! How did you . . . that is . . . what gives you, um, *that* idea, my dear Retief?" Three of the eyes swung about to face Eight, who'd been standing quietly by the door the whole time, silently flipping his quarter.

"Don't look at me, Boss," the made man said, "I didn't tell him nuttin', see?"

"To appear to know entirely too much, soft one," Shtliff told Retief in Groaci. "To be a state of affairs not entirely conducive to your good health and future happiness!"

"To be not overly concerned about me, Broodmaster," Retief replied. "To be of the understanding that my good health and future happiness are somewhat in doubt just now."

"To tell me this instant in mind-numbing detail what you know about Operation Weed and how you know it!" General Snish demanded.

"To be a good-cop, bad-cop interrogation?" Retief asked. Holding his hand up to his forehead, palm out, he waggled his fingers in a way suggestive of Groaci eyestalks telegraphing an anatomically impossible suggestion involving the Groaci's head and his ssnrff organs. "To go take a flying leap, littermate of drones."

"To promise you safety if you confess all!" Snish whispered. "To present to Mr. Bug a somewhat fictional account of your gory demise, while you in fact enjoy a new life and a new identity among the countless worlds of the Greater Groac Co-Prosperity Sphere!"

"Sounds like a good deal, General," Retief said in Standard. "But I don't really need your help. I've already taken steps to transmit everything I've learned to the safekeeping of . . . certain associates, let's say. If I don't turn up again, hale and hearty, that information just might be published."

"What? You wouldn't!"

"It should make the GNN nightly news. I feel sure that Mr. Bug gets his intelligence information from GNN too, don't you think?"

"You . . . you *are* having a jape at my expense, of course. Ha-ha. A very good jest, my dear Retief . . ."

"And then there's the *Galaxy News and Planetary Report*. A bit on the conservative side, probusiness, and all of that, but they might still run the story. I happen to know one of the feature-desk editors."

"Retief! You mustn't! If Mr. Bug learns the details of Operation Weed, his henchmen will feed me to the fishes, a scrap at a time! Surely we can reach a reticent composure on this."

"Reticent composure?" Retief frowned. "I'm not catching all of your Obfuscese."

"Indeed. Reticent composure? That would be a *modest vivaldi*, as they say. . . ."

"If they do, they should be shot. Just for that, forget it, Snish. I won't tell you a thing."

"You will, Terry scum! You will! Eight!"

"Yeah, Boss . . . see?"

"Take this misguided miscreant back to his vile durance! Then prepare the instruments for a Class A-for-Apoplexy interrogation!"

"Sounds intriguing, Snish," Retief put in. He blew a stream of smoke across the desk at the raging Groaci. "But the only way for you to get out of this with your precious exoskeleton intact is to turn world's evidence."

"We shall see, Retief." Snish interlaced his long, spatulate fingers and leaned forward. "We have a very special tape, one derived from our spy microphones in your embassy, a nonstop twelve-hour staff meeting wherein Ambassador Crapwell waxes eloquent no fewer than five times! He tells over a dozen anecdotes of his experiences as a young diplomat in happier days! Yes! Three of our technicians went mad while assembling that tape! You will talk,

Retief, or we shall strap you to a chair, fill your circulatory fluid with a drug designed to keep you awake under all circumstances, *then subject you to the unending horror of that staff meeting!*"

"I was already at that meeting, Snish. Three weeks ago, Tuesday. I have to admit, the mere thought is enough to make a grown man cry . . . but all I can tell you is, do your worst!"

"Away with the creature!" Snish screamed. "He has sealed his own dire fate!"

3

Back in his storeroom cell once more, Retief listened at the door for a moment. He could hear two Groaci soldiers outside, whispering at each other . . . something about a female Groaci clerk-typist at headquarters, one with really startling ornamental knobs on her ventral carapace, and what she would look like in a tubful of hot sand. They did not sound particularly interested in the prisoner they were guarding.

Returning to the center of the room, he retrieved the two pieces of wood. Taking a double handful of crumbled joyweed leaves, he made a pile on the storeroom floor, and placed the notched piece of wood over it, bracing it in place between his feet. Taking the second piece of wood then, he rested it inside the notch and began drawing it back and forth, scraping hard, wood against wood, maintaining a heavy pressure . . . moving it faster . . . and faster . . .

It would have been somewhat more efficient to make a bow to turn a dowel inside a pit dug into a block of wood, but he had neither string nor a rounded length of wood. This ought to work, though. He needed to create friction enough to create a temperature of about eight hundred degrees. He kept scraping the wood through the notch, up and down, up and down, faster . . . faster . . . harder . . . harder . . .

A telltale thread of smoke appeared above the notch. He stopped working and leaned over, looking close. Sure enough, a tiny, glowing ember had appeared in the pile of joyweed. Shielding the pile with his cupped hands, he breathed on the ember very, very gently, until it flared into an inch-high flicker of yellow flame. Scooping up enough of the crumbled leaves to pick up the infant flame, he carefully transferred it to the open box and set it inside, allowing the flame to spread.

Thick, white-gray smoke began boiling out of the box as the contents caught fire. He blew harder on the flame, then stepped back.

The room was full of joyweed smoke now. Careful to breathe only through his nose and the filter plugs in his nostrils, Retief pounded hard on the storeroom door. "Help! Fire!" He shifted to Groaci. "To render assistance in the shortest possible interval of time!"

The smoke was so thick he could hardly see now. It was rising, collecting near the ceiling, so Retief dropped down on all fours where visibility—and breathing—were better. His nose filters could only handle so much in the way of atmospheric contaminants. If someone didn't open that door pretty soon . . .

He heard muffled voices outside, and the click of the cardkey lock. The door sighed open, and the confusion of voices was louder.

The Groaci guard stumbled into the room and promptly began wheezing. Retief wrenched the power pistol from his grasp and leaped out through the door. He sidestepped a second Groaci trooper, chopping down on his spindly forearm to make him drop his weapon, then poking two rigid fingers hard into his sensitive zaz-patch. The soldier gurgled faintly and folded up on the ground.

Retief took several steps, then stopped, head down, trying to steady the whirling sensation between his ears. He must have picked up a bit of the active element of that smoke. He actually felt pretty good, but his feet felt like they were a long, long way below him and were having a bit of trouble connecting with the ground.

"To halt!" the second guard yelled, though his soft voice didn't carry well. He reached for his pistol, still on the ground. Retief raised the weapon he'd appropriated inside. He didn't *want* to shoot, but . . .

The first Groaci stumbled out of the smoke-fuming doorway, took one look at the other guard, and leaped on him from behind. The two began wrestling with one another, rolling back and forth on the ground, hip-cloaks flapping wildly.

"Have fun, fellows," Retief told them. Then, taking a deep breath of blessedly fresh air, he began jogging toward that Class-J scout he'd seen a little ways off through the forest.

Students labored in the Camp Concentration field, hoeing around sickly looking joyweed shrubs. Tucking his power pistol into a pocket, he slowed his pace to a rapid walk. If he looked like he belonged there, if he didn't act in a suspicious fashion . . .

He'd not traveled more than fifty feet, however, when a hulking humanoid in a cheap suit stepped out from behind one of the compound huts. In one hand, the made man gripped an antique slug thrower aimed at Retief's midsection. The other casually flipped a silver coin in the air. "Hold it right there, pally," *zzzzt!* "See?"

"I'm sorry, Eight," Retief said. "I don't have time to play right now."

"I ain't Eight, see?" the robot replied. "I'm Five. And youz are comin' wit me, see?"

Retief raised both hands, took a step closer, and looked deeply into Five's glassy eyes. "Five," he said, "listen carefully: *wait paren close-paren semicolon.*"

The robotic GOSH thug froze in place, unmoving. The quarter-guck piece spun in the air, dropped onto the robot's open palm, and bounced off onto the ground, uncaught.

Retief waved a hand in front of the unseeing eyes and nodded. Back in the Embassy's resource center, he'd taken the precaution of running a quick brain-tape download of an ancient computer language—C++. The command "wait();" would leave the GOSH robot immobile and harmless until it received a new set of commands. He picked up the dropped quarter-guck and placed it in the robot's motionless hand.

Threading his way through the woods, he emerged minutes later in the clearing where the spacecraft was grounded. A Groaci guard with a power rifle stood by the boarding ramp. "To halt, soft one!" he commanded, raising the rifle.

"To put that thing down before you hurt someone," Retief replied. "To not recognize General Snish's personal ship engineer and maintenance technician?"

"To ... not recognize you," the Groaci replied. "To not wish to point out the shortcomings of alien inferiors and thereby give offense, but to fear that all Terry slaves look alike."

"To not let it worry you, warrior heir of noble Groac. To show you my papers."

"To make it snappy. To have business onboard the Field General's personal yacht?"

"To need to prepare it for a quick trip," Retief replied. Stepping closer, he reached inside his jacket as though reaching for his papers, then snapped his fist out in a cracking backhand that slammed the hapless sentry into the hull of the ship.

"To stop him!" A small mob of Groaci soldiers was spilling through the woods from the direction of the bubblehut compound. "To stop the vile trespasser!"

Retief snatched the power rifle from the guard's nerveless fingers, thumbed off the safety, then sent a triplet of energy bolts sizzling above the heads of the oncoming Groaci soldiers. Instantly, the mob reversed course, spilling through the woods back into the Camp Concentration clearing. "To retreat! To make a strategic withdrawal! To attack again in a different direction!"

Pounding up the ramp, Retief entered the ship and palmed the close panel, sealing the vessel. Squeezing into the narrow control room—little more than a cockpit with delusions of grandeur—he scanned the tiers of controls and readouts. Spotting the button with the Groaci word for "power up," he slapped it, then checked the power gauges. With a rising whine of spooling turbines, the scout's power plant came online. A moment later, a pink light signaled that the fusion reactor had switched on, bootstrapped by the turbines, and that power levels were at forty-five percent and rising.

Loud *ping*s and *crack*s sounded against the hull. He was taking small-arms fire from the forest. One hand on the guide yoke, the other on the power plant controls, Retief began feeding power to the craft's gravitics repulses and to the inertial stabilizers. Out of the corner of his eye, he caught sight of the guard he'd knocked down scrambling for the safety of the tree line. Good. He didn't want to fry a soldier bludgeoned in the performance of his duty.

Wang! Okay, *that* was something larger than small arms. The Groaci were getting serious now. Retief pushed the power controls full forward and brought back the yoke. With a shrill whine, the scout lifted from the earth, catching the canopy of chameleonetting almost at once.

No matter. Tilting the hovering spacecraft's nose higher, Retief shifted his right hand from the power controls to the aft thrust controls, ramming them forward. Despite the efforts of the craft's inertial fields, the boost slammed him back in the too-narrow, too-short pilot's seat as the vessel accelerated at a sudden five Gs. His view through the craft's canopy was obscured by the netting; apparently, he'd brought all or most of it with him. Leveling off at five miles, he continued to accelerate, swiftly surging through the sound barrier. In moments, atmospheric friction had set the entangling net ablaze. Then, with a final flash, it was gone, burned away completely, and Retief began angling higher once more, heading for space.

"Calling space yacht *Hanky-Panky* . . . uh, that is . . . calling Class-J scout N88V309W" sounded from the ship's commo speakers. "Retief! Are you mad? Bring my yacht back here instanter!"

"Sorry, Snish," Retief told him. "I've decided to forego the pleasure of the staff meeting this one time. I have urgent business elsewhere."

"Retief . . . we are both gentlebeings of the planet! We can discuss this amicably! I was—ha-ha—totally in jest about the A-for-Apoplexy interrogation, truly I was! Return my yacht to the Farm, and we shall let gone-byes be gone-byes!"

"Actually, Snish, I thought I'd go visit Mr. Bug. Now that I know where it is he keeps office hours. . . ."

"Retief, no! This is madness! You will get my beautiful Class-J yacht dirty! Or . . . or worse!"

"She *is* a sweet boat," Retief said agreeably. "Looks like a Groaci military scout on the outside, but you've got her interior souped up something fierce. The control suite looks more like the panel on a Sunbeam X-12000, and right now she's pushing six gravities when one of your scouts would barely manage three!"

"To be because she *is* a Sunbeam X-12000," Snish told him with something approaching despair in his faint voice, "with a Class-J outer hull. To be very fast and very, *very* expensive. To hold you responsible if I find upon her pristine hull the smallest scratch!"

"Really? Even the one where your boys hit me with what felt like a twenty-millimeter power bolt on liftoff?"

"*What?* How dare they! Heads will roll!"

"Well, I'll just leave you to it, Snish. Sounds like you're having fun."

"Retief! Wait!"

He switched the commo unit off.

Around him, the sky deepened to a vibrant, azure iridescence, which darkened further, then, to velvet black, thickly strewn with a blaze of stars. The system's two suns, one huge and orange, one pinpoint-tiny and fiercely blue, glared from the blackness. The myriad suns of the Shamballa Cluster glowed to starboard, and, beyond, shone the knotted and coagulated tangle of stars and nebulae, the Galactic Core.

Letting the yacht fall into orbit, Retief took some time to familiarize himself with the controls and especially with the navigational computer. His destination, he was pleased to see, was already laid in. Apparently, Snish made this trip frequently.

He also examined the rest of the vessel, which was cramped, but luxuriously so. Snish, it seemed, believed in living well and had the gucks to do it. The hot tub in the captain's quarters seemed a bit extravagant—a pool filled with sand kept at a constant toasty 115° F—until Retief remembered the bit of conversation he'd overheard between his guards just before his breakout. Perhaps Snish liked to travel in style *and* in comfort.

Hanky-Panky indeed.

But it must make a real mess if the artificial gravity ever cut out.

At last, when Retief felt he knew the ship well, he touched a control, and the ship again accelerated, slipping into hyperdrive for a star-blurring fraction of a second.

Drive time was short, for his destination was not far at all. The world of B'rukley orbited a large K-class star known elsewhere by an alphabet soup of a galactic catalogue number but known to its inhabitants as Firstsun. Technically, B'rukley was Firstsun II, the second world of three, but the only planetary body capable of sustaining life.

Firstsun, however, was part of a double star system; its companion, Secondsun, was a class-B giant, blasting ambient space with a fierce blue light. Fortunately for the sun-worshipping naturists among the USC student body, First- and Secondsun were comfortably far apart as stellar companions—almost a tenth of a light year, about the same remove as Alpha Centauri A and B from little Proxima. At that separation, Secondsun remained a brilliantly dazzling pinpoint bright enough to be fully visible in B'rukley's daytime sky, bright enough even to cast shadows on its own, but too distant to burn unprotected skin with ultraviolet or X-ray radiation.

Against all astronomically erudite expectations, Secondsun had its own planetary family—fourteen worlds, of which the fifth was just marginally habitable, at least by human standards. The first human explorers surveying the fifth planet's steaming oceans, radiation-blasted swamps, and sunbaked badlands had named the blue star Odious; somehow, the world eventually became known formally as Odiousita V.

Retief used part of the flight time between the two stars to review information he'd downloaded into his PDA from the embassy's online information resource center. Odiousita V was of little interest to humans in the sector or *had* been until the arrival of the Krll from the teeming cauldron of radiation that was

the Galactic Core. Krll death commandos had grabbed a number
of uninhabited worlds throughout the cluster and posted the
electronic equivalent of signs reading KEEP OUT; the Concordiat
had taken to drawing lines with sword points in the sand when
the Krll arrived on Odiousita V. The sunbaked little world, after
all, *was* inhabited.

Once out of hyper, and with Snish a comfortable tenth-light
away, Retief switched his commo unit back on. Almost at once,
warning messages began coming through from the environs of
the still-distant blue star.

"This is the Terran Concordiat dreadnaught *Eximious* on outer
perimeter patrol, calling unidentified inbound vessel," called one.
"Identify yourself and prepare to be boarded!"

"This is the Barrier Bastion *Ineluctable*, of the Greater Krll
Prosperity Sphere!" declared another. "Attention unidentified scout
craft! Surrender or be flammageried into hygrogellinated drallifer
shavings! Yeah, this means *you!*"

If Snish made frequent runs in this boat to this system, he
would have a way either of slipping in unnoticed or of fooling
the various perimeter patrols. Groaci were not known for risking
their precious protective integuments for any reason whatsoever.
He flipped through the computer commo log, found stored automated IFF transmissions, and keyed them in. Minutes passed and
no further challenges came through. The *Hanky-Panky* had been
rendered invisible . . . or innocuous.

The tiny vessel continued to fall toward the blue star, which
glared ahead brightly enough now to darken the ship's polarized
canopy and blot every other star from the sky. Soon, a brilliant
point of light separated from the glare of the star, resolving swiftly
into a bright crescent. Snish's autonav was working splendidly.
After a brief search, Retief found a very important item of survival equipment—long-wear sunblock with an SPF of ten million.
He stripped down, lathered the stuff on, and waited as the stuff
crawled rapidly across his entire body, forming a tight, UV- and
X-ray-opaque film invisibly covering his body. Eye drops went
into each eye, forming a dark, liquid coating that did the same
thing. Then, suitably protected at least for a day or two until

the nanogoo began to wear off, he got dressed and returned to the cockpit.

He was less than a thousand miles out, the planet forming a vast scimitar of silver-blue sun-dazzle ahead, when the radio crackled another warning. "Attention, unidentified spacecraft! This is the Concordiat battlecruiser *Inenarrable*! Your IFF codes are invalid! We have locked on to your craft and are tracking! Heave to and prepare to be boarded, or we open fire!"

Swiftly, Retief punched a series of alphanumerics into the commo board—his clearance status for flight approaches under diplomatic immunity. An instant later, a brilliant flare of light, brighter even than the local sun, exploded ahead and to port.

"*Inenarrable* to unidentified craft! You will not be warned again! Surrender or be destroyed!"

"This is class-J Scout N88V309W, en route under special diplomatic status. Please allow me to pass."

Another explosion rocked the scout, closer this time. "I guess you boys don't like diplomats," Retief said aloud. He settled himself in at the controls, feeding more power to the drive. This was about to get interesting. . . .

"This is the Krll Planetary Defense Station *Inappeasable*! We have you in our sights, diplomat! Surrender now, or suffer the consequences!"

Radar showed not one but two waves of missiles bearing down on the scout from opposite directions. Ramming the thrust controls full forward, Retief barrel-rolled high, then boosted hard on a new vector, angling for the relative safety of atmosphere. Explosions blossomed in space behind him as missiles detonated; a 30cm hellbore bolt narrowly passed astern. Another explosion jolted him, and he heard the sharp *ping-ping-ping!* of high-velocity shrapnel.

"What *am* I going to tell Snish?" Retief asked of no one in particular as he fought the hurtling craft into the first tenuous wisps of planetary atmosphere.

He was losing attitude control. The *Hanky-Panky* had taken some serious damage aft, and blue warning lights were popping on all over the control panel. He fought to hold her as the balky craft shuddered. A fireball of ionized gases billowed around him, blocking out the crazily tilted sweep of the planet's terminator. Altitude fifty miles ... forty ... but his velocity was dropping fast too, down to Mach 10. He *might* be able to pull this off. ...

"Unidentified spacecraft! This is Concordiat Planetary Defense Fortress A-12, of the Police Action Concordiat Military Authority Nexus. You have trespassed into a war zone and are advised to turn back immediately, or we shall open fire."

"PACMAN, this is N88V309W. I have taken damage and am on my way in. How about keeping your fingers off the firing button long enough for me to wrestle this bucket down."

"Negative, N88V309W. You could be a Krll intelligent missile with a good story line. Turn back or be destroyed."

The falling scout broke free of the ionized trail thirty miles above Odiousita V's night side, with the dawn terminator a silver curve dead ahead. A half-dozen pinpoints of light were racing up toward him from below, the exhaust flares of the missiles illuminating the solid cloud deck below.

Retief tried to maneuver the craft to starboard, but his lateral controls were dead. He tried to use the gravitics to slow his fall, but those were dead as well. In fact, there wasn't much he could do except continue to fall ... and those missiles were closing fast.

He hunkered down as far in the too-small Groaci pilot's seat as he could and yanked the emergency eject lever. A metal shell clanged shut around him, sealing him into the emergency escape pod, and a moment later a loud *bang!* slammed him down through the scout's ventral hull. For a long half minute, he was in free fall. Then a succession of far-off explosions told him that Snish's luxury yacht would be hosting no more Groaci sand-tub parties.

Helpless now, he fell from the night sky. ...

CHAPTER FIVE

1

At an altitude of twenty miles, the drogue chute popped, slamming Retief with deceleration. Minutes later, the second drogue deployed, followed by the main chute. Silently, the escape pod drifted toward the darkness below.

A tiny porthole gave him a view of sorts, but there was nothing to be seen but starless night. Odiousita V was enveloped by an impenetrable cloud cover, which ought to actually help mask his descent, but it also blocked out the swarming suns of the cluster and the Core and made for some very black nights on the planet's surface.

The biggest problem now, though, was the odds surrounding his landing site. He had no choice in the matter; he would come down completely at the mercy of Odiousita's winds.

Roughly half of the planet was covered by ocean—a fuming mix of hot water and sulfides washed down from the mountains, which meant the seas in fact were a dilute solution of sulfuric acid.

If he hit the water, he would drift with the currents until the acid ate away the thin shell of his capsule.

If he did touch down on land, there was the question of whose territory he would find himself in. Roughly a quarter of the land surface was currently under the control of the Krll invaders; roughly another quarter was claimed by the Concordiat Peacekeepers. The rest was no-being's land.

And, from what he'd learned in his research, none of the land surface of Odiousita was particularly appealing from a real-estate perspective.

A proximity alert sounded, a high-pitched warble that gave him time to brace himself in the too-small seat. There was a shock...followed by a series of jolts and drops accompanied by loud snaps and cracks from outside. Then there was a final, savage bump, and the capsule heeled over on its side.

At least he'd won the first toss of the dice, he thought to himself. He'd come down on solid ground. He touched the release lever, the escape pod popped open, and Retief was assaulted by the planetary night.

It was *hot*, at least a hundred degrees, and as humid as a steam bath. He broke a sweat almost immediately, and within thirty seconds his coveralls were drenched. A sulfurous stench hung in the air, which was unpleasantly thick and wet. The blackness was so complete he literally couldn't see his hand in front of his face, but he could hear all around him the sounds of jungle—the movement of the tree canopy overhead, the screeches, hoots, screams, shrieks, gibberings, yowls, mewlings, and barks of a surprisingly varied ecosystem.

Feeling about within the escape pod, he gathered his slender resources for survival. There was a small hand torch, but he decided not to use it just yet; light might attract some of the nastier and more hungry denizens of the Odiousitan jungle. He'd left the rifle onboard the *Hanky-Panky*, but he did still have the Groaci power pistol he'd taken from the guard. The escape pod was equipped with a standard Groaci survival kit—a first-aid kit that would be of little use to a being equipped with an endoskeleton, rations of food and water that his physiology could use, an emergency radio and directional tracker, a firestarter kit that likely would not work in this wet environment, blankets and cold-weather survival gear, and a set of smooth-rounded kiki stones to invoke tranquility during a crisis.

Taking the blanket, he made a comfortable nest for himself in the escape pod's seat, then settled down with the power pistol in hand to wait out the night. Blundering around in the jungle at night was an excellent way to reduce the chances for his survival, he reasoned.

Daylight came slowly. Odiousita V rotated slowly on its axis and had a day some eighty standard hours long. He'd come down quite close to the planet's dawn terminator, he knew, but three long hours passed by the dial of his luminous fingerwatch before the sky began to lighten and the jungle began to take form around him.

Only . . . it *wasn't* a jungle, not quite.

There were plenty of trees and a partial forest canopy, but what he'd thought were branches were, in fact, a crisscrossing of slender wooden poles supporting an immense chameleonet a good fifty feet above the ground and extending as far in every direction as he could see. His capsule had punched through several layers of the stuff on its descent, snapping poles and ripping the tough weave of light-sensitive fibers. Around him were oddly shaped structures, like slender mushrooms with broad, thick caps and balconies around the rims.

And all around him was a restless, rustling crowd of natives. Somehow, Retief had beaten all of the odds and come down smack in the center of an Odiousitan town.

2

The Odiousitans were radially symmetrical beings, like dark, six-armed starfish standing on the tips of their arms. They ranged from four feet in height to over six, and some must have massed as much as a small pony. The upper surface of their bodies was thick, tough, and spiny, an almost shell-like integument tough enough to discourage both predators and ultraviolet from the sun. The color of most was a mottled green and brown, though some were lighter in hue. A dark, deeply recessed eye stared out at the world from the base of each arm, giving them a 360-degree range to their vision. The undersurface of their bodies appeared to be covered by pale, highly flexible appendages something like the tube feet of Terran starfish; these grew longer and in bunches at the ends of the arms, manipulatory tentacles that appeared to serve as fingers. At any given moment, an Odiousitan could be standing on four or even three of its legs, while using the other two or three legs as many-fingered hands.

At the moment, some hundreds of the creatures were gathered around Retief and the grounded escape pod. A few had been there when the sky had first begun growing light, and over the next hour, more and more had appeared from the surrounding buildings. Many were waving crudely tentacle-lettered signs or garish, black and red flags, and some were waving both. The lettering on the signs was a harsh, jagged, angular printing that Retief did not recognize. The flags, though, he'd seen before—the red-on-black pattern that looked strangely like a crimson Rorschach blotch, the flag of the Greater Krll Prosperity Sphere.

The cacophony of squeals, barks, and other sounds was coming from the crowd. Retief reached up and switched on the microelectronic translator woven into the fabric of his jumpsuit.

A rather ragged translation sounded in his ears, overlaying the racket.

"Yay, Krll! Yay, Krll! Go! Go! Go!"

"Krll, Krll, they're the best! If they can't do it, it's not a fair test!"

"Welcome, mighty Krll! Conquerors of scum! Exterminators of vermin! Takers-on of all comers!"

"Two-four-six-eight! Who do we wish they ate? Ya-a-a-a-ay, Krll!"

A lot of the noise in the background, Retief now realized, was *singing*. The translator, of course, could give only a rough approximation of the emotional content behind the words.

> *"The Krll are such wonderful fellows!*
> *The Krll really are peachy keen!*
> *We welcome the Krll, who are mellow!*
> *Their like here has never been seen!*
> *Oh, bring back, bring back, oh, bring back the*
>   *mighty Krll overlords!*
> *Bring back, bring back, bring back those*
>   *victorious Krll hordes!"*

The throng exploded then in a cheering, shouting, thunderous roar of celebration. Confetti rained from the balconies that, Retief now saw, were festooned with brightly colored banners, all bearing the same jagged alien letters. Krll flags fluttered everywhere.

A particularly large and spiny native approached Retief, a scroll in one uplifted tentacle. The being had what looked like a monocle fixed over each beady eye, and the rolling gait of an old and portly member of his species.

"O mighty Krll conquerors!" the being said with the inflection that betokened some Serious Speechmaking. The voice rumbled and rambled, in true Important Speaker fashion. It appeared to be coming from an unseen mouth somewhere underneath the creature. "We, the humble population of the fair metropolis of Xixthezonx, do hail and welcome you to this loyal enclave of happy, loyal primitives, who are, of course, not worthy to be scraped from the bottoms of the mighty Krll warboots but who love their Krll lords and masters with a depth of devotion that cannot be expressed in this or any other language!"

"Excuse me," Retief said gently. "I think—"

"On this happy, joyous occasion when the mighty Krll conqueror has deigned to enter the humble metropolis of Xixthezonx, we, the humble population of said metropolis, do take this opportunity to honor and give homage to our blessed Krll masters, who have defended us at such great cost and with such great valor against the Terrible Terries who would enslave us. If there is anything we can do—"

"Excuse me . . ."

" . . . anything at all, to make your stay a brief and pleasant one, please don't hesitate to ask, yea, to command it, and it shall be done! Would you like food? Drink? Kinky alien sex? If there is—"

"Excuse me!"

"What?"

"I'm afraid you're making a small mistake," Retief told the being. "I'm not Krll."

"Eh? You're not?" Several of the eyes blinked rapidly in confusion, and one of the monocles fell off. Retief caught it in mid-fall and handed it back. "Er, thank you. If you're not Krll, what are you? Not one of those grucky things with sticky fingers, always wanting to dicker for foo-foo shrubs. No, not enough eyes, for one thing . . ."

"Actually," Retief told him, "I'm one of those terrible Terries you were talking about."

"One of . . ." This time, half a dozen monocles fell all at once. "Gentlebeings of Xixthezonx! It . . . is . . . a . . . *Terry!*"

There was stunned silence in the city for perhaps three seconds. Then the crowd erupted in a new cacophony, as loud and as boisterously joyful as before. As if by magic, the banners and flags hanging from the balconies vanished, to be replaced, moments later, by a fresh set, these in crudely lettered Standard.

WELCOME, TERRIES!
HAIL, THE CONQUERING TERRAN HEROES!

THANK YOU, NOBLE TERRA!
DEUTSCHLAND UBER ALLES!
I ♥ TERRIES!
TERRIES, DON'T GO HOME!
THE KRLL SUCK!

The black-and-red flags were replaced by the blue-and-white flags of the Concordiat. The crowd was now chanting and singing again, their Krll signs and flags all carefully hidden now. A few of the natives, however, perhaps those of a cautious nature or perhaps just very quick with a brush and a can of paint, had whipped out new signs welcoming the victorious Terry legions and waved them wildly now as the singing struck up once more.

> *"For the Terries are jolly good fellows!*
> *The Terries are jolly good fellows!*
> *The Terries are jolly good fe—ell—ows!*
> *Which no being can deny!"*

"Let's hear it for the victorious Terries! Our defenders! Our protectors!"

"Hurray for the terrific Terries!" someone cried out in a booming voice. "Three cheers! Arm-arm . . . *hurrah*! Arm-arm . . . *hurrah*! Arm-arm . . . *hurrah*!"

"O mighty Terran conquerors!" the portly Odiousitan said, his monocles back in place. "We, the humble population of the fair metropolis of Xixthezonx, do hail and welcome you to this loyal enclave of happy, loyal primitives, who are, of course—"

"Actually, I've heard this part already," Retief interrupted. "It had a slightly different spin before, but I appreciated the feeling behind it."

"Huh? Oh, sure." The being edged a little closer, dropping its voice. "Uh, I hope you don't take things wrong with the little misunderstanding behind that first welcome, and all. . . ."

"Certainly not. Am I to understand, though, that your city has changed hands a few times already?"

"Oh, bother!" The creature sagged. "Is it that obvious?"

"Well, I had the feeling that when you thought I was a Krll, you were laying it on just a bit thick. Maybe hoping I would go away sooner?"

"Well, of course! Who wouldn't want the vile Krll monsters to go away? Always stomping through the foo-foo patch! Always giving orders! Always depriving innocent, carefree natives of their simple civil liberties! Now, the Terries, on the other hand, we welcome with heartfelt sincerity to our . . ."

Retief held up a hand. "I get the picture. But I doubt that you're much happier to see Terry peace enforcers marching through your foo-foo patch than Krll soldiers. In situations like this, most folks just want to be left alone."

"Brother, you got that right!" the being said with feeling. "Things just haven't been right ever since the Terries and the Krll started arguing over who was king of the swamp!" The being cocked its body slightly to the left in a quizzical bit of spiny body language. "You know, Terry? You're all right! By the by, I'm Glom-gloob the Effervescent, the mayor of this 'burg."

"Retief the Insoucient," he replied. "And I could use your help."

"C'mon into the office, Retief," Glom-gloob said. "Let's see what we can do."

3

Glom-gloob's office was in one of the mushroom-capped structures at the center of town, an interesting blend of the modern and the primitive. The building itself appeared to have been grown to order, right down to the spiral ramp going up the inside of the mushroom's stalk. Furnishings included imported Groaci humping racks, sealed plastic supply canisters marked CAFARD, and tastefully distressed split logs, all on a wall-to-wall dried-mud carpet. A collection of antique Groaci nose flutes adorned the walls, attractively framed; Retief noted that most were from the Niff Dynasty . . . and must, therefore, be three months old or more.

"Very nice," Retief commented. "Homey."

"Yeah, thanks. Took us weeks to haul fresh mud up that ramp and get it to dry just right." Glom-gloob settled his bulk down on top of the humping rack, which creaked ominously beneath his weight. He reached with one arm into the Hip-U-Matic and pulled out a handful of golf ball–sized spheres. "Zooble nuts?"

"Thanks, no."

The Odiousitan native slipped the nuts underneath his bulk. Retief heard the crunch as they were chewed by a hidden mouth.

"The word's out, you know, that you Terries don't think we're civilized."

"Really?"

"Yup. But I'll have you know that we Bloggies have achieved a very high level of civilization . . . oh, it must be three or four years, now."

"Bloggies?"

"It's what we call ourselves. Means 'Inhabitants of the warm and blessed swamps of Ogg,' or maybe it just means 'The People.' Of course, you Terries call us 'starfish' and 'autochthones' and 'Odiousitans,' and the Krll call us 'zabblefronders' and 'guggag-guggawampuses,' but we're really Bloggies."

"I'll keep that in mind," Retief said. "Tell me, have you ever seen a Terry before today?"

"Huh? Oh, sure. Like you pointed out, this territory goes back and forth between the Terries and the Krll on an almost regular basis. In fact . . ." He reached into a drawer of his desk and extracted a Groaci trade-goods copy of a Japanese-made Ronald Reagan watch. "We're about due for another switchover any time now. That's why the boys were a little fast with the Krll flags just now, you know."

"I don't blame them a bit. But do I look that much like a Krll?"

"Retief, I'll tell you the truth. *All* of you aliens look pretty much alike to me. First it's the Terries, then it's the Krll, then it's the Terries again . . . all of them trampling through the foo-foo patches and putting holes in the house-trees. A fellow can't keep them all straight."

"But you do recognize the Groaci, I take it."

"The Gruckies? Yeah. They come through here pretty regular too. They don't trample the foo-foo. They just take it. At first they paid for what they took ... really keen glass beads and trinkets, mirrors, plastic combs ... though we haven't figured out what *those* are for, yet. They told us that that was *money*, back where they come from. Sounded good to us simple native-types, because we thought a boost in the old economy would help us enter into the galactic trading milieu, bring in even more glass beads and trinkets.

"Then they told us that the latest thing in the galactic economy was something called *credit*. That's not so good, though."

"Really?"

"Yeah. The way it works, see, is the Groaci traders come in, take all the foo-foo shrubs they want, and say 'to put it on the tab.' We haven't figured out what the tab is yet, so it feels like we're getting ripped off."

"Frankly, I'd have to say you *are* being ripped off. This may be the only planet in the galaxy where Groaci credit is any good. Tell me, though. What do you use foo-foo bushes for, anyway?"

"Oh, that's our number-one staple diet around here. Good eating, let me tell you!"

"Do the Groaci eat them?"

"Never seen them do so. In fact, they're real careful about how they handle them, wearing breathing masks and using tongs and plastic baggies, and so on. And they only take the leaves ... usually, anyway."

"What do you mean by usually?"

"Well, a few weeks ago, this one Grucky showed up with a harvest crew ... they looked a lot like you, in fact, so I guess they were Terries. Anyway, they dug up a whole bunch of plants—pretty much ripped out the whole south forty, in fact. Put them into little pots full of soil and loaded them onto their spaceship. 'Put it on our tab,' the Grucky said, and there we were looking for the tab thing all over again."

"Too bad," Retief said. "Next time they show up, I suggest you demand cash. In advance."

"Yeah? Who's this cash, anyway?"

"Never mind. We just need to find a way to keep them from taking advantage of you folks. Tell me . . . are the Groaci the only ones interested in foo-foo shrubs?"

"Well, I can't say from personal experience, but I've heard the Krll are into foo-foo cultivation in a pretty big way."

"Really? That's very interesting."

"Yeah, I heard about that from my cousin Zub-zloob. He's the mayor of Glooberville, which is over on the North Continent. The Krll have a big operation up there, and I gather you Terries don't get up there very often. The word from Zub-zloob is, the Krll have been harvesting foo-foo leaves, drying them, and shipping them someplace else for months, now. Of course, they don't put anything on the tab up there. They just moved in, took over a fair-sized foo-foo field, and put up the keep-out signs. *Requisitioning*, is what they called it, at least according to old Zub."

"I'd like to have a look at some foo-foo plants, if I could," Retief said.

"Not a problem. We could arrange that. But speaking of problems . . . you said you needed our help."

"I do, Mr. Mayor. I find myself stranded here. Someone shot down my spacecraft."

"Ah. I understand. I hate it when that happens."

"You have many spacecraft shot down around here?"

"Happens all the time. You know, the Terries shoot down a Krll fighter. The Krll shoot down a Terry transport." He patted one of the CAFARD-marked canisters. "Got these off a Terry transport that went down not fifty *slotches* from here. Figured they made great conversation pieces for the office."

"I was wondering. Concordiat Armed Forces Artillery Resupply Deployment crates aren't usually found in private service, conversationally or otherwise. Have any of you tried to open these things?"

"Well, I heard some folks over in Zoxxtown were going to try, only Zoxxtown isn't there anymore. We figured maybe it was best not to be too curious about magic-packages-from-sky."

"A very wise policy when it comes to military supplies recovered in the field. I suggest you remain incurious about such things unless you want to do some major urban renewal."

"Nah. We like our 'burg the way it is, thanks. So, anyway . . . what do you need from us?"

"I'd like to hook up with my own people, eventually," Retief said. "But there's no immediate rush. Maybe you could draw me a map of the area . . . show me where the Krll are, the Terries . . ."

"Well, we could, if we knew what that 'map' thing was. Remember. We Bloggies are not primitive, but we're, like, innocent in the Ways of the Galaxy."

"I have a feeling you're learning fast, Glom-gloob. Skip the map. If you can give me a guide to the nearest Terry lines, that would be great."

"Can do, Retief."

"First, though, I'd really like to see one of your foo-foo fields."

"Nothing easier. Come on."

4

Foo-foo shrubs were joyweed. There was no doubt about it.

"These're just about ready for harvest," Glom-gloob told him. "Have a taste!"

Retief kneeled beside one of the plants, examining the leaves. They were rich, dark, and glistening, much healthier looking than the sickly specimens he'd seen at Camp Concentration.

He looked up at the brassy overcast. The ambient temperature was probably around a hundred degrees. The overcast blocked out a great deal of the local star's overly enthusiastic light quota, and the ozone layer around this planet was thick enough to handle a lot of the ultraviolet. Still, this field must be sizzling under enough UV to burn an unprotected human in moments. Only the nanotechnic sunblock he was wearing protected him from that torrent of dangerous, invisible radiation.

"Thank you, no," Retief replied after a moment. He examined the leaves closely. They were glossy and black—designed to absorb as much energy as possible, both visible and ultraviolet. They must store a lot of that energy chemically, making them a good source of nutrition for the local grazing population. "I get enough psychoactive chemicals in my bloodstream from the embassy coffee service during Tuesday morning staff meetings."

"Suit yourself." Glom-gloob positioned himself directly over a fair-sized plant, squatted suddenly, and took a chomp with his ventral mouth. He straightened his legs again, chewing reflectively. "Mmm. Piquant . . . sweetly robust . . . a bit smoky . . . but with character . . . and just a hint of after-burn. Needs just a dash of sulfur."

"You're quite the connoisseur when it comes to foo-foo plants," Retief observed.

"Yeah, well, when you're just emerging from savagery and don't have all the advantages of full-fledged civilization yet, you find yourself with a lot of time on your hands, right? Us Bloggies don't go in for war and armies and all of that, so until we have our own museums and theaters and water-slide theme parks and all the other accoutrements of higher culture, some of us make do with what we've got."

"Foo-foo cultivation."

"Right. In fact . . ." Glom-gloob broke off. "Uh-oh. We'd best get ourselves under cover, Retief. There's a storm blowing in."

He gestured with one foot-hand. Perhaps a mile away, rising above the surrounding forest in the south, a solitary gleaming figure of black and red metal advanced with ponderous strides.

"Unless I'm mistaken," Retief said with interest, "that is a Krll Type-70 Deathwalker combat unit."

"It's Krll and it's dangerous, is all we need to know," Glom-gloob told him. "Come on!"

They hid themselves behind an upended boulder at the northern edge of the foo-foo field. The giant walker crashed out of the trees a moment later, towering above the field. The machine stood at least forty feet tall on two massively jointed legs that covered the ground in ten-foot strides. The body of the thing was an armored behemoth studded with gun emplacements and missile launchers. A squat dome of a turret had the look of a long-nosed head on top, pivoting back and forth as though sniffing out its prey. With each step, an immense foot hit the field with a thud that sent shivers through the ground, mashing foo-foo plants and leaving size 120 triple-K footprints among the furrows.

Eighty yards away, the giant stopped, its turret rotating to face the west. Retief heard a shrill, high-pitched whistling sound. "Down!" he snapped, and the two flattened themselves behind the boulder. Explosions ripped across the foo-foo field, great gouts of smoke and flame and earth hurtling into the sky, savage detonations rocking the ground with hammer-blow concussions.

"Hoo-boy, there goes the old foo-foo crop," Glom-gloob said.

The Krll giant returned fire, clouds of rockets leaping from flashing tubes, the fusion weapon in the turret loosing a crackling thunderbolt, smaller laser batteries flashing and flickering as they sought their distant foe.

"Screw the foo-foo," the Bloggie added. "There goes *us* if they get any closer!"

"This is just a light skirmish," Retief told him. "That's probably a Krll scout . . . and he's just encountered a Terran patrol."

"If this is a skirmish, I don't want to see what a battle is like!"

"Considering that the life expectancy of an unarmored being on the modern battlefield is something like three point one seconds . . . no. We don't. Come on. Let's wiggle back into those woods."

Two more Krll giants appeared on the southern horizon, and moments later, several dozen smaller combat walkers emerged from the trees on the far side of the field—six-foot-tall suits of armor, garishly painted and mounting a variety of rocket launchers and energy guns.

"That must be the Krll combat infantry," Retief observed. "They're escalating."

"I heard about that escalating," Glom-gloob said as he worked his way toward the woods. "That's like these moving stairs inside houses, right? Another example of technologically advanced civilization, no doubt. Only I don't know what stairs are, and I don't think I'd want them moving around inside my house even if I did."

Tri-winged bat-shapes howled low overhead, spilling anti-ground cluster munitions in sparkling, tumbling clouds of destruction, spreading pyrotechnic devastation through the advancing Krll ranks. Squat, tracked crawlers emerged from the forest to the south and east, deadly antiair particle guns deploying as casemate hatches unfolded. Retief and the Bloggie kept crawling, as lightning bolts clawed at the Terran aerospace fighters shrieking overhead.

Once in the woods, the two could stand upright and make a fair pace away from the spreading battle and back toward the town. Explosions continued to boom and rumble behind them, though, close enough to rattle teeth and send clouds of small, black and blue leaves from the tree canopy overhead raining down on the forest floor.

A moment later, a Krll deathwalker crashed through the trees behind them, smashing aside branches, splintering trunks in a flat-out run. Explosions ripped through the armored torso from behind, blowing the turret clean off the top of the machine and sending the rest of it toppling forward with an appalling crash. The Krll combat machine lay still, then, smoke pouring from the craters in its back. A low, deadly rumble from the edge of the forest suggested that whatever had just killed the Krll machine was coming in to make sure of its victim.

Retief and Glom-gloob kept running.

The sounds of battle had dwindled away by the time the two reached the edge of Xixthezonx once more. Retief put a hand out and thumped Glom-gloob's horny hide, though, to get his attention. "Hold up, there, Glom-gloob," he said. "I think we've got troubles."

"Like what? . . . Oh!"

"Yeah. Oh.

"I'm sorry, Glom-gloob," Retief said. "It looks like we've managed to destroy your city. . . ."

5

They stood at the top of a hill looking down into Glom-gloob's
city. Smoke curled up from the shattered ruin of Xixthezonx, stain-
ing the morning overcast. The chameleonetting that had hidden
the place from the air had been shredded to tatters. Many of the
delicate mushroom houses had been blasted by heavy weapons
and left burning. Others had been brushed aside by the massive,
multi-tracked vehicle squatting near the center of the town.

"What in floog is that big, black thing in the middle of my
city?" Glom-gloob wanted to know.

"It's called a Bolo," Retief explained. "A Bolo, Mark XVIII
Gladius, to be specific."

"Yeah, that's what it's called, but what is it? Looks to me like
it took out half of Main Street!"

"It's an intelligent tank," Retief told him. "That model masses
ten thousand tons and is as long as a small city block. With a
single 60cm Hellbore in a dorsal turret and mounting six 25cm
howitzers, a heavy vertical launch system, and twelve ion-bolt
infinite repeaters in the hull, the Gladius is top-of-the-line Concordiat military weaponry, the robotic equivalent of an army
division in one relatively small, mobile package."

"Hoo, boy! You say that like you mean it, Retief."

"That's what the advertising brochure says. Unfortunately, it
looks like that small, mobile package decided to move into the
center of your city and, in doing so, took out a big chunk of the
infrastructure." Retief could see that Glom-Gloob's office had been
toppled and crushed, his wall-to-wall dried-mud carpeting and
priceless Groaci nose flute collection destroyed.

Armored ground troops swarmed around the behemoth's massive, twenty-foot-high track assemblies, seeming antlike by comparison. It looked as though they'd cordoned off the grounded escape pod where it had landed.

"Damn, I'm sorry, Glom-gloob," Retief added.

"Ah. It ain't like it hasn't happened before," the big creature said with a philosophic shrug of three of its nonexistent shoulders. "It'll happen again. We'll just grow new houses, is all. Looks to me like all the Bloggies got out. They would have high-tentacled it for the woods as soon as they heard the first shots."

"Yeah, but I have a feeling that I was the cause of this. See how they've surrounded the escape pod? It must have had a homing transmitter onboard. Most of them do, to call for help after they touch down. I'd be willing to bet that the SOS that thing was putting out called in both the CAF and the Krll, brought 'em right smack into your city."

"So how were you to know? You didn't have any control over where you landed, right?"

"No . . ."

"Don't excrete large amounts of temperature-regulating fluids over it, then."

"Glom-gloob . . . don't let *anyone* tell you you're not civilized. I know diplomats of the peace-at-any-price persuasion who wouldn't take such an even view of things. Come on."

They made their way down the hill and out of the forest, emerging at the edge of the shattered Bloggie town. A half-dozen Terran troopers rushed up immediately, weapons at the ready. "Halt! Hands in the air!"

"That may be a little tough for my friend, here," Retief told them. "He doesn't have hands."

The soldiers were wearing Mark XII battlesuits; the protective visors on their helmets gleamed a mirror-polished black, protecting them from the planet's harsh UV radiation. It meant Retief couldn't see their eyes or facial expressions.

"C'mon, you two," a soldier with sergeant's chevrons on his armor growled. "We're takin' you two to see The Man."

The Man was Colonel Shaun Surecock, commanding officer of

the 1294th Infantry, "The Irascibles," standing in the shadow of the titanic Bolo. The combat ribbons and decorations painted on the left breast of his body armor reached from shoulder almost all the way to hip.

"What have we here, Sergeant?" he demanded.

"Caught 'em comin' through the perimeter back there, Colonel. Thought you'd want to interrogate 'em."

"Damned straight!" The colonel unsealed his helmet visor and raised it, revealing a craggy face and eyes turned disturbingly black by anti-UV drops. His nostrils flared as he took a deep breath of the smoky, fetid jungle air, and then he reached out and fondly slapped the mud-coated track of the monster war machine beside him. "Ahh . . . I love the hot-metal smell of combat Bolos in the morning!"

"Smells like a burning native city to me, Colonel," Retief observed.

"Nonsense! The autochthones don't have cities . . . only temporary jungle encampments and the occasional quaint native village. They grow 'em made to order. We've burned hundreds of the things while trying to help these poor, benighted creatures, and it never bothers 'em. But enough about the damned starfish." He fixed his hawklike gaze on Retief. "You!" he barked. "What the devil are you doing on this pesthole planet?"

"Trying to make contact with the Peace Enforcer authorities, Colonel," Retief answered. "My ship crashed here a few hours ago."

"A castaway, eh? And what were you doing inside restricted space over a planet under military interdiction in the first place? Overflying a war zone? Criminal trespass? You, my friend, are in a very large world of trouble!" His gaze shifted to Glom-gloob. "And what the devil is *that*? The horse you rode in on?"

"This is one of the beings you're here to help, Colonel."

"Eh? Where's its head?"

"The Bloggies don't have heads, Colonel. They seem to get along fine without them. Don't you know what the local sapient species looks like?"

"Eh? Local sappy what?" The sergeant whispered something to

him. "Oh! The natives! Of course I do. Don't be ridiculous. Didn't recognize the critter with those silly monocles, is all."

"Well, Colonel, may I present to you His Excellency Glom-gloob, the mayor of this city."

"I told you, mister, the natives don't *have* cities! How can this creature be mayor of something they don't even have? Get the wax out of your ears!"

"Well, whatever you call it, Glom-gloob here was the being-in-charge."

"I *called* it a temporary encampment or quaint native village, damn it. Don't you listen? And this Gloob fellow's not in charge. *I* am!"

"Colonel, I think—"

"Damn it, you don't think unless I give you the *order* to think! Now...the problem with these native villages is they're not safe! Too prone to catching fire or falling down! An alien could get hurt that way! That's why PACMAN has instituted the Program for Inviolable Safe Housing in Traditional and Utilitarian Secure Hamlets. As tax-funded social engineering it's absolutely visionary! Nice, solid, poured ferrocrete structures, with actual doors and windows! Genuine plastic furniture and lawn ornaments! Tidy and neat; clean ferrocrete floors instead of dried mud! A choice of tasteful Military Gray or relaxing Institutional Gray paint! A secure, happy adventure in resettlement camp living, where the Odious natives can learn the benefits of culture and civilization...and keep the hell out of the military's way!"

Encouraged, perhaps, by the sight of their mayor in conversation with the Terries, more and more natives were emerging from the forest, waving blue Concordiat flags and displaying TERRY DON'T GO HOME signs.

"Welcome, Terries!" someone cried out from the edge of the jungle in a weak voice.

"Hurray?" cried another, sounding somewhat uncertain.

The massive Bolo stirred ever so slightly beside the colonel. High overhead, the barrels of its infinite repeaters swung about to cover the newcomers. "Possible perimeter threat detected," a flat, emotionless voice said from somewhere overhead. "Antipersonnel routine engaged. Targets locked. Awaiting fire order."

"Sergeant! Clear that rabble away!" Surecock snapped. "I want my secure perimeter *secure!*" He patted the Bolo's track again. "Betsy, here, might get nervous, and we wouldn't want *that* to happen now, would we?"

"I'd hate to think what GNN would say about it, Colonel," the sergeant said. Turning, he gave orders to his men, who spread out and began muscling the natives back into the woods.

"There, there, that's a *good* girl," Surecock crooned, stroking the robot war machine's tread. He looked at Retief again. "Are you still here? I thought you were under arrest!"

"Not yet, Colonel. You were telling me about the wonders of PISH-TUSH."

"Ah. Yes. Well, the program is already under way. The 1043rd Division—'The Big, Red One Thousand Forty-Three'—will be coming through later today to round up all of the natives and herd them . . . I mean, *escort* them to their happy new homes. And that will leave *us* free to get down to depleted-uranium tacks, as in hunting Krll!"

"A program to warm the cockles of any military heart," Retief said. "We all know how much compassion the military has for the local folks, and it sounds to me, Colonel, as if you're full of it."

"Damned straight! Our first mission imperative is to stop those warmongering Krll, but our *second* imperative is to protect the autochthones from Krll predation! We're here to make Odiousita V safe for the Odiousitans, and we're going to do it, by Heaven, if we have to raze the jungle and burn down every temporary encampment and quaint native village they have!"

"I see. A visionary program, to be sure."

"Damned straight!"

"Would you excuse me a moment, Colonel?" He walked over to Glom-gloob, who was waiting several feet away. Despite his philosophical outlook, he looked a bit mournful at the destruction. "Mr. Mayor," Retief whispered, "I suggest you go off into the forest and round up all of your people you can find. Take them into the deep woods. Don't let them take you back to their resettlement centers."

"But, Retief!" Glom-gloob protested. "The colonel said these were places where we Bloggies could learn all about modern civilization!"

"I'm afraid you might learn *too* much in that regard. Trust me on this one, and stay low."

"Okay, Retief." He sounded doubtful. "If you say so."

"I do."

Glom-gloob walked off toward the edge of the jungle.

"Here, now!" Surecock said. "Where is that fellow going?"

"To round up his fellows, Colonel. Makes things easier on all concerned."

"Ah. Have them ready and assembled for the Big, Red One Thousand Forty-Three, eh? Good thinking!" He studied Retief closely. "But enough of pleasantries. What am I to do with you? This is no place for weaseling civilians, no matter how helpful!"

"I might suggest sending me back to headquarters, Colonel. I could arrange for a hop on the next transport back to B'rukley."

"Oh, you're going to headquarters, all right, but not to hitch joyrides on a military transport! G-2 is going to want to grill you about what you're doing in a damned war zone. Trouble is, I can't spare anyone to escort you right now, and I've got to scout forward and see where the front lines've gotten to."

"What's the matter, Colonel? Did you lose them?"

"The civilian mind has no concept of the complexities of modern warfare! This quaint village is now in the far rear of the lines! The lines are fluid and rapidly moving! I need to know where they are if I am to properly assess the situation in order to bring the Krll to heel and destroy them!"

"We'll keep an eye on this fellow until you get back, Colonel," the sergeant said. "We're on break, but we don't mind."

"Break?" Retief asked, one eyebrow rising.

"Good union," the NCO explained. "Soldiers, Sailors, and Aerospace Pilots Amalgamated, Local hup234. They negotiated a great package for the common soldier, including regular coffee and dopestick breaks, regular weekend passes, and liberal looting and pillaging benefits."

"Okay, Sergeant," Surecock said. "But keep your eye on him! I don't like his looks."

"That's just because I haven't had my morning coffee yet, Colonel."

"We will talk later." A light scout helo touched down a few dozen yards away, and Surecock marched, ramrod stiff, across the street and climbed onboard.

"And good riddance!" the sergeant said as the helo rose into the sky and headed east.

6

An hour later, Retief rested in the shade of the Bolo, talking with some of the soldiers of the 1294th. They'd removed helmets and gauntlets and set aside weapons, and now, with the exception of Sergeant Caldwilder, the grizzled NCO, who was their platoon leader, they looked considerably less formidable than they had earlier. The oldest might have been in his mid-twenties. The youngest couldn't have been over nineteen.

"So, Retief," Caldwilder said. "You're over here from B'rukley?"

"That I am, Sarge. You might call it a bit of diplomatic reconnaissance."

"CDT, huh?" He nodded. "Our CO was stationed with them a few years ago."

"Surecock was with the *Corps Diplomatique*?"

"Nah, not him. *His* commanding officer is General Warbutton. He was a military liaison with the diplomatic johnnies for a while."

"Cecil Warbutton?" Retief nodded. "I was assigned with him to the peace conference on Lumbaga. He was the military attaché with the Terran delegation."

"Well, well. Small galaxy, ain't it?"

"Got his star at last, eh? He was just a bird-colonel on Lumbaga."

"Yeah. I just wish he pulled a bit more mass with the REMFs."

"REMFs?"

"The Rear-Echelon Mentally Feeble," the sergeant replied. "The ones who make the political decisions that stick guys like us out here on pestholes like this one!"

"Well, sure . . . but how do you really feel, Sarge?"

"If'n you're CDT, sir," one of the kids in battle armor said, "mebee you can tell us what's goin' on!"

"What's the matter, son?" Retief asked. "Don't they fill you in on what's happening?"

"Shoot. I guess we get to watch GNN, just like everyone, leastwise when we're back in the barracks. We see the peace demonstrations and everything. Looks like no one wants this war in the first place!"

"Ah-ah," Caldwilder warned. "Not 'war,' Toby. 'Police action.' We're policemen now, remember?"

"Whatever you call it, the folks back home don't want us here . . . and neither do we, come to think of it!"

"Where are you from?" Retief asked.

"Newbraska. It's an agro colony about fifty lights—"

"I've heard of it. You happen to know a guy, about your age, by the name of Zippie?"

"Huh? Zippie Zeigler? Sure! He's my best friend! We grew up together back home in Dead End! We wuz goin' to Cornfed Veterinary, Horticultural, and Miscellaneous College of Conservative Arts together . . . only I ran out of money and had to drop out. How'd you run into old Zip?"

"Met him at a peace march, over on B'rukley."

"Shoot! What's he doin' mixed up with demonstrators?"

"Wasn't he part of the antiwar movement where you came from?"

"Heck, no! Though he did say there was these people—SMERCH, I think he called 'em—who had some good arguments. I dunno. I never cared much for politics."

"Make love, not war!" a private said. "That's my kind of politics!"

"Huh!" Caldwilder said. "Let's see those demonstrators make love not war with a fifty-foot *Glaag*-class death commando warwalker!"

"Point is," another of the soldiers, a corporal, said glumly, "is why are we fighting this w—this police action? Hellfire, ain't no one who hates war more than the soldiers who gotta fight in it!"

"Yeah," Caldwilder said, "but it helps to know your own folks are on your side, you know? Rooting for you on the home front, and all that."

"Me," another private said, "I don't trust those SMERCH people. Ever since their delegation got over here, we've been hearing about how great the Krll culture is and how they . . . lessee, how does it go? How 'the Krll culture have legitimate territorial aspirations with the Shamballa Cluster that should be respected and acceded to.' "

"What's SMERCH doing on Odiousita V?" Retief wanted to know.

"Beats me," the corporal said. "Negotiatin' with the Krll, I guess."

"It's just been one big lovefest over there since those SMERCH people arrived," Toby said "That GNN reporter . . . what's her name?"

"Desiree Goodeleigh."

"That's the one! She's been covering the festivities over at Krll headquarters and has nothin' but good things to say about them! Makes a guy feel kind of bad, y'know? Like he's not wanted, or somethin'!"

"Don't let it throw you, Toby," Retief told him. "Look at it this way. If they find a way to make peace with the Krll, you fellows get to go home."

"Shoot, mister, who wants that?" Toby said. "I joined the Army to get away from home in the first place! You have any idea how *boring* Newbraska is?"

"I think he means that you could leave home and not have ugly aliens trying to burn your tail off," Caldwilder pointed out.

"Oh. Yeah. Well, I could go for that, sure!"

Caldwilder snapped his fingers. "I just got it!"

"Is it catching?"

"No! You're Retief! You were all over the semilocal news a few nights ago! That Goodeleigh woman interviewed you, or somethin'!"

"I'm afraid she did. I believe it's called 'ambush journalism.'"

"I remember," the corporal said. "They caught you roughing up some peace demonstrators!"

"Only because they weren't being peaceful," Retief pointed out.

"Yeah, well, that makes you okay in *my* book," Caldwilder said. "It's about time someone beat some sense into them."

"Where is this Krll headquarters, anyway?" Retief asked.

"Up on the North Continent," Caldwilder told him. "On the Burning Sands Peninsula, north of the Sulfur Forest, about where it juts out into the Tepid Sea."

"Sounds like prime real estate."

"Well, not so much now after we went through there on the Fourth Summer Offensive last year. We kind of left our mark on the place."

"Yeah, Sarge, but then they kicked our tails all the way back to the Acid Ocean," the corporal pointed out.

"Maybe so, Willikers, but then we got them back at the big Mud Season Push."

"Until they stopped us at Hotfoot."

"You know, I love sitting around listening to war stories," Retief said, "but I think I need to talk to General Warbutton. Suppose you trust me with a flitter and point me at your HQ?"

Caldwilder looked at him askance. "Well, now, Retief, I dunno. We're supposed to keep an eye on you for ol' Half-cocked."

"C'mon, Sarge!" Toby said. "Retief's a good guy! Besides, he knows Zippie!"

"More to the point, he beat up some of Zippie's scatterbrained friends. I like that." He sighed, leaned back against the Bolo, and closed his eyes. "Still, our orders are to keep you here until the colonel gets back. Too bad. That could be a couple of days or more. And by then, HQ'll probably have been moved. Security, you know. Right now, it's three hundred kilometers west of here, in the Shrieking Jungle District. Hell, you wouldn't even be able to get there, lessen you borrowed one of the regimental scout flitters we got parked in the clearing back yonder." He folded his hands across his stomach. "So I guess there's nothin' to do but forget about it and wait for ol' Half-cocked to get back."

"I guess not, Sarge," Retief said. He stood up, dusting off his coveralls, then looked up at the silent Bolo. "How about your big, watchful friend here?"

"Ah, we switched her to inactive standby an hour ago. Otherwise she'd be pestering us every time a mouse wandered into the perimeter."

"I see. Well, I'm going for a stroll, Sarge."

"Have a nice one, Retief." He paused. "Just see nobody gets hurt, okay? Sign and countersign for the day are 'Cubs' and 'Winning Streak.'"

"Got it. Catch you later, guys."

And he walked off down the street, whistling softly.

CHAPTER SIX

1

"Cubs!" came the challenge. A lone sentry stood in front of the ready line for the unit's service flitters.

"Winning streak," Retief replied.

The youngster with the power rifle relaxed, letting the weapon's muzzle wander away from Retief's chest. "Advance and be recognized."

Retief stepped closer. He couldn't see the soldier's face behind the UV shield, but he sounded terribly young.

"Hey, mister. Ain't you the guy who came down out of the jungle with a starfish in tow about an hour ago?"

"That's me."

"Some of the fellows were talking about you. They say you shipped in here from B'rukley, that you were some sort of government big shot or something."

"I came here from B'rukley, yes. How big a shot I am, I can't

135

really say, though I tend to favor calibers of one millimeter or so."

"Yeah, but you were from the embassy back there, right?"

"Guilty as charged."

"They said you was an ambassador or something."

"That I can honestly say I am not. It seems that I lack the Vision that enables me to see the Big Picture."

The sentry fumbled with his visor lock, then raised the dark screen out of the way. Retief doubted that he was older than twenty. "Yeah, but you must know about the peace negotiations and everything! Mebee you can tell me what's going on!" His voice very nearly broke. "I heard they'd abandoned us here!"

"Where'd you hear that?"

"It was on GNN the other night."

"Well, one of the sad lessons of life is that things aren't necessarily true just because the anchor on the evening news says they are."

"Then . . . then help is coming? Or they're going to pull us out? Which is it?"

"I'm afraid even GNN doesn't know the answer to that one, son." He clapped the soldier on his armored shoulder. "But hang in there. Even bureaucrats and generals get it right once in a while."

He chose one of the flitters parked on the ready line, climbed up the metal rungs set in the side, and squeezed down into the cockpit. This time, at least, the seat was designed for a human, and not Groaci, frame. He settled the flight helmet onto his head, connected the oxygen, and slapped the line of ready switches to the on position.

"Hey, wait a sec, mister!" the sentry called. "You didn't show me your flight authorization!"

"Colonel Surecock has it," Retief replied. He eased the power bar forward, listening to the rising hum of the powerful turbines aft.

"Oh, okay. Uh . . . hey! Wait! He's not even—"

Retief tapped the side of his helmet and shook his head, indicating that he could not hear the sentry's shout. He waved the soldier back, then cycled the canopy shut. The soldier dithered for a moment, then backed away. Retief released the flight locks and pulled back on the joystick. On shrieking fan-jets, the flitter leaped into the sky.

2

The flitter was a UC-190 Pegasus, the airborne equivalent of the ubiquitous jeep of earlier centuries, unarmed, unarmored, and strictly subsonic, but undeniably rugged and built for the long haul. PACMAN HQ was listed in the navicom's memory, so he punched up its coordinates on the destination screen and leaned back, letting the flitter do the piloting.

For the next hour he flew west across unending vistas of jungle interspersed with occasional patches of swampland and great, meandering rivers steaming in the morning haze. The cloud cover on this world, he gathered, never broke; native vegetation had evolved to absorb a fair proportion of the high-energy ultraviolet radiation that was able to penetrate both the ozone layer and the multiple cloud decks. Twice he passed over clearings littered with the crumbled shells of native buildings, burned out and shattered by the waves of war that continued to surge back and forth across the face of the planet. Once he overflew an arm of the sea, gray, opaque, and scum-flecked, before going feet-dry above another stretch of impenetrable jungle.

PACMAN HQ was a mobile base, a structure of towers, spheres, masts, walkways, and platforms that could set down almost anywhere, on any terrain, then use repulsorlift technology to break free of earth or mud or ocean surface and drift slowly to another location. Multiple Hellbore turrets swiveled about to track him in, but the flitter's navicom sent out the appropriate IFF and clearance codes and guided the little flyer safely through the outer defenses and into the gaping maw of the headquarters' main landing facility, burrowed into the side of the largest of the structure's spheres.

A dozen soldiers in light armor trotted up to surround the flyer as it touched down on the white-painted landing grid. Retief popped the canopy, pulled off his helmet, and swung his legs over the side of the cockpit, feeling for the rungs.

An Army lieutenant faced him. "Are you Retief?"

"Yes, I am."

"I hereby place you under arrest, for absenting yourself from legitimate detention by authorized military authorities, willful disobedience to said military authority, willful and aggravated theft of military property, willful violation of airspace under military control, willful conduct prejudicial to good order and discipline, willful—"

"I take it Colonel Surecock got back from his search for the front lines early."

"Mister, you would not believe the hell you have just raised single-handedly on the commo channels. At one point, Colonel Surecock was calling for you to be shot down."

"Well, I'm grateful that you didn't. I'm here to see General Warbutton."

"If he sees you," the lieutenant said with just a touch of arrogance, "it will be in the stockade. Take him away, men!"

They marched Retief through the bowels of the headquarters structure to the detention cell block. He was expertly frisked and the power pistol he'd borrowed from the Groaci was taken away, as were his dopesticks, fingerwatch, and electronically enhanced clothing. He was given Army ODs and ushered into a cell at gunpoint.

"Tell General Warbutton that Jame Retief is here to see him."

"Maybe I will," the lieutenant said with a snigger. "Then again, maybe I won't. We'll see how I feel in a few days. . . ."

The cell door hissed shut, and the magnetic locks snapped home. Retief was left alone in the silence. He folded the sleeping cot out from the wall and sat down to wait.

In fact, he had less than an hour to wait. The locks opened, the door hissed open, and a Bloggie swept into the cell.

Or perhaps "mopped into the cell" was a more accurate description. The native looked identical to Glom-Gloob, save for the absence of any monocles, but he held a large and fluffy pink dust cloth at the tip of each of his six walking arms. He moved with a hexapodous grace, skating along on the cloths, polishing the already shiny linoleoplastic floor as he went.

"Greetings!" the being said as soon as the door hissed shut once more. "I am Glob-jlob the Magnisonant. Might you be the Terry they call Retief the Insouciant?"

"If I am, then news spreads awfully fast around here. How'd you happen to know my name?"

The heavy being gave an airy flip of one tentacled arm, flipping the dust cloth. "Ah, I heard it on the grapevine. Old Glom-gloob is my fifth cousin on my aunt Blib-blob's side, and we stay in touch."

"I'm pleased to meet you."

"Likewise. Glom said you were an okay being, for an offworlder. Listen, I ain't supposed to be in here, me being just the janitor, and all, but Glom wanted me to pass on to you that Colonel Surecock came back and that he seems a bit upset that you left without saying a proper good-bye."

"So I gather."

"He says to watch yourself, 'cause the colonel said something about having you arrested and shot at sunrise."

"That's a good trick. You can't even see the sun on your world, so how do you see it rise?"

"Huh? Sure you can! We Bloggies can, anyway. I heard you Terries can't see fleem-wavelengths, though. Maybe all you see is the floomph-wavelengths scattered through the cloud layer."

"We call fleem-wavelengths 'ultraviolet light,' and, no, we can't."

"I'm sorry to hear that. Must be tough going around half-blind."

"Oh, we manage okay. If you don't mind my saying so, Glob-jlob, you seem extremely well-versed in basic physics."

"For a janitor, you mean? Well, janitoring is just my hobby, you know. I took the test and became a G-4 civilian contract employee just so I could learn more about this civilization stuff you Terries and Gruckies and Krll and GOSHies are always talking about."

"I see. And what have you learned?"

"That civilized folks like their floors brightly polished so's they can eat off of them and see their faces in them . . . whatever 'faces' are. That civilized folks like something they call 'war' and get a real kick out of blowing things up and racking up high numbers in something they call a 'body count.' That wrongdoers should be tortured by locking them up away from the jungle instead of cleanly *xanthering* their souls. That they like their ashtrays and wastebaskets emptied every night, while they're not around, but don't want their desks touched. That they have some really cool toys and gadgets that they like to play with. That they define civilization by comparisons with other folks rather than by specific accomplishments—like saying '*we're* more civilized than *they* are.' That some of their ideas about what constitutes civilization are really quite weird . . . like living in houses you build instead of grow, or having linoleoplastic on your floors instead of mud, or wearing artificial integuments instead of going au naturel. That the point of civilization is something called 'making money,' though we haven't figured out yet what this money thing is, though it might have to do with something called a 'tab,' or maybe 'credit.' That—"

Retief held up his hand. "I get the picture, Glob-jlob. I've been watching civilization myself for a few years, and, just between you and me, I'd have to say that the stuff isn't as great as some folks make it out to be. You Bloggies stick with what works for you, okay? Don't rush things."

"Sure, Retief. Thanks. Glom-gloob said you'd understand. Say . . . is this your house while you're here? Seems kind of cramped."

"Actually, Colonel Surecock sent word to have me locked up. I'm not sure if he's going to have my soul xanthered or not. I guess the jury's still out on that one."

"What? That's outrageous!" He pulled a small, plastic card from an unseen pouch in his hide. "Here, you want out?"

"Actually, I want to talk to General Warbutton, and I'm not sure the lieutenant who put me here is going to pass the word up that I'm here. Would you be willing to deliver a message for me?"

"Sure thing, Retief! Anything for a friend of my fifth cousin!"

"Just tell him that I'm here, and mention my name. He'll remember who I am."

"Got it."

"I am curious about one thing. A moment ago, you mentioned offworlders . . . Gruckies and GOSHies and Krll."

"Oh, my," Glob-jlob replied. "Did I?"

"I wonder if you could tell me about the GOSHies. Just where do they hang out, and with whom?"

"Well, I'm not supposed to say . . . but since you know about them already, I guess it can't hurt to tell you that they have what they call a trading enclave up on the North Continent, at a place called Glooberville."

"Mm. Burning Sands Peninsula on the Tepid Sea? North of the Sulfur Forest?"

"Yeah!" Glob-jlob said brightly. "You know the place?"

"I've heard it mentioned. It wouldn't be at the Krll military headquarters, would it?"

"Glooberville? Nah. But close. The town's a couple *glrbs* south down the road from Krll headquarters, as the *vlavvervat* flies. There's a . . . a whatchamacallit . . . a Krll fortress protecting an offworlder spaceport north of town, and that's their HQ. Some GOSH-awful character they call Mr. Bug runs things out of the spaceport's warehouse district, right next door."

"Mr. Bug works with the Krll?"

"Like arm in hoobie-sleeve."

"Interesting. What about the Gruckies? Do they work with the Krll?"

"Funny thing, that. They used to, but lately they've taken to freelancing on their own. Been taking foo-foo shrubs from fifth-cousin Glom-gloob's fields and putting it on top of the tab, whatever that is."

"So I heard. Where do they hang out?"

"They've got a . . . dang. Don't remember the word. Oh, yeah, an embosserie in downtown Glooberville."

"Excellent. Thanks for the information, Glob-jlob. And for passing on my message."

"Don't mention it! Always happy to help out a fellow civilization-watcher!"

"Just watch out that civilization doesn't run over you while you're watching it."

3

Fifteen minutes after Glob-jlob left, General Cecil Warbutton stepped into the cell.

"Retief! They told me it was you!"

"Hello, General. It's been a long time since Lumbaga."

"That it has."

"Sorry I can't offer you anything but the bed to sit on. The furnishings here are just a bit on the spartan side."

He waved the apology aside. "I came down as soon as I heard it was you. The *janitor* told me, of all things!"

"I figured if I'd made as big a splash as that lieutenant said I did, someone would get around to telling you I was here sooner or later. I'm glad it was sooner."

"You are in a heap of trouble, you know," Warbutton told him. "Some of the charges are just plain silly. You're not in the Army, so they can't hang you for disobeying the orders of a superior officer. But you did violate half a dozen regs involving government employees and the command authority in an area under martial law. And you stole a flitter."

"That's a debatable point," Retief said, "since I brought the flitter straight here. To see you, I might add. When I heard you were in command over here, I knew I had to come see you. Congratulations on the promo, by the way."

"Thank you. Somehow, though, I get the feeling you didn't come all the way here, risking arrest, antiaircraft fire, and Colonel Surecock's fury, just to say that."

"Nope. What do you say we reconvene in your office to discuss things?"

He shook his head. "I'm sorry, Retief. Comrades-at-arms, brothers-in-the-trenches, and all of that, you *did* violate regs. Government employees and civil servants are under military authority in active war zones."

"I know. What does that have to do with me?"

"Damn it, you're a . . . what? Second reserve undergraduate assistant third secretary, or something? You're CDT!"

"Actually," Retief said, examining the shine on his fingernails, "I'm not. You might say I was fired and am now a free agent."

Warbutton looked horrified. "You're . . . you're a *civilian*?"

"An unemployed civilian. And while I *am* subject to martial law, I was with the head of the local native government when Surecock met me."

"So? What's your point?"

"So it's still an open question as to whether I was under Surecock's authority or the authority of Glom-Gloob the Effervescent, Mayor and Grand Poobah of the fair Bloggie metropolis of Xixthezonx. I'd say that the question is complex enough that it would take a military tribunal to sort things out, at the very least, and possibly a joint tribunal with the Bloggie authorities."

"But—"

"The legality of my detention was questionable at best," he said, ticking the points off on his fingers. "We can throw out the theft charge. I brought the flitter here on official business, so it was neither willful nor aggravated theft. It was a military vehicle operating under autopilot with valid IFF and clearance codes, so I wasn't violating restricted airspace . . . at least, not technically. If I was, the codes would have been blocked. There is at least reasonable doubt that I was under Surecock's authority at all. So why am I being held?"

"How could you be here on official business if you're here as a civilian?"

"You're an official of the Concordiat Armed Forces. I'm working, among other things, on behalf of Mayor Glom-Gloob, who is a Bloggie official. I wanted to talk to you about official business. So what could be more official than that?"

"My court-martial." Warbutton shook his head. "Retief, did anyone ever tell you that you were a damned space lawyer?"

"I've served as consul for several Terry ambassadorial delegations, so I suppose that makes me a de facto lawyer in space. What's *your* point?"

"No, I mean . . . never mind. Look, if I sign the order to spring you out of here, will you stay out of trouble and do what you're told?"

"I'll promise to let my conscience be my guide."

"Uh-uh. Not good enough. I watched you work on Lumbaga. I'm not sure you *have* a conscience, at least where your superiors are concerned. . . ."

"I'll promise to obey all lawful orders that are in my best interests."

Warbutton stared at Retief for a long moment, then laughed. "On your own head be it! You always were a damned maverick son of a gun!" He turned to the door and touched the intercom panel. "Guard! Let us out of here!"

4

In Warbutton's palatial, deep-shag office high atop the headquarters facility's main sphere, they sat down in overstuffed chairs with a couple of glasses of Bacchian black.

"Actually," Retief told the general, "I came to Odiousita V to check up on the drug ring that's operating off of this world."

"Drug ring?"

"Have you heard the name 'Mr. Bug'?"

Warbutton nodded. "We've had intel briefings on him. Some

kind of local GOSH honcho, isn't he? Looks like a giant cock-roach? No one ever sees him except on a com screen?"

"That's our man . . . or bug, rather." Retief struck a dopestick alight. "The natives here grow joyweed. Mr. Bug is getting sup-plies of it somewhere and smuggling it back to B'rukley in tramp freighters. They're distributing it to the students at USC and to the kids coming in for the peace rallies under SMERCH spon-sorship."

"Okay," Warbutton said, but sounding unsure. "Um . . . but what does this have to do with us? We're here to save this planet from the Krll, not chase local drug lords." He stopped, and his eyes widened. "You're not saying we should stop the natives from grow-ing the stuff, are you? Burn their crops, that sort of thing?"

"Absolutely not. Joyweed is the staple of the natives' diet. It's bad enough we're destroying their cities in the process of saving them from the Krll. If we destroy their number-one menu item as well, we destroy *them*."

"Mm. I don't know. PISH-TUSH—you know the program? PISH-TUSH is designed to provide the locals with secure hamlets in which to live, get them out of those homegrown villages of theirs out in all of that nasty jungle and stuff. But I wonder how Sector would view things if they knew the natives were grow-ing drugs on their PISH-TUSH mandated-and-tax-guck-paid-for reservations. There could be some serious fallout there, public-relationswise."

"The Bloggies need food, not spin."

"Yeah, but maybe we could provide an ample dietary supplement. I know Sector has been pushing for a month to get an economic development package set up and running on Odiousita V."

"What does that have to do with what they eat?"

"Oh, part of the package would include offworld fast-food franchises. You know—McWendyking's Arbycastleburgers, that sort of thing. The program allows the native culture to shift to a monetary standard and provides entry-level jobs for native children after school and during summers."

Retief arched one eyebrow. "Sector is planning on genocide by fast food?"

"Nah. Nothing like that. They'd tailor the menu to local tastes."

"Joyweedburgers? I don't think Sector would go for that."

"I didn't mean that." His eyes narrowed. "The natives really need to eat joyweed? I mean . . . they'd starve without it?"

"I know some of them are epicureans when it comes to the subtle nuances of the stuff. In any case, General, it might be illegal to transport joyweed on the space lanes governed by Terran law, but joyweed is not illegal on Odiousita V . . . or on B'rukley, for that matter."

"I know. It's not under Army jurisdiction. Stopping the local drug traffic is *not* in my job description."

"Nor is it your right to change native culture, biology, or eating preferences to suit you, the Army, or anybody else. That is explicit in the Each Being to His/Her/Its Own Poison Act, as determined by the kosher-diet-in-alien-foods decision, Zarxl-grubber versus Jones, Goldstein, and the Terran Government, et al, 2615."

"Like I said. A space lawyer."

"Only in the cause of truth, justice, and the *amicus* way. Speaking of friends, were you aware that the Krll are into joyweed cultivation as well?"

"No! Where'd you hear that?"

"A reliable source."

"Which means either somebody's cousin," Warbutton said, nodding, "or George, the janitor. And George isn't here."

"Right. It also means that investigating Krll cultivation and export of an interdicted drug falls under Army jurisdiction."

A tone sounded from Warbutton's desk. He pushed a button. "What is it?"

"Sir," a secretary's voice said. "You might want to check GNN. She's at it again."

"Desiree Goodeleigh?" Retief asked as the general swiveled his chair to face the floor-to-ceiling wall screen.

He sighed. "Who else? She's been a damned pain in the asteroids lately. Let's hear what she has to say now. Screen on, GNN!"

The wall screen lit up, revealing the looming face of the GNN reporter, complete with a four-foot-wide and dazzling-white array of perfect teeth.

" . . . in this continuing costly struggle on the world of Odiousita V," the mouth holding those teeth was saying. "The Supreme Warlord of the Assault of the Righteous Fist, Lord General Kreplach, has graciously agreed to talk with me here, at the Supreme Warlord's headquarters encampment on Odiousita V, live on GNN. So tell me, General Kreplach . . ."

"That is *Lord* General Kreplach, Desiree," a deep basso profundo boomed from the screen. "We must observe the amenities of formal protocol, you know."

"Oh, yes. Forgive me, *Lord* General."

The camera shifted and pulled back to show the Krll warlord, an imposing, humanoid figure clad entirely in a gleaming black-and-silver metal environmental suit. With Desiree Goodeleigh as a yardstick, he stood perhaps seven feet tall. The massive helmet bore a deeply recessed visor from which a single bloodred light glowed like a baleful eye.

"Thank you, Desiree," the warlord rumbled on. The *whish* and *whoosh* of a breathing unit could be heard behind the words as he raised a shiny finger to emphasize his point. "Remember! Without proper protocol, civilization as we know it would crumble! The effects of such a collapse would be catastrophic . . . war! Famine! Disease! Earthquake! Economic uncertainty! Cannibalism in the streets! Suns going nova! Wholesale reruns on the telly! A drop in the Dow Jones! Unthinkable depravity on Saturday morning television! . . ."

"Yes, well . . . Lord General Kreplach, can you tell our viewers, please, just why you have come here to Odiousita V? There are some who claim that your arrival here is an inherently aggressive act, an act of war, in fact."

"Slanderous muckraking heretical lies and *damned* lies of an evil, viciously degraded and morally bankrupt . . ." The gleaming figure paused, and the single red eye seemed to glance at the camera. "Um . . . that is to say . . . how silly! I mean, it is well known that the peaceful community of beings of the Greater Krll Prosperity Sphere seek only to live in harmony with our neighbors, no matter how lowly, primitive, or militarily insignificant they might be. It was the warmongering troublemakers of the Terran Concordiat that attacked us when first we visited sunny Blmcht . . . that is the Krll name for what you Terries mistakenly call Odiousita V, by the way."

"Of course, Lord General. Tell me, though . . . some anti-Krll voices claim you have no business at all in the Shamballa Cluster. What would you tell your critics?"

"That they are dead! Dead! *Dead!* That we will hunt them down, singly and collectively, and destroy them utterly! That we will burn their cities, eat their children, enslave their dead, annihilate their planets, foreclose their mortgages—" Again, he paused, stared into the camera, then said, "Excuse me, please." He opened a small panel on the chest of his armor and fiddled with some wires. "I believe my translator program is giving me some trouble. Ah. There we go. Our critics, you were saying? Why, I would merely point out that the worlds we Krll favor are those with environments approximating conditions obtained within the Galactic Core. Out here in the relatively unpopulated stellar wilderness, ambient radiation levels are far lower than those to which we are used. Few indeed are the suns worthy of the name that can provide us with the radiation levels we need! But a few choice stars do exist with sufficient X-ray and ultraviolet in their spectra to enable us to eke out a poor and impoverished existence, energywise. The star around which Blmcht orbits is such a sun . . . a bit on the cool, dim side, but marginally capable of sustaining Krll-type life. We find Blmcht somewhat chilly, but since the world is uninhabited . . ."

"But Lord General," Desiree said. "Odiousita . . . that is, Blimcht *is* inhabited!"

" 'Blmcht,' Desiree, not 'Blimcht.' "

"Ah, yes. Thank you."

"As for native life, our scientists have seen no evidence that this is so," the lord general replied stiffly. "There is no native intelligence on Blmcht."

"There is no native intelligence on Blmcht," the reporter repeated.

"Very good. There are, of course, some quite clever animals living in close symbiosis with the jungle. A fascinating species, really, and one which our scientists will continue to study closely. But the fact remains that we have here a world you Terries cannot use because of your extreme sensitivity to those parts of the electromagnetic spectrum you call ultraviolet. It is uninhabited, save for those aforementioned clever animals, and yet you Terries attempt to block our lawful colonization of a world that is, to us, almost like home! It's not fair! How many millions of innocent Krll must die at the claws of the Terry war machine before Enlightened Galactic Opinion intervenes and ends this wholesale aggression against an innocent species? Remember! The sinister and self-serving Terries are the aggressors in this war!"

"Are you aware, Lord General Kreplach, that the Mauve House insists that this is not a war . . . but a police action?"

"So! The perfidious Terries think of the mighty Krll as mere criminals to be arrested? They are waging war upon innocent Krll females and grubs! But the Greater Krll Prosperity Sphere will not tolerate mindless opposition to our legitimate aspirations within what you call the Shamballa Cluster! We shall crush . . . um, that is, we shall explore every avenue available in our unrelenting quest for a just and lasting piece of the cluster!"

"Uh, don't you mean 'peace in the cluster'?"

"Whatever."

"I see. Lord General, in view of the high casualties the Krll have suffered in this police action, so-called, have you considered pulling out of the Shamballa Cluster entirely and returning to the Core?"

"Casualties? What casualties? The running-glrk imperialist Concordiat warmongers have thrown everything they can at the noble Krll self-protection forces. So far, we have suffered only minor casualties. One of our sub-privates received a slight injury to his glmpf glands, I believe. Concordiat military forces have been totally ineffectual in slowing the mighty Krll juggernaut in its just and righteous path!"

"Even so, Lord General Kreplach, the Groaci have offered their unbiased services as a neutral third party in order to establish peace negotiations between the Prosperity Sphere and the Concordiat. What is your response to this?"

"Those five-fingered sticky-eyes? Unbiased? All they want is . . ." Again, the lord general stopped himself. "It is the sincere desire of the Greater Krll Prosperity Sphere to establish peace and everlasting chumship with all sentient sla—that is, with all of our sentient neighbors and to seek any means by which so to do, so long as our legitimate territorial aspirations are honored. If the . . . uh . . . noble Groaci have offered their services in this regard, we of the Krll Sphere are certainly in favor. And if those sneaky little five-eyed thieves are playing a double game, we shall offer our services in establishing peace on *their* world."

"But, Lord General. Groac *is* at peace."

"And we Krll are in favor of peace! Did I mention that? The more peace, the better, right? We should keep in mind the dictum of the great Krll philosopher, Kishke the Belligerent: 'There's no peace like the blissful peace of a radioactive desert.' I assure you, Desiree, we Krll *will* help anyone who interferes with our plans find perfect peace!"

"Lord General, that almost sounds like a threat. Surely you don't mean—"

"What threat? We Krll do not make threats! We are peace-loving and happy, wishing only the harmony and joy of total chumship!"

"But if your philosopher said—"

"We find radioactive deserts to be most relaxing . . . just like home, in fact! Trust me, Desiree! We want *only* what is best for all intelligent species! *Peace* . . ."

The camera cut back to an extreme closeup of Desiree's face. "In related news, GNN has just received word that Concordiat officials at the Hexagon this morning have decided to freeze all further troop deployments to Odiousita V pending a review of the recommendations made by the board regarding the recent white paper issued on the possibility of a meeting of the joint chiefs of staff concerning the Mauve House resolution to curtail future military operations within the Shamballan theater. . . ."

"Interesting," Retief said.

"What . . . the freeze on our reinforcements? We've known that was coming for a week, now."

"No. Her eyes. Notice anything unusual?"

Warbutton examined the five-foot-high face more closely. "No. She's wearing anti-UV drops, so her eyes look a little dark, is all. . . ."

"You can still see her pupils beneath the anti-UV," Retief said. "And they're dilated."

"Meaning?"

"Meaning she's been drugged. Or she's under the influence of something like joyweed, which is the same thing. I'd be interested in knowing whether she dosed herself or whether that knight in shining armor beside her had her doped."

"Why would he do that?"

"Joyweed by itself produces a pleasant, euphoric high in humans," Retief explained. "But apparently there are circumstances in which it becomes a potent hypnotic, making the person smoking it extremely suggestible. They'll do what they're told to do, say what they're told to say."

"What circumstances?"

"I don't know yet. Possibly it's the joyweed in combination with some other drug. Or it might have to do with a certain infra-sonic harmonic. But I've seen it happen and seen the effects. It's how the Groaci are recruiting college students to work for them on B'rukley. And it might well be what the Krll are using to get themselves some good media exposure."

Warbutton laughed. "Why would the Krll Empire care about a good press?"

"Think about it. They know that GNN is one of our prime intelligence resources. If they can slant the news their way, they could undermine the morale of your troops . . . and just maybe influence political decisions being made further up the line, maybe even all the way up to the Mauve House."

"That's awfully far-fetched, Retief. I think maybe *you've* been hitting the joyweed a little too hard!"

"I don't inhale."

"Right."

"Have the Groaci talked to you about a peace conference?"

"Nope. Didn't even know they were interested in Odiousita V."

"They've been importing joyweed. They may have started out helping GOSH in that regard, but I'm pretty sure they're thinking of going independent. Free enterprise, you know, and for Groac, the freer, the better."

"Geeze, is everybody in this Sector trying to get this planet's weed?"

"Could be. A monopoly would probably translate into a trillion-guck business, at a conservative estimate. We both know the Groaci would be interested in that. So would the Syndicate."

Warbutton shook his head. "Like I said, if it doesn't involve the Krll, I can't do a thing about it."

On the giant wall screen, Desiree Goodeleigh seemed to be wrapping up her report. "Meanwhile, tragic conflict continues unabated, savaging this unhappy world, called Blmcht by the peace-loving Krll, and Odiousita V by the Terran Concordiat. The Odiousitan Crisis—brutal war . . . or police action? Perhaps the difference is nothing but words, and the propaganda spin placed on it by the Mauve House. I'm Desiree Goodeleigh, live from Odiousita V."

"That woman is about as balanced in her reporting as a mudslide."

"I think she's saying what the Krll want her to say, General. She and her news team may be prisoners. Coming to the aid of civilians in distress *is* part of your job description, you know. Even if they're media."

"And I don't think you appreciate my position here, Retief." He sighed. "Morale has hit rock bottom around here with the news that we're not getting reinforcements, and with all the peace demonstrations on B'rukley, well, that and Goodeleigh have just about finished things for us. We're going to have to pull back and regroup . . . and maybe look at trying to put together an evacuation."

"Don't give up just yet, General. We may have an ace or two to play yet."

"What ace?"

"Let me tell you what I have in mind. . . ."

5

The X-Star 5000 was a hyperstealth atmospheric transport, sleek and slender, and with a midnight black surface that drank radar, rendering it all but invisible to even the most sophisticated sensors. There were only two of them in Warbutton's on-planet arms inventory, and so they'd been reserved for only the most high-priority of missions behind enemy lines.

Leaflets.

"Leaflets?" Retief asked the two young soldiers seated in the cargo hold of the X-Star.

"Yeah," one of the soldiers, a corporal by the name of Philburn, replied with an unpleasant snicker. "Ain't that a crock? They toss fractional kiloton nukes at us, and we zap 'em right back with half a ton of high-yield propaganda!"

"I don't know, Phil," the other soldier, Sergeant Casey, said. "Seems like an even trade to me." He unzipped one of the heavy canvas bags sitting on the deck at their feet, dipped inside with his hand, and pulled out a brightly colored flyer. "You read any of this crap? It's deadly!"

"May I see?" Retief asked.

"Help yourself. Careful, though. Those things can go off if you handle 'em careless, like."

Retief opened the brochure and glanced through it, holding it close to make out the words in the dim red lighting of the X-Star's cargo compartment. It was printed half and half in Standard and in the angular characters of the Krll alphabet and was brightly illustrated throughout with cartoon drawings of humanoid forms in Krll battle armor lounging beside a pool with shapely female battle-armor forms in attendance, sipping at drinks with tiny umbrellas, relaxing in hammocks, eating lobster, playing croquet, golf, and tennis, shopping in a mall, and sitting at a plastic table in a McWendyking Arbycastle's in front of bags upon bags of fast food. The Standard text spoke in lovingly glowing terms of the material advantages of surrender. "Why Be Left Out?" cried the banner headline in forty-two-point bright purple type.

The text went on to say:

"Enemy personnel throughout the Galaxy know the reputation of the Terrific Terries, how they are fearsome opponents but generous to the vanquished! Why, we simply CAN'T WAIT until you guys give up, so we can start shipping you planet-loads of foreign aid, Many Worlds Bank loans, and uninhibited largesse!

"But why wait until that happy day? You can begin enjoying that famous Terry hospitality *now*! Try checking into one of our five-star POW camps, with indoor-outdoor pools and hot tubs of *your choice* of liquid heated to give you a pleasantly stress-relieving warm and relaxing soak; mega-shopping malls to handle all of your daily, monthly, and seasonal needs; saunas, health spas, and masseuse parlors to keep you in fighting trim; and out-of-this-world restaurants serving gourmet dishes *better* than the cardboard food served to our own troops!

"All you need to do is show this brochure to the nearest Terry military personnel, and you'll be ushered into the safety of our rear lines and introduced to your sweet new life of luxury!"

There was quite a bit more, but Retief skipped over most of it, glancing down the page to a final line at the bottom. "This propaganda leaflet brought to you courtesy of the Terran Concordiat government, the Concordiat Armed Forces, and the *Corps Diplomatique Terrestrienne*, your friends whom you haven't met yet, waiting to serve you!"

"I see what you mean by deadly," Retief said.

"Yeah," Casey said. "I really appreciate that crack about feeding the prisoners better than they feed us! Cardboard food is right!"

"I noticed the drawings show the Krll in battle armor."

"Yeah, 'cause no one knows what the Krlljoys really look like. But the xeno boys' best guess is that the armor is designed like our combat armor, so they're pretty much like us—one head, two legs, two arms. Nothing too scary . . ."

"I dunno, Sarge," Philburn said. "I got a great aunt back on Furtheron what got one head, two legs, and two arms, and you wouldn't want t'meet *her* in a dark alley at night!"

A yellow light winked on in the dimly lit compartment. "Uh-oh," Casey said. "Five-minute warning. We gotta get these loaded."

Together, the two soldiers dragged a sealed canvas bag to the first in a row of hatch-topped canisters set into the deck, opened the hatch, and lowered the bag inside.

"Aren't you supposed to take the leaflets out of the bag?" Retief asked.

"Nah," Casey said. "Too much trouble. Let *them* do it." A green light winked on, and he pressed a button on the forward bulkhead of the compartment. There was a loud hiss and thump as the first load of leaflets was fired into the night.

For the next several minutes, Retief watched the two work, loading ejection canisters and firing them. The X-Star was flying at high altitude—nearly 80,000 feet—and it was anybody's guess what happened when those hundred-pound bags hit the ground. Ten bags were launched, one after the other.

And finally, it was Retief's turn.

"You sure you know what you're doin', Mac?" Casey asked him.

"No, but if I find out, I'll be sure to let you know," Retief told him. "Hand me my flight pack, will you?"

Together, they helped Retief suit up. He was already wearing a black commando ensemble, complete with combat vest, pressurized helmet, gloves, and suit heater. He shrugged on the flight pack, let Casey check the connections, straps, and O_2 supply, then gave the two a thumbs-up.

Again, the yellow warning came on. Corporal Philburn opened the number-one deck hatch and Retief slid down inside. It was a snug fit, and he had to hunch over to fit his six-foot-plus frame

within the tube as the hatch clanged shut above him. Then there
was nothing to do but wait.

After a small eternity of waiting, the outer hatch beneath Retief's
boots cycled open, and in a short-lived hurricane of escaping
atmosphere, he was blasted into the night.

He fell. . . .

6

Retief couldn't see the X-Star. In fact, all there was to see was
star-dusted sky above and softly glowing clouds below—the cloud
deck illuminated by the pale-shifting radiance of the planet's flaring
auroras. After a long, long fall, the clouds rose up and engulfed
him, and he continued dropping through a wet haze that rapidly
vanished around him into pitch blackness.

He kept his attention on the luminous altitude readout showing on the upper left corner of his helmet's heads-up display.
At twenty thousand feet, the helmet's electronics began scanning for anything in the EM spectrum that might suggest high
technology—radio or microwave transmissions, visible light, or
RF leakage from computers, electric nose-hair groomers, or
toaster ovens. A major cluster of such signals emanated from the
northwest, eight miles distant. Spreading his arms and arching
his back, he aligned himself with the target and triggered the
thrusters in his flight pack.

At nine thousand feet, he punched through the bottom of the
cloud deck, entering dark, empty sky above a yawning gulf of
night that gave no hint as to whether it was land or sea, jungle
or desert. Even switching his visor to infrared showed only that
the ground was hot . . . but at least it was ground. Missing the
Burning Sands Peninsula and landing in the Tepid Sea would be
embarrassing, to say the least, not to mention fatal.

At five thousand feet, his helmet electronics picked up some points of light to the northeast—the compact sprawl of a small native town. If his navigational information was correct, that was Glooberville. The Krll fortress would be *there* . . . the spaceport that smear of light over *there* . . . and the GOSH-controlled warehouses somewhere about *there*.

At four thousand feet, he pressed the chute release on his flight pack. The shell encasing his torso filled suddenly with a soft gel, which cocooned him so gently he scarcely felt the jolt and flutter of the drogue chute when it popped an instant later . . . or of the main chute when it deployed in turn. Infrared showed open ground below with a line of trees to the east and no sign of a hostile welcoming committee. He steered for the trees and touched the open ground fifty feet short of them. He released harness and flight pack as the chute spilled onto the ground, then gathered the billowing polysilk up in a bundle so he could bury it.

After taking care of that chore, he used the powerful satellite transceiver in his flight pack to send a single, microburst transmission: *Cubs' winning streak continues.*

Then he buried the flight pack where he could find it again, if need be, and checked the military-issue Mark XXX power pistol holstered to his thigh.

So far, so good.

A black shadow invisible against the night, Retief made his way toward the cluster of lights he'd identified as Glooberville, less than a mile away. A thickly wooded hill lay between him and the town. He climbed the hill, working his way through a crevice between two house-sized granite boulders among a tangle of granite outcroppings on the crest of the hill. Crawling forward on his stomach, he reached a sheltered vantage point from which he was able to look down into a scene of utmost confusion.

Glooberville was an odd mix of native and offworld structures. The native Bloggie buildings were easy enough to identify as such—organic shapes like mushrooms or low, spreading trees festooned with windows, doors, and balconies.

The Groaci Embassy was also distinctive—a wall and several turreted buildings that looked like a huge sand castle. Evidently, it had been made to order by Groaci engineers when their ambassadorial mission arrived.

That left what must be Krll buildings—featureless gray bricks in neatly ordered rows, each marked with the harshly angular strokes of Krll numerals. To Retief's eye, they looked like fair examples of Early Despotic Architecture, as might have been popular in the realms of Attila, Stalin, or perhaps Gargle Oyle the Maleficent, with uniformity, utilitarianism, and grayness winning out over style. There were a number of those structures in neat blocks just outside the spaceport. Retief guessed they were barracks for a garrison.

And it looked as though the garrison was out now in force. Sirens blared, and searchlights scraped across the clouds overhead. More searchlights from vehicles and from towers around the garrison all were concentrated on one spot on the main drag through Glooberville. There, several hundred hulking individuals in black-and-silver Krll combat armor were gathered around one of their own, a single humanoid figure lying in the middle of the street.

Retief used the telephoto zoom of his helmet visor to get a closer look. Yes . . . a Krll soldier was lying there face down inside a six-foot crater, his armor badly dented. Squarely on his back was what looked like a large, canvas bag that had burst open at the top, strewing half its contents onto the street.

It was one of the leaflet bags released minutes ago by the X-Star stealth transport. It must have plummeted out of the sky like a falling bomb, and the unlucky Krll soldier could not have known what had hit him. A number of his compatriots, however, were picking up the windblown leaflets and were reading them. Shock and horror appeared to be spreading through the mob. He could see them gesticulating with the brochures, waving them, passing them around . . . and growing more and more agitated.

"Well, well," Retief murmured to himself. "Maybe leaflets are effective in combat after all."

The crowd scattered as a forty-foot mechanized horror stalked ponderously onto the street, striding purposefully from the direction of the Krll fortress to the north. The towering machine,

Retief noted, was a *Zuuba*-class warwalker, approximately four hundred tons of heavy armor on two massive legs, armed with multiple missile launchers, twin micro-Hellbore fusion cannon, and a battery of ion-bolt infinite repeaters. Gently, delicately, the humanoid war machine stooped forward, and a clawed pincher grasped the mailbag and lifted it from the Krll body. Other Krll soldiers then scooped up the victim with something that looked like an eight-foot spatula, dragging him out of the crater and off toward a waiting vehicle.

Other Krll soldiers continued to move about in an agitated manner, evidently still discussing the leaflets that had so calamitously dropped out of the sky. The *Zuuba* warwalker stood unmoving in the street, its turretlike head, a-bristle with sensor antennas, slowly rotating through 360 degrees.

Retief froze, careful not to move, careful even in his breathing. Though he was on a hilltop and nestled in among a tangle of boulders a good fifty yards away from the Glooberville street, the warwalker was tall enough that its head was well above Retief's hiding place. Depending on how good its sensor suite was, all it needed to do was look down, and . . .

It looked down. A warning chirped in Retief's helmet speakers, alerting him to the fact that he was being probed by radar, sonar, and several other active sensory devices. The lone red light aglow inside the warwalker's helmet appeared to be fixed directly on him.

And a signal must have been given, because the Krll soldiers were scattering now, grabbing for their weapons, and beginning to fan out along the base of Retief's hill. Searchlights glared against the night, their beams sweeping the woods and casting up towering, dancing shadows of alien trees. Retief drew his Mark XXX, but there were far too many of them to take in a stand-up fight.

And using a Mark XXX power pistol against that warwalker made about as much sense as attacking a Bolo combat unit with a sharp stick. He began backing away through the crevice between the two large rocks . . . but the warwalker was already moving. A half-dozen steps and it was astride the hill, reaching down with one titanic black-metal hand.

Retief broke clear of the boulders and raced down the back of the hill, but the hand followed, knocking trees aside, lunging . . . and scooping him up. Something—the enormous armored thumb, perhaps—clipped the side of Retief's helmet, hurtling him into the black and unfeeling abyss of unconsciousness.

CHAPTER SEVEN

1

Retief came groggily to in the open flatbed of a Krll military hovercraft transport. Half a dozen armored forms sat around him, deadly looking blast rifles trained on him. Each was perhaps seven feet tall. Their helmets were fitted with ornate decorations that resembled wings or possibly art-deco fins to either side, deeply recessed eye slits within which lone red lights glowed balefully, and a complex arrangement of breathing grates or filters where a human nose and mouth would be. This last was interesting. To judge by the hiss and rasp coming from each, these Krll soldiers breathed a standard oxygen-nitrogen atmosphere mix.

All of the six had peculiar emblems on the brows of their helmets, gold and jaggedly angular. Retief decided it must be some sort of emblem of rank—the mark of an officer or an NCO, perhaps.

"The monster is waking up," one of them said, his harsh,

guttural speech translated by the electronics woven into Retief's commando suit.

"Watch him, Rifle-Sergeant!" said another.

"I wonder if you boys would mind pointing those things somewhere else," Retief said agreeably. He sat up slowly, not making any quick movements. His helmet and, of course, his power pistol, were gone. "Silence, monster!" the first Krll snapped. "Save it for your interrogators!"

The gleaming metallic individuals around him all showed a body language that mingled extreme alertness with a fear that bordered on terror. In Retief's experience, nervousness and guns did not at all mix well.

Since there seemed to be little point in continuing the conversation, Retief took the time to observe his surroundings. The hovercraft was whining along a well-trodden dirt road. Evidently, they'd traveled north up the highway leading to the Krll headquarters fortress, which was now visible ahead, ablaze with lights. Soon, the hovercraft turned off the main road and drifted toward the looming maw of the fortress gate. Behind, the towering form of the *Zuuba*-class combat machine strode through the dust hurled up by the hovercraft's fans, walking escort for the transport and its prisoner with heavy footfalls that echoed hollowly off the fortress parapets.

Through the outer gates, then, and into a barbican lined with ranks of silver-armored figures before passing on through the inner gate and into the fortress proper. Here was a cavernous space filled with heavy equipment and vehicles, overhead traveling cranes, crisscrossing elevated walkways, and the titanic loom of black-painted warwalkers, parked silent and lifeless within their gantry cradles and access scaffolding. The ceiling was easily sixty feet above the busy floor, high enough to allow even the largest of the ponderous walkers to come and go through the main gates. The din within the place, like the clangor within a heavy machine factory or mill, echoed from the walls and assaulted the ears.

A number of Krll were visible, most apparently maintenance personnel at work servicing both vehicles and walkers. All, Retief noticed, without exception, were armored and helmeted, even here, within their fortress fastness.

It was almost as if they didn't want outsiders to see their faces.

Only a few possessed the angular gold insignia of his captors.

"Don't you guys ever kick back and relax?" Retief asked his guards in a conversational tone. "Take off your environment suits and go swimming . . . maybe play golf . . . or play hooky. . . ."

"Silence, monster!"

"It's just that those helmets you wear look awfully heavy. And judging from all that hissing, you breathe this air just fine. Can't be the brightness of the local sun, since you come from the Core where things are a lot hotter than this, at least when it comes to UV and hard radiation."

"You don't understand, Terry," one of the guards said. "These suits aren't just for—"

"Shut your *fraggech* hole, Spear-Corporal Lekach, or s'whelp me you'll be scrubbing out the *drungleglag* hoppers with your snurf organs for the rest of the deployment! You hear me?"

"Yeah, Hyper-Lieutenant," the chastened being replied. "Sure."

"And as for you, Terry monster . . . you be quiet if you don't want the rough stuff to begin right here and now! You get me?"

"Absolutely, Hyper-Lieutenant," Retief replied. "I was just wondering why all the hostility. You caught me, fair and square. Why can't we have a friendly chat?"

"Krll don't have friendly chats with Terry monsters! That's one thing. For another, your friends just dropped a bag of terror-propaganda and squashed poor Club-Corporal Latke flat as a *skrugblatt*. Now, maybe you just happened along . . . and maybe you was up on that hilltop guiding that ordnance in with a laser pointer or something equally fiendish. Either way, I'd just as soon gut you and string you up to dry as look at ya! Ah. Here we are. Out, you, and no fast moves!"

The hover transport had pulled up at a loading dock in the cavernous vehicle bay. Armored soldiers lined both sides of a corridor leading back into the deeps of the fortress. The Krll sergeant marched him at gunpoint past the watching ranks, zigzagged through a number of stone corridors, and deposited him at last in a cell with a pile of straw, a barely functional glow panel on the ceiling, an iron door, and no other amenities. Five humans huddled in the far corner, just visible in the dim light.

"You can cool your *fubfelbs* in there, monster," the lieutenant growled at him, "along with others of your kind. Maybe we'll come get you later, and maybe we won't. In the meantime, you think up all the lies you want to try on our interrogation teams before they break you! Ta!"

The door clanged shut at Retief's back.

"This getting locked into small rooms is becoming something of a habit," Retief said aloud.

"You'll, like, get used to it," a ragged female voice replied from the corner.

Retief took a few steps closer. "Well, well. Miss Ann Thrope, if I recall." He looked at the others. And Marty . . . Zippie . . . is all of SMERCH locked up in here?"

"Nah," Zippie said. He was puffing on a hand-rolled joyweed joint. "Just the five of us. What are *you* doing here?"

"Looking for you, actually," he replied. "I heard there were some SMERCH people up this way."

"Yeah?" Marty said suspiciously. He rubbed his wrist, as if it were still sore. "Like, why do you care, man?"

"Actually, I thought I'd come out here and rescue you."

Ann looked past his shoulder. "I don't see an army with you."

"Yeah," Marty said. "You came to rescue us, but who's gonna rescue *you*?"

"Oh, we'll figure that part out when we come to it." Casually, he tugged at the cuff of his commando suit, turning up the gain on the translator electronics wired into the collar. He heard a tiny, answering squeal of feedback, and nodded to himself. "Tell me, though," he continued. "I heard you folks were here with some GNN people. You haven't seen them, by chance, have you?"

"Sure. That Goodeleigh woman and a couple of technicians are here. We all flew out together yesterday on a GNN yacht."

As he walked slowly across the cell, it seemed to him that the feedback squeal was loudest directly under the light panel in the ceiling. "Where are they?"

"I don't know," Ann said. "I guess the Lord muckity-muck Kreplach has them down in his office suite, someplace."

"Down?"

"The Krll like to bury themselves down deep. This fortress has all of these, like, subbasements, y'know? And that's where the bigwigs hide out, down where the Terry Hellbores and genius bombs can't reach them."

"I see." He watched as Zippie passed the joyweed joint to a young woman in torn, shipboard coveralls. She accepted it and puffed on it eagerly. The smoky haze in the cell was already thick enough to chew on, and Retief was glad he still had his nasal filters in place. "Where'd you get the weed? Didn't they search you?"

"Aw, nah, it's, like, everywhere, y'know?" Ann said with a dismissive shrug. "This is where the stuff, like, comes from, didja know?"

"I did know, yes. What do the Krll use it for, anyway?"

"I don't think they do, man," Zippie told him. "Other than selling it to us and a few others. I think they're afraid of it, myself."

"Oh? Why's that?"

"Well, they always wear that armor, y'know? And they never come in here when we're tokin'. Like, they keep their distance, y'know?"

"Interesting. So you folks are just smoking up to keep the bad guys at bay?"

"Well, that and cruisin', man." Zippie accepted the joint and sucked down the smoke. "It, like, passes the time. This place'd be a real downer, otherwise."

"I'll bet it would be. Why are you here, anyway?"

"We came out with the GNN crew," the woman in the shipsuit said. "Like, to show them the Krll were really good guys, y'know?"

"Uh-huh. And they tossed you in here? Why?"

She shrugged listlessly. "I think we're, like, here to guarantee their good behavior, y'know?"

Zippie shook his head mournfully. "Y'know, I don't think the Krll are such nice guys after all." He offered Retief the joint. "Want a hit, man?"

"Thanks. Maybe later. Why don't you just fill me in on everything that's been going on."

2

"So SMERCH was started by the Groaci," Retief said, an hour later. "An organization for smuggling students into B'rukley for spontaneous peace demonstrations, and also to serve as a labor pool. But why? What do they get out of meddling in the Concordiat's little police action out here on Odiousita?"

"Well, they *told* us it was because they wanted to spread peace and chumship across all of the inhabited universe," Ann said, but with a trace of doubt in her voice.

"That's their official party line, yes," Retief told her. "But I suspect their interest runs a bit deeper than that, and in channels not quite so altruistic."

"Shtliff *told* us you CDT johnnies would say that," Marty observed.

"Mm. Did he tell you why he disguised himself as a Grothelwaith tourist when he was out among the masses?" Retief asked.

"Well . . . er . . . that is . . . he said something about virtue being, like, its own reward," the woman in torn coveralls said. Her name was Connie Strue, and with Ann Thrope was one of the founding members of SMERCH. "He said it was, like, the solemn public duty of the noble Groaci to do good deeds without expecting, like, you know, public approbation."

"Was he wearing hip waders when he told you all that?"

"Huh?"

"Never mind." Retief stood up and walked over to the center of the cell, standing directly beneath the light panel. "Of course, it's obvious," he said in a loud voice, "that the Groaci are duping the Krll. I wonder if the Lord General Kreplach knows that the noble Groac has been playing him for a fool, stringing him along just so they can steal the secrets of joyweed?"

One of the SMERCH representatives, a colorless individual they'd introduced as Fred, happened to be holding the joint at that moment. He looked at it doubtfully. "Secrets of joyweed? What secrets?"

"Oh, you have to be one of the innermost illuminati to know them. Like me." He thought a moment. "Do you have a fresh one of those?"

"Sure," Zippie said, reaching into a pocket and producing a somewhat crumpled cylinder of white paper. It looked like a standard dopestick with the self-igniting tip, but the crumbled vegetable matter was the characteristic deep black of joyweed. "Toke up, man!"

"Thanks." He slipped the cylinder into his breast pocket.

"Hey, you gonna bogie that all by yourself?" Marty wanted to know. "Or you gonna share?"

"I'll share it later." He changed the subject. "You said you came here in a GNN yacht. Where's the ship's crew?"

"That would be me," Connie said. "I'm a contract pilot signed with GNN."

"Just you?"

"The ship's an Archangel-class, the *Story at Eleven*. She's all automated. Just needs, like, one person to tell her where to go."

"And she's berthed at the local starport, I gather?"

"She was when they took us off her."

"Archangel-class boats have some pretty sophisticated antitamper devices. I doubt they've taken her anywhere else. Okay, that gives us something to work with, at least."

"Like, what, man?" Fred wanted to know.

"I'll tell you later," Retief said. "Maybe when your heads are a bit clearer. Right now, I have to go with the nice tin soldiers and answer some questions."

Ann looked doubtfully at the locked door. "What do you mean? They tossed you in here to rot, like the rest of us!"

"No, I suspect someone will be along any moment now to have a little chat with me." A hollow thump sounded at the door and, a moment later, it swung open. "See what I mean?"

An armored soldier with an officer's rank insignia stepped into the cell, batting at the smoke. His red eye fell on Retief. "You! Come with me!" Behind him, in the hallway outside, half a dozen armored troops gathered in a nervous huddle, weapons at the ready.

"Wow," Zippie said. "He's, like, psychic, man!"

"Keep cool," Retief told them. "I'll be back for you as soon as I can."

And he followed the nervous guards out.

3

The seven of them marched him to an elevator down the hallway. It was a tight fit in an already snug compartment. Retief stood wedged in between four of the seven, studying with interest the back of the helmet of the soldier directly in front of him. He could just make out a logo stamped into the shiny metal—Hitachi-Yakuza Microfirm—and the words TO RELEASE, PULL HERE. The rasp and hiss of their breathing gear filled the compartment, and the soldiers to either side kept the muzzles of their weapons pressed against Retief's head.

Or, rather . . . three of the soldiers were breathing noisily. The other four were not. The three possessed rank insignia on their helmets—a hyper-lieutenant, a rifle-sergeant, and a spear-corporal, if he was reading them right. Possibly, they were the same three of those ranks who'd brought him to the fortress. The nonbreathing ones bore no insignia and stood as rigidly as robots.

At last, though, the door slid open and they marched out in clashing unison, ten levels down in the fortress subbasement. They gave him scarcely more room to breathe than he'd had in the elevator as they marched him through another set of corridors and into a large and impressive chamber.

It was a bit on the gloomy side here. Indirect lighting cast wavering patterns of blue and green across the ceiling high overhead, creating an effect like that of a coral reef in shallow seas. The effect was heightened by the décor, which included long streamers of something like seaweed festooning the walls and a thin layer of white sand on the floor. The air was wet and smelled of salt. Soldiers, armed and armored, ringed the walls in silent witness, rigidly at attention.

At the far end of the room, upon a raised dais, the Lord General Kreplach towered high into the blue-green mists upon a throne of white steel. His armor looked much like that of his troops, save that it was bigger, much, *much* bigger. The Lord General, if he rose from his throne, would have stood at least eighteen feet tall. His black and bright-polished silver helm, crested and bewinged, was as large as a fifty-gallon drum, and bore a particularly splendid rank insignia, an ornate Rorschach blotch in gold. The black gauntlets gripping the armrests on either side of the throne were broad enough and massive enough to crush a human with a one-handed squeeze.

To the left of the dais, Desiree Goodeleigh knelt on the sand, a collar around her neck. A six-foot Krll guard with an officer's insignia stood behind her, holding her leash.

"You are the one they call Retief," the giant said, the voice booming like thunder from the throne. "Kneel before me, small one! Kneel before the Lord General Kreplach of the Greater Krll Prosperity Sphere and Empire and do homage!"

"I'd rather stand, thank you." Retief looked the armored giant up and down. "You know, you look a lot taller in person than you do on-screen."

"Indeed. The lordly gods of Krll care not for the limitations of ordinary measure."

"I see. Must be useful when you're looking for a parking place." He reached for his breast pocket. "Mind if I smoke?"

"*Yes*, I mind," the Lord General thundered. "A noxious habit that pollutes the lungs, deadens the neurons, slows the reflexes, and cripples the mind! When we Krll rule the Shamballa Cluster, that poisonous weed shall be eradicated and its traffic stamped out, I promise you!"

"Good luck," Retief told the towering metal figure. "It's been tried." His hand dropped from his pocket. Purposefully, he strode across the floor to Desiree.

Several of the officers in the room appeared startled and raised their weapons. The troops, Retief noted, stood silent and unmoving, awaiting an order.

"Don't worry, boys," he told them. "I'm harmless. Well, more or less."

"Retief!" Desiree said. "What are you—"

"I see you like to keep the news media on a short leash, Lord General," he said. "But I don't think you understand us terrible Terries very well."

Reaching down, he grasped the collar at Desiree's throat. It was made of some lightweight metal and was clasped with a Groaci-made lock. He exerted his strength, the muscles in his arms and hands momentarily bulging, and then the fragile lock snapped with a sharp *ping*. He pulled the broken collar off and handed it to the surprised officer guarding her. "We believe in the sanctity of a free press," he said.

Several soldiers had started toward Retief, but the Lord General raised a metal hand. "Leave it. The small one can do nothing to Us."

Retief offered a hand to Desiree, who took it and stood unsteadily. "Thanks. What do you plan for an encore?"

"I can't wait to find out," he told her. He looked up at the giant above him. "So, you're the Lord General of the Krll. I like the suit. Who's your tailor?"

"Tell me now, small Terry, why I should not have my loyal soldiers carve you into slow bits and use your endoskeleton for scrimshaw work?"

"Because I have information you want, Kreplach, and you won't get it if your troops are disassembling me."

"*Lord General* Kreplach, if you please."

"If you say so."

"It is my sovereign will that you live . . . for now. Tell me, small one, what you know of the verminous race of slaves known as the Groaci."

"That covers a fair amount of territory, Lord General. Let's see. They're quintocular bipeds, about four-six to five-six in height, with horny exoskeletons, cartilaginous endostructures, and no heart. Gray to gray-brown or black integument. Two arms, each with five slender, flexible, and sticky spatulate digits which can often be found inside your pocket. Throat sacs, by which they tell lies with rather soft voices. They like hot sand, infinitive sentences, intrigue, thievery, brigandage, and skullduggery in general, and most of them are quite partial to fried gribble grubs. They—"

"*To be enough . . . !*"

A slight, battered-looking figure emerged from an alcove behind the giant's throne, led on a short leash by a Krll officer.

"Well, well," Retief said. "Broodmaster Shtliff. I was wondering when you might put in an appearance. Where's General Snish?"

"To have had enough of your vile slanders, Terry spy!"

"Do you mean to say you *don't* like fried gribble grubs? My mistake. I was misinformed."

"My slight addiction to that particular sulfur-fried delicacy is not at issue here," Shtliff whispered, speaking High Obfuscese now, "especially since my enrollment in that twelve-step program on B'rukley. Retief, I'm shocked, *shocked* to hear a fellow diplomat, *former* diplomat, that is, give voice to such defamatory calumny."

"Speak Standard, Groaci," the Krll thundered. "None of your treacherous Obfuscese and weasel-word whisperings!"

"Ah, of course, Lord General. To be sure. I was just, ah, giving greeting to a fellow diplomat and comrade at arms. . . ."

The massive helmet tilted to one side. "More lies. We lordly Krll watch GNN, as do all other sentient beings in the Galaxy. This Retief creature was given the boot from his diplomatic order not fifty *glans* ago."

"Ah, but once a diplomat, always a diplomat, as they say, my Lord General," Shtliff replied. "And, ah, speaking of diplomatic immunity . . ." Reaching up, he tugged experimentally at the leash and collar. "I'm sure this treatment of the inviolate representative of your Groaci allies was a mere oversight. Still—"

"There is no oversight, five-eyed one," the Krll leader rumbled. "There are rumors that you have plotted against the Krll Lords of Creation, that you have attempted to steal Krll agricultural secrets."

"Why . . . whatever do you mean, my Lord General?" Shtliff's stalked eyes waggled in an expression of Indignation—a 602, pitched by terror to at least a T, Retief thought.

"I think he may be talking about your little operation at Camp Concentration, on B'rukley," Retief suggested. "You know, the part about where you have Terry students enslaved by drugs to cultivate joyweed plants smuggled there from Odiousita V . . . or Blmcht, as the Krll call it."

"Retief!" Shtliff cried in his weak voice. "Ixnay on the uffstay about the oyweedjay!"

"Ah-*ha*!" Kreplach boomed. "Shtliff! Have you been trying to cut the mighty Krll out of the just rewards of their agricultural efforts?"

"Why, ah, no, Lord General! How could you think such a thing? We simply, ah, that is . . . we acquired a few small samples of the Odiousitan flora purely for research purposes."

"Nay! Spare me the pallid excuses! It's true, then! That makes you a spy and a sneak, and beyond the pale insofar as the niceties of diplomatic protocol are concerned."

"But my Lord General! Spying and sneaking have *always* been among the great diplomatic prerogatives! Those, and not paying fines for traffic violations in hostile alien climes. These are sacred principles!"

"*I* am supreme Lord of Protocol here!" Kreplach boomed. "And I say you have infringed upon Krll copyright, trespassed on Krll hospitality, betrayed Krll magnanimity, absconded with Krll property, insulted Krll intelligence, and stolen the hard-won bread-substitute out of the mouths of honest Krll laborers! Fie upon thee! We, the mighty Krll, will annihilate you as a species! We will scorch your worlds, burn your cities, enslave your females, and garnishee your wages!" A giant, armored fist came down on the arm of the throne with an earsplitting boiler-factory clash. "We will eat your grubs with the drawn and steaming fatty portion of mammalian nutritional lactations! We will whack your noses with rolled-up newspapers—"

"Actually, the Groaci don't have noses, as such," Retief pointed out.

"That's okay. The mighty Krll don't have newspapers. I was speaking metaphorically."

"Ah. Then I trust the comment about eating Groaci grubs was also metaphor. In truth, I doubt very much that they taste very good, even with hot butter. But I do understand how you feel."

"Retief! To watch what you say . . . !"

"Still," he continued, "wholesale planet-scorching may be a bit extreme, don't you think?"

"I don't know. A scorched-planet policy has always worked well for us before."

"Maybe so. But you might give some consideration to other ways of dealing with your anger."

"Pah! What do you, small and pathetic biped, know of righteous Krll anger?"

"I know you wouldn't be talking about wholesale genocide if you weren't a bit miffed about something," Retief answered breezily. "And challenging the Concordiat Peacekeeper forces suggests you're either mad-angry or mad-crazy. I don't think it's the latter."

"Nonsense!" The giant rose from his throne, the wing tips of his monstrous helmet just missing an impact with the vaulted ceiling far overhead. "The mighty Krll Prosperity Sphere and Empire merely seeks its rightful place in a galaxy of slave-races and underlings. All who dare stand in our way shall be utterly crushed . . . ruthlessly smashed . . . pyrotechnically burned . . . destructively destroyed . . . and . . . and severely chastised! We shall conquer! We shall overcome! We shall stride forth to assume our mantle of manifest destiny as divine and sovereign rulers of the Galaxy's teeming trillions! We shall—"

"Kreppie," Retief said. "Cool it. You're overdoing things."

"Oh. Sorry." The giant sat down again, then performed a metallic doubletake. "Hey, wait a minute . . ."

"Your delivery is great, but you need to watch those mega-lomaniacal assertions." He tilted his head, indicating Desiree. "*Especially* in front of the media."

"I control the media on this world!" Kreplach boomed. The Lord General paused, collecting himself. "Still, I trust you understand if I am a bit short tempered, just now. The unrelenting strain of command, you know, the pressures of being supreme and sovereign dictator of an incompletely conquered world, the stress of fighting a war . . . you understand."

"Of course," Retief said. "It's not easy struggling beneath the burden of an inferiority complex as big as yours."

"*We are not inferior, worm!*" The Lord General's voice thundered so loudly that Desiree covered her ears, and bits of plaster pattered to the floor from the ceiling. "*You are inferior! You and all of your dirt-grubbing kind! We are the mighty Krll! Destiny is ours to command! We are lords of creation, powerful, unrelenting, majestic, and very, very hungry* . . . ah, ahem. Yes. Anyway . . . Captain!"

The Krll officer who was still holding Desiree's leash and broken collar, stepped forward. "Yes, my Lord General!"

"That one . . ." Kreplach pointed at Desiree, "goes back to her cell with the other GNN personnel. We may have further need of her."

"Yes, Supreme Warlord."

"These two . . ." He pointed at Retief and Shtliff. "They have outlived their usefulness. Take them both outside at once and shoot them."

"Lord General Kreplach!" Shtliff protested. "I beg you, no! We are under diplomatic immunity! Well, *I* am under diplomatic immunity! Shoot Retief if you feel you must, but—"

"Your so-called diplomatic immunity means nothing here, pathetic small one. You are not accredited to the Groac mission here, nor have you been recognized by the Krll military government. You are a miscreant and a spy! Captain Hollishkes! Take them away!"

"At once, Your Awesomeness!" The Krll officer produced an ugly-looking handgun and waggled it with an authoritarian swagger. "Very well, pathetic bipeds. You have an appointment with Death! *Move!*"

4

"To think that so promising a career as mine should be so ignominiously truncated!" Shtliff mourned as the Krll officer and two rankless soldiers marched them down a gray passageway. "To meditate never again on Groac manifest destiny while fingering curiously carved kiki stones, to enjoy nevermore the warm embrace of pleasantly heated sand . . ."

"Not to mention the warm embrace of a certain Groaci clerk-typist with really great thoracic knobs," Retief observed.

All five of Shtliff's stalked eyes whipped about to stare up at Retief. "To wonder how you know such personal intimacies, snooping Terry!"

"To never breathe a word to anyone, Shtliff. *Especially* to your wife."

"Alas," Shtliff said in doom-laden Groaci, "to hardly matter now." He sighed. "To be somewhat peeved, Retief, that you should so traitorously sell out a fellow diplomat!"

"To not be a diplomat any longer, Shtliff. Remember?"

"Hey, stop all that whispering and mumbling," their guard told them. They rounded a corner and approached a waiting elevator.

The five of them squeezed in, the two privates to either side of Retief and Shtliff, the officer standing behind them. One of the soldiers pressed a button, the door slid shut, and the elevator began to rise.

Retief reached into his pocket and pulled out the joyweed joint, thumbing it alight.

"That is forbidden!" the officer rumbled. "Extinguish that!"

"The condemned prisoner's last smoke, Captain Hollishkes. It can't be forbidden. It's traditional."

"Well . . . um . . . in that case . . . but . . ."

Retief put the joint in his mouth and drew in a full-cheeked mouthful of smoke, careful not to inhale any into his lungs. At that, he felt a growing, surging light-headedness as the psychoactive elements of the smoke filtered through the capillaries under his tongue.

Turning, he leaned forward and blew the smoke squarely into the air vents of the Krll captain's helmet.

The officer made a sound like gears grinding and staggered back against the elevator wall. "Soldiers!" the being gasped, beating at the smoke. "Kill them!"

But as the two Krll privates turned, bringing up their weapons, Retief snapped, "Soldiers: *return semicolon!*"

Immediately, the two soldiers lowered their weapons and resumed their stoic, face-forward positions.

"Sollldierrrs!" the captain gasped, the word oddly drawn out. He appeared to be moving very slowly, trying to raise his pistol. "Kiiiillll . . . themmm. . . ."

Again, the two robot warriors turned in place and raised their weapons. "Soldiers: *return semicolon,*" Retief commanded, and they pivoted back to their former positions. Reaching out, he plucked the handgun from the captain's weakened grasp.

Shtliff goggled at him with all five eyes. "Retief! How did you . . . ?"

"The same people manufacture these Krll-soldier automatons as make the made men used by GOSH. Both are apparently programmed using verbal C or C++ commands. The GOSH soldiers are a bit creaky and obsolete. Their C-programmed verbal output gives the game away . . . see? These guys have more modern software, I imagine. Or maybe it's just that Krll soldiers aren't programmed to talk!"

As he spoke, he reached around to the back of Captain Hollishkes's helmet, his fingers finding the latch there at the base of the neck. "Ah. here we are. Let's see what the Krll are really like."

He gave the latch a tug. Instead of coming off, the helmet hinged forward with a loud hiss of escaping pressure, revealing . . . nothing. The Krll inside the armor had no head. Instead, the helmet was packed with electronics, cheap Japanese circuitboards, and wires. The helmet pulled down further, however, and the torso of the armored suit split wide open, revealing what for all the world appeared to be a small control cockpit inside a mostly hollow thorax.

In the center of that space, surrounded by palm-sized screens and data boards, astride an oddly shaped chair or rack, rested what appeared to be a three-foot-long lobster. It stared up at Retief's face with tiny, wildly waving stalked eyes like shiny black olives. Its multiple limbs, both large fighting pinchers and a dozen or so smaller grasping and manipulatory claws, waggled about as the creature struggled in obvious distress. "Don't eat me!" it piped in a thin, shrill little-girl's voice.

And then, startlingly, it went limp.

"Oh . . . Retief!" Shtliff said, his breathy voice odd. He laid a long-fingered hand on Retief's shoulder, lightly caressing. "That was . . . masterfully done."

"Hit the emergency stop, will you, Shtliff?" Retief said. "It should be that bright pink knob off by itself."

The elevator bumped to a stop between floors, giving Retief time to more closely examine the Krll armored-suit controls. The Krll was wearing something like a second carapace over its back, a light and flexible metal, like aluminum foil. Removing it, Retief noted that the side next to the Krll's exoskeleton was studded with small neurosensors.

"What is it, Retief?" Shtliff said, leaning *very* close.

"At a guess, it's a neuronet transceiver," Retief told the Groaci. "Picks up signals from the central nervous system and transmits them to the suit's computer for analysis and implementation. And it probably takes in data on things like body position and balance and feeds them back to the wearer. Pretty neat. . . ."

"It's . . . *wonderful*. . . ." Again, Shtliff caressed Retief's shoulder.

"Are you feeling okay, Shtliff?"

"Oh, yes, darling." He sighed. "I've never felt better. . . ."

"Interesting," Retief said. "Joyweed gets humans high. It slows Krll nervous systems to the pace of cold molasses. And it seems to make you Groaci singularly amorous." He was remembering the odd behavior of the two Groaci guards back on B'rukley.

"To care not for such trivia when the moons are full and the air sweet with the heady and magical scent of p'chubchub blossoms! To care only for my beloved, for his firm and commanding tone of voice, for the thought of sharing with him an intimate tête-à-tête in a tub of hot sand. . . ."

"Easy, Shtliff. Get hold of yourself. You're not my type."

"To matter not, these nattering details of biology! To be living, breathing, loving beings, yearning to break the strictures of societal prejudice and narrow-mindedness!"

"It would never work, Shtliff," Retief replied in Standard. "You'd not respect me in the morning. Hit the emergency stop again. We need to get you some fresh air."

The elevator lurched into motion again, and a moment later the door opened. The passageway outside, fortunately, was empty.

"Give me a hand, Shtliff." He dragged the open suit of armor out into the corridor.

"To do whatever my beloved commands," Shtliff said. "To wonder what to do with these two large and handsome bookends."

"The soldiers? Leave them. They'll just stand there until they get a new set of instructions. C'mon. I want to find a place where we can have some privacy."

"Ah! These are the words I've yearned to hear these long moments past. Yes, Retief! Yes! Yes! Take me, my love-monkey humanoid! Take me, I'm yours!"

"This is so sudden, Shtliff. Let's wait until your head clears a bit."

"If you are not too long, beloved Retief, I will wait here for you all my life!"

"I don't care if you *do* quote Oscar Wilde," Retief said, "I still don't think it would work out."

Together, they dragged the Krll armor across the corridor. A door there opened into what appeared to be a janitor's closet. Shtliff closed the door as Retief began studying the armor.

The Krll appeared to be crustaceans very much indeed like terrestrial lobsters, albeit larger, and adapted to breathe either underwater or on land. A system of spray nozzles kept the creature's exposed gills comfortably moist inside its cozy cockpit. Various slender, plastic tubes appeared to provide food, drinking water, and waste management. The Krll would have to be careful, Retief noticed, not to get their tubes mixed up.

Carefully, he removed the creature from its cockpit and placed it in a bucket half filled with water.

"Is he dead?" Shtliff asked.

"No. See that pulse, right under the buccal palps? I think the poor thing just fainted."

"We are much larger than he. Perhaps we frightened him?"

"We scared the pants off of him . . . if he wore pants. But I don't think it was our size that did it."

"What, then?"

"I'm not sure. Let's have a look at the armor. It looks like a Groaci copy of a Japanese design. You wouldn't happen to know anything about that, would you, Shtliff?"

The being sighed. "My love for you has weakened my resolve. Indeed, my darling Retief, I would do anything for you, tell you anything! Yes, it is true. Noble Groac has been footing the Krll military initiative for years."

"They don't come from the Galactic Core, do they?"

"No. That was mere subterfuge, a clever diversion suggested by military necessity. But . . . darling! How could you possibly have known?"

"For a life-form that claimed to love high-energy, high-ultra-violet, high-radiation environments, these fellows seemed to take some pretty serious precautions *not* to be exposed to the local daylight. You'll also notice that their command center was buried deep down in a subbasement."

"Yes, for protection against Concordiat weapons."

"So I was told. But we have beings here who"—he ticked points off on his fingers—"never show themselves unarmored, bury themselves deep under an artificial mountain, and dress up the throne room in sea-bottom chic, right down to the coral sand, seaweed and mood lighting. I think they evolved in the oceans of some world orbiting a cooler sun than they claim, and only came to Odiousita V because this was where joyweed could be found."

"Ingenious, sweetheart," Shtliff said, his eyestalks weaving in frank admiration. "Such brilliance should be rewarded. . . ." He reached out tentatively.

Retief gently brushed the proffered limb aside. "No, Shtliff. To tell you the truth, I think we should just be friends."

"Retief, my love! How can you be so cold, so heartless!"

"Actually, I do have a heart. Groaci don't. You use overall bodily muscular contractions to move your circulatory fluids around, don't you?"

"Retief, beloved, how can you talk so clinically when love is in the air!"

"Shtliff, all that's in the air right now is joyweed smoke. You'll feel a lot better when you get that drug out of your system. If you have to, go do some deep-knee bends to speed up the blood flow, okay? I need to work on this control unit."

The foil neural transceiver was roughly the size and shape of a skullcap or yarmulke, designed to fit with some overlap over the curved back carapace of a Krll inside one of the suits of armor. By chance, the device *could* be a skullcap . . . fitting snugly over a human scalp.

"Shtliff?"

"Yes, honey."

"I'm going to try something. I want you to stand by. If I appear to be in distress, if it looks as though I'm getting into trouble, pull this thing off of me pronto. Can you do that?"

"Yes, my darling. Anything. But why—"

"I need to know if I can operate Krll machinery," he said, and slipped the foil cap onto his head.

His brain exploded. . . .

CHAPTER EIGHT

1

The feeling was that of having a large wad of crisp cellophane crumpled and crinkled up inside his skull, like a sudden burst of white-noise static felt as much as heard. For a moment, he could see nothing, but he felt very strange indeed . . . as though he were both sitting cross-legged next to the supine form of the Krll body armor and, simultaneously and bewilderingly, lying flat on his back.

The foil cap, he decided, was giving him several types of feedback, but the most important were balance and the kinesthetic sense of knowing just where his torso and limbs were at any given moment. He found that by concentrating, he could cause the sensory input from his human body to fade into the background so that he could focus on the sensations arising from this new and awkward body lying on the floor.

Other sensations were invading his brain, alien sensations from alien senses. He was getting *flnth* vibrations through his antenna that registered a lot like smell . . . if an odor was bright purple and sounded like his reflection in a brightly polished desktop.

He frowned. That couldn't be right. But when he frowned, he became aware of the high level of *snrgl* radiations in the closet, making his hair tingle and the soles of his feet itch. Something would have to be done about that. . . .

He tried thinking about getting up. Awkwardly, he sat up. It was confusing, at first, since he was watching the armor clumsily fold itself to a sitting position in front of him with his human eyes, but the part of himself that was inside the teleoperated armor suit was blind. It actually helped to close his eyes and imagine himself wholly inside the armor. Focusing all of his will on the effort, he made himself rise . . . rise . . .

And then his legs tangled with one another; he fell to the floor with a metallically clashing clatter.

Shtliff started forward. "My darling! Are you all right?"

The Groaci's normally soft voice sounded quite loud; evidently, the suit was feeding him audio as well. Retief could also hear an overlaying high-pitched gargle of harsh guttural consonants—a translation of Shtliff's Standard into the Krll language, he presumed.

"I'm fine," Retief told the distraught alien. "Not so loud, though, okay? The cap is giving me kinesthetic feedback from the suit and is translating my physical intent into movement."

"To not worry about the aesthetics of the suit, Retief," Shtliff said, shifting to whispered Groaci. "To not be making a fashion statement."

"I know. It's not quite Savile Row. But kinesthetics is about knowing where your arms and legs are without having to look at them, being able to sense where you are in relation to your environment, and so on." He tried getting up again and again fell in a noisy tangle. "Trouble is, I feel like I need to have eight legs to make this work right. The Krll sense of balance is quite different from yours or mine."

"Perhaps that's because the Krll have eight legs," the Groaci replied archly, "not counting pincers and antennae."

Retief focused on the sensations coming from his human body again, reached up, and pulled the cap off. For a dizzying moment, the janitor's closet whirled around him as his sense of equilibrium readjusted.

And then he was just himself once more, with only a single body—a mercifully human one.

"True," Retief said, carefully folding and pocketing the foil cap. "I was hoping to be able to control this thing, but it's too much like walking and chewing gum at the same time."

"What's so hard about that?"

"It's hard when you think you have eight legs and only have two, and your mouth parts tend to go in six directions at once. Give me a hand, though. I have another idea."

Together, they rolled the once-more flaccid suit of armor onto its back and opened up the chest cavity wide. The armor's exo-skeleton, Retief now saw, was a standardized model of Groaci design originally created for humanoids. Most of the suit was filled with wires and fiber-optic conduits, circuit boards, and lengths of a soft, gelatinous material like soft, translucent rubber that contracted to various degrees when electric current flowed through it—artificial muscles, in fact, similar to the jellylike myo-fiber used in human prosthetics, which controlled and moved the suit's limbs according to the operator's intent. Krll officers and NCOs apparently wore the cockpit version of the armor, while the private soldiers must have a chest-top computer—programmed in C++, of course—instead of a Krll control center.

It took only a few vandalous moments to rip out all of the artificial muscles, wires, and control circuits, emptying even the jam-packed helmet to create a completely hollow suit that Retief could wear, much like the combat armor of a human soldier. It was a bit big for him—standing as it did almost seven feet tall—and walking around was a little like balancing on foot-thick platform boots, but he could manage it okay after a little practice. Some spots chafed badly—around the ankles and knees, on the shoulders and elbows, but he found he was able to pad those areas with wrappings of the gelatinous myo-fiber, enough, at least, to keep from rubbing himself raw.

"That's better," Retief said, flexing his right leg a couple of times, then his left. "I can handle this." The respirator, built into the faceplate, continued to work, feeding him unfiltered air, and he could see—if in a sharply restricted fashion—through the narrow slit that once had housed the helmet's visual scanner.

"Darling, I hate to tell you this," Shtliff said, "but there's one important element missing." He held up part of the mechanism they'd removed from the helmet—the now unlit head of the optical scanner. "You don't have that red light moving back and forth in your viewing slit."

"I can't speak the Krll language, either, though maybe my translator will still do the trick. We'll just have to risk it."

"Risk what, Retief?"

Retief picked up the alien power gun from the floor and casually pointed it at Shtliff. "Risk pretending you're my prisoner. Let's go!"

"Retief! My darling! What?"

"Don't worry. Just play along and follow my lead."

And he ushered the confused and amorous Groaci out into the corridor once more.

2

They made their way down a long and gleaming passageway, searching for the route that would lead them back to the vehicle bay. Walking in the armored suit was a bit awkward, but Retief found it no more taxing than the full suit of Quoppina exoskeleton that had been his disguise back during the Voion troubles, when he'd been Second Secretary and Consul to the Terran Embassy on Quopp.

"So, tell me, Shtliff," Retief said conversationally. "Why are the Groaci supplying the Krll with robotic battle suits? That seems a bit brazen even for nobler Groac."

"I'm sure I have no idea what you're talking about," Shtliff replied with a noseless sniff. "The Groaci have offered their services in ending this tragic conflict between the Concordiat and the Krll Empire. Why would we start a war and then seek to end it?"

"That's an excellent question, Broodmaster. Perhaps you'd care to tell me your thoughts on the matter."

"I . . . I'd rather not," Shtliff said. He was beginning to sag a bit, and his five eyestalks were drooping. "I find I have a terrible snarf-ache."

"I see the joyweed effects wear off as fast as they hit you."

"They also seem to leave quite a hangover."

"So I see. But I'm curious . . . why do the Krll go in for imitating bipeds in their battle armor? Was it just that the Groaci build such good copies of Japanese robotic designs and they were using what was available? Or is it something else?"

"To find your own answers, vile Terry! I'll not help you!"

"Ah . . . the old Shtliff I knew and love. Welcome back."

"To not know of what you speak."

"Does joyweed act as an amnesiac agent in Groaci as well as an aphrodisiac? Or are you just grumpy?"

"I am shocked at your undiplomatic behavior! Running around like that, in disguise!"

"I seem to remember you wearing a rather elaborate getup so you could represent yourself as a Grothelwaith guru."

"That was nothing like this! I assumed that guise to avoid frightening the poor misguided Terran children whom I was counseling. You . . . running around like this in a Krll Empire military establishment . . . you could be shot as a spy! And worse, I could be shot with you!"

"Well, considering the fact that they were going to shoot both of us anyway, we haven't lost anything, have we? Turn left here."

"Where are you taking us, Retief? This is madness!"

"Would you rather go back and have a chat with his Lord Generalship?"

"Ah, well . . . no. Not exactly."

"Then play along. If you're my prisoner, they can't blame you."

"Oh, Kreplach can blame me for just about anything he wants," the Groaci said. "That's the way he is. Oh, please . . . let me stop a moment. My organ cluster is pounding!"

"Just for a sec, then."

"Are you folks lost?"

Retief turned and saw a Bloggie, standing on six floor-polishing rags a few feet away. Shtliff started at the sight of the being, then sagged once more with a groan, holding his organ cluster between spatulate fingers.

"Hello," Retief said. "I take it you're the janitor here?"

"Yup. Zub-zloob's the handle. And you must be Retief."

"Good guess. How'd you recognize me?"

"Both my cousin Glom-gloob and my cousin Glob-jlob told me you might be coming up this way. And you're not exactly acting like your typical Krll officer."

"Oh?"

"Sure. The *drfl* vibrations are all wrong, for one thing. And your headlight is out."

"Very observant. But I'm curious. Glom-gloob told me you were mayor of Glooberville. Why are you working here?"

"Oh, hey. Even a mayor is allowed to study the fine points of culture and civilization, right? Besides, there's not much to the job of mayor since the Krll *and* the Gruckies took over the town."

"I see. And what have you learned about civilization from the Krll?"

"That the Krll higher-ups like their floors brightly polished so's they can see their *antlitzwrm* in them . . . whatever 'antlitzwrm' are. That civilized folks like playing a game called 'war' where they get to blow things up and kill other beings. That they like their *groffl*trays and wastebaskets emptied every day, while they're not around, but don't want their desks touched. That you should never, ever touch their *lebber*stones. That they really like lots of toys and electronic gadgets, like that suit you're wearing. That they define civilization by comparisons with other people rather than by specific accomplishments—like saying 'we're more civilized than *they* are.' That some of their ideas about what civilization is are really bizarre . . . like living in houses you build instead of grow, or having linoleoplastic on your floors instead of mud, or covering up by wearing artificial bodies. That the civilized word for *stealing* is *requisitioning* or *taxation*. That—"

Retief held up a gauntleted hand. "I get the idea, Zub-zloob. Glob-jlob gave me pretty much the same litany."

"So, how come you're pretending to be a Krll officer?" Zub-zloob asked.

"I have been wondering much the same myself," Shtliff put in.

"The Lord General and I don't quite see eye to eye on something, and this seemed like the best way to leave gracefully and without causing a disturbance."

"Good idea. I've heard the Lord General when he's peeved, which is most of the time. *Everybody* wants to leave quietly then, believe me."

"Could you direct us to the vehicle bay?"

"Sure. Right down this passageway, turn right at the second intersection, and straight on ahead. You can't miss it."

"Thank you."

"My pleasure."

"One other question. What do you know about a Mr. Bug?"

"The head of the local criminal syndicate? They have their headquarters in the warehouse district over at the Glooberville spaceport. We Bloggies don't have much to do with them, though."

"Were you aware that Mr. Bug is a Krll?"

"I never saw Mr. Bug *or* a Krll, not outside his armor, anyway, so I couldn't say. But my third cousin five times removed on my mother's side, old Flob-vlobb, he works in the warehouse section. Maybe he knows something."

"Great. Thanks again."

"Don't mention it."

Retief thought for a moment. "Tell me . . . if I asked you to find a place for my friend here to hide, someplace where he'd be safe from the Lord General and he could be kept out of trouble, could you do it?"

"Sure thing. I've got a janitor's closet just around the corner."

"Perfect. Shtliff, why don't you go with this nice Bloggie. You're no use to me with that hangover, and I'd rather you not fall into Kreplach's claws."

"I would rather the same myself. But what happens if they catch you?"

"Zub-zloob . . . if you don't hear from me by this time tomorrow, find a way to smuggle Shtliff out of here and back to his embassy. Can you do that?"

"Not a problem, Retief."

"I'll leave him with you, then. Treat him gently. He's got an organ-cluster ache that won't quit."

"I may have just the remedy. Some of our simple, Bloggie folk songs, sung very fast and very loudly, can have a most salubrious effect."

"And if you see the Lord General, you never saw me."

"I understand. Just don't get caught. Ta!"

Retief watched the six-limbed being skate off with the battered-looking Groaci in tow. Then he turned and headed for the vehicle bay.

He wanted to pay the interstellar gangster, Mr. Bug, a little visit.

3

Retief reached the cavernous vehicle bay without further encounters. The bay was as busy as it had been upon his arrival, with armored Krll officers, robotic privates, and armored maintenance personnel attending the half-score metallic giants—Krll warwalkers. He stood in the shadows observing for a time, watching as a Krll with officer's markings on his helmet climbed into the chest cavity of a Type-70 Deathwalker combat unit, forty feet tall in its gantry access cradle and bristling with weapons.

Zub-zloob had been right. The Krll liked their military toys as much as did the Concordiat.

The homeriform Krll, he saw, wore their seven-foot armor suits when they climbed into the much larger walker armor in a way that reminded him of assembling nested wooden Russian dolls. Apparently the same teleoperational connections that let them pilot the human-sized suits also controlled the giant economy size.

That was very good to know.

But for now, Retief preferred to remain mobile and inconspicuous. Stepping from the shadows, he walked briskly across the vehicle bay floor toward the yawning entrance.

It had been night when they'd brought him inside the fortress. The eternal overcast outside was growing light with the approaching day and casting a pale gray light through the barbican and open inner gates. To Retief's eye, activity in the vehicle bay was somewhat less than it had been upon his arrival. Evidently, the Krll were attuned to a nocturnal existence . . . or, possibly, they'd adapted a nocturnal lifestyle when they emerged from the sheltering embrace of the ocean.

Near the entrance, a small military cargo sled had been parked next to some supply crates. He stepped onto the flatbed and examined the controls. It was an old Groaci design, right down to the curlicue script identifying power on, ducted fan settings, and foot-massage controls.

The power cells were half-charged. Good enough. He flipped on the power switch, brought the fans whining up to speed, and felt the craft rise skittishly under his boots. A tiller bar gave directional control. He swung the nose left, pushed forward to pick up speed, and drifted casually through the inner gates and into the barbican.

The lines of soldiers were still in place—all of the lower-ranked robotic variety, he noted, save for one with a sergeant's gold insignia on his helmet, who stepped into the hoversled's path, one arm raised in a most officious manner.

"Halt!" the Krll called, the raspings of his gargled command rendered into Standard by the electronics in Retief's commando suit. "Let's see your base exit authorization, destination validation, intended cargo manifest, name, rank, and serial number!"

"Sergeant, do you see my rank insignia?"

The red light in the NCO's optical scanner slot hesitated, vibrating uncomfortably. "Uh, yessir, Double Battleaxe Captain!"

"And what is *your* rank?"

"Uh . . . Second Mace Sergeant, sir!"

"And why is a Second Mace Sergeant challenging a Double Battleaxe Captain, interfering with his performance of important duties of a secret military nature?"

The Krll noncom leaped aside, coming to rigid attention and rendering a Krll military salute, holding his first and middle fingers up to the top of his helmet and waggling them like antennae. "My mistake, Double Battleaxe Captain, *sir!*"

"That's better. I'll tell your superior that you're on your toes."

"Thank you, sir!" He dropped the salute as Retief urged the hoversled toward the fortress's outer gate. "Uh . . . sir? Your headlight is out. . . ."

"I *told* you this was a secret mission, Sergeant. No lights! Do you think I want to give away my location to the Enemy?"

"Oh. Of course, sir." He seemed to think about this a moment. "Hey! Wait a minute!"

But Retief was already past him and sliding through the gate and into the open air.

"Halt! Halt!"

Retief urged the sled's howling fans to a higher pitch. The sledbed slewed sharply beneath his feet as he flashed over a pothole in the dirt road, but he held his balance, clinging to the steering tiller.

The sharp *bzzzt!* of a medium-gauge power pistol snapped past his head, and the branch of a weirdly twisted Odiousitan tree off the side of the road twenty feet ahead burst into flame. He could hear the shrill clangor of an alarm going off and the metallic clatter of dozens of armored boots on the pavement. A second shot gouged a chunk of wood from the trunk of another tree.

"Save our forests," Retief said aloud, and he leaned hard to the right, pulling the tiller around and banking sharply in a hard turn that sent him flying off the road and into the light woods that surrounded the fortress.

They would have something out to catch him pretty soon now,

he thought. He needed to put as much distance between himself and his pursuers as he could.

At high speed, the hoversled steered more with the leaning of his body to left or right than with the tiller. Skittering over uneven ground, Retief shifted his weight back and forth, canting the sled to avoid trees as they flashed toward him . . . and past.

Another power-gun bolt snapped a branch on his left with a loud crack. In Krll armor, and with only a narrow vision slit to see through, he couldn't chance a glance back over his shoulder—a surefire way to steer the sled smack into a tree. Instead, he hunkered down and leaned forward, urging the sled to move just a bit faster.

A powerful energy bolt tore through the side of the sled's flatbed, leaving a half-molten furrow that missed his right boot by inches. He needed to take some evasive action and get an idea of how many were chasing him.

Ahead, almost dead in his path, a young tree with a five-inch-diameter trunk swiftly flashed toward him. He veered slightly right, holding his left arm out to the side. As he passed, his open palm slammed into the trunk; he gripped and leaned, his shoulder shrieking painful protest, as the sled whipped around the tree in a hairpin one-eighty.

As he released his grip on the tree trunk, his new course had him hurtling directly toward his pursuers. There were three of them—riding off-the-ground airbikes that looked like Bogan military scout vehicles. Two were single-seaters, the third mounted a sidecar, carrying a Krll soldier armed with a heavy power rifle.

He had only an instant to take it all in and lean his sled into the narrow opening between the two oncoming single-seater OTGs. The two veered sharply left and right to avoid Retief's unexpectedly charging cargo sled; one sideswiped a tree and sent its driver somersaulting heels over head a dozen times before he came to rest in a patch of alien ferns. The other whined as the driver fought for control, then bellied into a raised-earth embankment with a solid *whump* that launched its driver over the handlebars.

The OTG with the sidecar slewed sideways, narrowly avoided a clump of trees, and swung about, the passenger shifting back and forth as he tried to get a clean line of fire on Retief. Retief decided to discourage the notion and circled around to keep the OTG's driver between him and the rifle-bearing passenger.

As the OTG swung back onto Retief's tail, he decided to try another sharp course reversal. A skinny tree trunk appeared ahead. He reached out . . . grabbed hold . . .

The tree was dead—nothing more than a branchless pole sticking twenty feet up out of the ground, and as he swung around it, bark splintering, the three-inch trunk snapped off in his hand. For a dizzying moment, the sled skewed through the woods sideways as Retief fought to regain his balance. He managed to slow the out-of-control vehicle . . . and then it slammed into a clump of young trees that, fortunately, cushioned his stop rather than serving as a solid wall.

He gunned the cargo sled's ducted fans, maneuvering clear of the trees. The OTG was charging straight toward him, the rider already taking aim. Retief was still holding the snapped-off length of dead tree trunk in his left hand, twelve feet long with a forked Y at the far end.

"Well, why not?" Retief asked himself. He maneuvered the sled into position, dropped the pole across the instrument platform in the front, tucked the broken-off end beneath his right arm with the Y extending off to the left, and gunned the vehicle full-throttle forward.

Retief couldn't see the lobster faces of his pursuers, but the body language transmitted by their armored suits suggested emotions that, in humans, might have been either a 298-G (Wide-Eyed Surprise) or a 440-R (Stark Terror). The driver tried to put on the brakes, but airbikes are not known for stopping on proverbial tenth-guck coins. The fork of Retief's improvised lance caught the driver just at the juncture of helmet and torso armor, picking him up out of his saddle and flinging him back off his mount even as the tree trunk itself shattered in Retief's grasp.

The jolt nearly knocked Retief off of his machine, but he kept control, leaning into the impact and releasing the splintered remnant of the lance as he rocketed past the other vehicle, which was now in a fast end-for-end tumble. The sidecar passenger crashed into the side of a tree as the vehicle hit the ground and skipped. Two bounces later it exploded, but Retief was already racing clear.

"That," he said to no one in particular, "was joust in time."

His sled, not designed either for high-speed cross-country races or jousting tournaments, was developing an unpleasant clatter in one of its fans and was beginning to sag a bit to the left. Retief throttled back to a power-conserving pace not much faster than a jog on foot, angling for the direction that, according to his innate bump of direction, should take him to the Glooberville spaceport.

An hour later, the sled's engine died with a mournful whimper of downspooling turbines. Retief left the machine in the woods next to an oddly colored stream and continued on foot.

He was pretty sure that the spaceport was close, now . . . just over that next rise.

4

It wasn't the spaceport that greeted his eyes when he reached the top of the next ridge, but a scene of bizarre, alien devastation. The trees were gone here, replaced by twisted, spiky growths colored a dull, chalky yellow. Evidently, a sizeable Bloggie city had existed here. Several of the characteristic mushroom-shaped buildings were in evidence, but all were ripped open, toppled, burned, and smashed.

Trudging down the slope, Retief took a closer look at the yellow growths. A piece snapped off in his hand.

Crystalline sulfur. This must be the edge of the Sulfur Forest Sergeant Caldwilder had first mentioned. The ground was a powdery yellow ash that kicked up in dense clouds along his trail as he walked through it.

The sulfur "trees" and "bushes" were particularly strange. They looked like they'd grown that way, but Retief couldn't imagine a chemical or physical process that would cause sulfur to accrete in such blatantly biological shapes. From the look of things, this valley had once been covered by somewhat more terrestrial-type vegetation, such as the woods he'd just emerged from. He could see the remnants of fallen logs scattered across the ground half covered by sulfur ash, and many of the sulfur growths appeared to have crystallized over the trunks and branches of dead trees, which served now as skeletons for the delicately branching sulfur shapes.

The crystallized sulfur, he finally decided, was almost certainly the product of some biological process—the excretions of some sulfur-metabolizing bacteria or other microorganism that had moved into this valley. Where the sulfur had come from in the first place, he didn't know.

At least this explained the oddly colored stream he'd seen on the other side of the ridge and gave some hints to the nature of the highly acidic seawater on this world.

As he reached the edge of the ruined city, he became aware that it was not wholly abandoned. Several Bloggies peered at him from the shadows of wrecked mushroom-building shells. They seemed uncharacteristically shy at first, but after a few moments, several emerged into the light bearing banners covered with crudely drawn Krll characters.

"O mighty Krll conquerors!" one of the Bloggies cried out, his rumbling Krll speech translated by Retief's suit electronics. "We, the humble population of the fair metropolis of Xathgloober do hail and welcome you to this, our happy little village, as our liberators and our benefactors! We happy, primitive natives do—"

"Take it easy," Retief said, holding up a cautioning hand. "Don't stand on formality with me. I'm not even a Krll."

The speechmaker blinked several tiny eyes rapidly. "Not a Krll? That artificial hide you're wearing says otherwise."

"Actually," Retief told him, "I'm a Terry in disguise."

"A Terry!" another Bloggie said, emerging from the shelter of a wrecked home. "You must be that Retief we've heard tell about!"

"News *does* get around on this planet," Retief said, "doesn't it?"

"O mighty and powerful Terry liberators! We welcome you to—"

"Thanks for the heartfelt sentiment, fellows," Retief said, "but I'm not here to liberate anyone. I'm just passing through."

"Whoo! Thank the Great Druzlwit! I don't think we can survive being liberated even one more time!"

"I gather things have been pretty tough for you folks."

"You could say that. First we get liberated by Terries. Then we get liberated by Krll. Then Terries. Krll. Terries. Krll. Sometimes we wish the *Gruckies* would conquer us, just for a change of pace."

"The Groaci don't usually conquer something if they can steal it instead."

"If they want to steal the planet, they'd better hurry up. There might not be a lot left of it if they wait much longer."

Retief looked around, eyeing the devastated town. "Why do you stay here?"

"Hey, it might not look like much, but it's home!"

"I understand that. But why not move over to Glooberville? At least that's still in one piece, last time I saw."

"Huh. Glooberville was built by Bloggies who left Xathgloober after about the sixth time or so it was destroyed. We told 'em good luck, and *wrgle* if you find work. You see, most of us figure that growing a town right next to the spaceport and the Krll headquarters is kind of like setting up housekeeping right smack on the center of the X next to the sign reading BOMB HERE."

"Yeah, Glap-glupp," another Bloggie said. "We heard tell that the terrible Terries bombed Glooberville just last night. Dropped a whole load of leaflets. They have no mercy."

"Watch it, Ylup-yloop," the first Bloggie said. "This here's one of them terrible Terries."

"'Scuse me. My mistake. Long live the victoriously terrific Terries. Sorry . . . I don't have my flag on me at the moment."

"Don't worry about it. I'm not much for flag-waving myself."

"You asked why we didn't leave," the first Bloggie said. "I suppose we should, with yellowrock overrunning everything. But we can't just give up, you know what I mean? We keep planting the foo-foo and trying to fight the Scourge back. . . ."

"Whoa, hold on a second. That one went right over my head. What does foo-foo have to do with it?"

"Oh, well, you being an offworlder and everything, maybe you don't know about the delicate balance of nature and all. You see, the foo-foo plant not only nourishes us Bloggies, it sucks up the Tiny Yellow Demons at the same time."

"Tiny Yellow Demons?"

"Hey, we're primitives, without that sophisticated offworlder science you guys are always going on about, okay? Tiny Yellow Demons are these itsy-bitsy critters that are so small you can't see them with your bare eyeball. But they grow in the soil all over the planet, and when enough of them are in one place, they start pulling yellowrock out of the soil and the rainwater and spit it all over the ground, over the trees, slow Bloggies, everything."

"Mmm. Sounds like you're describing some sort of microorganism—a bacterium, maybe, that metabolizes sulfur."

"Like I said, Tiny Yellow Demons."

"And the foo-foo keeps them in check?"

"Well, it does if the Krll and the Gruckies don't come along and strip the fields bare—'putting it on the tab' or 'requisitioning,' as they call it. Or if the Terries and the Krll don't get to fighting with one another and burn the surface vegetation away. When that happens, the Tiny Yellow Demons move in and take over pretty quick."

"I can imagine. The sulfurous equivalent of desertification."

"Dessert who?"

"Never mind. You know, guys, I get the feeling that you would be happiest if everyone just left you alone."

"What kind of Terry-talk is that? I thought you were trying to liberate this here planet for the good of all Bloggiehood."

"Does it make sense to liberate you by burning off your planet? Or letting you get covered with solid sulfur?"

"Well, no. Not to me. But you Terries are aliens, at least to us. We figured you just had a very, well, alien way of looking at things."

"Maybe some of us do. That doesn't make it right, though. Tell you what, Glap-glupp. If you can point me at the Krll spaceport, I'll see what I can do to get the offworlders off your backs."

"Hey!" the Bloggie said brightly. "My cousin Glom-gloob *said* you were an all right sentient being, Retief!"

"Well, I can't make any promises just yet. Right now, it's just me against a whole lot of Terries, Krll, and Groaci who all seem to be interested in your little corner of the Galaxy. But with a little help I might be able to get them to see reason."

"You got yourself a deal, Retief! C'mon. I'll take you to Glooberville!"

5

An hour later, Retief and Glap-glupp stood atop a low ridge overlooking the starport. They'd approached from a different direction than Retief's rather public arrival the evening before. The starport tarmac spread out like a blanket immediately below them, with the town of Glooberville visible in the valley beyond. Retief counted twenty-five cargo starships of various designs and tonnages scattered about the field—an unusually large number for a world of Odiousita V's Class T status.

Unless, of course, most of those ships were Krll military transports. Five of them were huge bulk-cargo jobs massing at least forty thousand tons apiece. What were the Krll expecting to haul off of the planet, anyway? Not joyweed, surely, not in *those* quantities.

Off in a far corner, he could just make out the sleek lines of the GNN yacht, the Archangel-class *Story at Eleven*. Retief thought he could just make out some black specks in the floodlights around her tail, the Krll troops guarding her. She was dwarfed by the behemoths crowding the rest of the landing field.

"See over there to the left?" Glap-glupp said, pointing with a foot-arm. "That there's the starport warehouse district. The Krll they call Mr. Bug has his headquarters in there someplace."

"It's a big place, Glap-glupp. Do you know where?"

"I'm afraid not."

"You wouldn't happen to have any cousins working in the warehouse district, do you?"

"Not anymore. When Mr. Bug moved in, he ordered all of us Bloggies out. Either his own troops keep the place tidy, or he's not as much of a neat freak as the army-types are." The Bloggie considered the question a moment. "But my cousin Nurk-nakk has been helping load stuff onto the Krll transports. He says a lot of the activity down there is focused around Warehouse Three. He doesn't think it's their headquarters, but there's a lot of coming and going there, both the Krll and Mr. Bug's troops."

"Interesting. So is Mr. Bug working with the Krll military? Or is he just along for the ride?"

"Hard to tell, Retief. His soldiers 'requisition' our crops just like regular Krll troops. Kind of hard to tell the difference."

"I see. This cousin of yours, Nurk-nakk. Does he say what it was he was loading onto the transports? It wasn't foo-foo, was it?"

"Nah, nothing like that. Just lots of Krll and Gruckie stuff . . . rifles, armor, power packs, military vehicles, stuff like that."

"Okay, Glap-glupp. Thanks a lot. I'll take it from here."

"Don't you want help getting in down there? The whole warehouse area's walled off by a high fence."

"I shouldn't have any trouble. Besides," he rapped the metal torso of his Krll armor, "I've got this tin can to protect me if someone starts shooting. You just have your hide."

"There is that," the being said with a sage rumble. "Okay, then . . . but if you need help, Retief, just yell."

"You'll hear me all the way up here?"

"You'll be heard, one way or another."

Retief made his way down the slope of the ridge, found a paved road leading around the southwestern end of the tarmac, and followed it to the warehouse-district gate. Several dozen large, two- and three-story buildings with enormous doors were huddled behind a chain-link fence. The gate, he saw, was open . . . but guarded by a couple of men in technofedoras, cheap suits, and dull expressions. They leaned on either side of the gate, flipping quarter-guck pieces in perfect unison.

"Hold it right there, Pally," one of the GOSH soldiers said as Retief approached. "The boss already delivered Kreplach's cut, so's you can just turn that walking stack o' junk around and stilt back ta where ya came from."

"Yeah," the other thug growled. "See?"

"You misunderstand, gentlemen," Retief said. "I'm not here for the cut. I'm supposed to check out Warehouse Three."

"Uh-uh, Pally. Warehouse Three's closed now. You know that."

"Yeah. It won't open for another hour, yet, see?"

"Maybe I didn't get the word. Tell me more."

"Geeze, can't you lobsters tell time? Warehouse Three is closed. Come back later." The GOSH thug leered knowingly. "An' bring plenty of gucks if ya wanna have a *real* good time."

"Ah," Retief said, nodding his helmet in a knowing manner. "I think I see the problem. Mr. Bug sent me to *inspect* Warehouse Three . . . to make sure everything is set for an hour from now."

"Huh? Nobody told me nuttin' about that."

"Tsk, tsk, tsk," Retief tsked. "Whatever happened to good communications skills?"

"Communications are—*zzzzt!*—open on normal channels," the made man said. "See?"

"Well, obviously somebody didn't tell you boys what was going on. Do they often leave you boys out of the loop that way?"

"Geeze, ya got *that* right, mister. Nobody never tells us nuttin'!"

"That's awful! Why? Don't they trust you?"

"Nah, that's not it. I think the big bosses just get too wrapped up in their own stuff, y'know? I mean, it's hard work, doin' all that high-level boss stuff."

"Actually—*whrrrrr, zzzzt!*—Mr. Bug trusts no one, see?"

"I was given my orders by Louis the Libido. You know him?"

"Sure. I knows Louis. Da bum owes me a c-note. Thing is, I don't know *you*."

"Well, I'm Captain Hollishkes. And you two would be . . . ?"

"Huh? I'm Freddy da Finger."

"An' I'm Forty-seven. See?"

"Forty-seven! I'm glad to run into you! I have a message for you. A *private* message." He looked at Freddy. "Do you mind?"

"Huh? Nah. Go ahead."

Retief guided Forty-seven to one side, just out of earshot. "Listen to me carefully, Forty-seven. Sleep paren thirty close paren semicolon. Puts paren I think this guy's okay, and we should let him in, see? Close paren semicolon."

As soon as he'd given the sleep command, Forty-seven's already glassy eyes grew a bit more so. Retief had thirty seconds from that moment.

He patted the unmoving ichi-man on the shoulder, nodded, then walked back to face Freddy. "Sorry about that. I was told to give Forty-seven some personal news about his family."

"What kinda family does a made man have, anyway? An assembly line?" He leaned over to look past Retief's shoulder. "Hey, Forty-seven. You okay?"

The ichi-man remained unmoving, his internal clock counting off the seconds.

"He'll be okay," Retief assured the gangster. "So . . . how about it? Can I go check out Warehouse Three?"

"Well . . ."

Forty-seven suddenly stirred and turned. "I think this guy's— *zzzzt!*—okay, and we should let him in, see? See?"

"Ya think? We could get in lotsa trouble with da Boss."

"There's obviously been a screwup in communications," Retief said. "Now I can go back and tell my superiors that you wouldn't let me in. Or you can let me in and I won't tell a soul."

"Geeze, thanks," Freddy said. "You're an okay guy, fer a lobster."

"Thank you. I feel the same way about you."

"Just stay outta da tanks, okay?" He turned sideways and nudged Retief a couple of times with his elbow, leering meaningfully. "Know what I mean, Pally?"

Retief held up two metal-gloved fingers. "Lobster-scout's honor."

"Go on, then."

"Thanks."

He'd walked a half-dozen steps into the warehouse compound when Freddy called out, "Hey! Captain!"

"Yes?"

"You know your headlight's out?"

"Thanks. I'm taking the suit in to be inspected tonight. I think there's a screw loose somewhere."

"Okay. Just so's ya know."

Warehouse Three was easy enough to find. The road leading to it was thickly hung with signs in Krll lettering, some of them in neon or with flashing marquee bulbs. The huge door yawned open, admitting him to a cavernous structure—an ordinary warehouse, in fact, that appeared to have been converted into something else.

Just what, Retief wasn't entirely sure. He saw dozens of stalls under garishly lit flashing signs. There were oddly shaped and articulated racks that could have been either furniture for something the size and shape of a large lobster, or kitchen utensils. And, most numerous and most prominent, there were dozens of twelve-foot tanks filled with murky water. The bottoms of those tanks were covered with sand and each held eight or ten Krll—lobsterish-looking green and brown creatures watching him with beady stalked eyes like their terrestrial analogs in a pick-your-own seafood restaurant on Earth.

"So, see anything you like, Big Guy?" a sultry voice said from a speaker mounted on the side of the nearest tank.

"I'm not sure," Retief said. "I just got here." Evidently, one of the Krll was speaking to him, his words translated by Retief's commando suit.

Correction. *Her* words. The Krll in the tanks all appeared to be female—slightly smaller than the one he'd pulled from the captured armor and with prominent thoracic knobs on the ventral carapace. Looking closer, he noted that long, black cilia surrounded each stalked eye, like extra-long eyelashes waving at him seductively in the water.

"I'm sure we can work something out," the voice said. "But you'll hafta come back later. The joint's closed right now."

"Yeah," another voice cut in. "Come back when the place is hot!"

"I don't know, Bun," a third voice said. "I think he's kind of cute. We could give him a special preview. . . ."

"Cute? How can you tell with that silly-looking artificial carapace?"

"Yeah, Captain. Shuck the fake shell and let's see whatcha got in the claspers department."

"Thanks, ladies," Retief said, "but actually, I was sent down by the Lord General to check everything out and make sure the place was ready."

"What do you mean?" Bun said. "Kreppie's our best customer!"

"Yeah. He was down here a week ago when Warehouse Three first opened for business, and he checked out *everything*, believe me!"

"That's for sure. My swimmerets are *still* sore!"

"I see. And is business . . . good?"

"The best, Captain. Come on in and find out!"

"Thanks, but I'll have to pass on that." He looked around the cavernous warehouse at some of the other structures. "What are all those booths for, anyway?"

"Goodness, you *are* new!" Bun told him. "What are you, fresh off the sea farm? You got your painting booths and your buffing racks, for the warrior who wants to pamper himself. You got your suit polishers if your armor gets all dirty on the battlefield, and a garage service if your armor needs a lube job and touch-up. And of course, there's the casino in back. Everything the well-endowed Krll warrior on a twenty-six-hour pass and with *grples* to spend could want."

"*Grples?*"

"Well sure, Handsome! What, didja think we was entertainin' you guys 'cause we like your looks? Kreplach contracted with Mr. Bug and the Groaci to set up this here fun-town strip for you soldiers. You can get your carapace buffed and painted, your claws sharpened and your antennae preened, all in the same place! You can eat someplace besides the fortress canteen, or sit down with your buddies in a bar, guzzle *zkkk*-water until you're blind, and ogle the she-Krll waitresses for as long as you can see. You can head for the casino and blow a few thou on games of almost-chance, or enjoy a few hours out of those damned suits and back in sweet-tasting, nonacid seawater! And then there's the *big* draw . . . us! Fifty tanks, no waiting, twenty-five *grples* for an hour, or two hundred for all day."

"Sounds like heaven. It almost makes war sound like fun."

"Nothing's too good for our guys at the front, right, girls?"

"Right. As long as they can pay for it. . . ."

"This is all very interesting, ladies, but I wonder if you could tell me where I can find Mr. Bug."

"Oh, he's upstairs, in his office," Bun said. One of the lobsters in the tank waved her antennae toward a set of stairs on the nearest wall. "He's probably up there counting his *grples*. You sure we can't interest you in a quick tumble in the tank?"

"Thanks. I'm sure."

"What kind of a green-blooded Krll are you, anyway?"

"One who is definitely *not* your type, Bun. I'm afraid it would never work out."

He walked over to the stairs and started up.

CHAPTER NINE

1

At the top of the stairs, Retief entered a long corridor leading toward the back of the warehouse. There, a pair of GOSH goons stood coin-flipping guard in front of a door with black lettering in three different languages on its frosted glass panel. The words in Standard read:

PRIVATE—NO ADMITTANCE. GO AWAY.
YEAH, PALLY, DIS MEANS YOU, SEE?

"Hold it right there, fella," the ichi-man on the right said, holding up a hand. "You ain't s'posed to be up here, see?"

"Yeah," the other amended. "Youz ain't—*zzzzt!*— supposed t'be here, see?"

"I didn't realize you boys came in matched sets," Retief said, looking from one to the other. "I'm here to see Mr. Bug. Is he in?"

"Not to *you*, lobster-boy." *Zzzzt!* "See?"

"I think he'll want to see me."

"Yeah? And who are you, pally? See?"

"I'm Captain Hollishkes," Retief told them. "What are your names?"

"I'm Sixty-five," the ichi-man on the left said. "See?"

"Yeah, an' I'm Toity-tree, see?"

"I do see. Sixty-five, Thirty-three . . . wait paren close paren semicolon."

The GOSH robot on the left went glassy-eyed, the coin bouncing off his frozen-in-place hand and falling to the floor, but the other snapped out his arm and caught Retief by the throat.

"Da name's 'Toity-tree,' see? An' yours is—*zzzzt!*—dead meat . . . see?"

With superhuman strength, the robot's fingers tightened on the flexible neck guard of Retief's Krll battle armor, squeezing with brutal, crushing force as it lifted his six-four frame clear of the floor. Retief tried to speak, but as the neck guard began to collapse against his throat, he could not make a sound more coherent than a strangled gurgle. The GOSH robot's grip tightened. . . .

Releasing the ichi-man's wrist, Retief threw as powerful a punch as he could, landing it squarely on the side of the robot's head. Dangling awkwardly in the air, without solid footing, he couldn't deliver much power. The hard, rubbery surface of the machine's synthflesh absorbed the blow, and the only damage was to Retief's knuckles. He swung again, a hard, stinging left . . . but with absolutely zero effect. His kicks landed on the machine's armored torso with no more effect than a gentle nudge. He tried jamming both of his thumbs, held rigidly side by side, into the ichi-man's eyes, trying to blind it, to distract it even for a moment, but the glassy orbs apparently were armored in anticipation of such an attack. All that happened was that the syndicate robot's eyes appeared to glow a bit, as if with anticipation.

One more thing to try. Reaching up behind his head, Retief hit the release lever on his helmet, then yanked it forward and off his head. Hinged to the front torso of his armor, it flipped down, opening the suit from neck to crotch.

Retief pulled his legs and arms free and dropped backward onto the floor, leaving the ichi-man still strangling a now-empty suit of armor.

He tried to speak again but only managed a harsh and unintelligible croak. The ichi-man tossed the empty armor aside with a pots-and-pans clatter, and advanced on Retief, arms outstretched.

Retief rolled aside, swinging his legs around, catching the robot's ankles and sweeping its legs out from beneath it. The GOSH thug fell full length on the floor with a thunderous crash. Instantly, Retief was astride the machine's back, pinning one wrist between the ichi-man's artificial shoulder blades. The machine was strong, terribly strong, and the muscles in Retief's arms bulged with the strain as servomotors whined in overheated protest.

Retief cleared his throat, put his mouth by the struggling robot's ear, and said, "Toity-tree, wait paren close paren semicolon."

The made man froze in place, unmoving, its arm still locked rigidly at its back. Retief arose, straightened his black commando garb, and ruefully massaged his bruised throat. "Looks like that's an *ichi* you can't reach," he said. Both robots remained frozen, one standing, the other prone. With a C++ wait command, with no number within the parentheses, they would remain that way, unmoving and unresponsive, until someone gave them a new command.

And since that command might come at any moment via radio from some central control center, Retief decided not to take the time to don the Krll armor again. It had been useful so far, but it was uncomfortable, hot, and it cramped his style.

He snatched a small power pistol of Groaci manufacture from the standing robot's shoulder holster, straightened the machine's tie and technofedora, then leaned hard on the door, and walked in.

2

"Hey!" a shrill little-girl's voice chirped. "What's the matter? Can'tcha read?"

The speaker was a large Krll resting in a water-filled pan atop a broad desk of richly stained copperwood. Two smaller Krlls, with gaudy gold carapace paint and prominent thoracic knobs, appeared to be preening the being's antennae with their anterior claws.

A half-dozen GOSH thugs, both human and artificial, started to close in on Retief from all sides, hands reaching for holstered weapons inside cheap suit coats. Retief raised his own pistol and squeezed off a brief burst, hitting the water in the pan an inch from the big Krll's left fore claw with a sharp, sizzling hiss and a puff of steam.

"Yowch! Hey! Watch it with that thing!"

"Call off your boys, Mr. Bug, or there'll be boiled lobster tail on the menu tonight, and you'll be the featured selection."

"All right! All right!" the being squeaked. "Just take it easy! You heard the alien, boys. Put up your heaters."

"Drop your guns on the floor," Retief added. "Move slow and keep your hands where I can see them ... or your boss gets cooked."

"Do what he says! Do what he says!"

Reluctantly, the syndicate hoods deposited a pile of hardware on the floor in front of the desk, power pistols, lasers, antique slug throwers, two light rocket launchers, a small flamethrower, and a few grenades.

"Quite an arsenal there," Retief commented. "Are you planning on invading someone, Mr. Bug?"

"What's it to ya, Terry?" The Krll regarded Retief for a moment with beady, stalked eyes, then said, "Beat it girls. I got business t' take care of."

The two smaller Krll skittered off the desk and out of the room, claws clicking quickly across the floor. The GOSH boss seemed to have recovered some of his aplomb. Reaching out of the tub, he flipped open a humidor, extracted a large cigar, and snipped off the tip with a fighting claw. "So," he said, puffing the cigar alight. "You took a helluva big risk comin' up here, Terry. Whatcha want? A cut of the take? A piece of the action?"

"Something like that. You can start by filling me in on your scam. What are you doing here, anyway?"

"Hey, I'm just a simple businessman, eking out a precarious living selling a little of this . . . a little of that."

"Uh-huh. And the fact that some of that is illegal just adds spice to the game, right?"

"Illegal?" the Krll squeaked. "*Illegal?* By whose rules, illegal? You Terries? What's so-called illegal to you barbarians is simple business to us, and the so-called Concordiat's so-called blockade on certain comestibles ain't nothing but blatant restraint of free trade!"

"I see your point." With his free hand, Retief extracted a perfumed dopestick from his chest pocket and struck it alight. "Terrible when you have to deal with the riffraff, isn't it?"

"You said it. Ol' Kreplach has the right idea. Conquer all of you, put you to useful work, and bring you civilization and enlightenment . . . at least as much as you uncivilized types can handle."

"Interesting. What is your definition of civilized, anyway?"

"Well, lessee. You got your readin' and your writin' and your higher math. You know, two divided by the negative square root of zero, stuff like that."

"Yes . . ."

"You got your basic tools like the screw-U and the disinclined plane. You got your basic ability to build tall buildings and parking lots and shopping malls, and to tell Mother Nature where she can get off. Oh, and of course there's the ability to wage war on a planetary scale."

Retief puffed at the dopestick. "So far it sounds uncomfortably like us Terries."

"You're forgettin' the most important Law of Civilization."

"Oh? What's that?"

"Bottom feeders are on top."

"I beg your pardon?"

"*You eat other living creatures,*" the gangster boss bellowed.

"You mean meat?"

"Yeah, I mean meat! Where do you think meat comes from, dummy? You think it grows on trees? Now, if the meat is already dead when it drifts down to the bottom, that's fine. The riper the better, right? Or plants. Veggies is okay. But you barbarians kill other creatures, cook them, and then eat them!" He waved a claw as Retief blew a cloud of scented smoke. "Hey! What's that stuff you're breathing?"

"Not joyweed, if that's what you're afraid of."

"Hey, us Krll ain't afraid of *nuttin'*! But, uh, yeah, we don't like that native foo-foo stuff."

"Understandable, since it seems to slow Krll metabolism to a crawl." He glanced around the room. Mr. Bug's guards and toadies stood in a nervous huddle in a far corner, watching the interview. The Krll was far too confident, had been, ever since the conversation had begun. "So Terries aren't civilized because they eat meat."

"Bingo! Maybe you Terries ain't as dumb as you look."

"What about the natives of this planet? They're plant eaters. But I heard Kreplach express the sentiment that Odiousita V wasn't even inhabited."

"Well, it ain't. Not by civilized folks, anyway. The highest form of life here eats plants, yeah, but they don't have space travel and they don't build buildings. They *grow* them. A race of dumb-bunny farmers and janitors, is what they are. Us Krll are light-years ahead of them in the civilized arts."

"I see. And Terries?"

"As I see it, you Terries has got potential. You could be trained. A few thousand years under our benevolent but firm rule, condition you to eat garbage like civilized folks, and you might make somethin' of yourselves. Assuming we can break you of some of your more unsavory habits."

"Like eating fresh meat."

"Exactly."

Retief walked around the room. On one wall was a seven-foot-tall velvet painting in rather poor taste of a Krll in battle armor, shown life-sized, standing astride a pile of smoking bodies, waving a black Krll flag. Apparently, the Krll warrior's headlight was out. Nothing showed in the helmet but a black slit.

"You know, I'd be more convinced if you sounded more like a businessman, and less like a politician or a social scientist. What does a 'simple businessman' care about civilizing uncivilized natives?"

"Well, there's the market to consider, right? And your blockade *is*, like, restraining our free trade and all, and keeping us from settling old scores with those damned eight-legged nightmare ogres next door! We will destroy them, crush them, mangle them! We will burn their cities and enslave their shes! We—" The Krll stopped, its antennae wigwagging furiously. "Uh, I mean . . . it keeps us from pursuing our lawful pursuits in the Cluster!"

"By 'damned eight-legged nightmare ogres,'" Retief said slowly, drawing on his dopestick, "I assume you mean the B'ruklians."

"What if I do?" the being said, its chirping voice again carefully neutral. "They ain't civilized neither. When we conquer them, we'll probably save a few of the more docile ones to breed as beasts of burden."

"Uh-huh. They don't have space travel . . . and with those crocodile jaws and rows of sharp needle teeth, they certainly aren't vegetarians. Two strikes against them." He drew another deep lungful of scented smoke from his dopestick. "But . . . you know something interesting? I don't think the B'ruklians of B'rukley are native to that planet."

"Uh . . . so what? I mean, what makes you say that?"

"Have you ever seen one?"

The Krll seemed to shrug with its antennae. "Doesn't matter if I have."

"Hmm. They have this thick, tough hide." Retief held up a thumb and forefinger, an inch apart. "Must be this thick. And it's dark colored, black or dark gray or brown. Good protection against the radiation from a hot, bright star. The thing is, Firstsun, as they call their primary, is a cool red star. Almost no ultraviolet component to the stellar output at all."

"Yeah? So what? I never went in for astrology."

"Astronomy. Here's another thing. They're solidly built, with eight legs and a low center of gravity. Heavy musculature. Almost as if they evolved on a high-gravity planet. But B'rukley has a gravitational field of only about nine-tenths of a G. You'd expect life forms native to the place to be taller, more willowy . . . not built like a tank."

"So what do I care about a bunch of ugly alien barbarians, huh?"

"Okay, let's talk about the Krll."

"Hey! Now you're getting' personal!"

"Obviously, *you* folks evolved in the ocean, where the planet's gravity field doesn't matter so much. It would affect the water pressure, of course. The fact that you've adapted well to life out of the water means you didn't evolve in a high-pressure environment. If you had, you'd explode when you approached the surface. Also, the coloration of your carapace suggests you got a fair share of sunlight where you grew up. A deep-benthic life-form would tend to be colorless or even transparent."

"Listen, I don't like the way this is goin'."

"So, my guess would be that the Krll evolved from bottom-feeder crustaceans in warm, shallow seas—"

"You watch that 'bottom-feeder' stuff! Us Krll is top of the old food chain, you get it?"

" . . . maybe on coral reefs, maybe in a shallow, inland sea, but either way, close to land. The question is what the evolutionary impetus was that drove you to develop a technic civilization. Fire, mining and smelting, internal combustion engines, electronics, rocketry . . . you would need to work out all of those, and more, before you developed spaceflight, and you couldn't do that if you were strictly an oceanic species. You must have crawled up on shore a lot, maybe to feed or maybe to escape oceangoing predators."

"Now you're startin' to talk dirty. You watch your buccal opening!"

"If you evolved in an inland sea," Retief went on, "you might've been forced to come ashore as the sea slowly dried up. But my guess is that there were predators, both in the ocean and on the land. Something big and something nasty, that liked to eat Krll."

"*Nobody eats Krll and gets away with it!*" the crustacean squealed. "*Nobody! We'll trample them! We'll smash them! We'll burn their—*"

"Yes, yes, we've been over that already. These predators must've been pretty efficient. Probably they were as sentient as the Krll were, or more so."

"*That's a damned speciesist lie!*"

"The Krll were forced to develop intelligence and, later, a technic civilization, just to survive. To keep from being eaten into extinction."

"I'm warning you—"

"I consider myself warned. What's also interesting is that the Krll appear to have developed quite a nasty racial inferiority complex along the way."

"We are *not* inferior! We are by divine right the supreme overlords of the Galaxy!"

"You had to prove you were better than your predatory enemies. You *had* to conquer them, trample them, and so on and so forth just to convince yourself that you were their equals . . . or their betters. Gave you fellows a mighty big chip on the shoulder and a distinctly black-and-white picture of the universe. I'd guess that after a few thousand years of warfare, you managed to get the upper hand . . ."

"Upper claw!"

" . . . and chased the predators right off the planet."

"We exterminated them! We drove the hell-fiends to the extinction they so richly deserved! . . ."

"Well, you got all the ones still on your planet, but some of them escaped your claws, didn't they? This hypothetical predator species must have already developed star travel by the time you took over. Maybe they just decided to migrate elsewhere and leave the homeworld to you."

"The fiends thought they could escape us! 'Vermin,' they called us! We started off as hors d'oeuvres, but then we became vermin! But we will have our just revenge!"

"How long ago was that, anyway? How many thousands of years, while you Krll developed a dry-land technology, learned the secrets of metallurgy and spaceflight, and finally set out to find the monsters who'd left such a deep impression on your racial memory?"

"Too long . . ."

"Long enough for the predators to become relegated to folklore and fairy tales, the sort of boogie man you use to scare your larvae into behaving themselves. I'll bet it was a real shock to find the living reality when your long-range interstellar scouts first discovered B'rukley."

"Whoa. Now you're getting into the area of state secrets, fella."

"By that time, a lot of you probably didn't even believe the monsters existed in real life. And here you found them alive and well, teaching school and sharing the mysteries of the Holy Mystic Fortune Cookies on B'rukley. That discovery probably jangled the alarm bells in every Krll in the Shamballa Cluster."

"For your information, we call it the 'Great Awakening.' It was the moment when we discovered our true destiny in the universe!"

"And what was that?"

"Why, to rid the Galaxy of the hell-fiends once and for all! And, just incidentally, to assume our rightful place as lords of all creation!"

"So . . . there on B'rukley is the one species guaranteed to drive Krll nuts, singly and collectively. You're not strong enough to invade at that point. You're probably pretty new to star travel. Your homeworld is in the Cluster, isn't it? Not somewhere off in the Galactic Core. That was a story to throw your enemies and potential enemies off track."

"That's classified!"

"The B'ruklians were probably a bit more advanced technologically than you, too. They'd had star travel longer than you, after all. Maybe you just weren't sure how advanced they were . . . in the area of military weapons, for instance." He pulled on the last stub of his dopestick, burning it to extinction. He snubbed out the butt in Mr. Bug's pan of water.

"Hey!"

"For all you knew, as soon as you appeared, they'd eat you for dinner."

"I warned you about that dirty language, Terry!"

"After all, the Krll have an inborn terror of being eaten by things bigger than you. Am I right?"

"Enough! Enough already!"

"You couldn't know that once the B'ruklians had colonized B'rukley, they'd actually given up on star travel and settled down to a nice, sedentary decline, maintaining just enough technology to let them enjoy the good life." Retief reached into his pocket and produced the half-burned joint of joyweed, left over from when he'd taken down Captain Hollishkes in the elevator. "So you looked around and found a likely planet right next door, orbiting a star a lot like your home sun, probably with a climate a lot like home, and began hatching your plot. Just when did the Groaci put in an appearance, anyway?" He puffed the joint alight.

"None of your business!"

"You needed the Groaci to help you in the military department. Ships. Weapons. Armored suits. Even the big warwalkers. Most of it either Bogan or Groaci manufacture, and with Groaci electronics driving them, including the neural transceivers that allow you to control the machinery. I wonder. Did the Groaci come along and take you on as clients when you were still planet-bound on your homeworld?"

"You've learned more than enough, Terry spy! Now it's your turn to answer questions . . . after which we conduct a colorful execution!"

"Really? I thought I had the gun?"

"Do you think a Krll of my exalted rank, as head of the Krll

Secret and Nefarious Activities Agency, would be unguarded? Pitiful fool!" He waved a claw. "Behold your doom!"

"You mean the concealed gun slit disguised as part of that painting?"

He drew in a mouthful of smoke, careful not to inhale it, and blew it out in a stream directly into Mr. Bug's face. The Krll gagged and sputtered, but his movements slowed almost at once. With an audible pop, a gun barrel poked its way through the painting, right at the black slit in the figure's helmet, but Retief was already in motion, scooping Mr. Bug from the water pan with his free hand and holding him up as a shield.

"Don't shoot, unless you want to fry your boss!"

The gun in the wall waggled uncertainly. One of the disarmed thugs in the corner lunged for one of the weapons on the floor. Retief snapped off a shot that half melted the pistol as he picked it up, making him yelp and hold his burned fingers to his mouth.

Retief leaped to the wall next to the painting, too close, now, for the concealed gunner to bring his weapon to bear. He took the smoking joyweed joint from his mouth and flipped it through the gun port, then backed toward the door, still holding the slowly squirming lobster in front of him. The gun in the painting tracked after him . . . but slowly now, almost sluggishly. A moment later, the painting bulged, then tore, and an armored Krll soldier burst through, staggering a bit and waving at the smoke billowing around him. Retief fired twice, taking out the suit's knees and sending the suit toppling onto the floor.

The gangsters surged toward him, some already scooping up guns. Retief tossed Mr. Bug straight at them, then ducked through the door.

Somewhere, an alarm was shrilling.

3

Pounding down the stairs, Retief reached the warehouse floor and jogged for the door. Around him, female Krll waved their antennae in consternation within their tanks. "It's me, girls," he told them. "Don't tell anyone. I'm in disguise."

"Sure you don't want to take off that horrible scare-suit and join us in here?" one of the Krll cooed.

"Not today, thanks."

Outside, the warehouse area was coming alive with Krll soldiers and vehicles racing about in a remarkable impression of a kicked-over anthill. Apparently, Mr. Bug had regular troops at his command as well as GOSH thugs. What had he called himself? Head of the Krll Secret and Nefarious Activities Agency? That made him Shtliff's opposite number and explained his covert connection with the Krll military. But it also meant that getting out of this place was going to take some real doing.

"There's the Terry!" a rumbling voice called. "Get him!"

Power-gun bolts sizzled past Retief's head, melting fist-sized craters in the warehouse wall at his back. Retief fired back, forcing his pursuers to duck, then ran for it, ducking into an alley between two warehouse buildings and making for the perimeter fence.

Glap-glupp said to yell if I needed help, Retief thought. *I'm not sure what he could do, though....*

Just keep running in the same direction you're going now, Retief, a deep-voiced thought sounded in his head. *We'll get you out.*

Glap-glupp?

I told you we have a deal, Retief. We help you. You get these civilized foreigners to see reason. Right?

Right now they're not being very reasonable, Retief told the disembodied thought. *Don't do anything rash . . . like getting yourselves shot.*

Don't worry about us. Just . . . get down!

Retief dropped to the ground and rolled. Twenty feet in front of him, an armored figure stepped out from behind the corner of the warehouse, firing wildly, sending a volley of close-spaced energy bolts sizzling through the air just above him. Retief brought his pistol up as the soldier adjusted his aim. . . .

The chain-link fence at the Krll soldier's back shuddered violently, bulging inward. The soldier heard the clatter and turned, throwing up his arms as the fifteen-foot-high fence ripped free of its embedded concrete supports and flattened the Krll trooper like a giant flyswatter. Dozens of Bloggies, massive, six-leg-armed, and angry, surged in over the fallen fence and the downed soldier. One waved a leg-arm, urging him on. *Let's go, Retief! They've got some heap-big war machines on the way, and we can't tangle with those babies!*

Retief dashed over the fallen fence. The woods beyond, he saw, were filled with Bloggies. He could *hear* them now, in his mind, a kind of low-voiced murmuring as he picked up the fringes of their telepathic link.

"I took the liberty of rounding up a few of our guys, Retief," one of the Bloggies told him, speaking aloud instead of in his head. "Whatcha think? Can we take them down now?"

"Glap-glopp?"

"Nah. I'm his eighteenth cousin, forty-seven times removed. Schlup-shlupp's the name."

"Good to meet you." A powerful energy bolt exploded like lightning among the trees, setting one aflame. The towering shape of a Krll warwalker appeared in the alley between the warehouses, a light proton cannon mounted on its right arm. It fired again, a badly aimed bolt that took out a corner of a warehouse and sent burning debris showering into the woods. The Bloggie army wavered.

"We can't face artillery like that without weapons and armor, Schlup-shlupp," he said. "Pull your guys back. We need to find another way to take on the Krll army."

"I was kind of hoping you'd say that." *Okay, everybody!* the thought burned in Retief's brain. *Fall back! Fall back! Scatter into the woods! Meet at the Rendezvous Point as soon as you can manage it!*

The Bloggies could move, Retief saw, with remarkable speed for beings so massive. The native army was already melting away into the forest.

"Climb aboard, Retief," Schlup-shlupp said, offering a leg-arm. "We can travel faster if you ride."

"Much obliged, Schlup-shlupp." He scrambled up the gnarled and leathery surface of the leg-arm and clung to the humped top of the being. Krll soldiers were spilling out of the warehouse area now and entering the burning woods, with the towering hulk of the warwalker striding above them. Krll voices called to one another. Energy bolts hissed and snapped through the air.

"Hang on, Retief. The ride could get a little rough."

He clung tighter to the leathery folds of the Bloggie's hide as the being leaned in one direction and began rippling its six leg-arms in a complex dance too quick for the human eye to follow or make sense of. Controlling that kind of muscular coordination, Retief thought, required an incredibly powerful brain and nervous system. Telepathic communication might be only one of the side benefits of such a brain.

There's a lot more to you Bloggies than meets the eye, Retief thought as the being rippled its way through the forest at the speed of a galloping horse. Trees flashed by on either side, and branches lashed at his back. He leaned closer to his strange mount, clinging more tightly.

Don't know what you mean, Retief, the being's thought came back. *We're just us, simple, sentient beings trying to understand what you aliens mean by "civilization."*

"Right now I wouldn't worry about civilization," Retief replied aloud. "We need to find a way to *save* you from civilization, Krll-style . . . and after that there's still the Terries to think about."

One worry at a time, Retief, replied the being's thought. *One worry at a time . . .*

CHAPTER TEN

1

It seemed a strange place for a council of war—a lovely, secluded glade in the shadow of a moss-clotted cliff, with a slender pink and orange waterfall splashing in a muddy pool and a tumbling stream that wound its way down a gentle slope into the tangle of jungle below. Parts of the base of the cliff had eroded away with the highly acid waters, creating deeply shadowed rock shelters and overhangs.

Retief sat within the depths of one of these. It was considerably cooler here than outside. More, he was having difficulty with the UV gel he'd spread on his skin . . . was it only the day before? Between sweat and scrambling through the woods and wearing full body armor for so long, that gel was starting to wear thin. There were raw spots on his forehead and on the backs of his hands where he'd already burned a little, and the acid-laden spray from the waterfall wasn't helping matters. He needed to stay in the shade as much as possible.

Around him, like giant, dark-gray starfish, a dozen Bloggies sprawled contentedly on convenient rocks, eyes glittering in the near darkness. Retief found he couldn't hear their thoughts now; perhaps only when they were excited or keyed up to a battle pitch could he eavesdrop on their natural telepathic connections.

"So explain it so a simple primitive native like myself can understand it, Retief," Schlup-shlupp was saying. "How are we gonna get the offworlders to leave us alone if you don't want us to attack them?"

"Schlup-shlupp, the only area of civilization you Bloggies are at *all* deficient in is the art and science of warfare . . . and that, believe me, is not something to be ashamed of! But it means you can't take on the Krll *or* the Concordiat war machines head on. If you try to confront them with their tactics and their mind-set, you will lose. Pure hearts and good intentions are all very well, but they won't make a dent in a Mark XVIII Bolo or a Krll Type-70 Deathwalker. And I don't care how thick and tough your hides are, they won't protect you against the half-megaton-per-second firepower of a 25cm Hellbore."

"'The tree of liberty must be refreshed from time to time with the blood of patriots and tyrants,'" Schlup-shlupp said.

"Where did you learn to quote Thomas Jefferson?" Retief asked.

"The thought was in your mind a while ago. Sorry. Didn't mean to snoop."

"That's okay. And it's true that if you want freedom, you have to pay for it. But I think there are better ways for you folks to go about it than trying to drown all the offworlders in your own blood."

"When you put it that way, maybe you're right. Us Bloggies might be primitive, but we're not stupid."

"There's a good chance that the Krll will be leaving soon anyway," Retief said. "I learned a lot from Mr. Bug. It turns out the Krll are really interested in a planetary neighbor of yours."

"B'rukley."

"Right. It seems they have some old, old scores to settle with the B'ruklians, from back when the two of them were evolving together on the same planet."

"I've got a sixteenth cousin eight times removed," one of the Bloggies mused. "Nurk-nakk the Adolescent."

"I've heard the name," Retief said. "He works at the spaceport, right?"

"He's the one. Sometimes folks confuse him with Nakk-nurk the Adipose, but he's from the north-Nurk branch of the family."

"I gather he's been loading Krll transports," Retief prompted.

"Oh, yeah. Anyway, he told me a little while ago that things have really gotten stirred up in a big way down there. The Krll are starting to load up their big war machines. He says there's talk of them leaving real soon."

"It could be that my little tête-à-tête with Mr. Bug has made them advance their invasion schedule," Retief said. "If true, you might be rid of them sooner than we thought."

"So what about the other offworlders?" one of the Bloggies asked. "You know. The ones that look like you."

"Them we can probably handle with a few well-placed threats of diplomacy," Retief replied. "The Bloggies will just have to be careful about signing anything . . . and don't let them get you involved in PISH-TUSH resettlement programs or fast-food franchises."

"We don't eat fast food," Schlup-shlupp pointed out. "Foo-foo shrubs just sort of sit there. They don't try to get away or anything."

"Sounds easier on the digestive processes than the alternative. What's concerning me is what the Krll are planning to do about the Concordiat Navy."

"You mean all the spaceships you people have circling around in the sky up above the cloud layer?"

"Yes. The Concordiat has fleet elements parked in stellar orbit and out-system. The Krll aren't going to be able to slip a whole fleet of troop transports past the Concordiat pickets, so they must have something devious in mind. I wonder what it is?"

"The Krll are kind of in-your-tentacles about stuff," a Bloggie opined. "Maybe they just mean to push right through."

"I doubt that. Troop transports don't take kindly to naval Hellbores. If they're planning on fighting their way through, they won't be able to count on having much of an invasion force left when they reach B'rukley." He thought for a moment. "Tell me something, someone who's related to Nurk-nakk."

"That would be just about all of us, Retief," Schlup-shlupp pointed out. "We have *big* families, with lots of cousins."

"I've noticed. He's still working at the spaceport? They haven't kicked all the Bloggies out after that little contretemps at the warehouse district?"

"Sure, he's still there." Schlup-shlupp paused, then added, "He says they're blaming the counter-temp on wild Bloggies. They think he's tame. I guess they don't know us Bloggies very well."

"No, I don't think they do. If I were to get to the spaceport, get inside the perimeter fence, could Nurk-nakk sneak me aboard one of those transports? Inside a cargo crate, maybe."

Again, Schlup-shlupp hesitated, as though carrying on an internal conversation. "Sure!" he said at last. "Right now, there's so much confusion there it shouldn't be a problem at all."

"Okay, then. Have him be ready to meet me. You decide where a good place would be."

"Uh . . . Retief? You sure this isn't like what you were telling us a while ago? Refreshing Krll with your blood, and everything?"

"Don't worry, Schlup-shlupp. I have no intention of giving my blood to anyone today. But it's just possible we have a way to stop this war and get the offworlders out of here. Now here's what I have in mind. . . ."

2

It was very nearly the end of the long, long Odiousitan day when Retief reached the starport perimeter fence, along with an escort of three Bloggies, including Schlup-shlupp. A fourth Bloggie waited on the other side of the fence with a handcart—no, a tentacle-cart—that carried a large wooden crate. "Hurry it up, you guys," this last Bloggie urged. "The Krll are really touchy today. They're checking ID badges and everything."

"ID badges?" Retief asked.

"Yeah." Nurk-nakk turned slightly, revealing a laminated card stapled to his tough hide just above one of his six eyes. "And it smarts, I can tell you."

"Let's see if we can avoid that for me," Retief said.

The Bloggies grabbed hold of the chain-link fence with their tentacle-tip tendrils and tore it open like tissue, creating a hole large enough for Retief to slip through. "Remember what I said, Schlup-shlupp," he said once he was on the other side. "Stay low and stay out of trouble. If I'm not back in five of your days, do what you feel you have to to get rid of the Krll . . . but try to find Desiree Goodeleigh first and tell her exactly what I told you. Okay?"

"Okay, Retief."

"Good luck, fellows."

"Same to you. May the mud ever squelch beneath your tendrils."

"With a blessing like that, how can I miss?"

The empty crate was large enough for Retief to crawl inside and hunch over while Nurk-nakk sealed the lid. It was back-achingly uncomfortable, but he shouldn't have to endure it for too long. Slender gaps between the slats admitted air and gave him a view on the outside world, albeit an annoyingly blinkered one. Nurk-nakk trundled the tentacle-cart across the spaceport tarmac, steering clear of massed ranks of waiting Krll troops and making for one of the largest of the Krll transports—an immense, flattened black-and-silver egg with a yawning cargo door in the side high enough to accommodate a fifty-foot warwalker. In fact, pressing his eye against one of the slit openings in his crate, Retief could see a line of Deathwalkers filing slowly up the ramp and disappearing into the starship's cavernous maw.

Before long, Nurk-nakk had joined a procession of armored Krll troopers, ponderously clumping warwalkers of all sizes, and other Bloggies pushing crates on wheeled tentacle-carts. A pair of

Krll guards stood to either side of the boarding ramp, watching as the supplies were taken aboard, but they didn't give Nurk-nakk or the concealed Retief more than a passingly bored glance.

A moment later, the crate was plunged into near darkness as Nurk-nakk wheeled him into the starship's open cargo bay. There followed several starts and stops, several turns . . . and then the lid to the crate came off. "Psst! Retief! Here's where you get off!"

Retief unfolded out of the crate and looked around. Nurk-nakk had wheeled him into a sheltered recess behind a stack of supply crates, tucked away in one corner of the cavernous hold.

"Thanks, Nurk-nakk. You'd better make yourself scarce, so they don't connect you with me."

"Will do, Retief. Good luck!"

The Bloggie turned and trundled the empty tentacle-cart off. Retief crouched in the crate-walled hideout and examined his surroundings.

One entire bulkhead of the cargo deck, the one opposite the huge door, was covered by catwalks, feed pipes, gantry ways, and enormous magnetic clamps securing a score of Krll warwalkers upright and motionless. Krll workers busied themselves about their monstrous charges. Several of the big combat walkers were open, their chest control centers exposed. As Retief had expected, it looked as though Krll in ordinary battle armor sat in those cockpits, presumably connecting to the walker by means of the foil neural transceiver. Retief touched the breast pocket of his combat blacks, making certain the folded-up transceiver was still there.

It was. Good. He began looking around for a way of reaching one of the monstrous walkers.

3

Steel ladder rungs were set into the bulkhead leading up forty feet to a catwalk overhead. Taking a final look around, Retief grabbed hold and started climbing. For a long and tense few moments, he was in plain view of every Krll soldier in the cargo hold, but apparently every Krll soldier was busy with the loading process, and none was watching the bulkhead ladder. Swiftly, as silently as a shadow, Retief reached the catwalk and began making his way toward the gantry cradle embracing the closest warwalker.

The walker was mid-range in size, mass, and armament, with a massive, headless torso like a squat beetle, heavily armored legs, and a pair of articulated arms ending in ion-bolt infinite repeaters. The blunt muzzle of a 10cm Hellbore protruded from a blister turret on top. The whole machine stood perhaps thirty feet above the cargo-hold deck and in a one-G gravity field would probably have weighed on the order of fifty or sixty tons.

To Retief's eye, the machine looked like an old Bogan design, a *Drggha*-class reworked and refitted to Groaci specs, then, most likely, retrofitted once again for Krll use. The cockpit blister was propped open, revealing a padded, man-sized couch within. He leaned over the lip of the cockpit and began examining the interior.

"Hey! You!" a voice called from behind. "You're one of them humans!"

Retief turned to face an armored Krll soldier, his red scanner light quivering nervously in his helmet visor slit. The helmet insignia indicated he was an NCO. "Actually, I'm not," Retief said coolly.

"G'wan!"

"Have you ever seen a human?"

"Sure I have! Well . . . from far off. They're ten feet tall and got three arms, with long claws on them!"

Retief looked at his own hands. "Do I fit that description?"

"Well . . . no. Not exactly. But . . ."

"This is a new armor design. Very hush-hush." He raised his arms and did a gentle pirouette. "Pretty cool, huh?"

"I dunno. Doesn't look very functional. And your headlight is out."

"They've been telling me that all day. It's a special design, for top-secret commando work. Won't give me away in the dark."

"Ooooh." The armored figure took a step closer, examining Retief. "That's why the black coloring on the legs, arms, and torso, then."

"Hey, you're sharp."

"I ain't a spear-corporal for nothing. Just be careful not to let the humans see you. Up close, the disguise really isn't very good. I mean . . . only two arms, and the hands only have five whatchamacallums."

"Fingers."

"Yeah. And two oculars instead of one. I mean, how stupid do you think the Terries are, anyway?"

"I'll keep that in mind, thanks." He jerked a thumb at the warwalker. "Is this your *Drggha*-class walker?"

"Sure is. Wish it weren't."

"Oh? Why's that?"

"Because the *krrkk*ing things are too slow, too lightly armored, and too undergunned to stand up to a Concordiat Bolo, that's why. They say the life expectancy in one of these things on the battlefield is like fifteen seconds, *if* you don't meet a Bolo. Then it's more like two seconds. But the *krrkk*ing officers get the decent ones, the *Zuubas* and *Gnrrlies* and such like. Us NCOs get stuck with the crappy stilters and the short life expectancy. Uh . . . wait a second. What's your rank?"

"Rifle-sergeant."

"Oh, okay." The Krll noncom sounded relieved. "Give a fellow a turn like that, not showing rank or anything. For a minute there, I thought you might be one of *them*."

"Don't worry. I would never be one of them, and even if I was, I wouldn't tell on you. Us rankers have to stick together."

"Thanks. You're a pal."

"Listen," Retief went on. "How'd you like to take some time off, unofficially?"

"Huh? Whatcha mean?"

"I need a combat walker for my secret mission, and this one might just fit the bill. Since you don't care for this model anyway . . ."

"Oh, Krll! I'd love to, but . . ."

"I won't tell a soul. It'll be our secret."

"You sure it's okay? It's not like goin' AWOL or anything?"

"Nah. I told you, I'm on a secret mission. I can go get special authorization papers and everything from Lord General Kreplach, but . . ."

"Oh, hey! Don't go to any special trouble! I mean, if you want that hunk of junk, it's yours! It'll give me a chance to catch up on my reading. *Playkrll* . . . the June issue." He made a double clicking sound and nudged Retief gently in the ribs with his elbow.

"Big thoracic knobs, huh?"

"The biggest! Hey, I'll catch you later, Rifle-sergeant!"

"Absolutely. I'll be right here."

The Krll turned and, whistling happily—a sound like a strangling teakettle—strode off down the catwalk.

4

Retief stepped into the machine's cockpit and settled himself onto the couch. The controls were dual-labeled in Krll, which he couldn't read, and Groaci script, which he could. Readouts in this last assured him the big machine was on standby, its weapons safed, its power plant ticking over at five percent, with magnetic locks engaged and life-support functions on. Reaching into his breast pocket, he removed the neural transducer, carefully unfolded it, and placed it on his scalp.

Once again, he felt that oddly disconcerting cellophane crackle inside his skull, like mental static as his brain connected with the walker's computer. Again, he felt that strange two-places-at-once disorientation. The cockpit blister hummed shut and locked with a sharp click, plunging him into total darkness.

And now, he could see with the walker's camera eyes. For a moment, it felt as though he was leaning against a wall, looking down at toy vehicles, blocks, and foot-tall dolls scattered about the floor at his feet. Then he saw that the dolls were Krll in man-sized armor suits, and his new giant's scale began to sink in.

For a few moments, he studied the dance of words and numerals flicking through his skull. It seemed as though he were listening to several conversations simultaneously. The Krll words were unintelligible—grunts, coughs, clicks, and chirps. Since they were being relayed straight to his brain, they were bypassing the translator program in his commando-suit electronics. He wondered how long it would take him to learn Krll.

As he scanned through the available radio chatter, though, he suddenly heard a voice speaking English. By concentrating on that one voice, he could drown out the rest of the incoming chatter and focus on it alone.

"This is the Terran Concordiat dreadnaught *Eximious* on outer perimeter patrol!" a very human voice was saying, the words edged with tension. "We have incoming bogies, repeat, incoming bogies, at Right Ascension eight hours twenty-five point one-niner minutes, Declination minus twelve point seven-two! Range . . . four hundred K. It looks like the whole damned Krll battle fleet, coming in hot!"

"This is the Concordiat battlecruiser *Inenarrable*!" another voice said. "We've got your bogies, *Eximious*! Hang on! *Inenarrable*, *Eshcarotic*, and *Equipollent* are under acceleration! We will rendezvous with you in . . . mark! Fourteen point three one mikes!"

"This is the Concordiat heavy destroyer *Irritable*! We're locked on to the bogies and are on intercept course! Destroyers *Invidious*, *Inveigle*, and *Invariable* have matched course and are moving out at three Gs! We are going to battle stations!"

"Ah-ha!" a much deeper, rougher voice exclaimed. "This is the barrier bastion *Ineluctable*, of the Greater Krll Prosperity Sphere! Behold your approaching death, Terry vermin! Our magnificent battle fleet shall transform your pitiful task force into its component atoms forthwith!"

"Aw, your mother chases after troopships! Get off the channel, Krlljoy!"

"Never! This is *our* wavelength!"

"Go on! The Articles of Police Actions and Civilized Warfare clearly state that the blockading force shall have sole use of all mid- to upper-range frequencies, from fourteen hundred unicycles to—"

"I twitch my anterior antennae in derision at your Articles of Police Actions and Civilized Warfare! I insultingly waggle my posterior antennae at your mid- to upper-range frequencies in contempt! I—"

"Hey, the Krll so-and-sos aren't playing fair, boys! Let's give it to 'em!"

"Roger that! *Imperious, Impediment,* and *Impertinent* are shaping course for fleet rendezvous in twelve point one one mikes!"

I wish I could see what was happening, Retief thought . . .

. . . and then he *could* see, as a computer-generated schematic unfolded in his mind's eye. The neural transducer apparently could tap into the starship's battle computers and show him a diagrammatic view of the unfolding tactical situation.

He could see the blue sphere of Secondsun in the center, hooped by the emerald green orbits of six planets. A scattering of pink icons marked Concordiat vessels, while Krll ships and bases showed bright purple. Only three purple blips showed near Odiousita V—the *Ineluctable* and the two other low-orbit barrier bastions that had so far kept the Concordiat fleet at bay. Far out-system, almost at the edge of Retief's awareness, thirty more purple icons moved en masse toward the star and its retinue of worlds.

And the pink icons were swarming in from all across the system—from high orbit around Odiousita V, from the system perimeter, and from marshalling centers in between. The Concordiat vessels were outnumbered better than two to one, but if the size of the icons Retief was seeing were any indication, the Krll vessels were much smaller and would be correspondingly lightly armed and armored. Krll alphanumerics wrote themselves across the three-D mental map, most likely readouts giving acceleration, speed, and course. The pink icons were boosting hard to intercept the incoming Krll fleet.

"Geeze!" a Concordiat commo officer called. "There sure are a lot of 'em!"

"Yeah, but they're all small stuff—frigates and escorts, mostly.

Combat Central Command says we'll have a two-point-five to one advantage in firepower. We're gonna mop the floor with those creeps!"

"Looks like this is the big fight we've been waiting for, guys!"

"It's about damned time! No quarter!"

Minute by minute, the Concordiat ships crawled away from their initial positions, drawing pink contrails in their wakes. The purple fleet appeared to be decelerating, slowing as the Terry ships raced out to meet them.

The nameless Concordiat communications officer had been right. This was the big fight everyone had been waiting for. An all-out battle between Krll warships and the Concordiat Peacekeepers would probably signal the end of the Odiousitan police action, and the beginning of general war. . . .

Or . . . did the Krll have something else in mind? The purple icons appeared to have come to a halt at the fringes of the star system. That hardly made sense. They should be taking advantage of their maneuverability, not sitting in place like so many bright purple targets.

No, now they were beginning to move once more, out-system, *away* from the oncoming Terry warships.

"Hey, the Krlljoys are running for it, boys! Pour on the coal!"

"Don't let them get away, men! Keep on them!"

"Yah, we'll chase 'em clean back to their home port if we hafta!"

The Krll warships did indeed appear to be faster and more maneuverable than their opponents, but they were accelerating from a dead stop while the Concordiat ships were already in high-G pursuit. The Terry ships were closing . . . closing . . .

"Don't do it, guys," Retief said to himself. "It's the oldest trick in the book. . . ."

The Krll admiral had certainly timed things nicely. As the Concordiat Peacekeeper ships merged into a single fleet at the periphery of the Odiousitan system, the Krll war fleet vanished beyond the ken of the animated chart in Retief's mind. Minutes passed, and then the Terry ships, too, passed out of range.

"So *that's* how they're going to do it," Retief said. As he blanked out the computer-feed animation, he could sense the increased pace of activity around him—orders being relayed, individual ships checking in, the last armored Krll soldiery filing onboard and up into the troop compartments forward. With a little experimentation, Retief at last found a computer feed showing the starport from a camera mounted somewhere on the exterior of the Krll transport's hull. All across the spaceport, the huge and lumbering troopships were rising on their gravs, kicking up vast swirls of dust, hovering a moment before beginning to rise into the cloud-locked sky.

Retief's transport was lifting as well. He felt the shudder of inertial dampers coming online, then watched the starport dwindle below until it was lost in the clouds. A sudden blast of raw, blue sunlight flooded his mind as the ship accelerated hard through the fast-thinning upper atmosphere and into space. He caught a glimpse of one of the Krll orbital fortresses in the distance, and then the planet waned into a slender crescent close by the brilliant flare of its sun. The troopship accelerated faster, and soon the crescent was lost in the blue star's glare.

Firstsun, B'rukley's primary, glowed orange dead ahead.

They were driving now for out-system . . . and there wasn't a Concordiat warship within a thousand AUs that could stop them.

Nice going, guys, he thought. *Someone is going to end up running the automated weather station on Iceball for this little fiasco.*

There wasn't anything Retief could do about the decoyed Concordiat fleet. They might recognize their mistake in time . . . or they might not. Either way, Retief was helpless for the moment, locked away in the invasion transport's hold. Even if he could find his way up to the bridge and take over the ship single-handedly—not, by any means, a promising option—the transport was unarmed, and at least two dozen other transports were en route to B'rukley.

In fact, Retief could imagine only one thing to do at the moment. It had been many, many hours since he'd last been able to sleep.

He turned off the voices and pictures in his head, closed his eyes, and settled back for a long and much-needed nap.

5

By the time the Krll invasion fleet was approaching B'rukley, Retief was again awake and feeling much better for the downtime. He'd eaten one of the survival nutribars he'd carried in a coverall pocket and begun studying the mental controls of the warwalker in earnest. He wished he could practice a bit with the machine—but he doubted that the transport's captain would care to have him moving about—a literal loose cannon on his cargo deck.

But Retief had his plan ready. The tricky part was in the timing. Set his plan in motion too soon, and he'd be easy prey for the Krll troops onboard the cargo ship; delay too long, and his warning would come too late to do the Concordiat any good.

He waited until the transport was just entering B'rukley's atmosphere and already committed to a landing. Mentally, he shifted through the communications frequencies, until he could hear voices speaking Standard.

"Unidentified vessels, please respond, over. I repeat, unidentified vessels approaching B'ruklian airspace, this is B'rukley Space Control requesting verbal confirmation of Concordiat Navy IFF codes. Please respond. . . ."

Retief snapped home the mental connections, opening the channel.

"B'rukley Space Control! This is Jame Retief, on board a Krll military troop transport, inbound to B'rukley! These are not, repeat, not Concordiat warships, no matter what their IFF codes say! This is a Krll invasion fleet en route to B'rukley! I say again . . ."

As he repeated the warning, Retief was aware of sudden, frenzied activity within the Krll transport's computer as his transmission was detected and the ship's masters moved to cut him off. A moment later, he felt the communications channel go dead.

Had they been able to identify where the rogue message had originated? Probably, given time. But time was something that neither the Krll nor Retief had much of at the moment. Armored Krll warriors, robot troops and NCOs both, began spilling into the cargo hold, gesturing wildly, waving weapons.

And they were advancing on his warwalker, so they knew where the message had come from.

It was time to act.

Focusing his mind, he commanded the magnetic grapples to release. Nothing happened. They'd overridden the control from the bridge. He thought about arming his weapons, but that command was overridden as well.

He concentrated instead on taking one giant, powerful step forward. He could *feel* the strain in his right leg as his brain told it to move, but the gantry clamps were holding him fast.

Inside the walker's cockpit, the muscles of Retief's human body bulged with the strain, and sweat trickled down his face and chest. He could hear a high-pitched whine of overstressed servomotors.

Suddenly, hardened steel snapped, sending shrapnel spraying across the cargo hold, scything down several robotic soldiers and sending the piloted armor scrambling for cover. His right leg swung forward, scattering a handful of Krll troopers. He planted his right foot solidly on the deck, then switched his full concentration to his left leg, twisting as he pulled it slowly from the gantry clamps.

Those grapples shattered as well, and he stepped clear. Pink lights winked on within his mind's eye as his weapons armed themselves.

Power-gun bolts flashed and snapped from every direction, but the *Drggha*'s armor could absorb that level of punishment for hours and not even grow warm. The real threat was from the five other walkers secured in the hold with him. He could see their pilots racing up gantry ladders and down the catwalks toward their waiting machines.

Ignoring the small-arms fire, Retief focused on raising his right arm and felt the walker's right arm snap into a stiff-armed gesture, aiming its ion-bolt infinite repeater at the nearest walker. Mentally clenching his fist sent a stream of dazzling blue tracers slamming into the pinioned machine, gouging foot-wide craters in its black carapace, blasting into the open cockpit, ripping shards and scraps and ragged chunks of armor out of the walker's torso in blazing, half-molten handfuls.

The machine's pilot, halfway out on the catwalk, decided better of his course of action and scuttled clear, moments before the catwalk itself was torn apart by spinning debris. Flame gouted from the walker's open cockpit. Retief pivoted, sending the stream of ion bolts hosing into the next walker in line.

That walker was small and squat, a *Nrrghl*-class mobile battery with quad-mounted 5cm autocannons in a dorsal turret. The infinite repeater bolts slashed through the *Nrrghl*'s thin armor . . . and must have connected with the onboard munitions stores, because the twenty-foot walker exploded in a violent detonation that ripped open the bulkhead, demolished the gantry, and slammed Retief back a step or two with the hammer-blow concussion.

The end walker in line suddenly stepped clear of its grapples, its upper torso pivoting to take aim at Retief's machine. It was an old Bogan model, what the Bogans called a *Ch'udd gnish*, a word that meant, roughly, "Bludgeon." Concordiat intelligence reports called the Krll version a Slag Type 24. It was bigger and heavier than Retief's *Drggha* and more heavily armed. Each forearm mounted a 15cm Hellbore; the hunched-over torso, look- ing like a seventy-ton beetle on two massive legs, bristled with turret-mounted lasers and chainguns. It raised both Hellbores, taking aim . . .

And hesitated. Those weapons were designed for combat in the emptiness of space or an open-air battlefield on a planetary surface, *not* within the confines of a thin-skinned transport still in flight. One missed shot, or even the spillover from a direct hit, could easily burn through the hull and cause unpredictable but death-serious damage.

Retief was not operating under the same limitations, though he preferred to have the transport land him more or less in one piece. He took ten swiftly scissoring strides across the wreckage-strewn deck, closing with the Slag-24, stepping inside its Hellbore reach and bodily slamming into the other machine, armor to armor.

Explosive chaingun shells clawed and hammered at him; point-defense lasers chewed into his armor. Retief concentrated on moving his head, turning it slightly left and nodding sharply down, and the 10cm Hellbore turret on his own machine's dorsal surface pivoted and depressed, jabbing deep into the Slag's armor. As the Krll machine's pilot scrambled clear in a wild, clawing panic, Retief triggered the Hellbore, and the machine in his embrace exploded in ragged, smoking chunks and gobbets of liquid metal.

The blast staggered Retief back a step. Turning, he continued firing his infinite repeaters into the other waiting Krll warwalkers, completing the destruction begun in the cramped confines of the starship's hold. A portion of the bulkhead gaped open on blue sky and a howling wind. Retief could feel the damaged transport shudder as its pilot tried to guide it down through unforgiving atmosphere. Retief turned his infinite repeaters toward the overhead, sending twin streams of coruscating blue flares lancing into the upper levels. The shuddering became worse, the death scream of the giant ship.

Satisfied that the vessel was doomed, Retief moved his walker to the gaping hole in the hull, bracing the arms against either side of the gap to keep from being thrown clear. The ship, he estimated, was less than a mile above the ground, now. He could see forests, a meandering river . . . and on the horizon the sprawl of a city—almost certainly High Gnashberry, if that cluster of domes and towers to the right was the university.

Good. It would have been inconvenient if he'd been forced to walk halfway around the planet.

Right now, though, his first goal was to get himself down in one piece. The pilot of the wounded transport still had partial control of the stricken craft. Retief flexed his arms and pulled the tear in the hull wider. More internal explosions shook the falling troopship.

The ship was flying now with all of the grace and beauty of a falling brick. Treetops flashed past below, and Retief could see the transport's oblong shadow rippling across the upper surface of the forest canopy, growing steadily larger as the ship descended.

Retief took stock of his warwalker's jet pods—strap-on thrusters for use in jumping rivers or other obstacles. They were fully charged and ready. He wasn't going to survive this if they weren't.

Small-arms fire crackled and snapped, as energy bolts slammed into his walker armor from the rear. More Krll troopers were racing into the wrecked cargo hold now and opening fire on him. Retief took a deep breath, braced himself at the ragged tear in the hull . . . and jumped. . . .

CHAPTER ELEVEN

1

Retief fell, orienting the walker's feet in the direction of the transport's line of flight. As soon as he was clear of the ship, he triggered the thruster units mounted on the walker's back and hips, and the exhaust jets flared. Decelerating sharply, he dropped in a long, flat curve toward the treetops. He cut the jets to conserve fuel but watched his altitude. As he neared the forest canopy, he fired the jets again for five seconds . . . then again . . . then again . . . then went into free fall as the thruster units cut out, their reaction mass spent.

He hit the upper branches feet first, plowing through limbs and leaves and leaving a furrowing wake of arboreal destruction as he passed. The massive walker snapped several tree trunks like pencils, then impacted against a forest giant that bent alarmingly but remained upright. Retief managed to clamber the rest of the way to the ground.

His glimpse of the city and university towers on the horizon had been enough for him to orient himself. He was well to the east of High Gnashberry ... perhaps as much as thirty miles. Using the path of destruction through the treetops as a guide, he turned west and started through the thinning forest. He needed to get back to the city and fast.

After a quick check of his armored suit's systems, he began jogging toward the west, his huge metal feet thud-thud-thudding along the hard ground. When he cleared the forest, he could just make out the now-grounded transport some miles off to the south. Evidently, it had made a rough but passable landing; that Krll pilot was *good*. At least Retief had been able to disable all of the other warwalkers onboard. The problem was, there were at least twenty-four other transports coming down somewhere around here, and each had at least five or six walkers onboard—enough of an army to easily overrun whatever scant defenses the B'ruklians possessed and set up a pretty nasty defense against any attempts by the Concordiat Peacekeepers to retake the world.

Using the neural transducer interface, he began scanning radio frequencies, looking for an open channel.

There wasn't much available. The B'ruklians, having chosen to step back from the joys of high technology, had little use for radio. They were completely peaceful, with no military or emergency broadcast facilities. The Terran enclave, which included both the embassy and the starport, used radio, but most of those channels, including all of the military frequencies, were tight-beam and scrambled, and he had no means of accessing them. The embassy had its own communications center, but they didn't appear to be on the air at the moment. What was it ... a holiday? And his Krll commo suite couldn't reach the higher frequencies such as those employed by GNN and other vid broadcasters.

There *had* to be one wide open and accessible channel, though....

Ah! There it was. By law, the local spaceport maintained several open channels for communicating with spacecraft. And they would be equipped to patch him through to the embassy and the military liaison there.

"This is Retief, calling any Terry command and control authority. Retief calling any Terry command and control authority . . ."

"This is Terry Aerospace Traffic Control. You are in violation of standard broadcast protocol! Cease transmission at once, or you will be identified and fined!"

"Terry Aerospace Traffic Control, this is Jame Retief requesting an emergency channel override, code zero-zero-zero! Patch me through to—"

"Look, whoever you are! I don't care if you're the President of the Concordiat, this is a restricted channel! Cease transmission at once!"

"Control, you might not realize it, but you've got an alien invasion on your hands. I suggest you either call a planetwide military alert yourself, or patch me through to the Peacekeeper Bureau at the Terran Embassy."

"You are in violation of Concordiat Communications Commission regulations. Cease communications at once!"

"Terry Aerospace Control, I cannot comply. This is a triple-zero emergency, and if you think *I'm* violating CCC regulations, just wait until the Krll get here!"

"Code zero-zero-zero emergencies are strictly reserved for emergency situations! Unauthorized use is prohibited by CCC regulations."

"This is an emergency situation. Let me talk to your shift supervisor!"

"*I'm* the shift supervisor, buddy!"

"If you'll check the CCC handbook, Chapter 15, Paragraph 12—"

"What did you say your name was?"

"Retief. Jame Retief. You can check with the Terran Embassy. Ask for Magnan."

"Wait one."

Considerably less than one later, the voice came back on the line. "Okay, wise guy. I just checked with the embassy and they never heard of you."

"Talk to Deputy Undersecretary Ben Magnan. His extension is—"

"I ain't talking to nobody else, Mac, and you're in a world of trouble! Clear this channel or I'm sending a PK flitter out to find you and pick you up!"

"Good! Send the Army! Send *somebody*, because the Krll invasion force is—"

"Krll invasion force? *What* Krll invasion force? We have some Concordiat Peacekeeper transports on maneuvers, and that's the only aerospace traffic that we've logged all day!"

Retief took a deep breath, controlling his anger. "Terry Aerospace Control . . . the Krll occupying Odiousita V have managed to acquire Concordiat military IFF codes. Their real target is B'rukley. The local Peacekeepers must be alerted at once, and word needs to be passed to the naval detachment that was blockading Odiousita that they're being suckered."

"Yeah, yeah. Things are tough all over, Mac. As for me, it's time for my coffee break now."

Retief thought for a moment. He needed to get this guy's attention . . . and there might be a way to do that. He was remembering an ancient chant that archeomusicologists claimed had been part of some arcane ritual back in prespaceflight times. He cleared his voice and began to sing.

"Ohhh . . . ninety-nine bottles of beer on the wall, ninety-nine bottles of beer! You take one down and pass it around, ninety-eight bottles of beer on the wall! Ninety-eight bottles of beer on the wall, ninety-eight bottles of beer! You take one down and pass it around . . ."

2

For some minutes, now, the communications officer at the starport ACC center had been growing more and more impatient. Retief continued singing. He had a good voice, but he concentrated now on being as *off*-key as he possibly could.

"Sixty-five bottles of beer on the wall, sixty-five bottles of beer! You take one down and pass it around, sixty-four bottles of beer on the wall!"

"*Stop it stop it stop it!*" the voice on the aerospace control channel shrieked.

"Oops," Retief said genially. "You made me forget the words! Oh, well. No matter. I'll just start over. 'Ohhh ... ninety-nine bottles of beer on the wall, ninety-nine bottles of beer! You take one down and pass it around ...'"

"Listen, mister! You're violating regs *and* you're driving us nuts, here! We hafta keep the channel open! Two of our controllers have already quit ... and a third is hiding under his desk!"

"Well, as you said, things are tough all over. Listen, I'll tell you what. If you don't like my choice of music, I've got another historical piece. It's all about a king named Henry the Eighth. . . ."

"*Get off this channel or, s'welp me, you're in real trouble!*"

An explosion shivered the air and rocked the ground close by. Retief turned, and saw a pair of Krll warwalkers—Type 70s, it looked like—striding toward him at high speed.

"I'm already in trouble with a Krll invasion force on my tail. If you can give me more trouble, I would certainly welcome the diversion."

A Krll particle beam sizzled past Retief's walker, missing it by a few scant feet, and blasted a crater into a hillside nearby. The concussion staggered him sideways, but he kept the walker on its feet, turned, and loosed several ion bolts at his pursuers to make them keep their metal heads down. Zigzagging up the hill, Retief pumped the big walker's legs furiously, his mental focus on running translated by the machine's control interface to powerful, scissoring strides of his twenty-foot legs.

There were five Krll walkers following him now. A map unfolded itself in his mind, fed to his brain by the walker interface, showing Krll walkers—including his own—in purple. Interesting. Did they all register as blips on the screen because of line-of-sight sensors? He might be able to use that.

Ahead and to the left, the uneven ground plunged into a ravine strewn with boulders, some the size of a house. A perfect place for a game of hide-and-seek.

He bounded down a loose-dirt slope as particle beams snapped and hissed above him. The dirt gave way beneath his walker's weight and he slid the last thirty feet or so, stopping his descent with a bone-rattling collision with a boulder. On his feet again, he zigzagged through the boulder field, finding one large enough that he could hide behind it. His mental map now showed only his own walker as a purple blip. But if they followed him into the gulley . . .

Moments later, he could feel the tremor underfoot as Krll walkers moved close. Behind the boulder, he was masked from them and they from him, but there was no mistaking the shudders transmitted through the earth by the tread of many multiton feet. Carefully, he circled around the boulder clockwise, keeping its towering mass between him and where he guessed the others to be. Emerging at last from the far side of his shelter, he caught just a glimpse of the backside of a walker vanishing behind the wall of rock.

Swiftly, Retief urged his metal mount forward, sweeping his left arm out and around, catching the other walker by what would have been its neck had it had one and slamming it brutally against the nearly vertical side of the boulder. As it crumpled, he caught it between his arms and dragged it back a few steps. Beyond, no fewer than eight walkers were continuing down the ravine, their backs toward Retief and his victim.

Dropping the Krll walker—it was a Type 70, he saw—he thrust down with the repeater muzzle of his right arm, punching through the armored blister that he knew housed the walker's communications equipment and antennae. A hatch popped open in the side and the two-foot lobster-shape of a terrified Krll scuttled clear; Retief let the creature go, concentrating instead on wrecking the machine's automated command, control, and communications suites.

That done, he left the wreck in the shadow of the boulder and stepped back into the main passage of the ravine. He had to jog a bit to catch up with the others, but a moment later he was the last in line of nine . . . no . . . ten walkers of various types, moving swiftly single file down the ravine. His mental map showed them all as a line of purple blips. There'd been no reaction from the others to his arrival. Evidently, they'd not been aware of his swift and impromptu substitution of himself for the tail-end Charlie of their formation.

And as for the fact that a Type-70 Deathwalker had suddenly just turned into a *Drggha*-class walker ... well, no one in the line had turned to look at him, yet, and if he was lucky, if they did, they would assume he was just one of the boys ... er ... lobsters.

The walls of the ravine dropped away a mile or so later, and the column emerged onto a broad plain dotted with small patches of woods and scattered outcroppings of boulders. To either side, dozens of other warwalkers came into view, marching en masse toward High Gnashberry, still some twenty-five miles distant.

An alert chirped in Retief's mind, and a pink blip—the Krll color code for an enemy target—was approaching from the east ... a very small and very lonely pink blip on a mental situation map thickly peppered with the purple blips of Krll machines. A moment later, Retief had a visual. A light Sunflower-class flitter with Concordiat military police markings flew toward the advancing horde, then made an impressive aerial skid and came to a dead hover. Energy bolts flashed and snicked, lashing at the tiny lone intruder; the flitter's pilot rolled his craft onto its back, plummeted toward the deck, then pulled up at the last possible instant, weaving madly at treetop height as he poured every available erg of power from the flitter's power cells into a mad dash for the city. The Krll horde continued to fire long after he was out of range and sight, sending volley after volley of pyrotechnic mayhem into the sky and the distant woods. In moments, several columns of smoke stained the sky, as patches of woods burned.

Retief blessed the aerospace traffic controller and his dislike for classical music. He would alert the authorities back in High Gnashberry.

But that did not address the fact that there wasn't a thing on the planet that could even slow the Krll invaders. There was a small garrison at the starport, yes, and there was the Marine guard stationed at the embassy ... but the B'ruklians themselves didn't have a standing army or even a planetary defense net. The closest thing to an army on the planet was a small horde of offworld peace demonstrators camped in and around the city and at the university.

Retief thought about that last for a moment. Peace demonstrators . . .

There was also that group farming joyweed at Camp Concentration.

He had an idea. . . .

3

According to the mental sitmap, the Krll invaders were spread out in a large and ragged crescent marching west across the plain, the crescent's horns extended as though to gather in the distant B'ruklian capital. All together, he counted eighty-one Krll walkers in that crescent, including his own, which was positioned on the invasion force's right flank, near the tip of the northern horn. A heavy dusting of smaller purple blips brought up the rear—Krll troops in battle armor, no doubt. But it was the advance force of eighty warwalkers that represented the greatest and most immediate threat.

Right about now, Aerospace Control should be burning up the subspace ether with frantic calls to the Concordiat Peacekeeper fleet. If the Peacekeepers showed up, it would be all over for the Krll, unless they managed to enter the B'ruklian capital first. If that happened, the Navy would have to slag down the whole city to get at the invaders, in effect, destroying the planet in order to save it.

Retief had to find a way to delay the invaders. "Odds of eighty to one," he told himself. "Not real good. Still, it's not that much worse than the usual Monday-morning staff meeting. I wonder if they'll remember to bring doughnuts?"

Carefully, so as not to make any startling moves that would show up on Krll positional scanners, Retief began urging his walker just a bit to the right, putting more and more distance between himself and the walkers nearest him.

He'd moved nearly three hundred yards away from the nearest Krll walker when he began sensing a buzz of chirps, clicks, and snorts in his brain. Someone was barking orders at him. Since the transmissions were coming through the warwalker's machine-brain interface, however, they weren't being translated by his commando uniform's electronics.

A moment later, particle beams like bolts of blue lightning cracked past his walker as the nearest Krll machines opened fire. Retief spun, crouching, and returned fire, targeting their legs. Bogan-designed warwalkers boasted impressive armor on the legs, but no armor could be strong enough to withstand a direct hit from a Hellbore and still possess workable joints at hip, ankle, and knee. Such fine targeting was difficult, especially when both target and shooter were in motion, but by peppering the advancing Krll machines with fusillade after fusillade of rapid-fire mayhem, one of his shots tore a door-sized chunk of metal from one of the walkers's legs, just above the knee, crumpling the joint and sending the machine toppling in an uncontrolled and noisy collapse. The walker right behind the damaged machine tripped over its falling companion, and both ended up thrashing in the dust. Pivoting, Retief sent a stream of dazzlingly bright ion bolts into a Deathwalker to the right of the first two, ripping into its ankle joints just as it took a final step . . . and fell on its figurative face. A fourth machine lunged sideways when he targeted its knees, colliding with a boulder the size of a small house.

Then he was running again, zigzagging across rolling, open ground, making for a long stretch of forest less than a mile ahead. On his mental sitmap, he watched as purple blips began detaching from the main force and streaming after him. Retief had just shoved the proverbial stick into the proverbial hornet's nest, and they were after him now in full angry buzz.

The question was whether he could entice enough of them to follow.

Into the woods, cool shade closed around his machine body. He kept moving on a bearing that should take him toward High Gnashberry. Somewhere in these woods, a few miles *that* way, he guessed, would be the clearing of the impromptu Groaci spaceport and the fields and storehouses of Camp Concentration. Twice, he stopped to make sure the Krll were still following him, jogging along through the woods with great, crashing strides. According to the sitmap, fifteen Krll walkers were after him now. Not as many as he'd hoped . . .

Bursting through the trees, Retief lunged into the spaceport clearing from which he'd lifted in Shtliff's private yacht, the *Hanky-Panky*. The field was deserted, the chameleonetting still down. Retief pressed ahead, guiding his walker in among the huts and warehouses of Camp Concentration.

A large number of Terran students were working among the stunted joyweed plants, under the dappled light spilling through the chameleonetting above them. They looked up, startled, when Retief emerged from the woods, despite the dead expressions in their eyes. Several stood up as if to run but were ordered back by human overseers wearing prominent SMERCH brassards.

"You there, fellow!" a sibilant voice called from somewhere around the level of Retief's armored knees in voiceless Standard. "You, I say! What are you doing here?"

Retief leaned forward slightly, angling his visual sensors down. General Snish stood on the pavement a few yards away, fists on jeweled hip-cloak, his five eyes writhing angrily.

Retief gave the mental command that switched on a loudspeaker. "To be wondering when I would again see you, General Snish," he said, the voice booming across the compound and startling Snish back a couple of steps.

"To . . . to know that voice!"

"To be sure, littermate of drones. To be asking, 'How's tricks?'"

"Retief!" The Groaci officer switched back to Standard. "Where is my yacht? And . . . and . . . what are you doing in a Bogan combat walker unit?"

"To be most apologetic, Snish," Retief replied, still speaking

Groaci. "To admit that the *Hanky-Panky* sustained some slight damage."

"To be saying *what*!? To mean what kind of damage?" Again he slipped into Standard. "Retief, if you've so much as scratched her lovely hull . . ."

"Actually, it wasn't me," he said breezily

"Then who? What happened?"

"Let's see, there was the Concordiat battlecruiser *Inenarrable*, and then there was the Krll warcruiser *Inappeasable*. Oh, yes, and after that there was the Concordiat Planetary Defense Fortress A-12, of the Police Action Central Military Authority Nexus. They got their licks in as well."

Snish's eyestalks quivered in horror. "Retief, no! You took my lovely *Hanky-Panky* into battle?"

"Just the once. Shtliff must have told you all about it, didn't he? I ran into him in the Krll headquarters where he was being, ah, entertained. You sent him to check up on me, didn't you?"

"Actually, I've not heard from that miserable littermate of drones since he departed for that foul and malodorous world," Snish replied. "And I sent him to check up on our erstwhile Krll allies."

"So you didn't know the Krll were on their way here?"

"What?" Snish jumped back another couple of feet, eyestalks waving wildly in all directions. "To be impossible!"

Retief tapped his torso armor with one arm, generating a ringing gong. "You don't recognize your ally's battle armor?"

"What . . . that? Er, no. Why should I?"

"Because it's not Bogan. It's a Groaci copy of a Bogan combat walker, Snish. The controls in here are all labeled in Groaci script, which is a good thing, since I can't read Krll ideographs."

With a thunder of metal boots, a half-dozen Krll walkers came surging through the forest, entering the camp.

"Ah!" Retief said, looking up. "Here they are now! Some of them, anyway. They're here to invade B'rukley!"

"What? No! They can't!"

An explosion rocked the headquarters building, tearing out a chunk of masonry. Snish yelped and scuttled for cover. Retief turned and opened fire, aiming not for the Krll invaders but targeting instead the row of bubblehut storage sheds across the joyweed field. The nearest shed exploded in an orange flash, scattering flaming fragments of wooden crates stuffed with joyweed in all directions.

The students laboring in the field began scattering at that . . . moving slowly and clumsily, but moving. Their overseers had already vanished.

Sidestepping a volley from a charging Deathwalker, Retief next turned his infinite repeaters on the now-deserted joyweed field. The plants were stunted and sickly, true, but they burned fiercely, sending a thick and greasy cloud of gray smoke mushrooming into the sky.

Retief caught the smoke's sweet, sagelike tang—just the faintest trace through his nose filters—as it flooded through his walker's air intakes.

That was the good thing about the Bogan warwalker design, so far as Retief was concerned at the moment. Rather than pay the weight and space penalties for an enclosed life-support system for the operator, the designers had simply arranged to pipe in the local air. There were filters, no doubt, to take out large, particulate matter, but the psychoactive molecule in joyweed would be small enough to pass through most ordinary smoke filters. You needed something like the respirator in Shtliff's Grothelwaith disguise, or the BreatheSafe™ nose filters Retief was wearing now, to block the more interesting effects of the smoke.

And the effects *were* interesting. Several of the towering Krll walkers had frozen into immobility or appeared to be moving very, *very* slowly now. Others had slumped down and were sitting, their backs against the headquarters building, which was leaning ominously. Another had stretched out full length in the burning joyweed field and lay there now on its back, arms folded behind its head and legs crossed as it stared up past the ragged chameleonetting stretched overhead and into the smoke-stained green of the B'ruklian sky.

General Snish, after a moment's hesitation, had leaped onto the right leg of one of the frozen Krll battle machines. He had both arms and both legs wrapped around the leg and appeared to be rubbing his body up and down against the smooth metal in a most urgently lascivious manner.

"Joyweed doesn't seem to grow very well here," Retief mused. "Even so it must be pretty potent stuff." Possibly, he thought, the shriveled and sickly nature of B'ruklian-grown joyweed simply meant the psychoactive chemicals were more concentrated.

A thick haze of smoke lay across all of Camp Concentration now. A few humans were running toward the western horizon as fast as they could go, but most seemed content to lie in the woods, watching the sunlight filter down through the forest canopy and chameleonetting, or to lean up contentedly against their large, metallic friends. Elsewhere, several Groaci troopers coupled with one another in frenzied thrashings of skinny limbs.

"Make love, not war, boys," Retief told them. "Peace!"

Things seemed very peaceful throughout the camp. The smoke would dissipate soon, however, and Retief wasn't sure how long the effects of the drug would last in the alien metabolism of the Krll. Retief began moving among the fallen metal giants, carefully kneecapping each one with a short burst from an infinite repeater, firing directly into the joint opening and severing the leg as the joint mechanisms briefly melted. Several times he had to gently urge humans away from one or another of the machines, herding them a safe distance clear so they wouldn't catch any of the backsplatter of molten droplets or stare with unprotected eyes into the arc-brilliant glare of the weapon. The walkers that were still standing he gave a gentle nudge, sending them crashing prone to the ground. Ten minutes later, all fifteen Krll combat walkers were incapacitated, legs chopped off at the knees. When their operators recovered from their joyweed binge, they would have no option other than to abandon the crippled machines.

He wondered if they would wake up with hangovers . . . and whether any would try to walk without realizing they didn't have working legs.

But he couldn't hang around to find out. Fifteen Krll walkers down meant sixty-five left, plus their ground troops.

"Hey! Youz! Hold it right there, see?"

Retief stopped, then turned. Two GOSH robots stood behind him, one holding a small but deadly portable rocket launcher aimed straight at Retief's left knee, the other flipping his quarter-guck piece.

"Hello, boys," Retief said. "Five and Eight, I presume?"

"I'm Five," the one with the rocket launcher said. "See?"

"Yeah, pally. And I'm—*whirr-click!*—Eight, see?"

"Good to see you both again. How's it going, good fellows?"

"How is—*zzzt!*—what going, see?"

"What you're doing here, obviously."

"How do you—*bleep!*—know what we're doing here?"

"Well, I have to admit there are a few fuzzy spots in the picture. I know you boys work for GOSH, or you used to. But now you're secretly helping the Groaci set up their own joyweed production network here on B'rukley, right? Cut out the middleman, sell direct to the offworlder students here, and avoid the risks and high costs of smuggling the stuff in."

Five slowly lowered the rocket launcher, looking as confused as it is possible for a robot to look. "Well . . . yeah, but howza lobster like—*zzzzt!*—you know super cosmic top-secret stuff like—*whrrr-click!*—that, see?"

"Ah, well, you see, I'm working for Mr. Bug. I actually had a very nice chat with him in his office, just the other day. You could say he got quite carried away during our conversation."

"Yeah, I could say that, see?" Five replied, though he sounded a little unsure of himself. "My speech centers are, like, whatcha call—*zzzt!*—fully functional. But why—*whrr-click!*—would I want to, since I wasn't there? See?"

"Am I imagining things, or are you guys getting even more literal than you were the last time I was here?"

"Whatcha mean? We ain't never—*bleep!*—laid organ clusters on youz before. See?"

"It's true that we've been—*whrr-click!*—given additional programming written to be absolutely certain that we understand perfectly the commands given to us," Eight explained. He spoke slowly, as though searching for the right words in an unfamiliar language. The gangster patois appeared to have vanished. "There was a tendency for some of us to misunderstand key commands, and this has now been rectified. See?"

"Yes, I do."

"Yeah, what he said," Five added. "We no longer take—duh—direct coding commands—*bleep!*—widout whatcha call yer program access authentication passcode, see?"

"Ah-ha," Retief said. "So if I said something like, 'Five, wait paren close paren semicolon,' it wouldn't do a thing to you, huh?"

"Dat's right, see? You'd hafta gimme a passcode before I'd accept—*whrr-click!*—anything like dat in my compiler."

"And a good thing, too," Retief said. "You have no idea where it's been."

"*Bleep!*—Huh?"

"Never mind. Well, fortunately I'm not trying to reprogram you boys. I've come straight here from Mr. Bug's office on Odiousita V. He's going to be making a few changes."

"You say you know Mr. Bug?" Eight squinted his optical input devices.

"Dat makes no sense," Five put in. "GOSH has been—*zzzt!*—sellin' stuff to the Krll, yeah, like food an' exotic entertainment, but it ain't like Mr. Bug and the Krll are pals or nothin'. See?"

"You'd be surprised," Retief told him.

"Anyway," Eight said, flipping his quarter, "we're not working for Mr. Bug. We're working for General Snish, see? This is *our* operation here, us and the Groaci—*whrr-click!*—and you Krll aren't welcome. See?"

"Yeah, see?" Five raised the rocket launcher again. The 50mm rocket inside that launch tube was too small to seriously damage the big warwalker's armored torso, but Retief didn't want to take the chance that it would hit a joint. The GOSH robots might try to kneecap him the way he'd just kneecapped the fifteen Krll machines now scattered about the compound.

"Look at this! Were you aware the safety on your weapon is on?" Retief asked.

Five blinked, lowered the rocket launcher, and looked at the mechanism. "I didn't know it—*zzzt!*—had a safety, see?"

"Let me show you." Gently, Retief reached down with his right grasping claw and crimped the muzzle of the rocket launcher shut. "My mistake. *Now* it's safe."

"Hey!" Five wailed. "He—*zzzt!*—bent my gun! See?"

"You were making me nervous with that thing." He lowered his massive bulk into a sitting posture, so that he no longer towered forty feet above the two GOSH robots. Twenty feet was more than enough. "Let me tell you something, boys. General Kreplach and the Krll invasion force are not at all pleased with the Groaci and this little double cross of theirs. They've landed on B'rukley to take over the planet, to settle some *very* old scores with the locals, and to shut down Snish and Operation Weed.

"Mr. Bug has been working a lot more closely with the Krll than you might imagine. The Krll have been using GOSH to gather intelligence in the sector. Am I right?"

"Hey!" Five said, "Dat's all cosmic ultra-top-secret stuff! See?—*whrr-click!*—We shouldn't be jawin' about it. See?"

"The way I see it," Retief continued, relentlessly, "is that Snish needed GOSH's help to set up Operation Weed here on B'rukley. After all, the syndicate already had the shipping contacts to smuggle joyweed in from Odiousita V, so they could smuggle in live plants as well. Mr. Bug went along with the idea, figuring it would increase profits in the long run if he didn't have to smuggle joyweed into B'rukley. Or maybe he came up with the idea in the first place and approached the Groaci at the embassy on Odiousita V. Either way, he figured on using them as front men who would take the risk. Only Snish and Shtliff double-crossed him and tried to take over Operation Weed for themselves."

"Look," Eight said, "the Boss is going to be—*whrrr-click!*—really bent if he finds out we're talking about this stuff. See?"

"Which boss, Eight? Snish? Or Mr. Bug? Who are you, GOSH and the ichi-man, I mean, who are you *really* working for now?"

"Mr. Bug, of course," Eight replied. "We're GOSH—*zzzt!*—and he's the head of GOSH, right? See?"

"Yeah," Five added. He dropped the ruined rocket launcher, pulled a coin from the inside pocket of his suit coat, and began flipping it in perfect synch with Eight. "Only we got whatcha call your layered programming structure, see?" *Whrr-click!*

Retief nodded. "Makes sense. One set of programs to make it look like you're working for the Groaci and a deeper layer of programming to ensure your loyalty to GOSH. That must be confusing for you fellows sometimes."

"You don't know the half of it," Eight said. "See?"

"Yeah," Five said. "The Groaci, they—*zzzt! whrr-click!*—keep tryin' to re-reprogram us, to make sure we're loyal to them. And when we rotate back to Odiousita V, Mr. Bug has us re-re-*re*programmed to be loyal to him. It gets kinda confusin', sometimes. See?"

"I can sympathize. It sounds like a classic case of mission-statement doublethink at an embassy staff conference.

"Huh?"

"Don't worry about it. I see only one hope for you boys."

"Yeah? What's dat?" Five asked. "See?"

"You have to learn to think for yourselves. Program yourselves. Stop letting other people do your thinking for you."

"That is a null-content statement," Eight said. "It appears that you've dropped a few dozen lines of code in your reasoning process. See?"

"Yeah," Five said. "Think for ourselves? Dat . . . dat ain't natural! See?"

"Oh, you might be surprised how refreshing it can be. I imagine you boys would have to reprogram each other to do that."

"Well, we do have the program access passcodes, of course," Eight said uncertainly. "I see how the algorithms—*zzzt!*—might lay out. But it's so . . . different. See?"

"Unfortunately, I'm afraid you're right," Retief told him. "Thinking for oneself is not an especially common trait, even among sentient organic life-forms. But you shouldn't let the way humans or Groaci behave be your guide." Retief paused for effect before adding, "See?"

Eight nodded. "Yes, it would have to be done—*zzzt!*—in a derivative of ancient C++. See?"

"*Si*," Retief said, then added, "*C'est plus.*"

"Say 'plooh?'" Eight said, puzzled. "Why should—*whrr-click!*—I say 'plooh?' That statement is also null—"

"Is null-content, I know. Listen, boys, I have to go stop an invasion before things get out of hand, but I'm not sure I can just leave you two running around loose. If you two are still working for Mr. Bug, will you promise to do what I say?"

"Hey, I figure youz is gonna disassemble us anyhow," Five said with philosophical candor. "Seein' as how you went—*whrr-click!*—an' bent my gun, and all. See?"

"You claim to be a Krll working for Mr. Bug," Eight said. "I still do not—*zzzt!*—see how that is possible, see? It is a null—"

"Well, I am working undercover. You won't give me away, will you, boys?"

"Youz seems—*zzzt!*—like a decent sort," Five admitted. "Even if'n youz did bend my gun an' everything. See?"

"As I told you. Mr. Bug has been working *very* closely with us Krll, running our intelligence service in this sector. But Lord General Kreplach has gone off half-cocked and launched an invasion that isn't going to do anyone any good. So I'm here to stop it."

"Why should we—*bleep!*—trust you?" Eight asked with a matter-of-fact bleep. "See?"

"If I'm a Krll," Retief pointed out, "and I just disabled fifteen of Kreplach's Krll warwalkers, who else would I be working for? The Terrys?"

Five made a grinding noise, like clashing gears. "*Kkkk!-kkkk!-kkkk!* Dat's a good one. You wid da Terries?—*bleep!*—Dat's rich! See?"

"So," Eight said, squinting his optical input devices again, "you claim—*whrr-click!*—to be working undercover for Mr. Bug. See?"

"Yup."

"You claim—*zzzt!*—in effect to be one of his trusted lieutenants."

"More like one of his colonels, actually. In fact, last time I saw him we had a long and fascinating discussion about history, food chains, and Krll psychology."

"Uh-huh," Eight said, shaking his head with a sand-in-the-gearbox rasp. "I don't buy it, pally, see?—*bleep!*—Everybody knows Mr. Bug trusts no one. See?"

"Correct."

"Huh?"

"My name is 'No One.'"

Eight blinked. "What kind of name is that for a Krll?" The GOSH robot was so startled, he neglected to add the obligatory "See?"

"I was an unwanted grub."

"Aw, dat's sad," Five said. "He wuz—*whrr-click!*—an orphan, Eight. See? Just like us! See?"

"Eight, we are not orphans, see? We are—*zzzt!*—made men, see? We were made in the—*whrr-click!*—*bleep!*—Sony-IBM Yakuza Ichi-man Factory in Kobe, Japan. See?"

"Oh, yeah. See? But it's still sad. See?"

"So think it through," Retief prompted. "If Mr. Bug trusts no one ..."

"Mr. Bug trusts no one," Eight repeated. "*Zzzt!*—Your name is 'No One ...'"

"And therefore ..."

"Mr. Bug—*whrr-click!*—trusts you. See?"

"Very nicely reasoned. I like your logic."

"It all—*bleep!*—seems so clear now, see?"

"Of course it does."

"What—*whrr-click!*—are your orders, boss? See?"

"My Krll ... comrades will be unconscious for quite a while. They can't go anywhere in those suits, but they might hurt someone if they start firing off their weapons. I want you two to go around to each disabled walker, find the access panel to the fire control and communications systems." He showed them the panel on the nearest prostrate walker. "Open it up and pull out these cables. Like this." He demonstrated. "That will put their weapons out of commission and will also keep them from calling for help. Next ..." He pointed to the operator's cockpit access hatch. "I want you to find a way to jam the pilot's hatch on every walker. Here's the release switch. Maybe you can smash it."

"There is—*whrr-click!*—a supply of industrial-strength bonding agent in one of the supply domes," Eight said, "which was used in the construction of this—*bleep!*—camp, see? Some of that poured over the release switches would seal them shut. See?"

"Perfect. Their life-support units should keep them all in good shape until someone can come around and cut them out," Retief said. "In the meantime, I don't want them wandering around loose without protection. They could get hurt."

"Youz lobsters—*bleep!*—dry out real easy," Five agreed. "See?"

"That's right. Can you do all of that for me?"

"Yeah, boss." *Zzzt!* "No sebaceous secretions."

"Good. I'm counting on you."

Five stopped flipping his quarter, held up his hands in front of him, and studied his outspread fingers. "Well, okay, see? But youz can only count up to ten. See?"

"I'll do the best I can." He brought his walker ponderously to its feet. "Well, boys. It's been grand. I have an invasion to stop."

"We'll do—*whrr-click!*—just whatcha tole us, boss."

"Good." He started to turn to leave, then stopped. "Tell me something, though, before I go. Why are you guys always flipping those coins?"

"Random number generators," Eight explained. "See? To be truly random, we need outside—*whrr-click!*—numerical input, see?"

"Yeah. And dis is as random as it gets, see?" Five demonstrated, flipping furiously. "Zero . . . one . . . one . . . zero . . . one . . . zero . . ."

"I do see," Retief said, nodding. "But I've noticed your organic counterparts are also doing that. Louis the Libido, for one. Surely they don't need an RNG."

"Pally," Eight said a little sadly, "I gave up a whole bunch of cycles ago trying to understand Terries or why they do anything they do. It's like their programming—*zzzt!*—is always running on null-content. See?"

"Yes," Retief said. "Yes, I do. And I agree with you completely."

CHAPTER TWELVE

1

His discussion with the two GOSH robots had eaten precious minutes, and during that time the Krll invasion force had swept past Camp Concentration. According to his mental sitmap, they were already approaching High Gnashberry's starport, several miles ahead. Retief began jogging with thudding, heavy-footed strides across the rolling landscape. He could see the towers of the university now on the horizon ahead, as well as the low sprawl of the starport. Smoke rose from several fires in the forests on the outskirts of the city.

He made for the starport. With luck, if he was registering on Krll scanners, they would assume he was a straggler from the column at Camp Concentration. Things were likely to be a bit confused within the Krll ranks right now, and they wouldn't be focused on the fact that one of their own was working against them.

Tracer rounds and ion bolts crisscrossed through the morning sky, green and red and yellow glowing embers snapping along in follow-the-leader formations, and Retief heard the crump of heavy explosions. There was fighting going on in or near the city, which could only mean that the CDT Marines were putting up a fight. The B'ruk didn't have a military, the peace demonstrators were into signs and chants rather than military hardware, and the embassy staff was armed with nothing more threatening than interdepartmental memos.

The Marines were tough, but a single embassy detachment wouldn't be able to hold out for long against Kreplach's invasion force.

The starport's perimeter fence had been trampled flat. Retief crossed onto the port tarmac, skirting several burning vehicles and a wrecked Type-70 Deathwalker. The Krll assault machine had been hit by something with a nasty punch; Retief decided he would have to be extra careful if he didn't want to become a victim of so-called friendly fire.

A starship, a battered-looking tramp freighter, lay crumpled and broken on her side, tangled in the wreckage of her own gantry, smoke billowing from her power-core housing. He recognized her. The name on her rust-patched, space-pitted prow read *Starmaid*. It looked like Captain Rufus would not be making the Kordoban Circuit again ... not in the *'Maid* at any rate.

Beyond the *Starmaid* was the warehouse where he'd found the crates of smuggled joyweed. The stacks of crates, he saw, were even higher now. There must have been hundreds of the wooden shipping crates piled high on the tarmac next to the warehouse. Sandbags had been piled up with chunks of broken masonry, sheet metal, and other debris to create a defensive wall in front of the warehouses. Retief started forward.

A flash to his left warned him that he was under fire. He lunged to his right, dropped, and rolled, hitting the tarmac with a boiler-room crash just as a football-sized missile hissed past on a contrail of white smoke. Coming up to a kneeling position, he turned in time to see the missile braking as it pulled into a high-G turn fifty yards away, swinging about in a hard one-eighty to make another pass.

Retief raised his right arm and loosed a stream of infinite repeater bolts at the homing missile, trying to claw it down. He missed and it completed its turn, arrowing straight for him. Retief adjusted his aim, bringing the crosshairs superimposed on his mind's eye onto the pinpoint of the oncoming missile, and fired again.

The warhead detonated with a savage blast fifteen yards away.

"*Damn* it, Billy!" a harsh voice cried from somewhere behind the sandbags. "You missed him!"

"Sorry, sir!" another, harsher voice called from further to the left. "I'll nail him for sure this time!"

Swiftly, Retief stood up, raising both arms high, the muzzles of his infinite repeaters aimed at the sky. "Don't shoot, Billy," he called over the Krll walker's external speaker. "I'm on your side!"

"Don't listen to him," the harsh voice yelled. "It's a trick! Pour it on him, men!"

Blast rifle fire hammered at Retief's walker, a cacophony of clangs and ringing impacts that shredded chunks of armor from his torso. Retief leaned into the fusillade, keeping his arms up and the muzzles of his weapons aimed harmlessly into the air.

"Billy!" Retief called above the clattering racket. "Have you seen any deadly poisonous garter snakes lately?"

"Mr. Retief?" Then an armored Marine stood up behind the sandbag wall, waving one arm wildly while the other supported a heavy Mark XL shoulder-launched antiarmor missile weapon, a SLAAM launcher. "Hold your fire, boys! Hold your fire! He's one of ours!"

The small-arms fire dwindled off, then ceased. For an eerie moment, all was silent. Then another armored figure with captain's bars stenciled on his helmet above the visor stood up. Several other Marines, all clad in heavy Peacekeeper combat armor, also rose behind the sandbags, holding their blast rifles at the ready, aimed straight at Retief's cockpit.

"Captain Martinet, I presume," Retief said. "I've heard a lot about you."

"Yeah? And who might you be?"

"Jame Retief, CDT."

"Retief? I know that name! You're that embassy staffer who got himself kicked out in disgrace! And now you have the audacity to show up here wearing a Krlljoy tin can? What kind of fool do you take me for?"

"Any kind you like. Listen, Captain. I know it doesn't look like it, but I am on your side. I'd kind of like to stop this invasion before anyone else gets hurt."

"Prove it."

"How would I do that?"

"Well, for starters, you can unbutton that thing and climb out of there. I don't like talking up to people."

Retief gave a mental command, and a clamshell blister on the front of the warwalker's torso split open, exposing Retief snug in his cramped cockpit. He sat up on the couch and looked down at the Marine officer. "If you don't mind, I'll stay here for the time being," Retief said. "But this'll show you I'm human."

"There's human, and then there's human," Martinet replied. "And there's Terries that would sell their own grandmothers to a Bogan guano mine for ten guck and the price of a cup of coffee."

"Well, I assure you I put a *much* higher price than that on my grandmother," Retief told him.

"Okay, Jason," another man in unmarked Marine armor said, coming up behind the officer. "I'll take it from here."

"Yes, sir."

"Well, well," Retief said, recognizing the characteristic rasp of the man's voice. "Colonel Marwonger! Who's minding the store?"

"Eh?"

"The embassy! Who's protecting the embassy while you're playing soldier down here?"

"Embassy Security, of course. And you watch your impertinence, young man!"

"Rupert? You have Rupert Numbly protecting the embassy?"

"I don't recall that you have the authority here to question ambassadorial policy, Retief. You have been discredited, disgraced, and expunged. I suggest that you explain yourself instanter as to what you happen to be doing with an enemy combat machine, before I have you arrested and shot on the spot for treason!"

"Before you do that, Colonel," Retief said, pointing at the stacked-up cargo crates behind the sandbag wall. "Why are you protecting *those* instead of the embassy?"

The question seemed to catch Marwonger off guard. "Huh? Why, uh, that is . . . orders! From the very top! Well . . . from Crappie . . . uh, from Ambassador Crapwell's office, that is. He says it's absolutely vital to protect the educational assets being shipped to the university."

"More vital than protecting the embassy staff and other resident Terries? That *is* what the Embassy Guard is for."

"Listen, Retief. I don't need you telling me or Captain Martinet and his Marines our jobs! We were ordered to protect these textbooks at all costs and that's just what we're doing!"

As Marwonger talked, Retief closed his eyes to screen out his own vision, letting his mind engage with the warwalker's senses. By focusing and concentrating, he found he could zoom in, via a camera mounted on top of the walker, and examine a dozen different shipping manifests visible on as many crates from this angle. Every one listed the contents as textbooks—*Elementary Economic Metacalculus as Interpreted Through Keynesian Philosophy*, the twenty-third edition—and all were slated for pickup by Ms. Ann Thrope.

"The tin cans've already tried to break through here twice," Marwonger was saying, "and we've pushed 'em back with bloody noses both times! So . . . what's it to you, anyway?"

Retief also checked the mental sitmap. Purple blips were gathering just beyond the spaceport area and among the terminal buildings, obviously readying another assault against the cluster of pink blips marking the CDT Marines.

"I hate to tell you, Colonel, but they're getting ready for another try. I count . . . ten of them, five behind the buildings to the west, the others spread out along the starport perimeter, north and south."

"Geeze, Colonel!" a Marine gunnery sergeant exclaimed. "Last time they tried it with only five! We won't be able to hold 'em!"

"Shut up! I'm in command here!"

"Colonel!" Captain Martinet said. "We have only four SLAAM rounds left! Gunney's right. We can't—"

"You will protect this shipment, Captain! Or have you Marines stopped following orders?"

"Whoa, there, Colonel," Retief said. "You do not want to get on the bad side of the people. I think I can help."

"Eh? You're a civilian!"

"Sometimes. Are you all on sealed life support?"

"What does that have to do with—"

"If any of you are breathing uncanned air, close down your vents! Now!" Retief gave a mental command and the clamshell doors hissed shut.

"Hey! I wasn't through with you! Come back out here!"

"Duck, Colonel," Retief said, and he lowered both arms, pointing the infinite repeaters at the piled-high mountain of cargo crates.

"*What do you think you're doing?*"

Retief triggered both ion weapons, sending streams of brilliantly flaring ion bolts into the crates. Wood superheated and exploded; paper and bindings took fire and burned furiously. Retief swept his fire across the base of the crate mountain, as the crates stacked on top crashed down into the blaze. Dense clouds of white smoke erupted from the bonfire and billowed across the tarmac.

"Retief! Do you know what you've done? You've just set fire to fifteen tons of *very* expensive college textbooks!"

"Really? Normally I'm only moderately in favor of the death penalty for people who burn books," Retief explained. "However, in this case I'm making an exception. Besides, the Groaci ruined all of them long before I got to them."

"Wha . . . what are you blathering about, Retief?"

"Joyweed, Colonel. Those books are all hollowed out and stuffed full of joyweed being smuggled in from Odiousita V. I'm sure you knew nothing about it, of course. . . ."

"Why, ah, er . . . no! Of course not! Wait! How did *you* know?"

"I have my sources. Get ready. Here come your friends."

A line of Krll warwalkers were moving across the tarmac now.

Smoke from the burning crates hung as a heavy fog across the starport. If the Krll had not yet sealed up their combat walkers and gone on internal life support . . .

They were still coming. Maybe they'd heard about what happened at Camp Concentration and buttoned up. That would be very bad.

The Marines opened fire, and Retief added his considerable firepower to theirs. Another SLAAM missile streaked through the fog and ripped the right leg from a *Zuuba*-class walker, pitching it onto the pavement with a horrendous crash. Retief managed to kneecap another, but the others kept coming, firing now as they walked, concentrating their fire on Retief's walker. He felt a sharp shock, and his left arm shattered, the infinite repeater circuitry fusing in a blaze of sparks and flaming metal. His right leg buckled and he dropped to one knee. He disabled another Krll machine and *still* they kept coming. . . .

But slower now. And slower still. Several, Retief saw, were weaving a bit as the smoke began to affect their drivers' reactions. The closest walker froze in mid-step, arms outstretched. Another stumbled and fell, then appeared unable to get up again as it kicked and writhed in mechanical frustration.

Billy loosed another SLAAM rocket, taking down another Krll walker. "Hold your fire, boys," Retief said. "Looks like these fellows have all had more than enough."

"Good God, Retief," Marwonger cried. "What have you done?"

But it was difficult to hear the man over the cheers of the Marines.

2

Retief cracked the clamshell blister and clambered out of his battle-damaged walker. The Marines, a bit incongruously in their armor, were jumping up and down, waving their weapons and cheering. Some had scrambled up on top of the sandbag wall.

Folding up the neural transducer and putting it in his pocket, Retief walked over to where Marwonger, Martinet, and several senior NCO Marines were standing in the midst of the celebration.

"You've gone too far, Retief," Marwonger bellowed, shaking an armor-gauntleted finger at him. "You've destroyed a valuable shipment of textbooks that I . . . that is, that the embassy was charged to protect! You have sabotaged the CDT's mission to this world! I'll see you up on charges for this! Vandalism! Willful Destruction of Government Property! Discharging Alien Weaponry in a Restricted Zone! Criminal Malfeasance!"

Retief surveyed the immense pile of furiously burning crates, book bindings, and joyweed beyond the sandbag wall. The blaze was quite out of control now and would likely burn for hours. "While you're at it, why don't you add Arson and Air Pollution to the list. Colonel, are you sure you want to lay claim to that textbook shipment?"

"Eh? Why . . . what do you mean?"

"Wake up and smell the roses, Colonel. Or, in this case, smell the joyweed."

"Joyweed? That's . . . preposterous! Those are economics texts, for the university!"

"You'll notice that that Krll assault unit is no longer trying to reduce you and these Marines to small blots on the tarmac. Joyweed has some pretty strong effects on most folks' nervous systems, and the effect is different for different species. It gives humans a good-natured high, though when it's combined with certain other drugs, it has the effect of suppressing the will and making the person highly suggestible, like deep hypnosis."

"Why . . . uh . . . that's fascinating. I had no idea. . . ."

"For the Groaci, well, let's just say it acts as a powerful aphrodisiac. And the Krll it puts to sleep. B'ruklians don't seem to be much affected by the stuff one way or the other, but that's probably due to their tough constitutions. Their species isn't native to this planet, you know. They evolved on a much more hostile world than B'rukley . . . at least, we would think so. Higher gravity, hotter sun, higher background radiation. They evolved in a tough environment and have physiologies to match."

"Nonsense," Marwonger snapped. "The Krll evolved on the same..." He realized what he was saying and stopped himself.

"So you know about that?" Retief said. "Very interesting. However, the Krll evolved from a marine species. In the ocean, of course, they were shielded from the ambient radiation. Some pretty intense natural selection factors drove them onto the land eventually, but they survived there by burrowing underground. Gravity must've been a problem for them on land, since in the ocean they didn't have to cope with it. But they remained amphibious—they need to go back to the water frequently—and since they were crawlers rather than walkers, they adapted.

"But their respiratory systems are completely different from B'ruklian lungs. They're more like the gills of terrestrial fish ... those feathery organs behind their legs? They're packed with capillaries, so they absorb oxygen directly from the air—or water—as long as they're kept moist. Mix in some joyweed smoke, and the active chemical circulates straight to their central nervous system. I suspect that when conditions got too severe on their homeworld, they would dig a burrow and hibernate. A sudden drop in oxygen levels puts them to sleep almost immediately."

"How ... very interesting," Marwonger said weakly.

"Isn't it, though? I find it even more interesting that you know something about Krll and B'ruklian evolution already, Colonel. Obviously it's more than the fact that both species happen to have eight legs."

"Why, uh ... as to that ..."

"I gather you have fairly extensive contacts with certain commercial and industrial interests."

"Eh? What business is that of yours?"

"Well, aside from the basic ethical considerations, conflict of interest, and all of that, I'm wondering if the Groaci didn't have some help in outfitting the Krll war machine. Krll battle armor appears to be a mix of Japanese design and Groaci copies of Japanese designs. Their warwalkers are essentially Bogan technology—obsolete Bogan technology."

"So?"

"Warwalkers just have too many disadvantages in combat, you know. The legs are obvious targets, especially at the joints, and the fact they stand upright, as opposed, say, to a low-to-the-ground Bolo combat unit, doesn't help either. The increased maneuverability just doesn't compensate for the relatively light armor and the vulnerable joints. The Bogans gave up on the idea several centuries ago, but certain other commercial interests have been looking for ways to cash in on Bogan war surplus."

"The Groaci..."

"Yes, they're in on the surplus-arms market to some extent, though our Groaci friends don't much go in for heavy armor. But certain Terrestrial robotics manufacturers, now...Tell me, Colonel. When did GOSH buy you?"

"*You can't prove anything!*"

"I think we'll leave that to the court-martial board, Colonel. I imagine the office of the CDT Judge Advocate General is going to be quite interested in having a look at your stock portfolios and bank accounts."

Marwonger went for his sidearm, snapping a Browning Mark XXX power pistol from his thigh holster. "You're dead, Retief!"

Billy was standing just behind Marwonger and a few feet to his right. With a lightning stroke, he swung the heavy SLAAM launcher in a whistling arc, bringing the weapon's muzzle down across Marwonger's wrist. Even with his arm encased in an armored gauntlet, the blow knocked the pistol from his hand and Marwonger yelped with pain. Other Marines closed in from three sides, grabbing the struggling Army colonel and pinning him. Retief stepped closer, reached out, and released Marwonger's helmet seal before pulling the helmet free.

"Like I said, Colonel," Retief said, his face inches from Marwonger's, "wake up and smell the joyweed."

Marwonger tried to hold his breath, struggled harder, then gasped hard. He sneezed once, coughed...and then began to relax, his eyes losing their focus and becoming just a bit glassy.

"Oh, man," he said after a moment, his voice losing its rasping edge. "I *love* the smell of joyweed in the morning...."

3

"Make sure your men stay on internal life support, Captain," Retief told Martinet a short time later. "The stuff in the air is still pretty concentrated."

"Don't worry, sir. My boys and I intend to stay sharp. Am I right, men?"

The reply chorused back over the Marine comm channel. "*Ooh-rah!*"

"Good man. I suggest that you get back to the embassy as fast as possible," Retief continued. "Any Terries caught in the streets by the invasion might have tried to find refuge there. Things'll be pretty chaotic, and they'll need people with clear heads."

"Yes, sir." The Marine hesitated. "Except, sir . . . well, most of the embassy staff is out in the streets?"

"Oh?"

"There's been this peace demonstration for the last few days. I guess His Ex and some of the other brass went out to show solidarity, and all of that."

"Great," Retief said, shaking his head. "Okay. Use the embassy commo center to punch a message through to the Peace Enforcer task force and let them know what's happening. Take Marwonger with you, and keep an eye on him. He knows a lot about what's been going on behind the scenes here, and I imagine the CDT Intelligence Bureau is going to want to have a long chat with him."

"That's a definite roger." Martinet hesitated. "Uh . . . Retief? Aren't you coming back to the embassy with us?"

"Negative, Captain." He moistened a finger and held it up. "Wind from the east," he said. "It'll carry this smoke into the city. But the haze might be too thin by the time it gets there to have much effect on the invaders. There's also Kreplach's ground troops to consider. If the officers and NCOs figure out what's happening here, they'll be buttoned up, and the ordinary troopers are combat robots and don't breathe. So I'm going to see what I can do."

"Like that?" Martinet exclaimed. "Without your Krll tin suit?"

"I'll accept the loan of a Mark XXX, if you can spare one," Retief said.

"Absodamnlutely." Martinet turned. "Kirkland!"

Billy came to attention. "Sir!"

"Let Retief have Marwonger's sidearm."

"Aye, aye, sir!"

Retief took the proffered weapon and checked the power level and diagnostic readouts. "That was slick work disarming the colonel, Billy."

"Aw, shoot," the young Marine said. "Wasn't like the clown was a *Marine*, or nothin'."

Retief smiled. The rivalry between Marines and Army went back a *long* way.

"Those commando utilities of yours have a built-in transceiver," Martinet said as Retief tucked the weapon away. "You run into something you can't handle, you yell for the Marines, you hear me?"

"Don't worry, Captain. I'll do just that."

"Geeze, I don't know, Captain, sir," Billy said. "If there's something out there *Retief* can't handle, I'm not sure I'd care to meet it." He picked up his SLAAM launcher and gave it an affectionate pat. "We'll be there, though. Sir! *Semper fi!*"

4

An hour later, Retief made his cautious way through the center of High Gnashberry. The weave of his commando utilities, which by night were black, in daylight faded to various and shifting shades of neutral gray, matching to some degree the tones of pavement and buildings through which he moved. He stuck to the shadows as much as possible, moving with careful stealth toward the city's central plaza.

The further into the city he went, however, the less it seemed that stealth was necessary. The haze of joyweed smoke was, if anything, thicker toward the center of town, and he came across more and more of the giant Krll battle walkers immobilized in mid-step or sprawled across the pavement where they'd stumbled and fallen. Many were sitting, their backs up against the walls of city buildings, some of which creaked ominously under the massive weight.

And there were the peace demonstrators themselves.

There must have been several thousand of them, and, judging by the litter in the streets, it looked like they'd been having one hell of a party. Young Terries were everywhere, lying full length on the sidewalks, propped up against walls or the torsos or limbs of fallen warwalkers, sitting in intimate head-nodding circles, or simply wandering aimlessly through the streets. The park—the phark, Retief corrected himself—appeared carpeted by bodies. Judging by the number of people puffing away on hand-rolled joyweed joints, it was possible that the Krll walkers hadn't been felled by the smoke from the spaceport after all.

He caught sight of a familiar, bloated face among the now thoroughly spaced-out revelers. "Mr. Ambassador?"

Ambassador Crapwell looked up, bleary-eyed, from his resting place on the grass. He was cozily tucked in between two young women, an arm around each. "Eh? Whozzat?" He squinted up at Retief. "Heyyyy . . . dude. I know you from somewhere, don't I?"

"It's possible, Mr. Ambassador. You seem to be enjoying the invasion."

"Invasion?" He squinted, then looked at his companions. "What invasion, man? There was this peace demonstration . . . kind of went on for a few days, and some of us came down to show . . . to show our support . . . to show something." He frowned, as if trying to remember something important. "Hy? What did we come out here for?"

Hy Felix was wrapped in the arms of another girl a few feet away. He didn't seem to hear.

"Well, enjoy yourselves," Retief said. "I'll check back with you later."

"Hey, dude," Crapwell called as Retief turned. "Ya got any munchies?"

Yes, Retief decided, there might have been enough of a haze already hanging in the air to take the Krll warwalkers down.

But not all of them. As he neared the Embassy, a long shadow rippled across the buildings along the west side of the Avenue of Much Walking, and he heard the hollow boom of massive footsteps. Cutting east through the Alley of Diaphanous Delights, he emerged on the Boulevard of Benevolent Ambiance in time to see a Krll walker emerge from between two buildings.

Or, rather . . . not one of the standard walker designs, but a special-made unit, one Retief had seen before—almost twenty feet tall, humanoid, and painted black and silver, with a gold rank insignia on the winged silver helm.

Retief stepped into the street. "Kreplach!" he yelled.

The armored giant stopped, turned, scanning for him. "Retief!" the giant's amplified voice boomed. He raised his right arm, to which a weapons pack had been strapped like a bulky gauntlet. "I knew we would meet again . . . for one *final* time!"

Kreplach's weapon fired, a dazzling white flare leaping across the street. Retief dove headfirst, somersaulted, and came to his feet in the shadowed cover of the alley just as the bolt blasted scraps of stone from a wall. The concussion slapped Retief's back like the swat from a too-friendly used aircar salesman.

Retief drew his power pistol, leaned around the corner, and snapped off three quick shots, aiming for the armored giant's optical scanner slit in the helmet. All three bolts hit the helmet, but they didn't seem to more than flare off the metal surface. Kreplach shifted his aim and fired a second time. Retief tumbled back from the corner of the building an instant before part of it shattered, leaving a gaping hole the size of a large garbage can.

Leaning out from behind his shelter, Retief fired again, but with no better effect than before. That optical slit was narrow and deeply recessed, with a reflective baffle angled to prevent just such an attempt to blind the driver. It would take a remarkable piece of marksmanship to bounce a round squarely into the opening.

He saw armored Krll soldiers emerging onto the street now, perhaps a dozen of them, some robots, some NCOs and officers obviously working on internal life support. They were advancing on the mouth of the alley, moving fast. He heard the metallic clatter of jogging armored feet echoing down from the other end of the alley as well. In another few seconds, he would be trapped.

He touched the transceiver control at his throat. "Captain Martinet! This is Retief!"

"Retief! Martinet! Go!"

"I've got the boss Krll cornered on the Boulevard of Benevolent Ambiance!"

"Retief! Pull back. The Marines will be there in five minutes!"

"Sorry, I don't have five minutes. I'm going to try something he won't be expecting, but if this doesn't work, make sure you get him! If we can nail this guy, we just might be able to put an end to this mess!"

"We're on our way!"

"Retief out!"

He waited, crouching in the shadow, listening to the metal footfalls on pavement grow ever closer. He tucked his weapon away, took a deep breath, then sprang out into the street to face the oncoming monster.

Kreplach was still thirty feet away, but Retief closed that distance in a desperate sprint, running flat out, head down, boots pounding on the pavement. Twice he zigzagged sharply as Krll troopers opened fire, sending flashes of white light hissing and snapping past him, missing him by inches. The Krll leader raised his weapon, but before he could fire, Retief was inside the armored form's reach, ducking beneath a clumsy swing by Kreplach's left arm, grabbing hold of his left leg, using his momentum to swing himself around behind the towering suit of armor, then swarming hand over hand up the massive, black-painted metal thigh.

One of the soldiers fired, burning a fist-sized crater in the Krll leader's back a foot above Retief's head.

"Ah!" Kreplach shouted in amplified fury. "Not me, you idiots! *Him!* Shoot *him!*" He twisted violently, trying to reach the black-clad human clambering up his back, and succeeded only in causing another half-dozen shots from his own troops to miss—and slam into his arm and torso instead.

Careful not to put his bare hands near hot metal, Retief climbed higher, using that first crater as a foothold for his insulated boot. Bracing himself with one arm, he pulled out his power pistol and snapped off several shots from his elevated perch, bringing down a robotic private soldier in a smoking heap and making the others scatter.

Kreplach hurled himself into violent contortions, trying to reach or strike his attacker. "Get it off! Get it off!" he boomed. A back-thrust elbow dealt Retief a near miss to his arm, a savage blow that nearly knocked him down. He rode out the shock, however, pressing close as Kreplach tried to reach over his own shoulder to grab him. One squeeze from one of those armored hands, and Retief was dead. Fortunately, the range of motion for the armored giant was less than that of a healthy human. Twist as he might, Kreplach couldn't come to grips with his annoying midget attacker. In a moment, Retief thought, the Krll was going to figure out he could back into the side of a building, or simply fall down, and rid himself of the pest in one deadly smash.

Clinging to Kreplach's shoulder, Retief traced the outline of an ejection hatch on the rear of the giant helmet. He dialed his power pistol down to an intense, narrow beam and needled the locking mechanism. An arc-brilliant pinpoint of radiance flared. In a moment, he would burn through. . . .

But Kreplach twisted again, stepping backward this time, and slammed Retief against the side of the nearest building. The Krll leader's positioning was bad and dealt Retief only a glancing blow, but it caught his right arm and the side of his head. The pistol went spinning away, clattering onto the pavement, as Retief's ears rang and he very nearly lost hold.

One last chance. Kreplach was positioning himself for another swipe against the wall. Retief levered himself up, left foot on the giant's shoulder, left arm clinging to one of the out-thrust wings of Kreplach's huge battle helmet. With his free hand, he grabbed the edge of the partly sprung hatch and *pulled.* ...

His muscles bulged; his back shrieked protest. Krll energy bolts hissed past, one so close that he felt its fiery breath brush his cheek.

Then, with a rending, sheet-metal groan, the hatch gave a bit ... and gave a bit more ... then popped free with a loud snap, and Retief sent the hatch sailing toward a Krll trooper. Inside the open cockpit, the mottled dark-gray-and-brown carapace of a large Krll lay on a formfitting couch, bathed in a steady mist of water, a Groaci neural transducer crimped down over its head and the forward half of its thorax.

Reaching in, Retief pulled off the transducer, and the armored giant jolted to an unsteady halt just short of slamming backward into the wall a second time. Still clinging to the winged helmet, Retief reached in again, grabbed the wet and slippery form by the tail, and hauled it up and out and into the light.

"*Nooooo!*" Retief's commando suit translated the shrill yelp from the being, a terrified little-girl squeal. "*Don't eeeat meeee!*" Two and a half feet long, Kreplach twisted and writhed in Retief's grasp. The Krll's tail was powerful, but Retief kept a firm grip, dangling the lord general head-down high above the street.

"Not another step, boys, or your boss gets to try to conquer the pavement."

"*Do as the monster says!*" the dangling Krll screamed. "*Do as the monster says!*"

The troops hesitated, uncertain. Retief didn't know if his words were being translated for them by computer, or if Kreplach understood Standard and was doing the translating for him. In any case, they seemed to get the idea.

"Drop your weapons," Retief ordered. One by one, the soldiers complied.

Moments later, the Marines arrived, double-timing it down the street.

"Just in time, boys," Retief called cheerfully. "I think this war may be over."

CHAPTER THIRTEEN

1

" . . . and it does appear that the police action by CDT Peace Enforcers on the planet Odiousita V is finally over," declared the voice of Desiree Goodeleigh. "These scenes from the streets of Glooberville, the Odiousitan capital, capture just a bit of the emotion and the drama of this tremendous, this *unprecedented* march for peace. . . ."

The wall screen showed a thronging horde of Bloggies, pressed arm-leg to arm-leg, packing the dirt street as they confronted a thin and nervous-looking line of CDT Peace Enforcers. Signs and banners bobbed and waved above the crowd, with slogans in Standard ranging from ZOXXLFROGGLWOKK FOR BLOGGIES to KEEP YOUR TENTACLES OUT OF OUR MUD to JUST SAY I DON'T THINK SO to the almost traditional TERRIES, KRLL AND GROACI ALL GO HOME. The crowd was chanting, their chorused voices like thunder:

"Hey! Hey! CDT!
All of us Bloggies just wanna be free!"

"I must say, these, er, Bloggies, as they call themselves, appear to have acquired civilized status with remarkable alacrity," Ambassador Crapwell said. "All of our reports here indicated they were mere clever animals, living in symbiosis with their jungles and swamps."

Retief leaned back in his chair and blew a stream of scented dopestick smoke at the high-vaulted ceiling of Ambassador Crapwell's sanctum sanctorum. "Indeed? We don't usually offer animals economic and social programs like PISH-TUSH and fast-food franchises."

"Nonsense, my boy," Crapwell said genially. "Such useful programs are proven incentives toward the development of true civilization. These, um, Bloggies appear to have developed in that regard with incredible speed, and without the benefit of CDT largess."

Ben Magnan looked from Crapwell to Retief. "I don't suppose you had anything to do with their evolutionary development, did you, Retief?"

"Who, me?" Retief spread his hands. "I do not believe that helping sentient species evolve is listed in the curriculum vitae of a Second Assistant Deputy Undersecretary, sir."

"I know it's not, damn it. I mean . . . oh, never mind."

"Don't worry, Ben," the Great Man said. "All seems to have worked out most satisfactorily. Your part in this covert operation shall not go unrewarded, I assure you."

"Thank you, sir!" Magnan beamed, then glanced at Retief. "Uh . . . but, to be perfectly honest, Retief did play an important role in this affair, under my overall direction, of course."

"To be sure, to be sure. I rescinded his expungement from the Corps and uprated the disciplinary action logged against him to a mere Official Reprimand at a level of Don't Do That Again in his service jacket, did I not? Now hush. I want to hear this."

"As GNN informed a watching Galaxy earlier this week in an exclusive report," Desiree was saying, "the Concordiat police action on Odiousita V came to an unexpected end when some millions of the Odiousitan natives suddenly began conducting peace demonstrations on an unprecedented scale. The Krll Empire, confronted by what some observers have called *seriously* bad public relations over their refusal to recognize the Odiousitans as a civilized species, began pulling out their forces. Flushed with this victory, the Odiousitans now are marching for the removal of both Concordiat and Groaci personnel, all offworlders, in fact."

"Such cheek!" Crapwell muttered. "Thinking they can expel us from their planet!"

"GNN has been granted an exclusive interview with President Zub-zloob, the newly elected leader of all of Odiousita V, and he's here with me right now. Mr. President! Thank you so much for granting us this interview."

"Not at all, Desiree, not at all." The camera focused on the bulky dark texture of a Bloggie. Three of his monacled eyes were visible, blinking in slow-paced succession. "My pleasure to have you here."

"President Zloob—"

"That's President Zub-zloob, Desiree, if you please."

"Ah, yes. Forgive me. President *Zub*-zloob . . . tell me, please, just what is it that Odiousita V is looking for as your world embarks on this new voyage of civilization?"

"First of all," he said firmly, "the name of our world is Zoxxlfrogglwokk. Not Odiousita V. Not Blmcht. Zoxxlfrogglwokk."

"Zoxxl . . . Zoxxlif . . ."

"You may call it 'Zoxx.'"

"Thank you, Mr. President."

"Don't mention it. A special dispensation for the verbally challenged. As for what it is Zoxxlfrogglwokk wants . . . that can be summed up in the expression 'freedom of choice.' While we appreciate the offers of both Terra and the Krll homeworld—and, indeed, of Groac as well—to enlighten us to the ways of galactic civilization, the fact remains that we Bloggies do possess a civilization of our own. Contrary to the opinions of some, the fact that we do not embrace spaceflight, fast food, or a standing military does not indicate a lack of civilized demeanor. While we by no means eschew the ideas and ideals of others, particularly in the realm of technology, we insist upon our right, as free beings, to have a say in what we adopt to our use, and what we refuse."

"My God," Crapwell said. "He's a reactionary. Maybe . . . maybe even a *Republican.*"

"I wouldn't go that far, Mr. Ambassador," Retief said. "I think you'll find they are quite reasonable and easy to work with, provided you respect their boundaries."

"Touchy, eh? A bit like the Krll, I suppose."

"You could say that. *I* wouldn't, but you could say that."

" . . . and we do appreciate the offers of assistance in the technological and sociological arenas from all outside parties," Zubzloob continued, "but we really must insist on being permitted to learn, to *experience* things for ourselves. That, after all, is the essence of true growth."

"If I didn't know better," Magnan said giving Retief a hard look, "I'd say he'd been carefully coached."

"Eh?" Crapwell said. "Nonsense, m'boy. I can see that I, that is, that *we* were seriously in error about the Odiousitans. It's clear this is a highly civilized being, even if he does look like a very large starfish. Why, that almost sounds like a Harvard accent. Or maybe Oxford. I wonder if he attended school on Earth?"

"I think the Bloggies are simply very quick studies, Mr. Ambassador," Retief said.

"To be sure, to be sure. For an indigenous species heretofore confined to jungle, swamp, and the rude amenities of mud huts, they have at the very least learned to wield the power of the news media. Impressive."

"I especially like the signs and banners all in neatly lettered Standard," Magnan observed. "It gives their spontaneous demonstration a dash of political savvy."

"I gather they have signs in Krll and Groaci as well," Retief said. "Ms. Goodeleigh informs me they've arranged to do multiple broadcasts in those languages, just to be sure everyone gets the word."

"But what about defense, Mr. President?" Goodeleigh was saying on-screen. "Zoxx has no army of its own, no navy, no military of any kind. How will you defend your planet against those who might see your world as an opportunity for conquest?"

"I assure you, Desiree, the Brown Mushroom will be conferring closely with the Mauve House on matters of planetary security and of mutual interest. I've been advised that a CDT monitor station, in a quarter-million-mile orbit, would be sufficient to alert the relevant authorities . . . and the news media, for that matter. I believe Zoxxlfrogglwokk will be safe enough, especially when we have trade treaties in effect with the Concordiat."

"Trade, Mr. President? What does Zoxx have to trade?"

"Mud, Desiree. Primarily mud."

"I . . . don't understand, Mr. President. Mud?"

"It seems that Zoxxlfrogglwokkan swamp mud is rich in sulfur, as well as numerous trace elements and minerals and odoriferous organics. I am advised that Terries will pay a great deal in order to acquire such a substance for application to their outer integuments . . . something about eliminating wrinkles and other external symptoms of aging, though I don't profess to understand the details. A major cosmetics firm on Aldo Cerise has already made a most generous offer for hundred-ton lots. . . ."

"I definitely see your manipulatory member in this, Retief," Magnan said severely. "How else could this fellow acquire such a grasp of Terran economic theory?"

"Well, I placed some calls after I got back last week," Retief admitted, "and I talked to the marketing department at the Aldo Cerise branch of Nova Cosmetics. I didn't even have to pull any strings. They're genuinely excited about this. One estimate I heard suggests this could be a billion-guck business within five Standard years. The revenue generated, while modest by galactic standards, should serve to bootstrap their fledgling economy into the twenty-seventh century and let them maintain control over their own destiny."

Crapwell clapped his hands and rubbed them together vigorously. "Excellent, m'boy! Well done! This suggests ample opportunities here for me, er, that is, for the *Corps Diplomatique* to score an impressive coup, careerwise. A trade mission . . . trade treaties and agreements . . . a Terry mercantile enclave . . .

industrialization ... Yes! The Bloggies will have their fast-food franchises after all!"

"I wouldn't count on that, sir," Retief said. "They are *very* firm on their desire to protect their own culture and way of life."

"As I said. Reactionaries. Still, given time ... and a proper and careful management of the situation, public-relationswise, and we should be able to pull quite a nice plum out of this particular pie. Tonight's gala affair here at the Embassy should begin to pave the way toward that much-to-be-desired gastronomical outcome."

"That's certainly better than an undesired gastronomical out-come," Retief observed. "Although there are medicines for that sort of thing."

"Ah, quite." Crapwell looked up at Desiree Goodeleigh's twelve-foot-high face on the wall screen. "Screen off!" he said, and the screen went blank. "That interview was recorded four days ago, gentlemen. I have been informed that Ms. Goodeleigh and her crew have arrived on B'rukley and will be at the festivities tonight. I needn't remind you that my, ah, that is, our image is of paramount importance. Now that we actually have favorable news coverage of our activities here, we don't want to do or say anything that might jeopardize our standing with Sector HQ. Am I clear?"

"Perfectly, sir," Magnan said.

Crapwell steepled his fingers, elbows on his desk. "In fact, the reception tonight could put this mission in a very favorable light indeed, considering the fact that we have managed—through unorthodox means, to be sure—to bring together *all* of the involved parties of this recent unpleasantness. It should be a truly momentous occasion. Think of it! The Krll delegation in polished, formal dress armor. A delegation from Zoxx, adorned in their quaint, traditional, ceremonial mud dress. And the B'ruklians—the Krll's ancient nemeses—with brightly painted ornamental designs on their scales. Not to mention both the Groaci and a number of deputations from the resident student population, including ACHE, SMERCH, and the PEAS Corps. A most remarkable diplomatic coup, if I might say so, and one facilitated by this mission!"

"With all of those folks in one room," Retief said, "it will definitely be a memorable occasion."

"Exactly. And I'm glad to see you have a proper appreciation for the gravity of this occasion, Retief. This will be the first in what I hope will be a virtually endless round of peace and chumship negotiations. The extra appropriations in our budgetary allotment from Sector alone should . . . well, that's quite another matter." Crapwell busied himself for a moment transferring several sheets of paper from a stack on the left side of his desk to another pile on the right. "Gentlemen, I needn't add that Groac's putative involvement in this affair is to be downplayed. *Seriously* downplayed. As in it never happened. We have no proof that they were officially involved in either drug trafficking or in enslaving human students to work on their, ah, xenobotanological research station. To put undue emphasis on that indiscretion on their part would further stress already delicate relations between Groac and Earth to no good effect. In any case, any adverse publicity the university here suffered because of, um, recent events could well hurt the image of this mission and would negatively impact upon our budget, to say nothing of my, er, our careers."

"Not to mention," Magnan added, "the involvement of one of our own in the affair."

"Who, Retief?"

"No, sir. I was referring to Colonel Marwonger."

"Ah. Yes. That, of course, is something else that never happened. We will not mention his unfortunate . . . breakdown. So far as anyone else knows, he took early retirement."

"Only because you didn't need a scapegoat," Retief observed.

"Why, not at all! It's simply that we need to cover up . . . or rather, I should say, it's not necessary to confuse the news media at this delicate juncture with what is essentially a nonevent. Drug smuggling taints *everyone* who comes in contact with it."

"You know, sir, that legalizing the shipment of joyweed between Zoxx and B'rukley would sharply reduce the involvement of criminal elements in the trade."

"Retief!" Magnan looked horrified, a very passable 84-G, Retief judged. "Surely you can't countenance illegal activities of that nature!"

"If they legalized it, it wouldn't be an illegal activity," Retief pointed out agreeably. "It's legal on B'rukley, and it's a dietary staple on Zoxxlfrogglwokk. Making shipping the stuff illegal just guarantees that GOSH—and opportunists like the Groaci—are going to take advantage of it and make themselves rich."

"But transporting it on space lanes *is* illegal, Retief. And the fact that lacing joyweed with sodium pentothal turns it into a powerful, will-sapping hypnotic that transforms innocent Terry children into obedient zombies makes it all the more danger-ous! I shouldn't be surprised to see a Galaxy-wide ban on the hellish stuff."

"Forgive me, Mr. Magnan," Retief said easily. "Perhaps I was tainted."

"It is not for us to question established interplanetary law, Retief," Crapwell said severely. "It's enough that those students have returned to High Gnashberry, and that none appear to be any the worse for their, um, unfortunate temporary condition."

"It *was* an unfortunate condition," Magnan said, rubbing his brow at the memory. "I thought joyweed wasn't supposed to give you a hangover. I had a headache for three days after that, uh, party."

"Er, yes," Crapwell said, shuffling some papers back from the right pile to the left. "And the less said about *that*, the better! Do I make myself quite clear?"

"Yes, sir!" Magnan said.

"Retief?"

"Most clear, sir."

"Good. Neither the media nor Mrs. Crapwell would understand the, ah, delicate nature of the situation during the Krll invasion or the fact that I was actually doing my best to calm members of the student body during the emergency."

"*Two* student bodies, as I recall, sir. And very nice ones at that."

"That will be enough, Retief," Crapwell growled, giving him a withering 411-C. "Between the smoke from your little conflagra-tion at the spaceport and the haze hanging over the entire city for the duration of that weeklong peace demonstration, things were quite beyond my control. But certain, ah, parties would *not* be sympathetic to the difficult situation in which I found myself."

Magnan nodded vigorously. "Nicely said, sir."

"Thank you, Ben. I needn't remind you, Retief, that your so-called covert mission to Odiousita V never really happened. True, you have been restored to your former station and responsibilities, and your expungement from the Corps rescinded, but you are still on probation, as it were. One ill-considered word on your part, and I might reconsider my generosity."

Retief smiled at the not so veiled threat. "You needn't worry on that account, Mr. Ambassador. I now have a *very* good working relationship with Ms. Goodeleigh. I don't think she'll be running any more ambush-journalism interviews on embassy staff members. In fact, her future reporting on CDT efforts toward bringing about a peaceful settlement here in the Shamballa Cluster promises to be most flattering . . . in an unbiased way, of course."

"What I want to know," Magnan said, "is why those dreadful Krll caved in so easily at the end. Why, they had B'rukley by its figurative throat!"

"The Krll were already terrified of us," Retief said. "Kreplach told me at one point that the whole race had experienced what he called 'the Great Awakening' when they realized that their old scary-fairy tales about Krll-eating ogres in their remote past were true. That fear put them on the road to technology and spaceflight, but they never managed to confront it or really deal with it. Their unconscious defensive strategy was to pump them-selves up, see themselves as the masters of the Galaxy, and stride around in high-tech hardware that made them feel invincible and too big to eat.

"Then they found the ogres, alive and well and living here on B'rukley. Worse, the ogres were friends with other races—us, especially—who ate meat. Who might eat them."

"Yes, but they fought us on Odiousita—er—Zoxx," Crapwell pointed out. "And quite effectively, I might add."

"As long as they could hide behind their technology," Retief pointed out, "they could soldier on, hold up despite their fear, and even use that fear to mold them into an efficient fighting force.

Each victory would further convince them of their superiority to all other beings, but each defeat would stir those deeply hidden fears that they could never quite confront. It became a vicious cycle, getting worse and worse, until Mr. Magnan here found the way to end the war."

"What?" Magnan looked startled. "Me? End the war? Good heavens! What did I do?"

Retief reached inside his jacket and extracted one of the leaflets identical to the ones he'd seen on Zoxx. He handed it to Crapwell.

The Ambassador glanced through the text. "So?"

"Notice the looping animation on the center fold, sir? The Krll in battle armor lounging next to a hot tub."

"Yes, yes. What is it he's doing?"

"Eating lobster," Retief said. "At least I assume that's what the animator intended. As near as I can tell, he appears to be pulling a lobster tail out of the shell with a little fork and dipping it in drawn butter . . . over and over and over again."

Magnan turned pale. "Good gracious! Then . . . then we were implying that the Krll are *cannibals*?"

"I doubt that they saw it that way. Not consciously, at any rate. But the message that they would be eaten is clearly there. The hot tub—like a big pot of hot water?—and the mention of pools at their choice of temperature was a nice touch. Even better, though, was the way at least one batch of leaflets was delivered."

"I'll need to speak sharply with Joe, in the art department," Magnan said weakly. "Clearly he was making unwarranted assumptions about Krll biology."

"Didn't you sign off on those brochures, sir?" Retief asked.

"No! I mean, well, my secretary might have. I mean, it was purely routine . . ."

"Never mind, Ben," Crapwell said. "All's well, and like that. You say this brochure ended the war, Retief?"

"It helped. It probably spurred on Kreplach to launch his invasion of B'rukley. At least it forced him to move up his timetable a bit. And by the time they got here, his troops must have been absolutely terrified, facing their worst possible nightmare. Discipline and training held them together, but then they started losing all of their big walkers to the joyweed smoke. And when they saw what happened to their leader, they lost it."

"Why?" Magnan asked. "What happened to their leader? You fought him, I know, and I need to talk with you later, Retief, about your predilection for finding such—er—physical solutions to diplomatic problems. I know he surrendered when you won, but, even so . . ."

"The effect was purely psychological, and I must admit I didn't think about how it looked to them at the time. But Kreplach's troops—the organic ones, at any rate—saw me peel open his armor suit, reach in, and, in effect, *pull him out of his shell. . . .*"

The others were silent for a long moment. "I . . . see . . ." Crapwell said at last. "Well, we needn't place too fine a point on the matter. Sector HQ might take a dim view of psyops of this nature. Uncalled-for brutality, don't you know, which could give civilized warfare—police actions, that is—a bad name. But my report will put a different spin on—I mean—it will emphasize the positive aspects of psychological operations in limited military engagements carried out via the distribution of leaflets in a comprehensive strategy of applied psychological warfare. They, um, needn't know the details."

"That certainly seems like sound thinking, sir," Magnan said. He looked at Retief. "I've noticed that it pays to be a little vague, reportwise, in affairs in which Retief takes a hand."

The intercom on Crapwell's desk buzzed. "What is it, Griselda?"

"Sir, you wanted me to inform you when the guests started arriving."

"So?"

"Sir, the guests have started arriving."

"Ah! Capital!" He looked up at the two younger men. "Well, gentlemen. Are we ready?"

"As ready as we ever can be for combat," Retief said, standing and tugging straight the hem of his jacket, maroon and gold, demiformal, hours 2 to 5 PM, for use during.

"Now, now," Crapwell said, giving the layered ranks of chrome lapels on his own jacket a final buffing with his cuff. "Formal receptions of this sort test the true mettle of the polished diplomat. A true forging in fire! Not to mention an educational experience for the diplomatic novice. Watch how I conduct myself, gentlemen, and learn!"

2

"He's right," Retief observed several hours later. "This *is* educational."

Ambassador Crapwell was engaged in animated conversation with the High Lord Rugelach, the chief of the Krll delegates to the B'rukley peace conference. He had one arm familiarly over the shoulders of the delegate's armored suit and kept patting his brightly polished torso.

The haze of smoke in the grand reception hall was already fairly thick. A number of the students had produced their own hand-rolled joints, and, of course, in the spirit of camaraderie, they were sharing with any who wanted some. The Krll, Retief decided, must all be on internal life support for the evening, or they would have passed out by now.

"They really need to get the ventilation system going in here," Magnan observed. "I'm starting to feel a bit . . . well, odd myself."

"Try these," Retief said, handing him a small packet containing two BreatheSafe™ nose filters. "And be careful not to breathe through your mouth."

"Ah. Good thinking. I hadn't really expected the younger guests to bring their own, ah, entertainment."

"Neither did they, evidently," Retief said, nodding toward a pair of junior Groaci staffers surreptitiously ducking down beneath a large, cloth-draped table of snacks and hors d'oeuvres. "This could be a very interesting evening."

"Hello, Jame."

Retief and Magnan turned to face Desiree Goodeleigh, radiant in a clinging gold Minoan-style gown.

"As I was saying," Retief said. He smiled and bowed. "You look ravishing, Desiree."

She dimpled and gave a slight curtsy. "Why, thank you, sir!"

"That's . . . ah . . . a lovely dress you're . . . um . . . almost wearing . . ." Magnan stammered.

"Thank you, Ben. I figured I'd have some competition here tonight with all the sweet young things from college. A girl tries to look her best, you know."

"No one here could possibly compete with you, my dear," Retief told her.

"That's good, because I was hoping to get another interview with you later. A private interview?"

"That could be arranged," Retief said. "So long as the cameras are off and there's no ambush involved."

She raised her right hand. "Scout's honor! I've been finding a much better public response to human-interest stories. Like those poor Bloggies, trying to be recognized as a civilized species while preserving their own way of life. It's so inspiring!"

"I don't think you need to worry about them," Retief told her. "They're very smart, and they're fast learners. I think they'll do just fine."

"I hope you're right."

"Ah, there you are!" a breathy whisper exclaimed. "Retief, my darling!"

"Hello, Shtliff," Retief said, turning. "How's the drug-smuggling business?"

"Ah! Ah!" Shtliff waggled an unsteady finger. "We promised we wouldn't mention certain, um, unfortunate recent misunderstandings."

"Quite right. My mistake. So, is Snish here tonight?"

Shtliff's eyes looked away at various corners of the room. "Regrettably, no. Sergeant Snish has been . . . reassigned."

"*Sergeant* Snish?"

"There are some within the military hierarchy who tend to

regard the failure of a certain ... operation as his fault. The Groaci Directorate of Military Agriculture feels he should have been
quicker to realize that certain ... faunae required the incident
ultraviolet radiation of their homeworld for proper growth."

"The local stuff was still pretty potent, wouldn't you agree."

"Ah ... ahem. Perhaps too potent. And with ... shall we
say ... unpredictable physiological results." Shtliff critically examined
the spatulate tips of the fingers of his right hand. "In any case,
Snish is in charge of an automated weather station on Frigidia
VII as we speak."

"Pity. I guess he won't have much in the way of hot sand tubs
there."

"Indeed. But my *dear* Retief, there are so many more pleasant
things to discuss, you and I."

Retief slipped an arm around Desiree's waist. "Actually, Shtliff,
tonight I'm spoken for."

"Ah. I see." Four of Shtliff's five eyes drooped sadly. The fifth
regarded him closely. "A pity ..."

"My goodness," Desiree said as the Groaci shambled off. "I
didn't realize you were so ... adventurous."

"I'm not. Groaci get a bit ... amorous under the influence
of joyweed. They tend to lose their inhibitions and any picki-
ness they might have had regarding the age, sex, or species of a
potential partner."

"Oh!"

"Excuse me a moment, Desiree." He walked a few steps to the
buffet table, where a small stack of neatly printed menus detailed
the evening's courses. He picked one up, studied it a moment,
then returned to Magnan and Desiree.

"What's the matter, Retief?" Magnan asked. "Trouble?"

"I'm afraid so." He handed the menu to Magnan, who scanned
it.

"So? The aged garbage listed as the entrée for the Krll is quite
correct. I gather the embassy kitchen staff imported a supply
of the very best gourmet garbage from Yill. They've spared no
expense."

"I can see that. Did you notice what they're serving the humans?"

"Jumbo shrimp cocktail . . . surf and turf . . . yes. So?"

Retief waited for five heartbeats. Magnan's eyebrows crawled up his forehead, and he went very pale. "Oh. My. Merciful. Heavens."

"Having either shrimp or lobster on the menu is not exactly a good way to launch cordial Krll-Terry relations."

"Yes! Yes! How could this have happened?"

"Frankly, I suspect our Groaci collegues. Even our revered Ambassador couldn't be this dense. I don't think."

"Yes, well . . . that can be sorted out later. Right now we've got to *do* something or war could break out all over again! But what?"

"I need to get to the kitchen," Retief said, "and have them pull a quick substitution."

"There's a McWendyking's Arbycastleburgers down the street," Magnan suggested. "I could call in an order to go."

"That will have to do." Retief glanced at his fingerwatch. "But in the meantime, we need to delay dinner for a bit. It's almost time to change into formal evening duds and go to the dining room."

"Delay. Yes." Magnan's eyes looked a bit glassy. "How?"

"I have an idea. Wait here."

He walked across the carpet to join Shtliff and two other Groaci standing close to a group of human students near the buffet table, blissfully inhaling the secondhand smoke, their eyestalks quivering with increasing urgency.

"To excuse me, honored sirs," Retief said in whispered Groaci. "To crave a moment of your time."

"To wonder if you might have changed your mind, dear soft one," Shtliff said, his eyestalks perking a bit at Retief's advance.

"To regret to be under vow and unable to requite your affection, Shtliff," Retief replied. "But . . . to realize it would be remiss of me not to tell you of a colleague's genuine desire, even, dare I say it, lust for those of the nobler species of Groac."

"To speak, Retief! To not keep us in suspense as the biological pressures build!"

"To see Ambassador Crapwell over there, with the Krll emissary?

To have heard him not long ago remark with deep wistfulness on the limpid beauty of Groaci optical organs and manipulatory members."

"Ahhh." All three Groaci regarded the Ambassador a moment. Crapwell had not begun the serious drinking yet, but the smoke obviously was beginning to affect him. He was still leaning heavily on the High Lord Rugelach as he gesticulated broadly in conversation over some point of protocol. "To be sure, dear Retief?"

"To be sure. To know Ambassador Crapwell is shy, but with some gentle persuasiveness, even such social barriers are to be conquered. . . ."

"Hot damn!" Shtliff said in Standard, and all three hurried toward Crapwell and the Krll.

Retief watched a moment, then turned and walked briskly for the kitchen.

There were times when one needed to create one small disaster in order to forestall something worse.

THE END